GW01271770

THE LAST QUEEN
OF HOLLAND

Josie Clay

For Vicky

CONTENTS

UPTURNING THE OBSTACLE (PART 1)

♻

May 16th 2166

Y oshi grinds the pills to powder with tools unchanged since the Ice Age. Copper bangles jangle. She looks out over blackening water. Out to distant realms. Out to where stars still relay their dead message. *What conceit*, she thinks, *what conceit that we should matter to any of it.*

This island, this house, bequeathed by the wrecking ball. Land-formed from pulverised cathedrals, shopping malls, tower blocks. She shakes her head at stupid hope. Coaxes the powder down a funnel into a fine Merlot, watches poison nebulae bloom and collapse in a ruby universe.

All matter is conserved. This is immutable.

Take stars; four hundred million born each day, while the same amount die. *Oh, those astro-boys and their thrusting certainty.* It might be true, she supposes. But counting stars has to be the mother of all displacement activities. *Fiddling while Rome burns,* she mutters.

She glances at Breeda, poised and shambolic as the driftwood arrangement on the kitchen table before her. Yoshi remembers the turn of the century. Seen in with starbursts and glut. When they had fucked night and day. Such appetites long since sated.

The candle flame dances in Breeda's uncommon eyes. Eyes that would always entrance. One blue, the other dark brown. They seemed to regard you as if you were a marvellous surprise. Everyone felt it. Yet it was Yoshi they had settled on. And though she had never felt more alive, it had been a kind of dying.

The wine bottle chatters against the glass. Yoshi's heart clangs at the wrongness of it all. But it is not wrong. Their decision to end this life is unimpeachable. Yoshi's struggle is in outwitting her heart. Much of her early life had proved her expert at this. Yet she feels shame at the betrayal; that brave sack of blood has faithfully cached her love, coralled her terror, all while keeping her alive. The heart is a miracle. In order to trick it, she thinks of the brioche buns she loves to bake; a batch of speckled breasts. Only to prompt a vision of brisk little birds, inconsolably weeping around poor cock robin, a tiny arrow stuck in his breast. Crosses for eyes. A merciful vision, given her extensive library of potential horrors.

Still, she can't shake the feeling her heart is trying to show her something beyond the obvious. Breeda, on the other hand, is unswayable; *let death be our midwife,* she had said, with standard gothic Dutchness.

Tonight they must die. A primal part of her tears at the bloated, bobbing fact. She senses the island scanned by hollow eyes, the derelict, turf-clad dwellings appraised. Hard around them the seas will converge and the world will continue, as remote from promise as the last egg in a cold nest.

"To new beginnings." Her arm describes a flightless gesture. She sees herself and Breeda unvarnished: two old women, profiles vague as wobbly-faced Georgians on thick pennies.

"What day is it?" Breeda looks around, bemused.

"Tuesday. Remember? We had that meeting today … in The States."

"Oh ja! The men's faces like pans."

"Uh-huh." Yoshi sips her wine. "And you know what we're doing now, right?"

"Tuesday…" Breeda frowns, "… a beige day to pop one's clogs." Her face brightens. "But we'll soon be back in the saddle."

Through the salt-smeared window, a sickle moon leers. Jupiter and Venus hang above it like eyes. Yoshi looks up. Leaves an eyebrow raised until Breeda notices.

"What?"

Yoshi raises the other eyebrow.

"Oh wow. Look at that. A perfect smiley." Breeda's own smile reveals remarkably good teeth. She licks her fingers and pinches the wick.

Hands held across the oilcloth, a ribbon of smoke unfurls between them. The celestial scene admired, until a rising cloudbank snuffs the show.

"Well, that's that." Yoshi stands, arches her back, pushes the chair in and takes the glasses to the sink. Her heart knocks in fierce awareness at the last doing of such things.

Yoshi lights the way, shielding the flame. Stairs creak in sympathy with the hoist of shot knees. And swimming beside them, her hand casts a shadow shark to cruise the uproarious mould blooms on the wall. Enfeebled by an old gravity they push on, sights set on the porthole of purpose.

The bedroom at last, as bereft of ornament as a plundered tomb. Only a bed and a printer's cabinet. (Originally purchased some sixty years ago to house Breeda's collection of shells and sea glass. She had long since lost the will to possess beautiful things.

And in renunciation, had thrown them into the sea, deeming them not hers to keep.) These days, the many small compartments proved ideal for storing something that truly belonged to them. Something, inarguably, their own. Something which, in the past decade, galloping technology had enabled them to hoard; dreams. Each housed in an oji; an unassuming, coin-sized device in which the dream is captured. Unlike coins, the ojis are identical, the assortment lies in the dreams, classified like any other collection, but oddly so. Labelled in a way that only has meaning to the owner. Similar to the emotion filed in our own complex systems, invoked by freshly cut grass or the haunting strains of '*Scarborough Fair*,' or the slant of a loved-one's smile.

And what of these syntheses we call dreams?

When we find ourselves in streets never walked in our waking lives, yet routinely our feet tread the cobbles. When the sword never held fits balanced in our grip. And when a person never met is familiar as kin. A good many actualities are portrayed of which we have no former knowledge, nor any business knowing. Things we should not know. And yet we do. We do.

"Remember how we used to ride?" Breeda climbs into bed. "So fast we nearly broke our arses."

But Yoshi is outside herself; evicted from her body by an age-old sorrow.

"I want that dream," Breeda says closing her eyes. "Horses."

Yoshi watches gnarled hands place the oji on Breeda's temple. Feels the cool sheets against her skin. Enfolds herself around Breeda's warmth. She could count on the fingers of one hand the nights they had not aligned themselves in this ancient, human furrow.

The roof must have vanished somehow, because she can clearly see two gulls gliding high in a greenish sky.

"*'tis cold*," Breeda says, "*'tis cold*." Though she doesn't get her horses, only a tangle of bracken, and swine paddling in an icy wallow. Such are the vagaries of dreams.

Breeda goes first. She had drunk more of the wine. *Always did,* Yoshi smiles faintly. Back in her skin at this last moment. Though death is incipient, she is sufficiently present to experience relief at Breeda's passing. And not dead enough herself to escape grief's deft evisceration. A blizzard of brain cells swirls and melts. She clings on, riding out Breeda's tremors until her arms make no sense. She has no arms, no legs. She is just a vast eye. A giant angler fish floating in space. *Unparticled,* she thinks. *I have become unparticled.* Suddenly, she is suffused in a bright and kindly light. *How do I love thee? Let me count the ways.* One hundred and sixty-eight trillion stars born since she was. She knows this is right. She knows everything. Her heart beats three times in quick succession. Knock, knock, knock, as if there is somebody at the door. Her last thought is for Breeda. *A life's work well done, my queen. Now rest awhile.*

BOOK 1: CHALK HORSES

Roman Britain A.D. 60

Each that had sought to vanquish and so lay with me as husband had returned to his land with his tail between his legs. It was our way; a suitor to a queen had to first overpower her in combat to prove himself worthy as her consort.

My blade had cleaved unsparingly flesh, then bone. Many souls withered and one was smote. And why did I thrash so, as if for my life? Because I lacked desire for a mate whose bristles would flay my face, whose odour, like the dark frowst of a bog, would offend my senses and whose manner in coupling was that of a battering ram intent on breaking the rampart.

I am Briga, Queen of the Cantiaci and I have no need

of a man.

I had been born into this world with a most singular attribute (I believe all things under the sun to be designed for a purpose). It was said of my eyes, one ice blue, the other black as a raven, that they were able to see the realms of both the living and the dead.

It may not be so in years to come when this story is relayed, but in my time, those of us with 'differences' were treated with reverence; we were deemed to have insight. Haska, our most sacred of healers, possessed six fingers on each hand, while her feet were as clubs. It was considered an honour to carry her. Another, Leffen, clad in galls like an old oak. Duin's head waggled as if in constant disagreement with himself and he did make beautiful song. All of us, opined touched by the gods. For myself, I believed I had been endowed with a divine gift, allowing not only comprehension of the surface picture, but an inkling of deep mechanisms hidden within and below.

The blue eye drinks in the colours of day and present; the fact of a high or low sky, whether it be specked with birds or like the sea, rolling grey overhead. Similarly, it takes in the skewbald horses, canted to the wind in the green grain. People, pink and hail. Drunken, golden barley. My own flaxen hair, dancing about my shoulders, woven with the azure feathers of battle kills. The silver bands on my wrists sending out coins of light, blessing all that is wholesome and alive.

While my dark eye watches within the moon shadow, it sees no edges and looks beyond the breezy child of day to crepuscular bogs and barrows, where centuries of grinning bones lay unaltered. Where toad squint breaches the black pool, where lizard laps at the moon and bats dip ... we were there. We came from the darkling depths, you and me. From frog pearls, containing a pattern like the twist of a corn dolly. One linking with another and another and another, until a woman was made. For there can be no man without woman and woman was there long before him. You were with me in that place, under that firefly sky, and have been many times since. So why do I thrash so, as if for my life? Because it is you I fight for and for you I wait. I am Briga, Queen of the Cantiaci. I see the present and the past, but I cannot see the future.

It is not that I had no liking for men; there was much to love: bravery, loyalty, heartiness. In our time, there was little between us strength-wise, both male and female honed by plough and sword. Girls and boys each learnt the ways of the warrior and were equally proficient. The equality would have been complete were it not for the crude ambition that some men harboured, taking them beyond their own control and rendering them inferior to beasts. One such as this took his pleasure once.

I was but eleven years old and had not yet bled, cutting birch for arrows in The Wood of Evening (named so because the mantle of twilight remained constant upon it). A foul smell, like the remains of Haska's offerings on the altar stone. Dismissing the kitten rabbit impaled on my spear, I peered into the gloom. It seemed to beckon; a white tusk in the dusk. A solitary stinkhorn nestled between an elm's roots. My sister, Andua, a healer, would be pleased with my find. I knelt before it and observed the black flies drawn by the stench, squabbling in its slime. Then, as if to spare me, a rough hand cupped my mouth and pinched my nose. I had no breath as I had already held it, and he dragged me down to the leaves. In my sight, the fetid fungus and beyond, just out of reach, my spear, winking ruby with the blood of my kill. I watched the moon ride through bare winter limbs, his urgency in me, it seemed, giving pace to her transit. His hand pressed hard on my mouth, shredding my lips against my own teeth and I saw my neck as a twig on the brink of snapping. He beat an incantation, muttering to his sordid deities and all the while, my head met and met again, the base of the elm. The goddess rode on, oblivious, or so I thought, until with a sudden pulse, she let loose all her starry sisters, which blurred into a thousand crosses as I wept for that baby rabbit, and how it had screamed. For baby rabbits know nothing, other than their mothers, how to find food and the thump, thump, thump of danger. And with that, the drum of fear in my heart shifted to anger.

The man spat on his hand and wiping the blood

from his cock with his cloak, he tucked it in his garment and strode off whistling into the woods.

He was easy to track, but then he would not have imagined that I had the temerity to do so. I blended myself with trees and had he turned, he would have seen nothing but the woody knot of my eye. His scabbard creaked and he coughed often (perhaps he had the cattle disease). He crashed over deadfalls and sighed heavily, sending roosted gamebirds carping. The breeze of a white owl brushed my cheek with the tenderness of a mother. At length, his commotion ceased, except for the splatter of piss. The last he would ever take. My heart hastened in recognition of what I would do, and the owl hooted a sage verdict. The goddess rode higher and brighter, silvering all about me, including the man ... asleep, bound in his cloak like a shroud.

His garb was that of a Roman, probably a messenger and as such, I knew his breastplate would not allow my spear to penetrate. So I stuck him in his loins and as his eyes widened, I stuck them too, so that he would never look upon his ancestors in the afterlife, nor would I have to witness his terrible comprehension. It was with great satisfaction that I unsheathed his short sword, suitable for a child, a trophy for my little brother, Bevin.

I am thinking about this now, some five and twenty years later. The crawl of bees on a troublesome nick on my thigh, which Andua is pressing with prickly leaves. Fleet, my hound, lifts his shaggy head, whimpering sympathy. The fire, fretting in the hearth, unleashes a whip crack. The wood smoke carries me down the years and elevates me to the thatch, from where I gaze down on my mother, herself a queen, and my father, both long since dead. Her bronze hair burnishes the pillow. Her hand, dyed red, forefinger singled out with a copper ring, strokes the broad back of my father as he pants and sweats upon her. I know it is their wedding night and that they are making me. Her passive expression turns to surprise and for an instant, I think she sees me, but she's only reacting to some secret craft my father is practising beneath the skins. Their shadow beasts loom on the wall and her cheeks are aflame, teeth clenching.

"Goddess," she gasps, "I beseech you. Let this be the girl child ... the vessel."

And the wood smoke twists itself around the rooftree, two spirals intertwine to form that harmonious pattern I have imagined all my life. Its secret hid from me.

I returned with a start to Andua, eyeing me with amusement.

"What did you see Briga?"

I stared at the guttering flames. "I saw our parents."

"An auspicious omen," she nodded, "especially on the advent of one's wedding."

How could this be so? Had I finally been overmastered? The truth was, yes ... and willingly.

Andua had foretold this. The gift of seeing, strong in our line. At only nine years, she had returned from The Wood of Evening to announce that her spirit was the kingfisher, the mote of the dream still in her eye. No-one doubted it. The flicker of fast feathers about her hair and in her fist, a single blue one. In celebration, father fashioned a silver cloak brooch in the bird's form, with agate wings, polished mother-of-pearl for its breast and two beady, little turquoise eyes. Being two years her elder and having no inkling of my spirit guide, the envy glowered in my throat, as a malady.

Keen to determine my creature, I tranced in the woods often. Choking on sage smoke until my eyes blurred. I willed wolves, she-cats and mythical, made-up beasts, whose dangerous characteristics, I felt, would embody me well. At length, I returned with a countenance sullen; the gods had scorned me. My vanity betrayed.

The vision had been too clear to deny. Two creatures locked in mortal combat. The larger, tawny and haired, long legged. His jaws clamped on his foe, nay, prey. The lesser, with fur of yellow and black, beads of gold caught on her coat, stabbing, until both lay lifeless. But no. One stirred, and with care, the bee extricated herself from the spider's web and flew up into the morning.

"But I don't want to be a stupid bee," I cried.

"Hush, child," my mother stroked my head. "Why,

the bee has respect of all the creatures. She can bring down a horse and it has been known for great warriors to lay swolled and frothing from one stick of her point. She is the hardest working of creatures and gives her life to ensure her line flourishes."

I began to feel a little better.

"She treats her subjects fairly," mother continued, "they value their queen above all. One day, Briga, you will be queen and would do well to portray her fortitude and perspicacity."

My despair was further mollified when father placed around my neck, a torc of twisted gold and black bronze, to ensure everyone, far and wide, would know "Briga, Queen Bee of The Cantiaci," he chuckled.

The morning was thick with rain when Andua, running the gauntlet from the women's quarters, burst in, skidding on the strewings. Fleet's tail thumped a welcome and I lifted myself from sleep. Seldom had I witnessed her demeanour so urgent.

"Get clothed," she said and shook off the droplets

like a fisher bird, free of the stream.

I flung back the bed skin. "How many?" My hand finding my sword belt. She placed her damp claw on mine.

"No, Briga … with calm." Her eyes beyond me, recalling back and forth her night flights. She sat on the bed. Often this had happened; a warning of marauding tribes. Or pretenders who would vie for my hand. Her hands caressed her own thighs and she rocked in beatific trance. "Everyone knows that bears have a tooth for honey." Her eyes found mine, as if I should understand this random statement. She resumed her rubbing. "There is love, oh there is love, Briga." She shuddered in vicarious rapture and lifted her chin as if harkening to a message born on the wind. Then the purblind eyes unclouded and fixed me. "The one who would be your equal is nigh," she said. "Fact."

It is not that I did doubt her gift but sometimes, her interpretations were slightly off-target, nonetheless, rarely had I seen her so adamant. And truth be told, that night, I had slept in an unusual complexion of ease. The source of which I felt was gaining. But despite the signs ...

"Andua," I said. "That's impossible. No man will subdue me." I casually examined my eyes in my blade. "How does he look?"

She slipped under the blanket as she did when we were youngsters, fidgeting with gossip. "I see five riders, all have helmets. Cloaks of green."

"Vortigae?" I was puzzled. "I thought I'd taught them lesson enough when Bax made his challenge."

"It's not Bax." She balled her fists and pressed them to her eyes. "'Tis another of his line." Her body twitched like a hound in sleep. "Bax is slain, there is a new leader. I cannot see him, save for the mark of the bear on his shield."

I began to feel a mite concerned; Bax had been dogged and so too would be his clan. "Tell me at least, is he a fellow of bulk?"

"Aaagh! No!" she screamed. "More of a gelding than a bull." She appeared perplexed for an instant before diminishing into giggles. And I laughed too to obscure my disquiet, because there crouched inside me a secret so deep, it was almost hid to myself. A shameful vanity but braided with fear. A bane at once salve and gall: one day they would stop coming. Although I maintained the vigours of spring, I was at the wain of my thirty sixth year, senior by our standards, battle worn and childless, with the knowledge I would never find the solace I required in any man. When I no longer had iron enough to lift my sword and spear, or handle my chariot pair, I would need the alliance of another to defend my people. This notion weighed heavy. Perchance this day I would succumb. Not to the blows of my suitor, but to my own burden.

Thankful for the warmth of my mount between my legs, we sat without motion. Some forty paces behind me, the warriors' steeds raked up clods with truculent hoof. The jangle of horse furniture and regalia garb as their necks nodded impatiently while the rain assaulted us in gusts. The wind screamed through my braids, whipping them about my head. My right fist draining as it rested, shoulder height on the shaft of my spear. The left, on the reins and gripping the mane of Ankou, my beloved, grey war stallion. His ears switched forward and he snickered a warning. "Shhh," I soothed. "Steady, boy." Five riders breached the horizon and the grassland between us took on the swell of the ocean as the rain fled to meet them. They halted, and although distant specks, I clearly saw one raise his arm in greeting. This gesture excited in me an inexplicable fondness, the like of which I generally reserved for kin. The hill steepish, they angled their horses with care to the foot and, once on the flat, proceeded at a canter.

The Vortigae were horsemen, and it was said, were able to make their mounts dance. Together, we could defend the southlands. I quickly shut my mind to further thoughts of this kind. They were also traders who sailed to Gaul and beyond, and, in consequence, their blood was well mixed. I reminded myself that no manifestation of manhood would be equitable to me and yet a small voice remained. "Briga," it whispered, "see with your true eye."

As they drew near, the helmets so designed to protect the head and face also described the countenance of a warrior already dead; the cheek and nose guard suggesting the eyes to be gaping maws and removing all semblance of humanity. Most aggressive that they should approach me, obscured in this fashion. I canted my spear in displeasure. Stopping at an adequate length, two dismounted and strode towards Ankou and me, their green cloaks snapping in the wind, which also moved the clouds apace. The sun broke through, prompting the Vortigae horses to steam and the Great Mother to cast her bow of colours in the sky. Of the two who had come forth, the taller bore the mark of the crescent moon on his shield and the shorter, the mark of the bear; he who would be my husband?

"Hail, Briga, Queen of the Cantiaci," brayed the thin moon in the voice of a newly broken youth and both, I noted, were yet without beards. What jest was this? As I dismounted, they sunk to one knee. And placing their right arm across their chests, they bowed their heads.

I circled them for a while, my hand caressing my hilt, and cleared my throat.

"Vortigae," I said. "What is your quest?" Thin moon raised his head.

"Why, Majesty, we come to fight for the honour of your troth." His ambition amused me, and I let forth a hearty guffaw.

"What, the two of you?"

"No Majesty, only I," said the shorter bear, whose frame, I noted, was good. Although his voice was gruffer, it did not resonate with the growl of a seasoned man of war. I looked to my tribe, who remained stern, except Andua, whose expression revealed a mischievous wisdom. I stood, a tower of confusion above the genuflecting.

"Vortigae," pitching my tone weary yet patient. "Are you men or boys who would fight for my hand?"

With this, the bear lifted his helmet and steam curled from his smooth face and black hair, which was cut short in the Belgic fashion. His eyes met mine and within me all the tumult of my soul subsided as the answer became clear.

"Neither," she said.

Pushing on her shield, she stood to her full height. "Ysolte, Queen of The Vortigae wishes your hand." Her hot words billowed in vapours, fogging her features until her dark eyes materialised, fixing mine. Her countenance, at once disorientated and moved me; as if peering into a glade pool, to see the reflection returned, though familiar, is not one's own. The curve of her cheek, the chisel of her rather large nose, suggested the abstract lines a traveller would seek in the landscape, indicating the kindly configuration of home. Clouds issued from her open mouth, formed in a bow, showing white teeth intact, with a central gap, hinting humour and magic. Although of a similar age to me, a silver streak blazed in the night of her hair.

The implication rattled between us, turned the tumblers and slid home. Our various versions incarnate, playing out as fleeting fish, twisting in a cataract. We fluctuated in height and colour; the journey of generations passing in an eye-blink. Young, granite giants stirred and shouldered the horizon, then, just as quickly, melted to bones. Great forests sprang up and toppling on their sides, blackened to char. The frozen rivers we had traversed, now under the sea. The perpetual darkness we had endured when the gods were reshaping the world. After that crimson sky-storm, we held each other in hope, bearing witness the sun's rebirth.

The dogs that ever nagged at my heels, the secret that winked just out of vision, now furnished me with understanding; we had found and lost each other a thousand times, and just as a dream on waking, the message eludes us. The truth is buried under the morning and we are consigned to forget, yet again, that which is too complex to hold in our daytime eye. It remains in our pocket; a shiny, indeterminable object, that our fingers fall upon from time to time. It was you and had always been: my rooftree, my answer, my purpose, my own heart.

The moment overtook me, and I was compelled to act in an unaccustomed way. Taking her hand in mine, I knelt and pressed it to my lips. "Have you sought me long?" the words choked in my throat.

She removed her hand from mine and placed it on

my head. "Aye, my queen," she said. Her voice held the peace of prayer. "Many lifetimes over."

"The one who would be my equal is nigh," I said getting to my feet and drawing my sword. Two of my maids ran forth and as they unbuckled my cloak and set my shield on my arm, I was unable to take my eyes from Ysolte's, nor her mine.

We touched blades and circled each other, part in wariness and part in a private game. Her legs were long with hide boots to the knee. She wore the plaid breeches of a man and resembled one most closely but for the leather chest guard, shaped to accommodate her breasts. We had no will to fight each other, but understood the custom had to be seen to be observed ... and well.

I struck a blow, which I did not pull. She batted it away with her shield, exposing her midriff and my sword sliced not one inch from it. She sprang back, her brow fusing. I could have finished her then: she knew it and nodded an acknowledgement. And so ensued a cunning exchange of two warriors communing at once in battle and agreement. The clang of our mettle ringing our ears, pleasing both ourselves and the goddess. Now under a blue sky, we turned as hawks, folding and striking in the sun, until it hung directly overhead. My eyes were slits, dazzled by glinting metal and salt sting. Ysolte's shape imprinted upon them as a phantom.

"Hold," we panted as one. And catching our breath we armed at our brows and rested on our swords.

"I would rather have you at my side in battle than opposite," I said.

"And so you shall," she smiled, setting about me once again.

Her entourage had removed their helmets, revealing themselves to be women all, and shouted hoarsely their encouragement to her. Their dialect rolled with round sounds and burrs as if they were gargling ale and they punched their palms with their fists in ebullience. My clan remained silent but for Bevin, soothing Ankou, who reared in distress as the tip of Ysolte's sword punctured my thigh. We had to be convincing and while she had barely grazed me (a skill in itself), I felt the fever of battle corrupt my senses. And realised, for the first time, the sensation was closely akin to lust. Our mouths drew wide in a leer. My sword wagged a reprimand and as she glanced at the blood issuing from my wound, I suspected she had a notion of another flow she had provoked.

We found ourselves sweating in stalemate, impatient for a climax. It was up to me to contrive a subtle supplication if I wanted her. I'd never wanted anything more. So casting my shield aside, I took my blade in both hands and hacked relentless at hers, to distract the onlookers from the fact I was now vulnerable and inviting defeat. She understood; driving forward, her jaw set resolute, she growled as a bear and butted me with the boss. My foot caught a rabbit hole and as I fell, I knew the moment had arrived for which we both had hoped. I lay spread-eagled in the wet grass, her shield pinning my sword arm, her hot face above mine. Quite forgetting their burly bluster, her women erupted into jubilant screams and whoops.

"Yield," she snarled. The screams ceased and there was not a breath, save the weary wind. Her eyes flamed but mine reflected a mocking calm.

"I yield," I whispered, and the women, placing their fingers in their mouths, let forth piercing whistles and linked arms in a whirling dance.

Loosening her grip, she kept her weight upon me and bore down with emphatic menace for the crowd, and for my benefit, ground her mound against mine, our mouths almost meeting.

I had seen nothing of Ysolte in the two weeks since our exchange. She had returned to her people, proclaiming her victory and to gather suitable tokens of her intent. I knew she would have difficulty with this, as would I; no amount of trinkets, however rare, could express our unprecedented connection, nor were they needed.

Tormented by desire, I absorbed myself in summoning the landscapes we had inhabited in our former incarnations.

As a child, I'd often depicted lands beyond my ken to my mother: a place where there was sand but never sea. Where great rulers, clad in gold, were entombed in smooth mountains. And a different mother looked down upon a different Briga. Occasionally, I'd wept for my other family, moreover, my other self, and for something else which I couldn't identify.

"Don't fret, child," she would console, "I'm your mother now and you're my Briga."

Even in maturity, I would often wake with a start, shot from a realm of inexplicable grief and horror. Accompanying me in this place was an abstract presence, which I endeavoured to make out. It emanated love and a complete knowledge of myself, but the only tangible impression I could glean was that it was more on the female side. Naturally, as an infant, I took it to be my mother. But no sooner had I beheld Ysolte, I understood it was she I'd been trying to fathom. In other lovers, I'd merely been seeking her. So familiar: the swagger, the strong grip, how our bodies fitted together as two babes in the womb. I saw gold and black bronze, twisted in a torc. I saw wisps of woodsmoke intertwine. I saw plaited stalks of grain, the linked necks of swans and the circle of a serpent, consuming its own tail. In all things I saw her.

We, The Cantiaci, as with all you would call 'Celts', followed ways which we judged natural and pervasive. We did not view each other as simply men and women, although most identified themselves as one or the other. There were several degrees betwixt, sometimes based on the body's urges, but more often, on an emotional sensibility. We did not think it wholesome that all should be tarred with just one brush or the other. As such, it was not uncommon for a man to lay with, or be joined with another man, nor woman with woman. In fact, it was considered unremarkable.

Furthermore, it was of no concern that Ysolte and I would not directly produce heirs; we had siblings whose children carried the royal line. Bevin's twins, Luki and Signa would be as our own. The druids stumbled from their hemp-smoke huts, relaying visions of the bee sustaining the bear and its reciprocal protection, so condoning the union. While the elders rubbed their chins and nodded at the political advantages.

"Besides," said Haska, "a male warrior, even a king, will remain just that ... a man. Whereas a female warrior ... a queen, is something over and above man and woman, engendering all things admirable in both."

They all agreed the joining of two such rare entities would be auspicious indeed.

The brew Andua had concocted surely calmed my nerves but had also unleashed an ardour below that needed little stoking, rendering it barely containable.

"By the goddess, Andua. Am I poisoned?"

She hummed and thoughtfully re-dressed my wound. "The mighty murmur, I call it," she sang. "It relaxes, provokes the desire and makes sweet the breath, all in one little measure ... marvellous." She patted my thigh. "I drink it all the time."

"Ha," I said, "that explains much."

I stretched, cleansed and fragrant on the bear skin. Fleet lapped at the bath water in which my sister had me almost boiled.

The Vortigae horses had thudded upon the woodway outside my window at daybreak. Their harness bells danced a subtle celebration as did the jess of a hunting bird, which I imagined tethered to a leather mitt. Ysolte resided somewhere nearby. The very thought of her prompted an exquisite ague in me, which Andua's draft enhanced

"She's bathing," she smiled, as if picturing her. "She's travelled long for you, Bee."

"I know," I replied. "Make sure she gets to sup your mighty murmur."

Andua leant in and took one of my braids in her fingers. "And be sure she gets to sup yours," she giggled annoyingly, painting my lips with my own hair.

"You're such a nit," I hiccupped, and we laughed.

"And you, my sister, are caught on the horns of love." Her eyes gleamed moist and merry.

I'd lain with others before and once or twice had felt the flutter of hands that might steal my heart. But I was a girl then and had since myself resigned, that I would never know the true nature of that which makes us at once slave and mistress.

Tomorrow, Ysolte would bestow me with gifts: jewels, trinkets from far lands, tapestries, soft fabrics for our bed, surely a horse, perhaps that bird. As would any husband, as would I. It was as if giving presents to oneself. But hold, was she my husband and I the wife? An inequality prickled the language. Could we both be husband, both be wife? The roles, like the gender allotted to us were insufficient. However, our people, most pragmatic, refusing to subscribe to any law which we felt compromised us, had an alternative word – 'gade', which was nearer kin or partner.

"Now," Andua fussed. "There are plenty of logs, more draft is in the jug, meat and ale on the dresser ... water. Oh." Ears pricked. "Your bear approaches."

I was aware of this already, for not only had I sensed her, but her tread was not careful. A gentle rap on the doorpost and my heart knocked in response. Ysolte's fist drew aside the curtain and she stooped to enter. No longer dressed in her armour and trappings but in a plain white tunic, as if for bed. An intricate, blue tattoo escaped her upper arm and snaked under her clothing. I beheld her face, which mirrored my own; nerves, elation, and the high blood of passion were drawn upon it.

"Goodnight my queens." Andua bowed with unusual decorum and left. Fleet followed, giving Ysolte's hand a hasty nuzzle on the way.

We stared for a while, chests rising and falling, lips forming a similar, sinuous smile. Almost nostalgic. Her eyes fell to the dressing on my leg and she frowned.

"Worry not," I said unwrapping the bandage to reveal a mark, pink and almost healed. Then pulling my garment over my head, I presented my body, which her eyes travelled gravely, alighting on the many scars and welts. "We have done well," I said, "to last long enough that we might find each other."

She nodded and knelt before me. My vitals clenched as she moved her head towards my lap, brushing the wound with her lips in apology and reparation. She kissed my hand, inferring respect and devotion. Then, her mouth halted not a hand span from mine.

Emanating the whiff of mighty murmur, our smiles met quietly. The gallop of my heart kicked up, as if bent on unsaddling me, and reared up in my breast as her rough hand closed upon it.

We kissed gluttonous, eager to feed. The singular sensation of a dream, when one is tumbling through the abyss overtook me; falling not to one's death, mind, but returning to a much longed-for, simpler state. I realised the abyss was within me. Too long we had waited for gentle rediscovery; an urgent exchange was desired.

She mauled my neck and fell upon my breasts, a ravening beast, where she gorged and suckled, but with tongue most cunning. Hungry, barbarian growls issued from her stuffed mouth and she pulled back to observe her own thumbs working her drool over my teats. This crude handling prompted me to sweat and buck in fevered rapture and her gaze swept down my body to the heart of the contagion. Nostrils flaring as a filly, her expression roguish as she charmed forth the briny humour from my cunt, her fingers wallowing in their anointment. My senses half crazed.

"Do it," I commanded. "Now!"

Pulling her tunic over her head, she leaned forward and guided her own teat to my essence, producing there, a lathered sound. This caused me desire beyond mind. Measuredly, as if painting herself for battle, she daubed left cheek then right, and revisiting the palette, she passed her glistening fingers over her lips.

"Please, Ysolte. I beg you."

I knew this would give her satisfaction; the subtleties of this game long established when we had played in another time. Bracing the heel of her hand between my breasts, to halt my thrashing, she entered me with slick assurance, holding me fast, so that we could witness both, her tender onslaught. Hastening her motion, she contemplated my cunt, until we struck upon a rhythm. All the while examining, treasuring. Reviving me.

Her sword arm continued its thrusting, gilded in the lamplight, which also described the orbs of her breasts. They jostled amid the knots and ropes on her chest and arms. The gold cage of her ribs, the yoke of her shoulders. As handsome a person I'd never seen. And as she plied, faster and deeper, that flicker of eternal recognition passed between us. She was bringing me back to her, bringing me home.

Noting the spark had caught; she lifted her chin in summons and uttered for the first time in this.

"Come to me, Briga," her voice hoarse. "Come to me, my queen."

Resonating in the half light, her countenance shock-shifted: a diminutive, furred beast to a slender necked, dusky being. From flint-eyed crone to a slant-eyed woman, apple-cheeked and ancient. Shaman, hunter, slave, nomad and many others, too fleeting to catch. Each regarding me through the same glade pool eyes. I felt I had known and loved them all, just as fiercely as the one inside me now, the queen known as Ysolte. I cried out, unable to contain the divine ride. Suddenly the gods snatched me up and confronted me with a blinding prospect, but all too cognisant of my mortal limitations, I let the knowledge slip to the wind. Mercifully, they set me down, quaking and sobbing in the arms of my love and all those beings I must have shook loose, returned to the hub, as bees to the hive.

Ysolte and I wept for our reunion and the understanding that our completion would be all too brief. But for now, we were whole. Our pledge; to further our story in this life and to keep hold the thread till the next. A pact we had made countless times over.

The grave tamp of bone upon skin in the great hall, beat the chants of the sacreds. Sparks spat to the rafters at the flutter of Haska's oil-glazed fingers over the fire cauldron and beasts stared stricken from the tapestries. The song soared with the smoke, redolent with pine pitch and sulphurous nose-pinch and died in the thatch, only to be reborn in fervent roundelay.

Bare-breasted and blue we stood, Ysolte and I. Hair, lime-raked white. We returned to each other, stars in a black firmament; eye sockets painted as a death's head, symbolising a union beyond life. A stag's sinew binding us in the hand-fast, from which the letting of our blood loosed droplets to a gold chalice. First leaving Ysolte's lips grinning gore and then my own.

"Thou art blood of my blood and bone of my bone." Her voice rose true and clear. The gap in her teeth reassuring me from the distortion. "I give thee my body, that we two might be one." Her ribs bleached, and then the rafters as Haska angered the flames. "I give thee my spirit, till our life shall be done." We lifted again, our blended iron to our mouths and she fixed me as a gimlet-eyed hawk.

"Thou cannot possess me, for I am my own." I picked up the vow and amid the clamour, my voice sounded to my ears a distant echo.

"I give thee that which is mine." Our words finding purchase together and her fierce grip wrung further rubies from our palms. "I shall serve thee in all ways, for thou art life. And the honey will taste sweeter from my hand."

Haska summoned luteous clouds from the cauldron. "Let it be known," she proclaimed, "that Briga and Ysolte are henceforth joined as gade, and in that marriage, Cantiaci and Vortigae are one clan.

We were bound. Our lips met and we tasted the salt of each other. The drums became a frenzy, in which our people engaged themselves in increasingly intimate forms of unification. As she resonated before me, I fought to stop this moment sliding to the past, but it was a memory already.

I saw your body; a soot-smeared carcass. Blue and immortal, marble white. Skin pricked with greenwood figments. Beautiful you shimmered. Your tattoos danced and my eyes found the trick of salvaging your visage from the death mask. We unwound the sinew and I branded your breast red with my hand.

That night we rode our mounts to the sea (Ysolte's, a well natured, roan mare named Gildas), wherein we threw our oathing stones, which contained our pledges, so that the gods might keep them safe for eternity.

Ghosts in the surf light, lathered with soap weed, we washed each other clean of woad and lime. Of woe and time. Unfettered, we rolled in the brutish swell, a game both dangerous and exhilarating, losing and regaining each other with much relief, as if taunting the forces that would drag us apart. While above sparkled a million, mute messages, the origins of which we pondered from the shore.

"Perhaps they are souls," Ysolte mused, "as ourselves in waiting." The wind almost snatching her words. Her thoughtful countenance gilded by moonlight, and the fire we had made from antlers of driftwood.

"Do you claim we were once stars?"

"No, well ... maybe." She scratched the silver streak at her temple, as if thinking much had made it so.

Now, I was pleased to be able to share a long-held concept of my own. "I believe stars to be still present in the day," I whispered to her ear, for fear of the eavesdropping breeze, "even though they are hid from us."

"Me too," she said, grasping my hand. "Like people when they die; even if we cannot see them, we know they remain somewhere."

My mind tipped on the brink of a notion, terrifying

in its enormity. "And they reside in the sky and not beneath?" I was bordering territory heretical.

"It matters not where they reside," she said, "whether it be above, below or within us. They are as bears in their winter sleep, until they are awoken and set down in this life once more."

"Set down by the goddess?" I asked.

Ysolte surveyed the night sky. "Call it what you will," she said, "but this ... all this." She spread her arms wide. "It's all set on a wheel; sunset, moonrise ... set within a greater wheel of season and solstice. We are born, we die ... another wheel."

I pictured the water mill, our most complex device.

"A machine?"

"I think it so," she said.

I paused, my face hot with panic. "But who operates it?"

"Briga," she shrugged, "who operates the river?"

My mouth opened but shut abruptly, holding at bay, 'the goddess', my initial response, and I stared as the

THE LAST QUEEN OF HOLLAND

tentacles of another idea breached the surface.

"Ysolte, do you believe you and I to be on a separate wheel to other folk?"

She sighed heavily. "I believe it to be a riddle that, someday, I will have the wit to fathom," she brought her face close in to mine, "but not in this life," she smiled, "for I am solely employed in the duty of your love."

"And I yours," I said, kissing her mouth. "But sometimes I am confounded by my own scant comprehension of it all. I may as well be an ant, traversing the vast planes of a tabletop."

She laughed, "I agree. But each time we return, we glean a mite more."

"But we are destined to forget it all again," I said.

"Not quite all," she said, "or else I would never have found you."

My limited mind, which consigned me to plough the same thought-furrow and harness my reactions, sensed the goddess' frown to have shifted to a smile, as the coal sky began to burn at the edges.

I knew well the cycle of dusk and dawn, of seed time and harvest, but had glimpsed a greater dance playing out. Blood-dashed clouds retreated from the rising sun, pursuing stars already fled. Suddenly, the bickering waves, obeying a higher nature, bowed to the horizon. Whereupon a path so solid seeming was formed, I reckoned I could ride to the heart of the machine itself. I looked for an answer in Ysolte's face, lashed with pieces of gold and fell, yet again, on that immutable fact; we had been first in the darkness and, at the end of days, we would be the last.

Smoke filtered through the stubble-snout roundhouses and mingling with mist, drifted to the ground as an exhalation. Our stride swirled the vapour as we made our way to the great hall, wherein the Roman procurator, Livius, awaited our arrival. Ysolte's march moved the woodway underfoot and her goose-fleshed arm brushed mine. The trees shivered, I fancied, at the recollection of how her fingers had touched me, like the willow meets the water.

A steady clang from the forge fashioned the

morning, while a skylark unseen, had it embroidered. We passed neatly tended gardens; fat hen and turnip emerging in lines and a chicken sent flapping by the clap of old hands. A man bowed

"Good morning your majesties," a gnarled fist against his heart.

After the fields to the south, further Cantiaci settlements were strung out. And beyond, Vortigae strongholds were now sharing their pastures with Astawegii and Tambartes. Surely our combined light could banish the long shadow of Rome. The thought weaselled my mind, but then as a sweet draft, the laughter of children; Luki and Signa had become most intrigued by Ysolte. But failing to draw a reaction, now tramped behind her as bellicose giants, in parody of her heavy step. She halted stern. And hand on hilt she turned slow. Screaming with delight they scampered off, their mission accomplished, Fleet barking and bounding in pursuit.

"If only it were so simple," I said.

Her tilted head requested elaboration.

"To see off the Romans," I explained, "with a single glance."

She smiled. "Aye, that would be a charm indeed," but her expression shifted to gravity. "We must tread softly, Briga. Our time will come."

It was no secret I despised them. The Romans had been in our land for some years; The Cantiaci, along with most others, had taken up their offer of protection and the promise of trade and for the most part, it had been equitable. But their terms were becoming increasingly unacceptable. It was a curious arrangement and although they generously allowed us to continue our old ways of worship and chieftains, some amongst us had begun to see it for what it was; an insidious occupation.

We were invited to store our grain in their granaries, to 'educate' our youth abroad. The grain, like our young people, was never returned. Cruel and humiliating punishment was meted out on those resistant, and women were subjected to that low act, the one which I, myself, had suffered as a child. For all our ferocious reputation, we were a largely benign people and, it transpired, had been duped as easily as children.

A rebellious breeze disgruntled the puddles and carried my gaze beyond the pig pens and paddocks to a distant field, where an oxen pair was turning the green ground to black. Brown rumps twitched under the ploughman's switch. Ysolte cast her hand over her eyes to follow my view.

"We are as such beasts," I said, "under the yoke."

"Your majesties." His extravagant bow a mockery. Close-set, furtive eyes and sharp, white teeth, which he tested with his tongue constantly, gave him the appearance of a fox, with slyness to match. Distinctly unnerving was the graceful dance of his hands and his slender frame; it produced in me a distasteful fascination.

It was rumoured that in Rome, women were closely tethered: banned from high office, unable to own land, pursue the sword, nor could they choose their own partners.

The procurator and I had met a number of

times and Ysolte had encountered him also. On each occasion, we concluded, he became a deal more odious; an opinion from which not even his pretty looks could redeem him. He adhered to the protocols, but the flit of his eyes betrayed an ugly art. That moist mouth, often overheard, boasting of acts most cruel, brought before a Roman audience for their pleasure. The screams of the unfortunate victims enhancing the spectacle.

"The Emperor Nero is most pleased with our cultural exchange programme." He paused, savouring the sanitised phrase.

"Cultural exchange," Ysolte sneered. "Is that what you call slavery these days?"

He sighed, as if addressing a wayward child. "It is of no concern what you think." His hand flapped dismissively. "It is my intention to expand the project. The Cantiaci," he assumed a benevolent air, "as are the Vortigae, are a fair people; strong of back and brave of heart."

The evaluation was meaningless. "Livius," I said. "Do you mean to flatter us into further subjugation?"

His eyes travelled my body. "Briga, Briga, Briga ..."

"You will address my face, sir," I hissed, "and not any other part."

He leant in, reacquainting me with his tainted breath. "It is only in respect of your customs ..." I detected garlic and rosewater, "that I address any part of you at all ... Now!" He clapped his hands. "This brings me nicely to the crux!"

The reason I associated Romans with a foul smell was not lost on me.

"Your women," he said, as if discussing horses, "they are of particular interest to the emperor." Ysolte stepped forth with such speed, I thought it her intent to butt him. The guard drew his sword, but with a waft of the procurator's hand, he repostured. "So feisty," he tutted and reached to touch her cheek, which flamed with indignation. "Your women, I mean," he goaded, "they pose a challenge which the emperor, and I must say myself, find most gratifying ... and then," he leered, "there are the children ... such beautiful savages."

My nostrils twitched at the onslaught of his breath. "I suggest you comply, Briga." His gaze roved idly over my breasts. "Or there will be consequences."

A picture appeared in my mind; myself, standing behind his prone person, steadily violating with my unsheathed sword, his hairless, perfumed arse hole.

Instead, I moved to his ear. "I suggest you get gone," I whispered, "before I cut your cock off."

His head snapped back with laughter and for a moment I believed this whole exchange to have been but a joke. Giggling, his eyes twinkled, but in a blink, returned steely. Mouth forming a sour bunch. "You have been warned," his spittle flecked my face, "you mongrel-eyed harpy."

We tried to keep them close. The children.

Ysolte turned by degrees, her feet planted in the dust where hens pecked. Her torso twisting with such stealth, the birds remained unperturbed, until the clack of her wooden sword upon Luki's sent them into a flap.

"Your wrist is now broke," she said, kneeling to adjust the boys grip on the hilt. "Like this ... and don't look at the sword, watch my eyes."

The beam of the unfinished chariot on which I sat, quietly creaked as Signa settled beside me. Fleet stretched a yawn as she gently dug about his belly with her practice sword and I was struck by the idea that Ysolte had completed more than just my own self. The disparate pieces had lain about me all my days, much like the parts of this chariot: the wheels propped against the side of the forge, ready for rimming, the axles, still trees on the hill. Not only had Ysolte fitted it all together, but she was a key constituent; her presence bringing order to kin, clan and perhaps a nascent nation. But whilst order was agreeable, I sensed a greater knowing could be acquired from chaos and struggle; without the challenge of adversity, there would be little expansion in understanding oneself. Ysolte and I were as two halves of a whole. A new token for our land had been minted, neatly housing this notion; our likeness imprinted either side of a coin. Two queens on a wheel.

Fleet sounded a vexed whine as Signa's petting with the soft weapon grew provocative.

"Do not taunt him," I said sharply, and her face fell. She had only meant to court my attention. Drawing her to my side, I took in her scent of wind-ratted hair and smoke. We both knew she would never invite me in that way again. Her small frame stirred in me a she-bear, who would rip from gut to throat any man who sought to harm her. She gnawed her nails and I guessed her nettle.

"Signa," I whispered, and she regarded me with bitter sorrow. "Ysolte does not favour your brother above you, you know." I knew this insufficient.

"But why then," her words burst forth as a fox unsnared, "does she always have time for his stupid games and why does she let him ride Gildas and polish her blade and let him wear her helmet and ..." reddening outraged "... he always has the place next to her in bed." I smiled at this unintended snub of myself.

"My child," I said, "she sees you as you are: a clever,

patient girl, who has little need for childish games and mollycoddling."

Her shoulders straightened. "Did she tell you that, Briga?"

"Yes, she says it often and I believe it true also." The scowl banished, her eyes shone to Ysolte. "Besides," I continued, "let me tell you something about boys," leaning in confidentially. "They are the squeaky wheel that gets the grease." Her faltering smile revealed the recent vacancy left by the milk tooth we had dropped in the stream. "Do you understand, kitten?" Her flaxen hair jounced upon keen nodding and we chuckled in female collusion.

Ysolte and Luki resumed their careful dance. The strong little boy stood; arms braced before his chest, sword out thrust, a picture of taut concentration. A beautiful child. Ysolte swung and he lithely squatted, jabbing against her shin his dull blade.

"Ouch!" She hobbled and cursed in a circle, while Luki bent himself double with guffaws. "Good ... that was good," she hissed.

"Do not venture beyond the river," a command which most children obeyed, but stifled by safety, Luki was a frequent exception.

He was easy enough to track; I had followed his scamperings, little bigger than those of a hare, all morning. At length I spotted him, his lime-stiffened hair at odds with the whispering tufts surrounding him, but closer to the chalky scree on which he scraped his belly. What the kitten was stalking, I was unable to yet see. The standing stones of our ancestors loomed beyond and with a clench in my gut, the object of his focus became apparent; a lone legionnaire relieving himself against a sacred slab. Luki jumped to his feet, brandishing his dagger and charged at the soldier, who, startled, drew his sword. In the next second, the soldier fell to his knees, gawping at my war spear protruding from his shoulder. Luki gave a whoop and finished him off with a slice across the throat.

"Filthy Roman," he snarled. The slaughtered man's neck gave an ejaculation, painting on the boy's chest a red flower. "The gods will see you gone!" Luki shrieked. "Briga and Ysolte will kill the eagle!"

We had tried to keep them close ... the children, even allowing them into our bed. And though Luki was not kin to Ysolte, a resemblance to her was discernible in his features. That, and the way he now wore his hair; cut short in the Belgic fashion.

A further puzzle was Signa's appearance; not because her flaxen hair and fierce expression resembled mine (we were kin after all), but that she should be as chalk is to cheese to her twin brother. Bevin's wife, Culta, a respected warrior, had died in their arrival on a morn of mixed blessings. And as is the way with our people, the babes were passed around all wet-titted women in the settlement.

Come leaf fall, the twins would be eight years and starting their warrior skills. And though they were not kin, Ysolte treasured them as such.

"The fault is mine," we would tell each other on those unending nights, when the children slumbered between us no longer.

You can believe that they were abducted if you

want. Taken to Rome, where they were clothed and schooled in a rich man's house. Becoming cultured pearls, well fed, well versed, far away from this land of trials. Such a version I would give my life to make true. I begged the goddess to make it so. Or to reverse the wheel so that I had not speared that pissing legionnaire, or after the children had arisen, Ysolte and I had not remained in our bed, gratifying each other and then, when dozing, the dream I had not cared to heed: of flying over dark fields, of a vast mouth gaping with black, broken teeth, of a phallus, full in its wood and crawling with flies. Of the screaming of baby rabbits.

"Wake up, my queen." The horrible scene assuaged by Ysolte's tender gaze. She brushed my cheeks and lips with the back of her fingers, on which my musk remained. "You were twitching like a rabbit." I buried the dream, preferring to bask in the safe sun of her face.

Of late, we had exchanged less our expressions of adoration. Not that after one summer our love was waning (if anything it was the reverse), but we were as blossom blighted by a chill wind; a circumstance we could little affect. A single thought harried our minds ....

"I would like to kill him [Livius], in a most excruciating fashion," I would say.

"I know, my queen," Ysolte's reply. "I have the compulsion also, but it would bring down upon us retribution so emphatic, that not one soul would be spared to tell the tale."

"Better dead than enslaved," I would mutter, and the conversation would progress no further.

On that morning however, the black dogs of strife had, it seemed, briefly silenced their baying. Her hands travelled my skin once more as she pressed the permanence of her close-packed body upon mine and we began a mutual gallop to that place of immortality. It was a sight I loved to witness; Ysolte, outrunning her woes (although it did not appear so): eyes screwed shut, mouth a gritted grimace, nostrils panting a fearsome labour. When it was time, the deluge of our heat bloomed between us and from her throat would rise a throttled cry, flooding her visage. Her veins stood garrotted and her eyes would meet mine, inferring a complex revelation; 'you have killed me, you have saved me, you have freed me.'

At length, leaving Ysolte to shift her ravenous appetite to breakfast, I donned my breeches and stepped into the hazy afternoon. A procession of ox-drawn carts clattered the woodway, making for the winter barns, their wheatsheaf loads lurching precarious. It had been an excellent harvest. Andua sat amid a dozen children, painting the death's head on each upturned face. A dull throb took up behind my dark eye, which very soon turned to a pounding to match, blow for blow, the hammer from the forge. I put my hand to it and stumbling towards the children, tried to pick out my own, only to be met with the blank stare of empty sockets. I looked to the sky as the alarm clang in my head was pierced with a distant scream. My blue eye took in the looping course of an eagle. I saw Andua stand.

"Bee?" she said, "are you alright?"

I saw my hands grab her shoulders. "The twins, where are they?"

I saw her shake her head, "I don't know ... are they not with you?"

I looked within myself and saw the ring of black, broken teeth; the standing stones of our ancestors. I heard myself shout.

"Ysolte! Ysolte!"

Poor Fleet; even though his ears and tail had been hacked off and he lay half flayed, his ceaseless barking had hastened us to the circle of stones, wherein an alien structure had been erected, casting a crooked shadow across the altar. A single stripped tree with a cross member, upon which was lashed, back to back, two small bodies, broken, lifeless and defiled.

Fleet licked my hand as Ysolte ended his torture. I wished she could have done equal to me.

My grief was as a storm at sea, making no matter to the bottomless waters into which it fell. Ysolte's tears did not come; her heart became a stone, enclosed around a tragic fossil.

Our suffering magnified through many pools of

imaginings. We dwelled on their demise and, as a mirror, reflected each other's grief and how I would do anything to annul the hurt, to carry the pain for her... anything, but the wheel must turn, even if we are broke upon it.

For six days she sat solitary by the shore, surveying the sea and sky. Perhaps to glimpse the stars in the day, the souls in waiting. I observed her from afar; a huddled rock, against the white gash of cliffs. She had shrugged off my touch and the food which I had brought to her lay gull-scavenged. I passed as a cloud across her face to place before her an offering; one which I considered to be our only route to redemption.

"We will raise an army."

Her gaze passed through me to the dim horizon. "Then I shall lose you too."

"No," I took her hand in mine. "You will find me."

The golden path was beginning and sea birds bobbed in its blaze. She hung her head and black locks, no longer Belgic, tumbled over her weary eyes.

"Do you know what it is you ask of them, my queen?"

And drawing my fingers through her silver blaze. "Aye," I said, "but better dead than a slave."

The candle I always left for her guttered at the window. I remained in red-rimmed torpor as the death dance of my dreams yawled and skittered across the wall. If I had not her, I would lose my senses, cut my blood to the ash and smear my face with the resulting paste. The eye of sleep took me to a hill, where I stood, emitting a plaintive whistle and swinging the lure in ever wider circles, scanning the sky for all that was lost. A grumbling, earthbound sound shut my sleep. I stared alert. A warm gold filled my heart and sent it riding out on yet another false alarm. But hold. The woodway continued its gripe particular, and my heart dared to soar. Her presence was restored, just as sure as the new sun was painting sharp all that the night had obscured.

Ysolte entered as a fact and stood before me, arm outstretched. The ashes hissed disgust at sprinkled blood. Her fist clenching a snatch of oiled coils and drunken laurels. The eyes, upturned in rapture, and from the incredulous mouth, spilled the blue, lollygag tongue of the procurator.

"I hope this gives you a deal of peace, Briga," she said. "It surely has for me. But relish it while you may, my queen, for upon this deed, there will be peace no more."

Cold painted into us it was; the way of the forest. Crouched in mossy hollows, we had returned to our quiddity. The reprisals had come thick and fast; eviscerated livestock lay flyblown in the pastures. Then, the winter barns became an inferno. This we had witnessed in a chain, stricken-faced, passing hopeless buckets. At length, the flames leapfrogged from paddock to stable, from forge to dwelling until, over our shoulders, the night sky raged. It was under that false dawn, an ashen procession of stumbling souls and blistered horses melted into the trees.

Now we thrummed with it; the hunger to fight burned just as keenly in our bellies as the want of a crust. There was no resentment that these punishments inflicted upon us were at Ysolte's instigation. I knew my people and their concern for our eroded integrity and that our blood would be milked until we were but lambs in the clutch of talons.

The forest's sanctuary rekindled us, and from it, was fashioned all that was necessary to sustain us. Our mounts blackened and limed, we stepped silent between shadows. The Romans marched the ravines below oblivious, only sensing the beady stare of birds upon them, and would offer up their shields in vain at the rumble of great boulders, sent down to crush their skulls. Any left pinned, were dispatched by the children. Dung-dappled, they darted in the leaf light, and blood-mottled they returned, picking over their haul of tinder boxes and spears, of fingers and ears. In our migration, we had reverted to the fluid force of our forefathers, who had seen off the strange beasts and clarions of Rome once before.

At night, huddled under hides stretched over saplings, the rain drummed of war as the Goddess gathered her black cloak about us and a medley of displaced voices floated from the trees. "It's not rain," exclaimed one, "tis the holy water of a desperate druid," and there ensued much good-natured banter.

"My people will have wind of this by now." Ysolte's forearms, grazed and grubby, hugged her knees. The flame flickering between us painted harsh lines across her face, grown lean, but handsome, nonetheless. "Those eyes of yours," she smiled. "I swear, it is as if I'm looking upon two individuals, bound up as one."

"I often think it so myself," I replied, "but not two alone. A score, a hundred, perhaps a whole tribe reside within me. Their clamour drives me spare."

"Would I could reach up inside you and pull them all free," she said. Her hand made a fist and I felt the clench of it. "An army of Brigas," she shook her head and for an instant, her face lifted clear from care. "What a sight to behold indeed. That would send the Romans packing, oliphants and all."

"Oliphants and all!" shouted a voice from above.

"Aye, oliphants and all!" cried another and laughter swelled the air, ousting the drizzle, and dissipated as smoke, until all was quiet and calm.

"What is an oliphant?" enquired a small child.

And I saw in the darkness, one wise, collective smile.

Steering clear of open land, we made our way south and west to the Vortigae settlement, colouring our skin with berries and bark, red and ochre, to rival the turning leaves. And though vanished from Roman sight, our numbers burgeoned with those of a similar livery and shrewder eye: Tambartes archers pitched their cloaks over bows as tall as a person. Long-shanked Astewegii women swung axes strung with fox tails, grim-faced druids, Epovantes, Kerallaunii, Sildora, pledged their allegiance all.

The woodland ended abruptly and raising my hand to the sun, the silhouette command took a while to reach the rear guard, but at length, all motion ceased and all fell silent, aside from the snicker of horses.

Ysolte and I surveyed the plain; flat and verdant with a vastness that unrolled towards a gentle hill, upon which was emblazoned a mighty white horse.

Its fabulous scale pronounced by tiny sheep dotted along its crest. An abundance of real horses grazed the foreground and, on the horizon as a slumbering giant, there nestled a green hump. Along its sides, the hill gathered at intervals like the folds of a cloak. Atop its back, timber palisades surrounded its heart, from whence a string of smoke unfurled.

"Go home," Ysolte whispered to the breast of the hunting bird upon her arm, and lifting its hood, let loose its tether. The bird launched herself, gliding close to the ground, before squaring up to the sky to find her bearings. High she circled, keen head switching left and right. I watched until she was indistinguishable from the motes that skated across my eye.

"How will we know?"

"Wait," she said, "they will give us a sign."

Our mounts, impatient for a good run, nodded beneath us.

"There," she pointed. "Look."

It struck me humorous and I began to laugh; the

languid smoke supplanted by vigorous billows, tinged green.

Ankou and Gildas, glad for the gallop, moved shoulder to shoulder. We hung low around their necks and the grass took on the blur of smoke. Many fine horses about, looked upon us placid, while others scattered with much elation, setting off this way and that on sprints of their own. The approaching land island in its scale, seemed the labour of the gods, not of man at all, and thrilled to be gaining on the marvel, I urged Ankou ever faster, outpacing Ysolte a mite. When, all at once ...

"Hold!" she cried "Hold!"

I looked to her, puzzled and she seized Ankou's reins, pulling me to a halt, not two lengths before the ground fell away to a steep, hidden bank, some hundred spans deep.

"By the goddess, Briga," she panted. "Do not shock my heart so."

"I had no knowledge of the ditch," I protested.

"You are right," she said, "I should have given you

warning," and leaning over, she kissed my mouth. "Come."

We ventured along the perimeter, where soon was encountered a grassy ridge, and on its crossing, ascended to a track, which coiled its way around the fortress. Round and up we climbed until I marked the distant forest (whence our army remained) five times over again. On turning the next bend, a rising creak unwound; the yawn of the beast, into whose gaping maw the path fed us. Our mounts adjusted their tread to the woodway, and we traversed a further timber rampart.

Once within, the scene unfolded as a dream; shrouded in the smoke of industry, a thousand green-cloaked individuals dropped to one knee, while a myriad more looked on with expectation. The air silent, aside from the squabble of fowl that appeared to be mustering also. A figure emerged from a roundhouse and heads turned to follow her dusty swagger. Her wild, silver hair restrained by the bronze crown of a chieftain, she regarded us with one eye, the other, drawn forever closed by a scar, catastrophic.

Her lips bunched under the rather large nose, but then grew wide, revealing amongst white, gapped teeth, one of gold. Her frame robust, despite her age. Leather armour and bindings stiffened her heavy gait. Ysolte stood her ground and boomed,

"Hail Vortigandua, clan chief of the Vortigae."

At this, the woman spread her arms. Her great hands met with a clap, startling the horses, and from her mouth erupted a laugh of rich friction.

"Yes, yes Ysolte, hail to us all." She motioned the warriors arise.

As we dismounted, Ysolte took my hand.

"Vortigandua, I present to you Briga, Queen of the Cantiaci ... my gade."

The woman fingered my cheek, not unkindly, and squinted. She smelt a great deal of bear.

"Aye, they said you were fair." Her voice swam in a western drawl. Next, her broad hand thumped at my breastbone, near knocking the breath from me, "and well strung together," she laughed. "A good match for you Ysolte!"

Well, I had never been treated in this way, but the umbrage I would have usually taken was not forthcoming. And as I stared at her damaged visage, there took root in my heart a fondness, our one dark eye apiece inferring a symmetry. "You are most welcome, Briga," she murmured.

"Briga, Queen of the Cantiaci," persisted Ysolte. "I present to you, Vorti ..." but before she could finish her formality, the woman grasped her in a tight hold and tears welled in that good eye.

"Hush child," she growled "and give your mother a hug."

The prospect of fresh bread, ale and a soft bed was much inviting, but until my people were ensconced safe in the citadel, I felt unable to indulge. From the watchtower, I followed the march across the plain, of persons both domestic and military, of cart and chariot, of child and warrior, of kin and stranger.

At length, the first in this rag-tag army reached the base of the fort and, crossing the grassy bridge, began their ascent, faces shining up to me. And returning my gaze to the distant forest, I was much surprised to not yet see the tail of the serpent. My vantage point afforded me the eye of a bird over the settlement; the picture covered some ten acres, wherein various elements laboured to ensure its well-being: a tall house atop which, turned sails as on a ship. This, Ysolte explained, was a wind-driven mill for grinding grain. An oxen pair yoked against a wheel, trod a circle, seemingly without gain. This, Ysolte explained, drew water from a source which flowed many hundreds of spans beneath the mound.

My people wound in a steady stream around the hill below and for an instant, I saw that twisting spiral of life itself, from which we were all composed and to which we were all bound. They appeared to me as oxen, treading futile circles. Perhaps, one day, I would fathom the purpose of it all.

As queens, Ysolte and I were of higher rank than Vortigandua, but her bearing, seniority and ample presence, commanded a respect to which we could only defer. Yet she bestowed all the soft-bosomed comfort and healthy ribbing a mother should. She had, like us, the female template, but appeared of a gender indeterminable. I had noticed that as folk did age, their sex became ambiguous; their frames paunching in parallel. Mild facial features brought to harsh lines in women. On men's visages, strong jaw lines and stern brows turned kindly and flaccid.

The Vortigae beacons had burned throughout the nights, giving reassurance and summons to other chieftains, whose bitter losses and humiliations at the causement of Rome, had smelted a rancour most urgent. Together, we Britons discussed terms of engagement and it was decided we should wait upon events. That was until Boudica, the Iceni queen, forced our hand.

"She was always a hothead," a pinch of Ysolte in her gestures, Vortigandua's hands collapsed, exasperated against her thighs. "She should have waited."

News had come that Boudica's forces had been routed. A panting messenger lay nose to the ground. The moon slid up Vortigandua's shoulder as she squatted and touched his hair. He cowered as a whipped dog. "Get up, you poor fellow," she said. "I am not Roman ... not yet at any rate."

The Romans believed that death held no fear for us. The propagation of this opinion made for a useful attribute in battle; one who has no regard for their own life will fight unflinching. But I can tell you it was not so. My very being was honey-combed throughout with the fear of death, my dark eye invigilating its approach. She who is unafraid of battle is a fool and she who overcomes her fear is the true warrior. Our fear shapes us; it preserves and progresses life. It demands us cling to each other in our beds and quaking, delivers us to that place where we can but glimpse it.

"I would gladly die for you." Ysolte's naked weight was upon me. Her mouth sucked at mine and catching her lip between my teeth, I switched her beneath me and held fast her wrists.

"Never say that." I quickly traded my fear for panic and a further transaction won me anger. "I will not allow it," and muscling her legs asunder, I obliterated her mannish assertions by plundering her cunt.

Wet and shocked, it acclimatised swiftly to the unhabituated onslaught. While her countenance, slack-jawed, struggled to comprehend the conflict. Her stiffened body began to capitulate as I reminded her of her position; that of my woman. "You will not die," I said, "not for me." My sword arm, good and strong, thickened as in battle and I prevailed. "For if you do, I am as good as dead."

Her breath hastened ragged, on the brink of the trauma as her spellbound eyes beheld the realm of the afterlife. A sound of a person walking on snow issued from her head until I realised it to be the grinding of teeth.

"It has been so," she gasped "and will be evermore." Her words hung in hoarse tatters.

"No," I cried, "I forbid it," my hand bringing her ever onward. "Yield!"

And then, she panted as a woman in birth, her body writhed in resistance. "You are my queen and I serve you," she groaned, "but you have not dominion over death."

My fingers held the silver blade within her and keeping her on the cusp, I dealt the final blow. Air and warm streams rushed from her and her back arched as a cleanly stuck beast. The bucks subsided to quivers and I remained inside her, gently plucking her strings. I gathered the hot, huddled person and drew her to me. Tears and sweat of my beloved warrior greased my breasts and also from there, came words which did heat my heart.

"I will always find you, Briga."

Positioning myself as a babe, I rested upon her. Where my mouth met her neck, there throbbed her essence. I listened to her workings internal; the rope and creak of her. The breeze that would swell her sails, inward … outward, inward … outward, feeding her fundament, fuelling her functions. The soft pump beating midmost, my ear to its message. Many a time I had witnessed the gobs and tripes of beasts (and people for that matter) dismantled before me and had pondered each part's purpose, and at who's devising we had come about. A notion struck me; most rightful was our design, most consummate. I looked within and saw the cogs and twine of us, the wheelwork, and grasped the nub of it.

"A parade of mechanisms," I informed Ysolte's face, but from her dreams no words came. "Multitudinous in complexity," I traced her lips, "but machines nonetheless," I whispered, fitting my finger perfectly to the furrow beneath her nose.

The glimmer on the horizon presented a second dawn. A keen-eyed sentry had shouted down and before long, hand over hand, we climbed the ladders of the watchtowers to see for ourselves, until the structures were all but clad in folk. Children hung by their fists in a game, fifty spans between their feet and the ground. While mothers below shrieked and wrung their aprons. A bear stood among the deer.

"Get you down off there, you young'uns!" bellowed Vortigandua. Pulling their weight up, nimble, they hurriedly complied and clambered as squirrels to the ground.

Her hand found her brow as she looked up to Ysolte and I with a question. My dark eye met hers with the answer, at which she turned away and spat in the dust. We levelled our gaze on the east, where upon the ridge, the confusion of glints had coalesced into shields and standards carried on a crimson tide. More they came and yet more, moving silent as a shadow, until borne on the wind, the intermittent tamp of drums was audible. The horizon bristled with a forest of javelins and clustered on the hillside, menacing, dark accumulations gathered as if, against nature, storm clouds had descended to the ground.

The grassland had lost its filigree of frost by the time the Romans had settled in squares just in front of the forest. We could not have hoped for better; for although the bay of it afforded them protection on either flank and from the rear, unbeknownst to them, a good number of our allies crouched latent in branch and ditch. This was not by design; there was simply no more room in the Vortigae hill fort, but a fortuitous happenstance, nonetheless.

Boudica's defeat had learned us lessons most useful and the clan heads and I were vexed to hear of the horror. Eighty thousand Britons chopped into pieces across the battlefield: warriors, babes and the aged alike. No-one was spared. While of the Romans, only four hundred or so had fallen.

"Each soldier did link his shield to the next man," explained the messenger, "then they moved as one beast, armour plated, spines of javelins atop its back and from its front part, swords protruded as teeth. We could not find a chink." Others amongst us who had escaped the massacre shook their heads in recollection. Boudica's force had been twenty times over that of the Romans'.

"Too many to command," muttered Vortigandua.

We, ourselves numbered thirty thousand with some two thousand secreted in the forest, while the Romans appeared a third of that.

"There is no question that those slain did fight with valour ..." I said, getting to my feet "... as will we." Stooping, I began to score plans in the dust with my sword, "but we must employ our wits as well as our hearts, lest we suffer the same fate."

We numbered too many for the great hall. Moreover, people spilled from every nook and cranny. Hammocks were strung below and betwixt the rooftrees of dwellings, some slept on skins in the open, or else it was bare earth for a bed. The oxen turned constant to raise water and the grain was dwindling. Aside from our honour, we had to fight before we were starved out. But this night, on the eve of Sahven, we would feast as best we could, and the throats of goats were slit for the spit as well as in offering.

Our ancestors were liminal; we sensed them move among us, drawn by the druids' drone and drumming and the mighty fires that blazed. Folk flitted around the flames like the fat bats that swooped upon the flies, attracted by the brimming midden. The stench of which was banished by burning mint and wormwood.

A sliver of silver resistance remained in the night sky; the waxing moon hung as a sickle, but the outline of its entirety did glimmer and as I stared through the smoke. I fancied I could see legions assembled on its hidden surface. We, of course, the silver, who would tomorrow in battle shine, flooding the land with light and reinstating the whole. There passed between the warriors, a great chalice issued by the sacreds. And as each one supped the revolting potion, we all did boil and sweat before a sensation most agreeable befell us.

I was immense, surpassing my frame and moving with the grace and stealth of a she-cat. My power burgeoning by degrees, I felt I could pluck the moon from the clouds and made a snatch at it. My hands found my thighs, hard as oak trees and as long. The hands, themselves, great paws that swept along the terrain of my arms, over tattoos like tributaries, spanned by gold bands and veins which burrowed blue into the meat and muscle. My mouth alive with herbs and char. I drew an in breath unending, which did rise me from the ground and screaming, I exhaled a gale to knock an army flat.

"I am Briga," I boomed, "Queen of the Cantiaci. And no man shall subdue me!"

The touch of men and women both, smearing my body blue. Fingers daubed lovingly my limbs, then lecherous, my breasts and buttocks and I found myself invoking the many armed deity, that indigo Indian, to whom I had given my soul in another life. She came and shimmered before me, her necklace of skulls rattling, arms braced as a crab. One hand flourished a curved sword and three others brandished nothing but enticing gestures. Lolling from her lips, her tongue made redder by her sapphire visage, described a language seductive and her black eyes glittered with the promise of death. A further hand gripped the locks of a hollow head which she thrust towards me, while yet another caressed against her leg, a finely tooled phallus.

"Come Briga," her voice had the creak of the raven and I was much aroused by the cant of her body and how the shadows served her shape. Spinning as a spider does a fly, I followed her dancing hands into the dark where they pulled me down and the anticipation of their touch concurrent, near drove my heart to breach. But they remained clutching the wet grass as it was her mouth she did apply to the place of my desire. I squirmed in her sorcery as she held me apart and devoured with much urgency. Her tongue wormed deep inside my being, coaxing from me the stars, and then withdrew in order to lap and flutter. The flash of her eyes met mine, underpinning a passion most pointed. And when the divine paint had been wiped from her face by my own lather, the gaze was that of my queen. And in the stead of many hands, there were but two.

She moved upon me and I felt still the false cock, but thought it my imagining, until reaching down between us, she greased it with my own humours and guided it firm. While the sensation was not unpleasant, my pleasure was taken in her face; awash with ecstasy and a deal of relief.

"Oh, my love," she said, "I thought you would not permit it." In truth, had I not been subject to the warrior's brew, I might not have. Her hips rocked ever faster, driving the device to my core, in a manner which seemed to her second nature. Stroking her shoulders broad, and jaw strong, it was as someone other than myself was watching through my eyes and I mused that were it not for the betrayal of breasts, she could appear a man. She stuck me for all she was worth and as that familiar expression of pain exquisite did colour her face and she let go a moan she could not contain, I knew that once it had been so, and that I had loved her as such.

Bare-breasted and blue, you sat aside me upon Gildas, her rump adorned with red hands, Ankou's to match. Our faces daubed with the death's head, concealing my pallor, nauseous. Great gold gullets spewed forth a harsh bray; the horns, referred to by the Romans as Carnyx (even under torture, no Briton had ever revealed their true name in our tongue) and known to strike their hearts with terror. Over our heads they droned with clamour enough to wreak rain from the clouds.

Throughout the night, the hill fort had disgorged its thousands. We stood scores deep; archer charioteers, warriors brandishing sword, spear, axe and sling and behind those, filed folk armed with pitchforks, cudgels, sickles and anything that would break heads. Employing warfare of the mind, many wore helmets with horns and wings; being mostly taller than the foe, this increased further their stature. Similarly, you and I elected to forego any armour save a shield (may the goddess protect us), knowing this unsettled the Romans greatly.

Bare-breasted and blue, the battle fury now upon us, we menaced the Roman lines. Back and forth we galloped. "Keep hold your cocks!" we goaded, "for they are first before your heads!" This allowed us to view at close range their formation. Also, that they might see the royal torc about our necks, which undoubted, would single us out for reckoning. Frightful, we taunted, and they did shift with much unease behind their shields. The warriors beat sword upon boss and again we rode, whirling our weapons. You streaked forth, stood in the stirrups, arms outstretched, green cloak streaming. Your cruciform frame inviting the fate of captured queens. But then, using only your legs you steered Gildas sharply from the Roman ranks, demonstrating a horsemanship unparalleled. They considered us wild maniacs and we would do all things possible to oblige that notion.

My blood was up, pumping my veins proud and expanding my ribs to their capacity. I flew along the Roman lines, fixing each man who would dare meet my eye. "Today you WILL die!" I thundered, thrashing the air with my sword. "Hark the horns that do announce it!" And with that, the Carnyx bleated with renewed tumult. "We will end you!"

"Bri – ga! Bri – ga! Bri – ga!" You began the chant which our army took up. "Bri – ga! Bri – ga!" Their voices resounded as a storm as thirty thousand hearts beat my name. And so I raced. Lime-shocked braids deranged, skin flourished with indigo swirls, shameless, naked. Terrible and vainglorious.

It was time.

Bare-breasted and blue we sat astride our mounts, your leg touching mine. The horses shook their wet manes, and all became still, save the thrumming rain. Your eyes from black sockets connected with mine.

"Live for me," I said.

"Always," your reply.

In the last diminishing seconds, we transferred our

spirits to a place of safe keeping and a thunder, at once in our hearts and overhead, was echoed in the ground below. Faint it began, but gained with an unbridled insistence. How the earth rumbled, and our mounts jittered, ears pricked in acquaintance of this phenomena.

The Romans remained in crouched complacency, but their ranks started to waver as they caught wind of the beast we had conjured; a sea of wild horses, their fluidity cleft by the hill fort, teamed past us. The Vortigae rode at their flanks, hollering and channelling the stampede. Some of the animals harnessed to carts with bushels of swamp tar aflame. Others to chained logs, but all tethered to one unshifting purpose as they were whipped to ever faster frenzy. The wild whites of their eyes rolling helpless in compliance to their compulsion. We stood safe in the elevation as the crazed tide washed past us to break on the Roman shore. Vortigandua's horse reared in distress, steaming and circling.

"Epona!" she cried, "forgive us for the sacrifice of your children. I beg that you do not ask for mine in return!"

Our army roared a great gale as some animals fell to javelins. Others charged blindly on, clattering over men and metal. Some flailed twisting to the ground, while the next wave over leaped to impalement or liberty as they filtered through the forest. The carts at their full inferno when they crashed into the Roman ranks, shedding their fire undowsable, despite the rain in torrents. The horses screamed as chains snagged on battered bodies, sweeping them asunder. Many Romans fled the scene and some lay stunned and dormant 'neath their shields. And we all did fret in hope and sorrow as the creatures that had not perished, sprinted onwards or pulled up, directionless and dazed.

Next, with a sweep of my arm, war chariots wheeled in from the flanks, veering this way and that. The drivers wrestled with the reins, keeping steady best they could, while the occupants released rocks from slings and drew their bows, harpooning the enemy at close range, as fish in a barrel. Many legionnaires retreated to the forest, where upon they were met with missiles from above. Centurions and prefects struggled with their mounts and berating their men, attempted to reconfigure the war machine. One fixed me with a glare that cleaved my chest and I knew I had been marked.

The Carnyx blared anew and looking to you for affirmation, you nodded. "Let it be done, my queen," you said, and spurring Ankou, I sped along the ranks.

"Brothers and sisters!"

"Bri – ga! Bri – ga!"

"See how the goddess is with us!"

"Bri – ga! Bri – ga!"

"Today, we fight for our lives!"

"Bri – ga! Bri – ga!"

"For our children! …For freedom! … Let us take what the goddess offers!"

"Bri – ga! Bri – ga!"

"My people! … Let us take it!" and marshalling Ankou, I drew my sword.

"CHARGE!"

The hoof-mangled mud churned up, and borne upon the convergence of sinew and muscle, I was swept forward, beside your galloping swagger. And as the clouds mustered once more above, so too did the legions, arising from the earth as a phalanx of spectres, clotting themselves in banks and hunched against shields. A swarm of javelins darked the sky, but onward we surged, the thud of them hit home in wood and flesh. Swathes of us stumbled and sank. You were still there and weathering the storm, we rode on, till a second sharp fleet did arc and glinting, rained down upon us. My shield took the brunt, and unwieldy, I let it go. Stuck in her chest, Gildas did somersault, hoof and fetlock thrashing, neck bent unnatural 'gainst the ground, she screamed, while you did roll and find your feet. Still the drums and horns. And still we were there. Approaching the line, Ankou reared over shields and my sword found neck and upraised arm and as he trampled and I hacked, I glanced but you were lost in the throng. Dismounting to find you, I turned. The scene was red and blue, gold and silver and our numbers had dismantled the machine. Now each part fought hand to hand and as a pestilence we moved, over the tripes of folk, which greased the ground. My feet floundered and all about, the press was upon me. A slew of arrows from our own Tambartes arched over head to the scattered Roman cavalry. Astewgii women sprang forth in packs of three, to fall upon the enemy with a fearsome shriek. Rending each man limb from limb, ululating grotesque, the chaw of their axe achieving a just atrocity.

Blue backs defending my own, I pushed them asunder to meet a giant, black-skinned man, the spotted head of a great cat atop his, its fangs fixed to his brow. In that dark visage, his teeth snarled while his curved sword did slash to get my guts, but it was into his, your sword plunged, and as you withdrew, his hot matter spilt, and your gore-flecked smile leered. Round I spun to hack at a neck till the head, full clear, did come from its housing. From the red-brushed helmet of the centurion I pulled out and brandished the dead head and bellowed greedy ... victorious. Back to back we fought and there also beside us, your mother, routing through men as a wild boar. The landscape of your back and all about us a world of warriors slashed and splintered with iron, resolute. There was only reaction and I employed a dead woman's axe to knock back blows, while my blade dug at belly and back. I gripped tight the hilt. My fingers bonded in a gauntlet of butchery. My arm before me a ruddy sleeve. Sword and axe seemed fused with my person, as if the goddess had devised of a warrior, at once human and machine, possessing neither ruth nor tire. I slashed and stuck until I'd cleared a space about me, which the next was loath to enter. My mind half corrupted in righteous bloodlust, dispatching one, then another to the afterlife. My zeal underpinned by the knowledge that I would, evermore, be swaddled in your love. "I am Briga!" I roared, "Queen of the Cantiaci!" and sinking my sword into the tripes of the next, "and no man shall subdue me," I informed his staggered visage.

"Get you from this place!" shouted Vortigandua, and gaining a spear, I did stick a Roman in the eye who would end her. "They see the torc!" she tugged at her collar and saw off a legionnaire with a thrust up into his jaw. "Worry not," she said, waving her arm, "we will prevail without you."

A space cleared as magic and in it I saw Ankou, dancing in the slaughter. Romans tried to cut me down in my mounting but Vortigandua severed tendons with expedience, rending sword arms useless. "Ride, Briga!" she commanded. Looking about me, I sought and found you and, in an eye-blink, you were up behind me, wet-hot and panting.

"Go, my queen! I will not let them have you! ... Ha!" she smacked her sword, broadside across Ankou's rump. He sprang forth but I hauled him aftward.

"I will not flee!" I barked.

"It is not fleeing!" her body thrust up against me, sword lost in the throat of a Roman, she butted him with her shield. "It is living to fight another day," she shouted, "they need you!" And seeing the logic, I urged Ankou over the remnants of his kind and mine alike. "Look around you, Briga!" and sure enough, the dead were mostly of Rome. The eagle had fallen.

THE LAST QUEEN OF HOLLAND

From the cohorts, "Sagittarii!" I heard a prefect bellow and I knew that word to mean archers. But the Roman auxiliary remained all about us; the black-skinned cat men still at their work. Surely, they would not fire upon their own comrades.

A Roman standard bearer, little more than a boy ... my sword hesitated at his chin. Sobbing, he thrust it to me, and I snatched the eagle, leaving him unscathed.

Then. "Aquila!" yelled the prefect. "Sagittarii! Aim for the eagle!"

"Look to the skies!" you shouted and bowing me down across Ankou's neck, you held a shield above our heads. Arrows rattled all about, one piercing my forearm clean through, I let drop the standard. "Ride, Briga," your voice vital.

"Are you hit, Ysolte?"

"I'm still here," you said, tightening your grip around my waist. "Ride, my queen!"

The prefect's message muffled, I did nonetheless, comprehend its meaning. Another deadly deluge and, once again I was shielded, but Ankou screamed, and I knew he had been struck.

"Onward Ankou!" I cried. He faltered and stumbled, but at length cleared the bodies.

"Ysolte! Are you hit?"

"I'm here," you said.

On my return to the hill fort, our domestic auxiliary hastened to meet me; the aged, the weak, small children. All sworn to the fight and it was with relief on my part that their effort had not been called upon. Pitch forks and pans could resume their usual service for now, at any rate. But the triumph I had at first seen reflected in their faces was supplanted by a flinching, an expression which evaded my ken. As I cantered along, each knelt, sombre of visage, and humble utensils clattered to the ground. What message lay in Haska's eyes? And why did Duin weep so?

"Ysolte," I said. "Are they not glad of our victory?"

"Aye, my queen," you whispered, "they are." Your arms hugged my hips and you restored your head to my shoulder.

My eyes met Andua's. And the collective demeanour I had still to fathom was writ large upon her; there lived pity. And yet something more; heartbreak.

I slowed to a trot but Andua shook her head "No, my sister," she said, "do not tarry."

I regarded her nonplussed.

"You must take her to the sea," she added.

It was then that I saw myself as a mote in her eye. Tilting back her head, she cast me up to the sky. "See with your dark eye," she said. And as an eagle I soared, viewing the scene below, familiar even from this vantage. The rounds of thatch within the hill fort, shrouded in a peaceable smoke. The steep, verdant sweep of its bank sloped down to where the folk did kneel, respectfully removed hats revealed bald patches and matted hair. Would I could, I'd have broke away then and embraced the clouds. However, my dark eye, bent on comprehension, fell upon my own chalky braids and I saw you at my back; the lime all but washed from your black locks and your silver blaze. I saw your green cloak, now changed to brown, and from it there bristled the fletchlings of a dozen arrows. I saw my own countenance, wreathed in shock.

Do not look back. I would ride and never look back. Ankou's jostle did stir you, for your knuckles clenched whiter at my waist, and your motion in the saddle was in accord with mine.

"Ride, my queen," you breathed, and I felt your star wane. My eyes blurred till all I could discern was a glimmer. I set a course to it.

"Stay with me in this world, Ysolte," the words caught as an arrow in my throat. Your grip tightened faint in response. Your love lingered as a brilliant rainbow. But after the passing of a few fields, the first gestures of evening painted the winter sky. I felt your leaving. Those blood-stained hands, most precious, fell to my thighs, and your body did sway lifeless. Lashing you to me with my sword belt, I urged Ankou faster, and gleaned the last of you with my cheek against your head. 'Ysolte, Ysolte, Ysolte, Ysolte.' I would repeat your name till my own tongue stiffened. I would keep you in this life by the rhythm of my gallop, and you would rock against me once more, as you did when we made our love. I would never cease my motion, until you were restored to me. I would ride you back from death. Just as I had ridden you to it.

Ankou shuddered under me, and much spittle foamed at his mouth; he would not see the night through. At length, the metal air of brine abounded, and I knew I could not outrun this. Desolation stretched to the horizon. I came to a halt some hundred poles before the cliff to witness the day's demise. Reaching your arms around me, I held your hands to my heart, their warmth departing.

It was you and always had been: my rooftree, my answer, my purpose, my own heart. We had been first in the darkness, you and I, and at the end of days, we would be the last.

The cruel cauldron was sinking on its wheel. How dare it!

"I am Briga, Queen of the Cantiaci!" I cried at its infernal indifference as it continued its descent.

But hold, the goddess must have heard me, for

at that moment, the waves did sort themselves into ranks before me. Linking their shields across the disquiet, they lay in a golden line, till a path, most solid seeming was bestowed, direct to the heart of the machine. A notion surfaced; would I could confront it and order the wheel be reversed! I kept your hands and leaning forward, I caressed Ankou's weary withers. "One last dash, old friend," and kissing his neck, I eased him to a canter. The thought that I had drawn the arrows to us by taking the standard had plagued me much. If I could have it replayed, you might live still. The hope climbed in my chest as we entered a gallop and a new star did wink in the welkin. If I could catch the path before it was dismantled, you would live. I gained on the gold, its blaze dazzling. And with a leap, we were upon it. "You will live, Ysolte! We shall both live once more!"

UPTURNING THE
OBSTACLE (PART 2)

May 16th 2166

Earlier that day, Doctors Breeda de Hoog and Yoshimi Kumagai had emerged from the Solstice Building, two pit ponies into the light. The rain had cleared, and the sun blazed a trail towards the gleaming boots of a synthetic chauffeur. His impeccable, black livery disconcertingly reminiscent of a stormtrooper, complete with gloves and peaked cap. A discreet fellow, nonetheless, with tea-coloured skin and ebony hair. He projected an air of aloof vigilance, perfectly befitting his designation as bodyguard and driver. Spines like wilted stems, they had clambered in.

"Thank you, Taal. Sorry to have kept you waiting." Breeda said, without expectation. (The Taal unit's conversational style, at best, terse.) However, as he nosed the car into traffic Taal sought her gaze in the rear-view mirror.

"Doctor de Hoog," he announced, "it is always a great privilege and a great honour to convey both yourself and Doctor Kumagai. And it is *I* who should be thanking *you*."

Quite a song and dance. Unlikely Taal had been updated while charging with the car. Yet his neural terrain had obviously undergone some modification. And while Breeda launched a subtle inquisition, Yoshi slumped, stunned with fatigue, and blinked into a place where, hand extended in mute prompt, a long-lost self stared up at her. The open expression, the glossy hair spilled over one eye. So fierce. So beautiful. A gap between the two front teeth the only evidence of a shared aspect. Had she really been so beguiling? Yoshi bit down on the memory, like a questionable sovereign. It was her alright. *Didn't I say goodbye to you already?* She'd thought her younger versions all tucked up. But this one, from the most pivotal point in her lengthy innings, was persistent. Oh, that lovely skin, those earnest eyes. *I know, I know. It's hard.* Yoshi reached out. *But we can never go back. Only forward. I'll see you again. Well, maybe not quite you.* The grip between them tightened. *We found her though, didn't we, Yoyo. You found her.* (An unspeakable stroke of luck.) Those urgent days fell in bright droplets around her. Days that would come again, she assured her selves. *Be gone, now.* Yoshi batted a hand as if fending off a cobweb. She detested vanity. Besides, it wasn't the daft, ugly mask of old age thrust upon her that she minded so much as the shrapnel joints, the strengthless grip, the lost threads. Her head bobbed, seeking the harbour of sleep. But the doors of Breeda's curiosity were flung wide; *Okay. But say, for example, I wanted to disable the safety protocols on my car.* Her voice swam. *How would I do that?*—A distant shout. Then. *Here you go, baby*—a close whisper. Yoshi's cheek greeted the cushion placed there. "Thank you, darling," she mumbled, and her mind curled up on it like an old cat.

Some six hours previous, speeding through a

sulphurous dawn, a poker-faced man stared ahead. Puckering guts momentarily appeased by a brisk volley of flatulence. The widening city refreshed, now and then, by a sluggish wiper. Sharp-shouldered elevations loomed like giant gangsters in the haze of a shoot-out. He started as an oncoming freight-transporter spritzed the windshield with murk. The notion he might be coming down with something, dismissed with the drizzle. Naked in the small hours, a pitiless light had him glassy-eyed. His urine churning up Olivia's in the toilet. Rubbing a porthole with his fingers in the bathroom mirror (Olivia hated it when he did this). A liberal splashing to his neck and shaven face of his private blend neroli. Why his brain seemed to rattle at the vigorous cheek patting with which he always completed his ablutions was a puzzle. Headaches, photosensitivity, the initial symptoms of the TOSA virus. Cloyingly exotic; the expensive scent crept from his collar.

He sneaked a glance at his aide beside him. Milo piloted the limo in silence. Oh, how he wished he could stay in this quiet reprieve, insulated from the pester of responsibility. He imagined himself instructing Milo to bypass the Solstice Building. Tyres sending up a befouled archangel to drench a bemused greeter. Then what? Where to?

No, he couldn't outrun them. That pair. Those two old duennas, tailgating his every manoeuvre. Monopolising his dreams (albeit by invitation). If only he didn't have to face them. Today of all days. The last half a dozen meetings they had attended virtually. Holograms you could put your hand right inside (if you sneaked up on them from behind), as if groping their spirit. But this time they were coming in person. Must have something special up their sleeve. He squirmed, abashed to admit he had hung them out to dry; his wife, his daughter ... all of them. He found refuge in a justification of sorts; it was for their own good. But an implacable truth grinned through; man was an animal that when threatened, would fight dirty. The road ahead suddenly glistened like the bright belly of some twisting creature.

The limo's interior dimmed as they entered a

tunnel. The city had no outskirts; you were either in or out. The man flipped open an attaché case, pointlessly housing a laptop shaped like an attaché case. The outer, leather-bound version had been a gift from his wife on his ascension to the Upper House. Olivia, like the moon in his peripheral vision throughout his college years. Olivia. As inevitable as winter. But it was Brynklee he had wanted. The sun of her smile beaming from trashy contouring, her true features as elusive as a dazzleship. How they had wept, helpless with laughter at their incompatible appellations; the man's surname being Brinkley. He'd sensibly plumped for Olivia, gate-crashing her influential dynasty, and promptly carried on with Brynklee. Until one day she told him—*Love was like the city; you were either in or you were out.*

The tunnel's CCTV tracked the VIP vehicle. The man's face, illuminated by the laptop, strobed past like a thoughtful comet. He was perusing the credentials of people far smarter than himself. A global delegation of the finest minds. Eight alpha brainiacs, appointed to redeem the situation. Plus, himself, John

Brinkley; a jumped-up bean counter, invested with the thumb up, thumb down jurisdiction enjoyed by Caligula. His decisions largely influenced by mood or prestige. Professors Harald Babbage, Noon Crick and Om Snyder were experts in Synthetic Development, Transmutable Resources and Micro-science Solutions. Doctors Manuel Hahn, Adrian Yang and Professor Titus Hewish, world leaders in ... even their sphere beyond the horizon of his grasp. Something to do with space.

He scrolled down. The mis-matched eyes never ceased to jolt him. One, a dense brown, the other, a glacial blue containing a black dot that returned your astonishment. The shrivelling gaze of Doctor Breeda de Hoog, nano *and* neuroscientist, quantum physicist, hydrologist, programmer, gamechanger. You name it. The maker of small things as he understood it. Teeny weeny things. Also, very big things. The picture taken perhaps twenty years ago, when she was a hot seventy-eight-year-old. He smirked, not without affection. And last, but not least, de Hoog's research partner, Doctor Yoshimi Kumagai, with the lucky gap-tooth smile, a pensive disposition, nonetheless. She, the seminal force in Climate Pacification, Ethical Technologies, Glacial Restoration. A keen ice swimmer (without wet suit). Yeah, and probably some kind of ninja to boot. Twelve years de Hoog's senior, making her an impressive one hundred and ten years old. Not unusual in itself, but to be at the rooftree of one's game at this age utterly was. Partners in every sense. It was common knowledge that these two old dames were lesbians. Together. A licentious swell broke out in his loins and flooded his chest. And weirdly, like it always did, ended in his mouth as a yawn.

"Tired, sir"? Milo inclined his head.

In truth, Brinkley was exhausted. Sweet Jesus, they were older than his grandmother. He tried to focus. Pushed the knot of his tie against his Adam's apple. Nipped a prime booger from his nostril. Assured himself it was a harmless perversion. "No," he blustered. "I'm good."

As usual, he was underprepared for this potentially

pivotal gathering and did not expect to understand anything. All he could do was nod along ... ask a few salient questions. Bluffingly conversant by now. *Just go with the flow* ... Olivia had told him last night, plucking lint from his lapels ... *like you always do.* He did have some form on this matter, admittedly. Still, the compulsion to punch her had been hard to override. He had never lifted a hand to his wife. To any woman. Except that one time in Bangkok. Hell, that woman had been as strong as a man. Anyway, Olivia would never appreciate the hard-won scope of power he managed. The precarious line he'd had to tread in order to gain it. She wouldn't understand. She *couldn't.* Because men and women were separate creatures. *Men have ten percent more cranial capacity than women.* He recalled the snooty way he had regaled Olivia with this fact. *I don't doubt it,* she had replied, *they have to store their over-sized egos somewhere.* Touché!

Saving the world was what they were shooting for. A small ask. But Doctors de Hoog and Kumagai always met him with hope, with reason. They were the real deal. Been around forever. Two people more harmonious, more made for each other, he'd yet to meet. He liked them well enough. Judged them good company. Even had them over to his summer residence three times, which was twice more than most invitees. Olivia adored them. But then he'd cracked that tasteless joke. A crimson banner unfurled in his mind, emblazoned in burnished letters; FAUX-PAS. Golden horns announced it. His face still heated at the memory with more than an element of cringe. After that they'd always found reasons not to come again, as if they'd intuited their sexual orientation had been requisitioned for his own base purpose. Women sensed that kind of stuff.

They had kept it in on the plane. Like all good Stoics, first updating their journals in frictionless silence. Breeda's thoughts flowing seamless with the ink. Their pens busy in synchronous waggle. Pausing now and then to rove the cloudscape, or to sip a Virgin Mary. Halfway across the Atlantic, Yoshi felt the shift of it in her gut; a magnetic constant losing its pull.

The glinting projectile in which they travelled, crested some stratospheric arc. Froze at the edge of stars under a perfect curve of midnight blue, before bowing to the physical laws that governed it. This was Yoshi's Icarus moment. Emancipated from gravity. Free from earthly cares. Until her wings began to melt, and she would plummet, once again, in the full knowledge that their journey could only end one way. Landing would be nothing—as a Stoic, she'd made room for that. But how the fall hurt. Every last fucking second of it. She'd agreed with herself, for Breeda's sake, to meet death with poise. And while Breeda wrote of bees and synths, of systems and salvation, Yoshi's was a letter of love.

She glanced at Breeda. Still discernible within the aged casing, the student of a platinum anniversary ago, and then some. Yoshi, inspired by her posting at such a prestigious institute, had sought asylum in the quads and turrets of that repository for the insanely intelligent. But it was the younger woman who had punctured the meniscus between figment and fact. For Yoshi had regularly encountered this person in the unknowable hinterland of her dreams. Her sleeping life infinitely more vibrant than her waking hours. Each morning she would stare at the ceiling, marshalling her grief as Breeda's flipside versions retreated to the cloud forest, the desert's warped heat, the tundra snow. Oh, for an oji in those days ... but then Yoshi would probably never have seen the light of day. Never have stepped out into the slanting, fresh-mown morning. Never have happened upon Breeda, corporeal, reading under the oak, whose roots snaked seven centuries deep beneath that hallowed seat of learning. Skirt bunched around her thighs, showcasing wonderfully artless legs, ticked with golden hairs.

Yoshi had been launched into a cosmos of sensations. And how right it would have been to slip off her shoes and sit beside her. To contemplate their toes pushing through the manicured lawn. *So here we are again,* Yoshi would have said as a matter of innocent routine. Threading a daisy crown for that poured honey hair. *I knew I'd find you again, my queen.* Instead, she had hung back, shyly. Casually obtaining her name from a colleague. Checking the registers and noting the woman's path of study, markedly parallel to her own. Similar disciplines, but never quite touching. Breeda de Hoog was ridiculously clever. More shocking than a sphynx. Sexy as fuck.

On first impression, Breeda looked Dutch because you knew she was. Otherwise, those curious heterochromic eyes, like jewels presented upon broad cushions of cheekbone, sheathed in monolid folds (not unlike Yoshi's), lent her a transcendent quality; the blue one suggesting the cooler, genetic outposts of Iceland, Finland and the Sami people. The brown (were it not for her champagne hair), could place her, quite unnoticed among the Uygur of North West China, the Cherokee tribes. Or perambulating the foothills of The Hindu Kush.

John Brinkley caught sight of a silver sideburn in the wing mirror. He'd been a handsome fellow in his youth—still cut a dash. Gifted from his mother, a Russian transmittal of plump lips that drew the eye. The kind of soup coolers women wanted to kiss, and men wanted to watch. Some compensation, he guessed, for the comically petite Brinkley feet. Good for the jig, as his father used to say, claiming Irish heritage. That mouth of his though, had gotten him away with murder.

Yet these two old dames seemed indifferent to his charms. Inferiority pooled inside him whenever they met; a feudal awe, inspired by royalty. What troubled him, partially at any rate, was that they had no requirement for men. Like so many women nowadays. Man's role in the reproductive process fast becoming an anachronism. Going the same way as God. The TOSA virus hadn't helped in that it only affected males. Sending them sociopathic, violent, especially towards females. And while the mind deteriorated, physical strength became amplified. Uncoupled from civilising inhibitions. Handy in some ways; the work camps got a good three years out of the super-pumped sick before they succumbed to irreversible wear and tear, or to a pre-mortem, vegetative state. In the past decade they had mined to the bottom of Africa's barrel. Despite the indigenous womenfolk digging their heels in. Getting all uppity about the defilement of Mother Earth. Nothing the introduction of a little Ebola couldn't fix. Regrettably.

Women would always love men, he guessed. But these two old witches embodied an elemental kind of love. Something of it swam within him, like a shark under ice: hard-nosed, greedy, indiscriminate. A love that could gobble you up like small fry.

Again, he glanced at Milo. More affably this time. He preferred to sit up front with his aide. Openly taking him in. Tunnel lights careened across his face. Crisper than human. Calmer. Poles apart from his own brutish son. He admired the golden hair, the eyes that tensioned at the corners in an approximation of geniality. Besides, he liked to see where he was going. Graceful fingers allowed the steering wheel to spin of its own accord, Milo's hands coming to rest at nine and three. Just like Brinkley, himself, had been taught. In fact, Milo reminded him of his younger self in many ways; open, keen to please, useful. Except Milo couldn't lie. He might have passed for a regular person were it not for the three black arrows set in a Mobius loop that branded his forehead, suggesting him completely recyclable. De-humanising Brinkley thought. Like so much garbage. Maybe that was the point. Thankfully, Milo didn't possess the capacity for chagrin.

A small bear growled in Brinkley's stomach. Last night at dinner, he'd covered his wife's hand with a repentant paw. *I love you, Olivia.* That normally did the trick. *I love you too,* she'd replied, but the absence of any light in her eyes implied he'd run out of chances. In bed they had slept in their customary 'Baron of beef' position. Rumps touching. Then, he'd fled the house at dawn, way before any potential breakfast recriminations.

"Milo, will there be any nibbles? You know those spicy nuts I like?"

"I'll call ahead, sir."

"No insect stuff, tell them that."

"No insect stuff, sir."

"I don't mind algae. Algae's okay."

De Hoog and Kumagai would have approved. A calorie-restricted diet, apparently, the secret of their longevity. Bullshit. He was a monkey's uncle if a little nanoscience hoodoo hadn't been employed to mitigate cellular degradation. Rake-thin they were. Olivia had taken great pains to accommodate them on that first visit. How he'd manfully masticated his way through oodles of vegan sushi, a vat of kimchi, his appetite remaining unsated. Their capacity, however, for his Chateau Margaux was enormous; literally drinking him under the table. After the women had retired, he'd squatted in the refrigerator light, tearing at a chicken carcass with his teeth, before negotiating the endless staircase to bed on all fours.

Yoshi checked the pilot screen on the back of the seat in front, where a little red plane was pursuing a dotted line across the ocean. *Your flight is seventy six percent complete. E.T.A. Weeze 19.07.* Yoshi looked at Breeda, completely. Though Breeda was not complete.

Not fully herself anymore. Yoshi recalled a time when there had been enough Breeda to inhabit them both.

More than three quarters of a century ago she had watched the tall, intense woman, obliquely, in the canteen. A woman in her entirety. Countenance hawkish in the company of cooing students, while her restless fingers shredded a napkin to confetti. Then, neither by coy degree, nor via any ceiling-searching overture, Breeda de Hoog had looked directly at her. Skewered by the stare, Yoshi had felt the hot needle of it lance an intimate organ. (The recollection still popped a bubble down there, to this day.)

Delivering a lecture in the auditorium that afternoon, a brooding Yoshi, in alternate pleats of defeat and relief, had scanned the upper circle to no avail. After a hit-and-miss session, she put on her coat and killed the lights when an electrical prickle raised the hairs on her neck. An urgent gravity almost forced her down on one knee. As a scientist, Yoshi rallied against unfounded compulsions, and dipped to place her briefcase on the floor instead.

There Breeda stood, green-tinged in the emergency exit light. *I'm sorry Doctor Kumagai. I hope I didn't scare you.* She hadn't. Yoshi's only surprise was that her expectation had been met. Having learned to live with the fact that nothing could be proven, only disproven. Despite the evidence, Breeda de Hoog was still only a hypothesis. Yoshi's data thus far, based on an abstruse feeling. A dark matter whose existence was only verifiable by its influence on the observable. Yoshi had observed herself over the years. Mindful of the lack of engagement, the absence of romance. She had supposed herself a lesbian, on the basis she found women mildly less disagreeable than men. The fact that she had never had sex, an irrelevant detail. Then as Breeda drew nearer, Yoshi felt her core temperature and density rise to infinite values. The singularity she had yet to experience, seemed increasingly likely. She worried she might be ill-equipped to reciprocate, having undertaken no previous fieldwork in this area.

That first embrace had been a collision between two membranes of reality in Yoshi's mind. All at once, some innate know-how surfaced. Like that instrument you used to play as a kid. That language you used to speak; the ability lost like early blossom to the frost. Until you found yourself drunk in downtown Kyoto, the ivories at your fingertips, and suddenly the acquaintance would boldly re-flower.

This was why Yoshi's mouth knew how to meet Breeda's. How her fingers moved over her with virtuosity. Exclamations rising in the dark auditorium, like the gasps of students at some smoke and sparks demonstration.

The surety that they had shared numerous lives, afforded them a foothold in this one. A prudent Yoshi had resigned her professorship without hesitation, recognising the limitations of purely observable data. The implications were immense. A reckless invincibility seized them. What of it could be attributed to love, Yoshi didn't know. Everyday anxieties evaporated and they faced the world with a renewed facility for wonder. In a constant state of elation, Yoshi sat on her hands, stifling the urge to clap. *It's cute,* Breeda would say. *Clap away ... just not after sex though, huh?*

Everything matters, Yoshi had said. *Yes,* Breeda agreed. *Therefore, nothing matters.* They slipped their collars, immersing themselves in the sensual rather than the rational. And there they stayed for a while, eventually arriving at a kind of optimistic nihilism. However, a framework was required to reign in their indulgent tendencies and help channel their intellect because, presumably, they had been set down again for a reason, though they had little idea of what it could be. They listened hard and found clues in mindfulness, which swiftly progressed to Stoicism. Of course, there had been more to it than this—details you think you will never forget. But you do.

Yoshi had never felt daunted or outshone by this scholarly Valkyrie. Not at all. Breeda had simply leaned down, offered her hand and pulled Yoshi up behind her into the saddle. And there she had remained these past seventy-seven years. Clinging on for dear life. Exulting in Breeda's vitality. Watching her back. It had been the ride of a lifetime. And though they hadn't yet discussed it, Yoshi was in no doubt that earlier that day, this astonishing woman, her queen, had accomplished their somewhat open-ended mission. She noted the smile playing across Breeda's lips and its infinite capacity to charge her heart. If the mission's outcome had been anything less than successful, Breeda would have told her by now. There being scant time to regroup, recalculate, press on … scant time.

BOOK 2: THE BLACK TREE

Germany 1943

I hadn't wept. There was too much to weep for: my country, myself, the children placed in my charge.

The sable coat smelt of death, and squatting in the dark I rocked, pinching the soft lapels against my throat, toes wincing in the painful patent, which I'd saved my coupons for yonks to acquire. We'd been herded into this boxcar, like so many cattle. And although we'd remained as docile as such, they hastened us with whips, allowing their dogs to snap at our calves. Memories pricking repeatedly at the fraying edges of my mind, like a needle run out of thread. I suck the fibres to a point and hold my breath. The thread goes through the eye. Yes. We were seamstresses, Mother and me. People will always need clothes, she said. And so we worked for the Rosenbergs.

Old Moshe had been a friend of my father, that's why we got the job. It was nice to be thick with a family, especially in a strange city. Josiah, the youngest son, really took to me. How he darted around my machine, replacing bobbins and sweeping up my snippings. A studious boy, often pressing books upon me as if to bring me up to speed for something. For him. His favourite was Doctor Freud, whose dream interpretations kept me up late. Josiah did make me laugh! Waddling about like Charlie Chaplin, whom he resembled. As soon as he'd approached me, height wise, he'd gone down on one knee, then and there in the factory, tugging a crumpled rose from his breast pocket. Oh no, he wouldn't do at all, not because he was a Jew I hasten to add, but because I knew I was meant for someone else. When I told him in the kindest way I could, he just sidled off, rubbing his eyes comically, as if it had all been part of the act. How the women laughed and clapped. There were no hard feelings and that was the measure of the man. Anyway, he soon married Clara, and twins quickly followed and when my mother was killed, the Rosenbergs paid for the funeral. So what else was I to do when he rapped softly upon my door, urging his children towards my dressing gown?

"Please Brigitte," every inch of his careworn face, a plea. "You're our last hope."

Think very hard. Think when it first started, this whole deepening nightmare. A saga so drawn out that barely anyone could remember its inception, and the conditions which had fomented this terrible storm. As far as I'm concerned, the clouds had first begun to gather when I was just fifteen; when the world had got depressed, and then father died. August Von Hoch, a descendant of Bohemian nobility, forced by his family to drop the 'Von' when he married my mother, a farmer's daughter.

Misty eyed when he recalled the romance. He'd been a gay Hussar, out on a boar hunt with his pals, when a disagreement erupted concerning the integrity of the Kaiser. My father, proclaiming him a posturing pudding head, rode off in high dudgeon. And as pride comes before a fall, his mount had thrown him, and he had lain all night alone in the forest. The pain in his leg causing the Perseid star fall to take on an apocalyptic significance. At length, dawn prevailed, bringing in its radiance, what he perceived to be a celestial being, sent to escort him to the pearly gates. 'Have you come for me, oh angel?' he gasped in awe. Well, my mother, unaccustomed to the Hungarian tongue and taking him for a Russian, promptly snatched up his musket and levelled it at his privates.

Ironically, he was killed in a riding accident. Mother and I dug in harder, but what with hyper-inflation and the high price of feed, we just couldn't make the farm pay. So along with thousands of others, we headed for Berlin.

A fairy tale to me now, my home village; a place so small it hardly qualified as such. A few red-tiled houses and tired barns set stubbornly against the Franconian forest. The trees shrouded in wood-smoke, so it always held the gloom of evening. At night it was the wolves' domain. Their mournful appraisal of things voiced my childhood. Informed my adolescence that there was no answer.

Father's passing was a blow, but mother and I took it with a stoicism typical of country folk. It was when Grusha, our beloved horse had to be sold to Herr Paulus, the baker that I cried for three days, even though I knew Herr Paulus was kind and Grusha's workload would be lighter. That's when I realised that you love something the most the day it is gone. Frankly, my protracted grief was a relief, for I was often struck by the notion that I had no feelings. I'd noticed small children would wail, if say their ice-cream fell in the dirt, but would not shed a tear over the death of a loved one. As if the concept was beyond their grasp, crouching in their psyche till they were advanced enough for it to be assimilated soberly. In order to stave off the trials of adulthood, I had adopted a similar policy. To say I hadn't bargained for it would be a lie. It was a part of me as much as any other. At fifteen I learned it was considered a shameful affliction. The joyful ardour with which I greeted the blacksmith's daughter suddenly paled to a cursory wave. Inside I howled.

Gangly, uncomfortable in my own skin; it didn't help when mother berated me for continually growing. Another condition over which I had no control.

"You're a veritable Titan," she said, cinching father's suit jacket around my waist, while I stood belligerent. Arms outstretched.

The 'what ifs' overwhelmed me. The train had snaked through muffled forests and then a key change as we smoked to open skies, a long exhalation over emerald fields. Here in the dark, I recalled each nuance of that journey to Berlin, like a symphony that conjures pictures in your head. I fold one frozen hand over the other to better concentrate. What if I had never come to Berlin? I wouldn't be in this stinking boxcar, that's for sure. Bound for god and the Nazis only know where. 'What-if- what-if-what-if', mocked the chuffing engine. But if I hadn't come to Berlin then I wouldn't have seen her. 'What-if what-if what-if' ... If only I'd spoken to her ... and now it was too late, I would never find her. 'What-if what-if what-if', the train hissed and then screamed.

Little flashes. My mother's knitting needles keeping pace with the clickety-clack and then stalling. The view as we approached the city demanded her full attention: river, sidings, boxcars, pylons, scrub, sooty brambles, wires, steam, the alternating A and N as girders flickered past, gyrating bridges, reeling us in, into Berlin. Two helpless fish. Stations, low, squat sheds, allotments, cranes and smokestacks, we'd taken the bait. Buildings loomed higher, and tracks divided and multiplied, gasometers, gothic tenements painted with advertising, scaffold and smoke, mountains of aggregates, faded messages shouted by. Roofs revolving around spires, turning us into Berlin. Domes, steeples. For a while the glittering river stayed with us but was soon obscured by dingy geometry. Winding ever tighter as if my hair were getting caught in cogs, wringing out the last forest and glade. Forget them. Arches and stained glass, clock faces, chimneys, buy soap, beer, chocolate. Tressled towers. Below, ranks of cars rubbed shoulders with horses. Black-windowed blocks and ancient tracery. Steel haunches surging, an indignant hoot, our seemingly static shadow rippled across an idling boxcar, fetching cattle to slaughter. We slewed through marshalling yards, causing the red ball of wool to escape Mother's lap. I watched it progress towards the carriage door before coming to a halt beneath the sole of a shiny, black boot. My eyes travelled up the impeccable, black breeches and alighted on three pips on a brown collar (the insignia, I know now, denoted a Stürmführer). Smiling broadly, he tossed the ball back to me, but then, as expected, the subtle and fleeting falter, almost a question, as he noticed my eyes.

"Good day Fräulein," he said, turning on his heel as if at once charmed and disgusted.

I'm not afraid of the dark; it's where we come from and it knows no discrimination. Mother put it down to my eyes; one oak-black like my father's and the other blue like hers. One for day-seeing and one for night-seeing she would smile. I pointed out that I was just as blind in the pitch of night as anyone.

"Ach," she said, and then mysteriously, "there's none as blind as those who will not see." It was to be years later before I was to fully comprehend her meaning.

We descended from the train under its sonorous clangour, burnished in the morning light which streamed through the vast glass roof. Then, swept on a tide of commuters we found ourselves clinging to a lamp post, and each other, as the human flood eddied around us. At the same time the city seemed to be eating itself; great jawed buckets bit into ballast. Bone-shattering pile-drivers shook the ground. Mother wrestled with the map as the wind picked up, spitting dust in our eyes. Hats and hems were clamped down but a straw boater, free of its crimped head, bowled gamely into the gutter.

Trams, trolley buses, bicycles, horses, all maintained an assertive but civil code. Pedestrians offered tentative feet to the road, which were sharply withdrawn at the kazoo of a motor car horn. As soon as enough people had gathered, they were beckoned on by a white-gloved policeman and swarmed between the traffic, looking neither left nor right at the furious fenders, like gnashing teeth. Mother and I were moving too slowly. Her, rotating the map, consulting scraps of paper, which were snatched by the wind. Me, spinning, bedazzled at the scale of the metropolis and all its complex circuitry. Everywhere humanity teemed, coolly mimicked by glass-eyed mannequins who skied, reclined, pointed and danced behind glamourous glass. Once the commuters had dwindled, other participants in this passionless play became apparent. A leather-faced crone set down a man's cap on the pavement and cranked up a hurdy-gurdy, while a hatless simpleton loped and jigged out of time. They possessed identical disarming smiles, both revealing gold teeth. Sturdy children with satchels on their backs scurried to class, while flinty-eyed, ragged kids darted towards and away from misdemeanours.

No, I wasn't ready for this. Barely sixteen and not

yet able to hold my ground. I would be consumed like a fledgling fallen from the nest. The panic was rising in my chest; I wanted to go home, where people were kind and caring and said, 'Good day to you.' There was no love in this city, I thought. Not one jot.

"Can you see where we are?" Mother shouted, setting her hand over her eyes. I looked about me and in the distant heat haze shimmered the Brandenburg Gate. Victory's horses, a furious scribble.

"I think this is Wilhelm Strasse!" I squinted at some gothic script, high on a building.

"Good," she nodded, "we're on the right track!"

We plodded on towards the monumental mirage before taking a left. Stone cherubs swooped in the architecture. Fossil curls anointed with pigeon excrement. Frozen faced at a column of soldiers marching through the street below. Their crunching footfall becoming cluttered. Slungshot back to them by petrified putti. On closer inspection, I noticed they weren't soldiers exactly, although they did wear a uniform: brown shirts, black breeches, a little black kepi on their heads. Much like that chap on the train.

They all sported an arm band upon which curled a motif I was sure I'd seen before; a sort of cross but with each of its arms bent at an angle. They looked vaguely ridiculous. Pompous. However, I did feel a little sorry for them when a group of bystanders began to jeer and scoff.

It seemed barely a minute could go by in this city without some incident, some drama, and it wasn't long before we encountered the next; the single most revisited episode of my life.

A crowd had gathered and with shameless, provincial curiosity, Mother had elbowed in. Oh dear, an upturned cart, a beleaguered mare on her side, whose nut-brown eye, rolling in terror appealed to mine. For a second, we connected, as if in recognition of mutual vulnerability. But as much as my heart went out to the poor beast, it was still grieving for Grusha, and I had to look away. It wasn't my place to get involved anyway, I'd only been here five minutes, for goodness sake. Surely there'd be someone who'd know what to do. The driver sat dazed on a barrel shaking his head. I wrung my clutch purse and looked around in anguish. Oh yes, yoo-hoo! Over here! Although I said this in my head, two of those brown-shirted gentlemen came sauntering over. Good, it was my concern no longer. I felt sure they would take care of it, with their polished boots and efficient manner. I picked up my case to move on but set it down again sharpish when one of the gallant fellows retrieved the driver's whip from the road.

"A good thrashing is all she needs," he said, brandishing it above his head.

No! This would not do at all and I found my feet stepping forward without my say so. No sooner had I committed to this intervention, when a striking looking girl, no older than me, held up her hand to the whistling whip and tugged it clean from the brown shirt's grip. She must have confused him as she herself was dressed in a brown uniform, but of trouser-overalls, and instead of a black kepi, a green headscarf contained her hair. Not too successfully as several black locks had escaped over her brow. This did not compromise her air of authority as she knelt beside the horse's head.

"Shhh," she soothed, "shhh," calming the neck. And her hands, I noted, were tanned and strong.

But the thing of it was, I was sure I knew her: the rather large, noble nose, teeth with a central gap. Dark eyes, narrow with concern. I quickly discounted her from the short parade of people I'd encountered at school or in the village; it felt like she pre-dated them somehow, as if the configuration of her features had been stitched into my fabric before I myself even existed. When I was someone else. My eyes searched my own brain as if it were a house, the contents concealed under dustsheets. The compulsion to stare at her was overwhelming. Mesmerised, I watched her lips purse in concentration. While her hands travelled forearm and fetlock, from hock to hoof. And all the time that velvet ear stayed cocked to her voice.

"Shhh," she whispered, "you're going to be alright," and something in me stirred as if it were my ear receiving her words. "You've just had a shock that's all." The old nag lay perfectly still beneath her touch, and gave an acknowledging snicker. "But you must get up, my queen," she said, "or you'll be done for." I shuddered as if it were my contours she was examining, me she was coaxing. I felt myself being led to a fence I had refused. This girl seemed to present the answers to questions I'd been too afraid to ask. A stubborn fear of adulthood and all that it entailed had kept me a child. Her movements were conducting a sea change. Miraculously, the transition was upon me. A shifting in the shell; a shadowy, fertile flicker, like when Mother and I candled the eggs. My skin prickled with the dawning revelation; my sexuality was hatching, wet, stubby and twisted, and I confronted what it was I had deflected for so long. The full understanding of this variance thudded through me and that I would be destined to a difficult life were I to pursue it. Nevertheless, this girl had inspired me. She hooked two fingers through the bridle.

"Up you come, my queen," she said, hauling hard. Flailing to gain momentum, the animal rolled to its knees, gathering itself. With a shake of its mane, hooves striking the cobbles, it scrambled to its rightful height, head and shoulders above the crowd. I found myself standing taller also.

"Brava," she said, "good girl," and the crowd applauded.

I was a woman transformed: broad, strong, fully fledged. A woman who thrummed with patient desires, imbued with the ardour of a queen, the spirit of a warrior and I felt completely and utterly entitled to my inclinations. This girl. No. Woman, had not so much induced this magnificence in me but restored it. I could almost taste her name, her skin. And while the cart was being righted, I blossomed with the certainty that I was in love with her, and always had been. A hundred images overlaid my eyes, like watching the trailer for a film in which one had inexplicably featured; now I am on horseback, the land flying past my head, now a night fire tightens my skin, now a golden ocean dazzles my eyes (I had never seen the sea), and now a face so close to mine that it is obscured, but I know it's her. Were these portents or memories? The chaos of the here and now reasserted itself and I was assailed by confusion.

"Brigitte, Brigitte," Mother's gloved hand harassed

my sleeve, "stop day-dreaming, child." I watched the green headscarf disappear in the crowd. And there went my answer. "Probably a gypsy, I shouldn't wonder," Mother said, following my gaze. "They have a way with horses."

I had undergone some kind of conversion, both physical and spiritual, and felt for all the world how I supposed an evangelist would when the scales had fallen from his eyes. The grey door grated on its hinges; not even the dilapidated apartment block we would call home could put a crimp in me. We were greeted by an atmosphere as stale and multi-layered as the peeling, ochre walls. As we climbed the steps, I mused that I'd been seeing only the surface of things, reading the words but not registering the plot. Each landing had its own stench. (Boiled cabbage.) I was infused with colour and light, my hormones, a kaleidoscope. (Perished rubber.) My bones glowing in a crimson casket. (Acrid fish.) And each time my mind glimpsed her, some secret muscle down below would clench in a thrilling spasm. Mercifully, our landing was relatively neutral, save the homely smell of baking, which emanated from the apartment next door. Downstairs, a potato masher struck up a brisk tattoo against a pan, prompting the squeak of plimsolls on linoleum and the sinister laugh of children to echo up the stairwell. Next door's step was scrupulously clean. On the doorframe was a notched, oblong charm about the size of a lipstick.

"Mezuzah ..." Mother hissed, "... Jewish."

Once inside, we surveyed our new accommodation: a kitchen looking out onto barracks of identical windows. From the courtyard below, criss-crossed with drab laundry, sprung grizzled goldenrod. A naked dolly lay abandoned, one open eye gazing up at a dab of blue. The perpetual motion of Kaiser Wilhelm Strasse percolated up to the living room window. The bedroom window framed, in abstract detail, the soot-mottled brickwork of the Marienkirche, little more than three metres away. The stained glass may well have been revelatory from inside, but all we got was a dull suggestion of saints. Suddenly, our eyes locked startled. Mother's hand flew to her chest; a fearsome clang rattled the windows and vibrated the floor. And as if in response, a milder, tinnier version peeled from the apartment next door. The muscular, midday toll seemed relentless, but by the eleventh chime, Mother was wiping down the kitchen table while I unpacked, lost in my own carillon.

The night before I started work was spent sleepless, inventing scenarios. With adolescent logic, I had massaged the possibility of her working at the factory into a fact. She might even show me the ropes. I imagined, or remembered rather, her hands on me; their solid tenderness moulding my hips, my buttocks, coaxing my breasts. The bells struck five and Mother, grumbling, folded the pillow around her head for the umpteenth time. The twin bed she occupied next to mine, a jumble of sheets. Her bedspread slid to the floor. As the first gestures of morning etched the room, the candlewick fabric appeared to ripple, like grass in the wind. The hallucination intensified lumping into life, it formed the shape of a figure, head bowed at the end of my bed. I regarded it for a while, and realised I was night-seeing. 'How I have missed you, my love,' I told it, 'please find me soon, my horse charmer, my Bärchen, my little bear.'

Of course, there was no sign of her. The noise deafening as we were shown to our machines. The women glanced at us with naked boredom and perhaps it was the pins clamped between their lips that made their smiles so pained. Seams were sewn steadfast, in brief overlapping bursts. All about me the insistent tacka-tacka-tacka of countless needles drilling countless dirndls. From time to time, I'd unhunch my shoulders and look to the glass roof where, beyond the roar, seagulls wheeled in peace. And humming to myself, I'd wonder where she was. From somewhere that is not yet a city, she might have looked up at that eternal sky, and down the aeons of time, she would sense me. That night, when I closed my eyes, I saw nothing but my own hands guiding an ocean of fabric under the feed dogs.

I'm grateful I'm not night-seeing. If I were to witness the crush of bodies all around me, I'd go quite mad. I can't help but feel the stench though.

And succumbing to an imperative to which most had already, I find the warmth of my own urine vaguely comforting. My organs are strung out along the track; first the heart had been jettisoned, the unravelling lites, the stomach entrails quivering in the moonlight, evacuated bowels a bag in the gravel. My dignity shredded and dispatched to the wind; I can do without them. Travelling light. Hell's waiting room, first class. It almost raises a smile. We've become the animals they always insisted we were. The constant, low level sobbing of a woman nearby, sporadically corkscrews into hysterics as bit by bit, her brain digests the fact that her father stopped responding some time ago. *'Daddy, oh daddy, you can't leave me here.'* He was just a baggage of useless old junk now. Worthless, like the cases of Reichsmark bills or silver candelabra that people still cleave to their chests, as if they were children. Poor old fellow grappled to the end of the carriage where the dead are mounting up. At least it means there is more room for the living. This is how I have begun to operate. I realised we never said goodbye, my father and me. No auf wiedersehen. I really want my mother but I'm glad she's not here. I think about Frau Karp and Josiah, and picture them on some remote desert island, clinking brandy sours, as far away from this as I can put them. Perhaps I should put my girl there too? No, because now more than ever I need her beside me. I need her where she always is, safe inside my head.

The train slows as if unsure of its direction. A chink in the roof allows a thin shaft of moonlight to illuminate lice on a black collar. The Hasidic Jews had it particularly bad, half-starved in the ghettos. I feel their perpetual sway, their thrumming focus; bony knees hugging the ribs of some ritualistic rocking horse, egging on the fervour, delivering them clean away from here. Can't say I blame them. Sometimes I wonder what it would be like to believe in something so far-fetched, so implausible; an eternal god in his heaven with his all-seeing eye, invoking in the pious, a rapture and humility. If only I could make that leap. But then of course I do, often ... when I summon her.

Glad eye. The phrase made me smile. According to Neunzig, (a name she had gained because she was always ninety percent sure of everything), Josiah held it for me. Or carried it, or rolled it, or whatever it is one does with a glad eye.

"I know," I said, pulling a sour face.

"You could do worse." Neunzig had a startle of red hair, which she kept in buns over her ears. She smelt of biscuits and wet cardigans, and her ham-like arms rippled slightly as she lined up a pocket to the needle. Her manner and elbows intrusive, and often I'd re-stitched after one of her nudges had sent me off course. "All I'm saying Bienchen (I had become little bee on account of my constant humming), is that you're not getting any younger." I was nineteen.

Despite the incursions, I thought Neunzig a good woman. My first friend in the factory. She'd taught me to run my thread through bees' wax, so it didn't tangle, and had regaled me with a dispassionate profile of all the women in our immediate vicinity: Sigrun, the hunchback steam presser, constantly in tears due to her phobia of buttons. Hilda, the hefty cutter, of whom it was rumoured, would lift men above her head in return for Korn gin. Fritzi, the scuttling production supervisor with the unplaceable accent, who Neunzig was ninety percent sure was a spy for the Nazi party. The more circumspect they appeared, Neunzig maintained, the more dramatic their past, the more florid their secrets.

"Steer clear of that one there," she said, nodding towards a woman who'd always intrigued me. The whiff of the Weimar clung to her like cigarillo smoke, and even in overalls she carried herself with the grace of an aristocratic panther.

Waiting till Neunzig had completed the hem, "Why?" I whispered.

A coral colour crept up from her collar to meet her expression of scorn. "Lesbian," she spat.

The word impaled by pins, fluttered in the air between us, and my face bloomed too.

"Really?" I concentrated hard on a seam. "How do you know?"

"Oh, she came sniffing around me once. Of course, I told her where to get off."

I regarded the woman's elegant, black, cropped hair,

the intelligent, cat-like eyes, the jaw made wide with a lazy smile, and doubted very much that she had any interest in Neunzig.

"Gräfin, they call her. She was a countess apparently. See that mark?"

I chanced a look when the woman was absorbed in trimming threads. Yes, her face appeared strangely abstracted, putting me in mind of an Otto Dix painting; a silvery line pinked her left eyebrow and slightly dragging down the eyelid, terminated like a tear on her cheekbone.

"Duelling scar," Neunzig barked, just as the machines lulled.

We stared furiously at our work, knowing full well we'd been overheard. That would have to be it for now, but I was dying for the story I knew Neunzig was itching to tell. But after we'd chatted a while on a different topic to cover our tracks, I thought it safe to hazard a look at the Gräfin once more. My heart tripped coyly in my throat and my overalls housed a blush, I knew had invaded my whole body. The grin that met me was challenging, affectionate, knowing.

Her entire visage focused upon the insinuation that I was most definitely, most undoubtedly of interest.

More snapshots. Mother and I on a bright, spring day, shaking out the washing upon which ash from the Reichstag fire had settled. Ash that would spawn a virulent fungus, although there was nothing organic about it.

President Hindenburg had made a pact with a raving madman. Shortly afterwards the grand surfaces of the city dripped and rippled with his crooked sign. His minions marched every street, and from each corner, his tinny voice could be heard barking electric bile. People stood obedient, harkening heads cocked, before jerking their arm skyward in salutation of his name.

"Well I'm not doing that," Mother snorted, "looks like you're hailing a taxi. Ridiculous." Poor Mother, she always did stick to her guns.

The picture I want in my head of Josiah has been superseded by a pale, dark-ringed mug shot.

Although he hadn't yet been rounded up, we both knew it was only a matter of time. Standing in my doorway, harshly backlit, a cameo, a Charlie Chaplin silhouette. He'd pulled the children into him in order to cover their ears, while he mouthed, barely audible, that most chilling of phrases; *concentration camp*. Something dense and sinister coupled with something gay but pragmatic. I'd struggled to grasp the true implication, too fearful of it perhaps. So he brought it home to me as clear as the midnight toll. "Death camps, Brigitte. They're slaughtering us wholesale."

No, I refuse to let them erase my memory; they can't control what goes on in my head. I will keep my friend in amber on the shores of the Wannsee, cuddled up with me in those basket dome chairs that resembled a congregation of Puritans. I will see him sun-kissed, vital, slicked back hair fighting loose in the breeze. Pretty, green eyes like a woman, crinkle smile, made roguish by an abutment of black whiskers. A kind man, a playful man, a clever man. I will picture him there with his charm intact, and those precious conversations I will never forget. It was as if we were in our own film, where I starred as his patient. He, the unorthodox doctor, capturing me like a bird, to be examined and set free. His mind hopped about like a magpie; extracting from me secret pearls, from which he'd string a necklace, and present it back to me with all the flourish of a suitor.

"I love you, Brigitte," he glanced at his pocket watch. The clear but cold afternoon had kept the bathers away. He always started a session with this sentence to monitor my mood, but my reply was invariably the same.

"I'm not interested in you that way, Josiah."

But today would be a watershed; I had decided to expose myself, in a metaphorical sense, naturally.

"Do I repulse you, Brigitte?"

"No."

"Do you have a fellow?"

"No."

"Why not?"

"I'm not attracted to men."

"But don't you want babies?"

"That is a different issue entirely."

"Hey, I'm Jewish, what do you expect?" He inched his eyebrows up and down, Groucho Marx style, forcing a giggle from me. Stroking his beard, he looked at me appraisingly and I knew he understood. Clearing his throat to restore gravity he continued.

"So, tell me Brigitte, do you have desires?"

"Yes."

"Have you liberated them?"

"Gosh, no."

"And why not?"

"It's someone I'm waiting for … I'll know them when I see them."

"Ah, love at first sight."

"No, that's not what I mean."

"Good, because that would be what we call projection."

JOSIE CLAY

I readied myself to employ the third person feminine.

"It's more like déjà vu. I've seen her in my dreams."

"A sense of familiarity?" He didn't miss a beat.

"Yes, definitely."

"Mmm, the unconscious fantasy that leaks through when you are sleeping."

I could see where I was being led.

"No, it's not that ... it's ... you'll think me quite mad."

"Let me be the judge of that."

"Well, I've met her before, more than once, in other incarnations. Josiah, I'm positive I've been here before."

"Transmigration of the soul, is that what you believe?"

"Perhaps, I'm not sure what you call it."

"Brigitte, let me ask you this. Are you afraid of dying?"

"Probably, aren't we all? But you see my biggest fear

is that I'll die before being with her again."

He steepled his fingers, indicating a further theory.

"I'd like you to consider this; there is a dislocation, whereby she is, in reality a manifestation of you, your inner self if you like, because you are afraid that you will live your life without ever fully having known yourself."

"I disagree."

"Time's up." He snapped shut the watch and returned it to his pocket. "And thank you for sharing that with me, it takes trust."

He fussed the blanket over my knees, and we reclined in the creaking structure holding hands. The evening tinted apricot as the sun attempted to boil the lake. A twitching in my dark eye, imprinted on my retina, a scorching halo of devastation. Tears cascading from a glacial eye in the sky. I saw black stars scrolling down the sunset like the end titles of an epic film …. FIN.

"I hope you find her," he said.

It's not because my family is gone … my friends, nor that I've been kidnapped. It is because I am without you that I am dislocated. And yet here in the dark, I feel you more than ever.

They'd played it out at night for optimum drama; the event morbid, hypnotic, an infernal crucible. Pallid spectres at the spectacle. Josiah and I hovered on the periphery. Their sleeves raised to the heavens. More and upward they thrusted like children of the Hydra's teeth, roaring for fire. The Minister for Public Enlightenment and Propaganda presiding, fuelled the fanatics. *'No, to decadence and corruption!'* as Brecht and Barbusse were consigned to the flames. *'Yes, to decency and morality in family and state!'* Freud and Kafka followed, together with Einstein and Engels, *'un-German all!'*

"Barbarians," Josiah muttered.

As if to grieve the cremation of a million books, a grey shroud unfurled over Unten den Linden. A swarm of cinders disseminated like confetti upon the saluting crowds. They chorused a manic mantra, zealous chins under lit, *'Sieg heil! Sieg heil!'* The chant audible yet from the door of my block, where Josiah and I batted the ashes from each other's coats. All about us, the 'decent' darted back and forth, eagerly fetching more books to burn, as if offering their own minds to the pyre. The Marienkirche chimed once, closely followed by Frau Karp's clock next door. I sat exhausted and bitter at the kitchen table, Mother dabbing smuts from my cheeks.

"Mark my words," she said. "They'll be burning people next."

Brothel lights; I'd walked these streets in the day, unaware of their existence. But then I had been unaware of many things. We strode along Budapester Strasse arm in arm, looking for all the world like two dandy fellows. A number of prostitutes had thought so, turning away in apology and amusement.

There was an inevitability about it … the Gräfin and me. It started when I'd taken on sewing jobs from home to earn a few extra marks. Like an art deco Dietrich, she stood in our kitchen, fabulously tall, arms outstretched as I altered the man's suit around her. My fingers remained unflappable, gathering the cloth about her intimate parts. A dart here, a dart there. Before long I was inundated with others of her ilk, who seemed to enjoy the whole procedure as much as the finished article. I attempted to arrange the fittings when Mother was out, but more often than not she'd bustle in, plonking the shopping ostentatiously on the table. They seemed to hold a fascination for her, these Anita Berbers, as she called them. And when a particularly handsome breeches role addressed her as 'Gnädige Frau', she'd blush quite deeply and giggle like a girl. After all, she was only thirty-six. Something I often forgot.

Propaganda papers chased about our brogues, our double step the only sound in the street. Gräfin had folded herself around me like an origami flower, but it was me who was doing the using. I had needed her to gain entry to those mystical, shadowy places I knew existed; an underworld that my horse charmer might inhabit. The factories, parks and cafes of the day, I'd investigated as best I could to no avail. Gräfin was a portal to where I felt our more common ground lay.

In the day I huddled stitched. Pleated with defeat.

Through the night however, I waded obscenely tall, the city swirling about my ankles, inhaling a higher air. This was my element, my atmosphere, where I was sure I would find her. If not this night, then the next. She wandered this realm. Come to me, Bärchen. Perhaps she was doing the same and circular, we would meet in the darkness. She may be just around that corner, just down those stairs, up in that blacked-out window. She was everywhere and nowhere.

In the meantime, I enjoyed the Gräfin's attentions. Her story; yes, she was a countess fallen on hard times, due exclusively to her excesses. Yes, she did suffer the scar in a duel, no honour to it; a sex game that had backfired. The details she said sketchy to her now and unimportant. Neunzig's account she concluded would probably be ninety percent true.

One place after another: glowing ribbed lanterns Japonaise. Amber alcohol, the slide of feet to smarmy violins, breasts pressing bandaged breasts. Stares, persistent or furtive from every corner, and beautiful hands adorned with gold and bloodstones, raising a toast. But nowhere my Bärchen. Not this time. Gräfin knew of my quest, had even put the word out and many a time I'd been presented with raven-haired, sultry-eyed women. Each crestfallen or nonchalant, depending on their assessment of me. Encouraging me to take refuge in schnapps, Gräfin's stern features would dissolve in a mass of jokes, and she would help my stagger, although I was no pushover. A faceless man, a prostitute, an empty banana stall, shouting people. We skirted down a side street straight into the SS. *'Here are my papers, I'm completely Aryan, do you see?'* A dubious squint at our trousers but they can't touch us for that, can they? *'Heil Hitler.'*

Dawn scraping the sky, a chiding blackbird, and back to Gräfin's with her hands and mouth. It brings me closer to you, my love. I remember you, hot cold, hot cold. Your hips on my flanks, your hot breath and your fingers charming that cold miracle from me. The steel-damaged eye penetrates. The pressing, the biting, the sweet, cold sweat, the heat inside me, the red flower, the cool bindings, the creak of my throat ... devour me. That red leer that for now is yours. Those white teeth testing the rose bud will do. Her tongue speaks the same language. We are all sisters and that is the crux. The glorious taboo that kinks my guts, the spindrift between my legs. Her touch will do it until you find me.

A stunted dawn is sketching out shapes on a black canvas. Wrestling with the morass of detail, my brain constructs an impossible mezzotint. A Gordian knot of grief encircles my chest. Round and round it goes and where it stops no one knows. The optical illusions of an Escher; now a hat is a head, now a bag a body. Now the living, the dead.

I wept at the deconstructed version of her imagined in the coffin.

I saw her legs walking around, the seam on the back of her stockings, the neat efficiency in her movements. First the baker's, a cake for Brigitte's twenty-fifth, tick. Fruit, yes, those plums look nice. I see her gloved fingers checking for ripeness, she smiles as they tumble into her basket, tick. Next, some wool for the mittens she will knit for the little Rosenberg twins. She heads for her favourite haberdashers.

The SS ranks had swelled of late allowing, with the addition of a uniform, your common or garden thug to terrorise with impunity. I see her step falter at the entrance to Schatzmann's at the discrimination of two such accredited cretins. Papers offered and scrutinized, she returns them to the handbag that smells of face powder.

"Tell me ..." one puffs up. "Why does a purebred German and, may I say, handsome lady such as yourself, wish to shop in a Jew store?"

"I will shop where I please," she retorts, pushing past them. Perhaps her heart tripping a little with indignation at the comment *'Jew-loving bitch,'* that is levelled at her. But once at the counter, the sanity of pristine, silver-edged glass, the worn, wooden pigeonholes, stuffed with soft rainbows, calms her. Blue and pink too obvious, she toys with lilac. Something rolling across the floor towards her catches her eye. She glances to the door where joking faces turn away, ears covered. The penny drops with a pikestaff of panic; stopped beneath her shoe, not the errant ball of wool she'd anticipated. And in a storm of shards and fibres, after forty-two years of trading, Schatzmann's and my mother are closed down forever.

The factory had been 'Aryanised,' and I was granted only a day's compassionate leave to get over the *'unfortunate accident,'* as the Gestapo put it. Were it up to the Rosenbergs, currently quaking under curfew in their Wannsee villa, it would have been a week or more. The stout winter coats and dirndls which we had manufactured were replaced by military wear; my task, to apply the various and many insignia to collar, cuff and pocket. God, how they loved their regalia. Coolly, I sewed with steel-thimbled fingers: the Hakenkreuzen wreathed in laurels. Sinister. Gold and silver oak leaves on grounds of orange, yellow, brown, red. Quite pretty. The twin black lightening scratch and grinning skull and cross bones of the Waffen SS. Plain terrifying. But the motif that disturbed me most of all was the eagle. Dark eye squinting, I'd hum to drown out the incessant scream it seemed to trigger in my head.

"Bienchen!" Neunzig would implore, "Shut up!"

It also conjured, quite clearly, a vision in my mind's eye; a circle of standing stones, the grim shadow of a crucifix falling, its arms fractured and bent upon an altar. And though I had no idea what this signified, it felt like a warning.

The nights when I wasn't with Gräfin, the apartment was brutal without Mother, so I sat in with Frau Karp. She had some nice things, and although on the same template as ours, her apartment gave off an altogether more opulent ambience. We sat hunched in plump, damask chairs with stubby, cabriole legs. Decades of baking lingered in the cushions. The dresser, table, piano and stool all crouched on similar squat limbs, and I spied a further set displaying themselves, coquettish, from beneath a viridian tablecloth. Verdigris glimmered in the brocade wallcovering, almost eclipsed by banks of books filed alphabetically, from Aristotle to Jules Verne. It struck me as a masculine library, too lofty for the likes of an elderly lady, keen on clothes and cookery. A dusty chandelier cast a dim light, making the task at hand even trickier.

"Thank you so much for your help, Fräulein Hoch." Her claws pinched up a needle which she examined myopically through pince-nez, "my eyes are not what they used to be."

It was a long way around the yellow stars when using the most delicate of stitches, so as not to damage the garments.

"It's no trouble," I said, although my thumbs pricked ominously for the old woman, forced to deface her own clothing.

"I tried to pin them, but they just kept falling," waving her hands about her turban, "off they blew into the wind and I said to myself, Sofia," chuckling, "you are much too old to go chasing stars."

I could see through to the kitchen where billows of steam were clouding a cast iron cooker (also cabriole legged). She levered herself up to pacify the kettle's insistence and the church bells joined in the alarm, leaving me to picture a runaway locomotive. Her mantle clock, always getting the last word, returned as the kettle capitulated. Soon there was rattling bone china on a silver tray, set down upon the flirty table.

"I'm sorry there is no sugar," she said. "I used the last of it in the plava, but with no eggs," she shrugged comically, "what a disaster."

Touched by her good humour, I managed a smile, and setting aside the sable coat, of which the yellow star made a mockery, the words were out of my mouth before I could stop them.

"Frau Karp, are you not afraid?"

She smiled as if charmed by my concern and I noticed that once she must have been rather beautiful.

"Ach," she said, with that trademark bat of the hand, "I escaped the Odessa pogroms, my dear. I've seen it all before," settling back into her faded shrug. "We live, we die and only God knows when and why. Maybe out of this mess some good will come."

I found her attitude perplexing, insane even.

On the piano, a photograph of a fabulously bearded

officer, sat astride a horse (clearly a stallion). He wore a hat that I associated with Cossacks, more brass buttons on his great coat than were useful. I thought of my father. I had assumed Frau Karp a widow and she followed my gaze.

"That is my brother, Abram ... killed in the Russo-Turkish war."

"He looks very gallant."

"Ach, he was an idiot," she said, folding her pince-nez as if she'd seen enough of him, "like all men," she added.

This intrigued me and I began to see the old girl in a new light.

"But why then, do you keep his picture if you didn't like him?"

"Oh, I liked him well enough. He couldn't help that he was a man."

"You don't have much time for men?" I ventured.

"Oh, women are just as bad, if they are not busy being victims of men's dysfunction, they are collaborating with it."

"Really? I hope I'm not included in your assessment."

"Oh, my dear, we are all one or the other or both, it is our nature. Just as it is man's to build and destroy. They will not be satisfied until they have burned everything down. And then they will train their sights on the heavens above, no doubt."

The idea of Nazis storming the pearly gates and mowing down angels was a disquieting one.

"You'd think God would finally intervene at that stage," I said jokingly, and then worried on several counts: I'd implied he'd abandoned his chosen people, or that he didn't exist at all, or that he didn't figure in my personal beliefs. Or if he did, I thought him cruel and manipulative, immoral even. In any case I may have unintentionally disrespected her faith.

"Oh, I'm sorry," I said, "I didn't mean ...."

But Frau Karp batted this away and positioned her thumb and forefinger, as if she were holding an invisible biscuit.

"We are tiny, Fräulein Hoch. Tiny, weeny little parts

in his plan. We cannot imagine the enormity of his perspective. The disparity is far greater than say an ant, trying to comprehend a human being; the ant is not equipped intellectually, if he were, he'd be a human being. Just as we are not equipped, otherwise we would be God. Some things cannot be measured, simply acknowledged."

This was certainly a most plausible argument. My throwaway remark was but a pebble bouncing off her armour-plated logic, and I did indeed, feel as tiny, weeny as the seed pearls on her slippers.

"Frau Karp, do you think Germany will win the war?"

"I hope not."

I thought about all those mothers' sons, both in this country and abroad, who would be systematically trained to commit acts deemed abhorrent in peace time. "Do you believe it is in everyone's nature to fight?"

"Fight? Yes, we can't help it; we are bound by evolution to wipe out another tribe in protection of our own, so that we might have sufficient resources to ensure the proliferation of our own kind. Survival of the strongest, and if that fails, we adapt. But I believe you are referring to warfare, a different beast altogether; warfare is about ideology."

"Do you mean religion?"

"Everyone thinks they are on the side of God. Don't you Fräulein Hoch?" I thought she'd skirted the question, but then realised she hadn't at all.

"I believe myself to be on the side of good. Of peace."

"Ah, but peace on your terms. In order to maintain peace, someone, somewhere will be subjugated, oppressed. Eventually the oppressed will rise up and become the oppressor and so on and so on ...."

"And where will it end? Is humanity destined to destroy itself?"

"That is when I believe God will intervene, he will not let his children be lost."

"A second coming?"

"Well it would be a first from a Jewish perspective, but yes, if you like." Sensing it was not really what

I would like, she took a different tack; repositioning her pince-nez, she leant forward. "There is only one way out that I can see." Her gaze seemed to scan the crystal spheres of time. "Hundreds of years in the future, when we are immeasurably more scientifically advanced than today, mankind will build God in his own image." She settled back into her chair, satisfied, allowing me to pick the bones out of that one.

The concept fascinating but a step too far, just beyond my reach. Was she playing with me? "And what good will that serve?" I said.

"We will have learnt by that point that mankind cannot be trusted to manage his own affairs, and so some overseer, like a parent will be necessary."

"But isn't that what God is supposed to be now?"

"Ideally yes, but there will be no room for interpretation of his word, and therefore, no differing ideologies. He will manufacture us, just as he did before, in his image, like machines ... Maschinenmensch, purged, cleansed, with only the best vestiges of humanity remaining within us."

"As in the Garden of Eden."

"You've got it."

She was either a woman of astonishing mental capacity, or quite mad, and if I decided upon the latter, I felt it would be as a result of my own mental shortcomings.

The bells struck a quarter to eleven, allowing me to extricate myself from her philosophical web.

"I should be going," I said, "it's been a most interesting evening, thank you, Frau Karp." I took the tray to the kitchen. "Please don't get up, I can see myself out," but she ignored this. When I returned, she was at the door, as motionless as the hat stand. We stood in the landing light and gnarled hands grabbed mine. The slack-skinned smell of talcum and hot Darjeeling breath warmed my ear with an urgent insight; news from another realm perhaps Frau Karp was nearing. A parting gift (for I would never see her again and I think she knew so).

"I beg your pardon?" I said, unsure if I had momentarily slipped into a daydream, but she fixed me with rheumy eyes.

"Good luck, Fräulein Hoch," she said, closing the door without a sound.

The gymnastics of her message tumbled through my thoughts and I reached for the handrail to steady myself as they froze, poised in a perfect Arabesque. I inspected the statement from all angles, smoothing out any ambiguity or miscomprehension, and then I began to tremble; how did she know? Moreover, what did she mean?

"Fräulein Hoch," she had said, her voice adopting a mystic's warble. "Listen well. The one you seek is with you in the darkness, but it is in the light that you will find each other."

The dawn is false, at least in this reality. Outside the air may sing a bright, clear matinal. But here in this cracked tomb is sung a mourning Kaddish:

'Yehei shlama raba min shmaya,' chants the rabbi.

'Amen,' return the weary.

I will see the light again. I will find the one.

"I would never hurt you, Bienchen." Gräfin's riding boots paced the lino and a leather crop spliced the air beside my cheek. This was not the love I wanted, but somehow it felt deserved. Over the years our games had progressed to arrive at this point; me, kneeling blindfold, wrists shackled to a belt around my waist. Each lash a starburst of angry bees turning to livid snakes. She would tell me I was bad; I knew I wasn't. She would say I needed to be taught a lesson. Maybe that was true. I would bow my head, penitent. We had an understanding, the Gräfin and I; while she needed to feed her fantasies, I needed a distraction from mine.

"Grubby ... stupid ... bumpkin." Red welts crosshatching my breasts and buttocks like netted peaches.

"Harder Gräfin," I'd gasp.

"Oh no," she would chide. "You have to earn it," and there would be no more until I'd found with my face, that stubbled wetness. The game would dissolve with her, my mouth and nose bubbling, drowning. Her hand pressing my head until teeth grated bone.

"Bienchen, my glorious girl," she would moan, "I

love you and that is very bad news." I thought so too because I imagined her the jealous type.

Friends were being picked off one by one. Neunzig, seduced by a Party member and his goose-stepping claptrap, appeared to have gone up in the world, her confidence and dress size had increased accordingly; the zeal with which she towed the Party line, only surpassed by her enthusiasm for bratwurst. Both passions she'd press upon me at every opportunity. Our meetings now bracketed by an earnest salute, and my refusal to respond in the prescribed manner had elicited a raised eyebrow or two.

"You are such a queer fish, Bienchen." Neunzig (or Tutta as she was called by her new fiancé, Hans-Peter) stabbed at a sausage. "How can you not agree?" champing down on the meat, mechanically separating. "Take yourself; tall. Beautiful blonde hair, Aryan in the extreme you might say," she paused. "Well, aside from that little bit when God ran out of blue," she giggled, her fork waving dangerously close to my dark eye. Hans-Peter slid his half-eaten meal towards her. "Thank you liebling," she said. "Anyway,

I'm not saying you Bienchen, but an Aryan woman marrying a Jew? Imagine the half-breed children ... no, it simply must not be allowed; our blood must be kept pure, do you see?"

Hans-Peter nodded, soberly.

I recalled, once upon a time, when she had told me that I could do worse than marry Josiah.

"But supposing you'd fallen for Hans-Peter here, and he turned out to be Jewish?"

"Gosh Bienchen," she laughed, conducting with the bratwurst, "you're so precious, isn't she liebling?" But Hans-Peter was eyeing me with distaste.

"For goodness' sake, Neunzig," losing my cool. "It's as if you've been hypnotised. Gobbling down all that propaganda as eagerly as that bloody sausage."

Hans-Peter's chair scraped the floor as he shot to his feet, "I suggest, Tutta," he hissed, "you tell your friend to keep her bloody mouth shut." And throwing down his napkin, he excused himself from the table with a click of his heels.

"Heil Hitler," Neunzig squeaked, presenting the

sausage sheepishly to his back. Lips tight with annoyance she regarded me. "And another thing ..." she flushed, her outrage so mismanaged her fork clattered to the floor and heads turned. "Bienchen, I'm saying this for your own good," bratwurst-breath cloying as she leaned in. "If you continue to knock around with that perverted witch, there will be trouble."

I studied the beads of meat sweat on her upper lip. Almost overwhelmed with sadness. "Are you threatening me, Neunzig?"

"Of course not! It's just that she's already down as 'unreliable' in the Party's books and between you and me, I wouldn't be surprised if soon she'll be regraded as 'degenerate'. When that happens, her and her 'close' associates," she nudged me hard, "can expect to find themselves in Ravensbrück."

'At your suggestion, no doubt,' I thought. I had worked beside Neunzig these past years and now understood all her gossip and snooping had found its raison-d' être.

"I'm telling you this as a friend, Brigitte,"

dispensing with my pet name. A slight delay as she realised, "but I have to do my duty, or else I'll be the one who's carted off."

"Yes," I said thickly, "we must all do our duty." At this her face brightened. "We must all do what we believe is right," I continued, and her auburn tresses jounced in agreement. "Neunzig, as far as I'm concerned, we haven't been true friends for a long time, and I miss that, sincerely," I patted her pudgy hand, "but now it's no longer necessary to carry on the charade. Goodbye Neunzig." And that's how I left her, staring into her sauerkraut. Perhaps for once, ninety percent unsure.

Please God! Don't let me be too late. After leaving Neunzig, a brisk march as running would have warranted a stop and show to the SS. Rounding the corner into Budapeste Strasse, ten past noon on a Saturday, the Gräfin still unconscious, no doubt. Hopping to a halt, I melted into a doorway; three leather-coated Gestapo consulting the name plates beside the door of Gräfin's block, hers conspicuously blank. I never did learn her real name. They randomly jabbed bellpushes until, all at once, the door was drawn wide from within. All three recoiled and then reflexive arms were offered to the hallway; one so emphatically that he dislodged his colleague's fedora, leaving it at a drunken angle. A stiff exchange ensued that sounded like a dog fight, before they piled up the stairs. Sheisse, my nails digging crescents into my palms, I looked up at her window, cursing the person who had let them in who, as it happened, stepped out into the day. An officer, Waffen SS, but not any old brass; he was Liebenstandarte, Panzer Division. Personal bodyguard to the devil himself.

Despite my loathing, I could not help but admire the smart Hugo Boss design. At work, we'd often commented on the elegant lines, the quality, ink-black cloth; the investiture of malevolent beauty. His collar tabs sporting SS runes winked in the sun, so too the sleeve eagle, silver bullion cuff detail, the one-star shoulder boards of an Obersturmbanführer, all of which I might have stitched myself. A tall, raven-haired fellow, he strode head down, his peaked cap, laden with more silver rope, obscured him to the chin.

Jet-black jodhpurs barely bunched as the oil-bright riding boots continued the silhouette that Gräfin had possibly machined. Something was missing though; no service pistol holster strapped to his belt, most unusual. He tapped the top of his boot with a riding crop and I smiled at the tip off. Pushing up the cap with the crop, that wide, wry grin was revealed. Duelling scar, the icing on the cake. Sauntering near, her step slowed casually, and she scanned the sky, as if for signs of rain.

"I'm making for Switzerland," she grimaced like a ventriloquist, "what a bore, all that hideous yodelling."

"Nice chocolate though."

"Not my vice of choice, darling," she purred.

"But what will you do? How will you live?"

Her gaze met mine, "I'll trip-trap over that bridge when I come to it."

A lump clogging my throat. "Good luck then," was all I could manage.

And with a blue twinkle, a flick too quick for the

human eye to discern, a final sting of bees as she swatted my behind.

"Be good, Bienchen," she smiled, and ambling off, nose scenting the air, she turned a good-natured corner and touched the crop to her peak at a pretty woman.

"Be safe, Gräfin," I whispered. "You old goat."

Morning buttered the kitchen table where I'd remained throughout the night. Motorcars fizzed in the street below, left wet by a pre-dawn deluge. The sun's rays sliced through the haze as I ground another butt into the ashtray, like a gambler, surveying the dangerous game before me: fake identity cards, fake ration cards, fake me, bluffing it out, I mustn't fold. I was to be Johanna Bixel, a Swiss national, taking her children to see an ailing relative. Not sure if I approved; the name sounded weak, apologetic, a little obvious. I attempted to saturate myself in all the potential scenarios, but at the same time a degree of vagueness was required, so I didn't appear too rehearsed. However, my attention was divided, partly working on the nag that something was not right. Something was missing from right here in this room. I jabbed my fingertips against my brow to drum it in ... to drum it out.

"You will take them to Bern. Leave in a week, the window is closing ... money," he rifled in his pockets. "Papers," his hands shook. "The children have warm clothes in their cases and if you get into difficulty," fear reared up inside me like a cobra, "use this for bribes." He rattled a tobacco tin containing gemstone rings and pearls. "Check into this hotel and wait. Clara and I will get as far as we can by motorcar, but since we can't buy fuel, we may have to walk part way." To this I nodded sharply. A sob blotted his voice as he knelt and hugged the twins to his beard.

"Rubin ... Miriam," he set them straight with his hands on their shoulders, "Aunt Brigitte is your new mummy now." They looked up at me blankly. "You will call her mummy, not aunty, do you understand?" They nodded slowly, "and you too have new, fun names ... Wolfgang," he dabbed Rubin's nose, "and

Ilse," he smiled at his daughter. "Isn't that pretty?" She seemed uncertain, but agreed, nonetheless. "You must do everything Aunt Brigitte, I mean mummy tells you, is that clear?" They understood the principle.

"Like a game?" Miriam brightened.

"Yes." Josiah's chest hitched grateful at what the little girl had gifted him, "yes ... a game, liebling, that's exactly what it is."

"So who will be the winner?" Rubin piped up. Josiah hesitated. "Why, the one who plays the game best of all, of course. Mummy will explain the rules." He grinned at me apologetically.

A curious expression of guile passed between them and with a gesture at once chilling and marvellous, each presented their right arm to their father. "Heil Hitler!" they barked with uncanny comprehension.

I looked in on them sleeping, limbs and hair entwined, angelic and oblivious to the Marienkirche alarm. And there it was, I realised what was missing, its tinny twin; Frau Karp's mantle clock had not responded all night. Perhaps she had neglected to wind it, or .... Keys in hand, I braced myself for the prospect of stockingless, stick legs, horizontal on the bedroom floor, seed pearl slippers turned heavenwards. Or maybe dull eyed she lay, mouth agape, a frail crow carcass beneath the candlewick. But when I entered nothing was upturned, no tablecloth dragged to the floor, no crumpled heap, no broken form, human or otherwise. In fact, there was nothing, nothing at all. The apartment echoed my own perplexion. A series of indentations on the carpet hinted a ghostly blueprint, so too the lustrous brocade preserved as new by now absent bookcases. No longer did the edges of the room crumble to dusty infinity as each alcove was picked out starkly by a shadeless bulb. There was not a single shadow in which even a tiny, weeny, bird-like Jewess could have hidden. And so, she had gathered herself together with all her belongings for one final flit. To where? Somewhere safe I hoped.

As I turned to leave, a sudden jolt, before my mind adjusted the watchful shape hanging on the back of the door into the harmless thing it was; a sable coat,

THE LAST QUEEN OF HOLLAND

a few threads on the lapel where the yellow star had been picked off. It didn't reflect her; so voluminous it would have dwarfed her even in the height of her youth. Besides, it looked almost perfectly new. I eased my arms into the silk-lined sleeves and its glorious weight closed around me, like being in the safe custody of a friendly bear. My fingers found a note in the pocket, in spidery copperplate; *'May it keep you warm in the darkness.'*

Without that coat I'd probably be dead by now.

A study in discomfort; Rubin fixed me with his father's eyes, his hair a cone of lather.

"This is the last time, I promise Ru-Wolfgang," (I had to stop saying that!) Bending over the bath, he pinched his nose as I sluiced the suds to the plughole. Miriam, having undergone this treatment already, repeatedly rubbed the steam from the bathroom mirror to admire her new blonde tresses.

"Can we go out tomorrow?" She traced a love heart on the glass. They'd been in for four days now and although immaculately behaved, I couldn't blame them for growing restless. And bless them, like shame-faced puppies when I returned in the evening, their small deposits mellowing in the toilet because I'd told them not to flush in the day.

"Yes," added Rubin, towelling his golden crown, "now we look like you, everyone will think we really are your children."

I thought for a while. When Paris had fallen the indifference was palpable. Eight years of hard work at low wages and long hours, of belt-tightening and censorship had dulled the German masses to good and bad news alike. The bombs had barely touched the city, the inconvenience of air raids was just that, and there had been none since Frau Karp had disappeared. On three occasions I'd helped her to the cellar to perch cramped between the Winklers, the Rupprechts and the unconcerned Herr Schenk. Once we counted the distant pump of eighty bombs landing on what we surmised was Tempelhof Airport. "A strategic target," asserted Herr Schenk, "they wouldn't bomb civilians."

A strange tug in my chest as I tucked the quilt around my wards; Mother Nature was casting her spell. I took in their smell and through the faint taint

THE LAST QUEEN OF HOLLAND

of peroxide, their fresh, natural perfume prevailed. The urge to keep them safe, overwhelming; a difficult exchange ensued between heart and head. Nurture's mare soon trampled any resistance and as I had grown accustomed to their careful obedience, their trust, their unguarded affection and, of course, their vulnerability. I was seduced. They could have been mine had I married him, and now, to all intents and purposes they were, if only temporarily.

"Where would you like to go then?"

"The zoo!" they chorused.

A grin crept across my face because in all these years I'd never been. But then concealing the smile's disintegration behind my knuckles; I wished my horse charmer were here to complete this picture.

Home from work early, a serious offence, but I was leaving in a couple of days anyway and whatever happened I sensed I would not be back. It was one of those winter days that never quite got off the ground; the sky remained close and leaden. The threat of evening tinting the air by lunchtime. By the time we reached the Tiergarten, the sun had all but given up the ghost. Rubin's gloved hand in my left. Miriam's in my right. They skipped along to keep pace with my stride, steam breath seething through Mother's knitted legacies. Branches underlit by sodium lamps made gold baskets above us. We headed further into the park, streetlights were fewer and it grew darker. Surging waves of traffic abated, along with the twentieth century and some exotic bird exclaimed a primeval screech. We heard, before we saw, the gentle bison tearing at the grass. Like munching boulders, their cave-painting shapes materialised in the twilight. We might have had the place to ourselves, were it not for the reassuring shadows strolling around the Pagoda Gate entrance, a little off in the distance. The shriek and whine of the animals within, sounded particularly querulous, I noted. The bison started to stir; getting to their feet, raised snouts snorting out vapour, plodding through the frost-silvered grass until they had gathered in a herd. Miriam let go my hand and danced into the gloom.

"Where have all the squirrels gone?" she shrugged,

raising a palm of nuts to a tree.

"They're probably hibernating," I replied, "like all sensible creatures on a day like this."

But something was wrong, and my dark eye winced at what sounded like the cry of an eagle. I scanned the black trees now shrouded in fog, just as the wail of an air raid siren cranked up. Sheisse. A distant popping already discernible. I grabbed their hands and we made for the gate at a pace, where the nearest shelter was situated, but the lights were killed at once, leaving us nearly blind and disorientated.

"Gnädige Frau! Over here!" A voice in the dim which I followed. The clouds suddenly ablaze with anti-aircraft fire spitting from the zoo flack tower above the canopy, and in the brilliant cascade I saw the beckon of a man in brown uniform. Thinking him Nazi personnel, I hesitated, but soon deduced that his overalls were that of a zookeeper. "Hurry!" he shouted, "I have a safe place!"

He ushered us into a concrete maintenance hut with the sensible smell of creosote and hessian. Lifting a trap door in the ground to reveal a vault, he lowered first the children and then me, before climbing down the metal ladder himself and pulling the hatch closed over his head. The strike of a match, and soon a paraffin lamp dimly lit our plight; our shoes wallowed in a liquid floor.

"It shouldn't last long," he said, his face a kindly woodcut, though etched with unease.

"Thank you so much, Herr ...?" Removing my glove, I extended my hand.

"Grunau," he said, taking it. His was warm and dry.

"Bixel, Frau Bixel," I said, "and these are my ..."

The children had pushed beneath my coat and he squatted, offering the lantern to their faces.

"Hello there," he said. "What's your name, son?"

"Ru, I mean Wolfgang," the little boy corrected.

"I see, and yours?"

"My name is Ilse," Miriam replied with a practised air. "But mister, won't the hippos be afraid?"

"Ah, you like hippos?"

Miriam nodded.

"Well, when this is over, I will take you to see them," he said, "because I am their keeper." This prompted a twin gasp. "And the elephants, I look after them too and we have a new baby, would you like to see him?"

"Yes please!" in unison.

The booms and blasts drew nearer. Between them, the shrieks and trumpets of terrified animals far from home.

"Do you have a family, Herr Grunau?" making conversation, and for some reason I expected him to say that he didn't. But, yes. He had a daughter.

"She's out there now," he exhaled. "She works at the zoo."

"She's most probably safe in the shelter," I said.

"Oh no, not my Yael," he shook his head. "She wouldn't leave her animals any more than you would abandon your children."

Yael. Something about the name, the shape of it. And then it hit me with the force of a shell; I recalled how she had handled the horse. The brown overalls! Brigitte, you perfect idiot. The clues were there in each condensation smeared bus where she wasn't. I would perch on the sill, a vigilant bird watching the bobbing Kaiser-Wilhelm Strasse heads. Hats, gloves fluttering on church steps. Lithe and louche in every bar alcove, the restaurant canopies, the dawn streets, empty barrows, the solitary footfall that wasn't hers. The factory gates, S-Bahn commuters. I expected her residual after each passing parade. In friends, in friends of friends, in friends of friends of friends. The stables, the sweatshop's tarnished livery. The riverboats, the bathers. In charge hands oiling the cities wheels. In tug-boat crew and orchestra. Bystander, activist. In slumped drunks. In vacant, cud-chewing diners. In dance classes. Every place I could have found her, every place I searched, every place ... except the zoo. This rumination flashed in a second but completed my life. I returned to Grunau with renewed interest.

"Loves her giraffes she does. Started in the reptile house and worked her way up, so to speak." A joke perhaps she had invented and there was pride in his voice. Running his hand through his hair, "as a matter

THE LAST QUEEN OF HOLLAND

of fact, young Ilse here is the image of her when she was that age ... uncanny." Winding the lantern wick up a notch, he examined Miriam with close concern. "I've told her to go," he said, "get herself safe," and then he stood, holding the lantern at his shoulder. He studied me with similar concentration, and in his features, I recognised someone I loved. "Her mother was Jewish, you see." This was not a confidence he should have shared with a stranger, let alone an Aryan, but I was glad he had. His sincerity was touching. "But as I said, she will not leave the animals."

Now the bunker was vibrating as if outside an angry giant was venting his spleen. Grunau, taking advantage of the pounding, moved to my ear. His extraordinary azure eyes drilled into mine. "When are you leaving?"

Completely wrong-footed "After the weekend," I blurted, and bit my lip.

"You must go tomorrow," he said. "Don't delay." I nodded, but still his stare would not release me. "Swear it, Frau Bixel," he said, almost with menace and

I found myself promising.

Our ears were suddenly assailed by a high-pitched whine. We crouched instinctively and Grunau covered us with his body. The children screamed; an almighty detonation, too loud for human ears to register, so that it played out in our lungs, our chests, exploded with apocalyptic satisfaction not yards from our heads. Dust and concrete rained down and the puddle in which we squatted slewed tidal; its surface simmered with rock falls, as if the entire planet had been knocked off its axis. The lamp snuffed and Grunau held us tighter. Immediately, the bombardment ceased as if stunned by its own intensity. Everyone was left mute to hear the teeth-clenching harmonic of a tuning fork struck to the skull. A dwindling hum. The flak guns stuttered to a halt and fell silent. Gradually we stood, coughing and dusty. Several matches hissed at our feet before Grunau was able to relight the lamp. With light returned our hearing; from outside a heart-rending cacophony: screams, roars, shrieks of terror and pain. The unmistakable trumpet of an elephant in distress, overriding the all clear.

The air thick with sulphur and smoke as we emerged, and thankfully, I retained the presence of mind to engulf the twins in my coat, concealing from them the carnage all about. Split, splayed trees and blasted against them a tangle of bison. The children hugged my sides and sidled warm against me in the understanding that they would not look, they must not look.

Shocked, shambling shapes, us amongst them, drawn to the Pagoda Gate, like mud-caked natives to an oracle. Against a backdrop of orange smoke, a nonsensical limb flailed feebly; the wavering trunk of an elephant. Grunau broke into a jog in response. I looked to the flaming trees, screaming with monkeys, and skirted around something almost human smoking on the path.

The elephant lay on its side, its belly burst in a pool of purple. Grunau disappeared behind one huge flapping ear, his hands clawed in anguish, his face contorted. I saw him place his tiny man's skull against the massive brow of the beast. I saw him offer his hand to the dying trunk. I saw him look into the crusted, tear-stained eye. I saw him weep. It was then I saw the pulpy remains of the elephant's calf and beyond that, the extreme wrongness of a giraffe on its knees, its neck bent abnormal across the railings. I knew she was there, somewhere in the eye of this nightmare, and though it was not my intention to approach her, I had to see her; it would be my last and only chance.

Out of body, I set the children down by the ice cream stand and covered them with my coat. "Stay here," I said, "don't move, I'll be back shortly." Brown uniforms were everywhere, mostly attending to people who lay like sunbathers in their own patch, clothes blown clean off. A cavernous rumble, like a stone rolling from a tomb; a tiger, skulking, limping and she would pause like an Indian Kathakali dancer, to snarl at each threat, real or imagined. With stealth she loped, taking refuge behind the ice cream stand, perilously close to the children. I could see their black shape. Turning my back on the havoc and my horse charmer, the heat on my neck, I returned to the twins, the tiger watching from the shadows. I had them warm against me once more. We would leave tomorrow. I frowned at the sky; dark shapes in a V formation were moving against the clouds. Reflexive I hunched, but looking up again. Purposeful, pink wings under-lit; a skein of flamingos was flying away.

I am biting the sides of my tongue to make the 'Ya.' It writhes through the word like a salt-dowsed slug, arching against my teeth and ends up a stubby peg behind the incisors ... 'el ... Ya-el.' Without any conscious effort, that muscle performs all the oral gymnastics required to speak; I suppose we learn that when we are babies, unless we are deaf of course, in which case the process must be mystifying. Never have I enjoyed so much, wrapping my tongue around a word, 'Yael'. The flexing stimulates saliva. I'm parched. Grief occludes my throat.

I sighed out a cigarette to calm my nerves as the train lurched away. The children instantly curled into sleep either side of me, having got little the night before. Although I had managed to shield them from the sights of the zoo bombing, the sounds and smells had germinated in their imaginations conjuring visions terrible enough. Their limited concept of things gruesome extended to the beheading and dismemberment of biblical or fictitious characters, often meted out with a semblance of justice. But in their realisation that such cruelties were not confined to The Old Testament or The Brothers Grimm, their world had suddenly turned vicious, untrustworthy.

I attempted to impress upon them that while such atrocities did happen, it was rare and that I believed most people were kind and good.

"Do you think those airmen flying up there, dropping those bombs on us are kind and good?" said Miriam, pinpointing the paradox of war. I had no answer.

"Ladies and gentlemen, your tickets please!" The approaching conductor sent a needless wash of fear through me. A woman, perhaps in her late fifties sat opposite, expertly knitting. 'Beautiful,' she mouthed nodding towards the sleeping children, at least that's how I interpreted her strangely over-lubricated annunciation. Should I thank her? What would a mother do? It wasn't down to me that they were beautiful, even if were their mother. So I just smiled. The conductor, a jovial fellow, chatted with the passengers as he progressed along the carriage.

"Thank you kindly," he punched the ticket of the knitting lady and then indicating to the wool on her lap, "I want to see that finished by the time we get to Bern." Concentrating on his mouth, she let out a breathless titter. I noticed she had a hare lip, eyes that turned down at the corners and a wide nose; an odd but not unpleasant face. Her nostrils whistled as if she had a head cold and she seemed unaware of the croaky, keening sounds she intermittently issued. I gathered she was deaf. Chomping noisily on radishes which she fished from a brown paper bag. I graciously declined her offering, but Rubin plucked one dozily, then instantly fell back to sleep with it clutched in his hand.

"Ba?" she said, nodding and smiling enthusiastically. A few seconds of puzzlement passed before "Yes," I replied, nodding. "We're going to Bern."

Placing the needles on her lap (a gesture strongly

reminiscent of mother), she embraced herself, "Brrr," she shivered theatrically. "Ca."

"Yes," I agreed. "Cold". She mimed that she was knitting a scarf and hat.

"Ca in Ba," she frowned, laughing delighted at our conversation. I suspected she might be dim-witted. And with a disquieting instinct, pitying and misanthropic in equal measure, I fought an impulse to both kiss her and punch her. Again, her eyes danced to the children "Byooful," she mouthed once more and resumed her knitting and keening. Soon we would be nearing Frankfurt, then I would wake the children for their lunch and downgrade to yellow alert. However, my thumbs prickled as the train slowed before idling at an unscheduled stop, to pick up water I assured myself, but the metal-headed soldiers standing at arms along the platform suggested otherwise. Sheisse. My heart kicked up savagely in my throat as a gaggle of officers climbed aboard, bringing with them a cold gust that swirled about my legs. I wondered if I should tell the knitting lady who now slept, head slumped against the window, a strand of drawl escaping the crevice of her mouth. But all I could do was lean forward and reinstate to her lap the ball of wool that was also escaping. With this movement the children stirred. "Are we there?"

"Not yet, lieblings, try and go back to sleep," I said, arranging the fur coat around them.

The knitting lady startled, eyes wide. "Funfa?"

"No, not Frankfurt yet." She trusted my eyes.

The train shuddered and the stationary soldiers inched past the window, signalling a resumption in our progress, albeit at a walking pace, allowing me to study each earnest, young face. We cleared the station with a clank as the track diverged; we remained southbound while the other continued westward to Cologne. The engine huffed as if bored with the dawdle, breaks squealing to stifle its momentum.

"Papers! Show your papers!" A soldier marched swiftly down the aisle bouncing the floorboards and jolting my pulse to a gallop. The knitting lady's eyes met mine in panic.

"Wha?" she said, stuffing away her wool.

"Papers," I mouthed, not least because I was unable to find my voice. We rifled in our handbags as the children knelt up on the seats to look down the flustered carriage.

"What's happening?" Rubin had sensed the change in atmosphere.

"Nothing, liebling," I said. "They just want to check our tickets again," but he eyed me unconvinced. A fugue of terror struck up in my head as a Sturmbannführer approached; the type of middle rank that carried with it an air of self-importance and a degree of autonomy. I noticed he had incredibly small feet. I tried to remind myself that he had probably been nothing more than an accountant, but war had elevated the status of many an insignificant bean-counter to that of a minor deity. Perhaps I could appeal to the bespectacled, tubby, little boots he once was, not the Caligula he had become. No chance of it. I could see it in the way he removed his gloves, better to pronounce judgement, and the way they fluttered impatiently, like crows' wings at his back vent. I saw it in his strut, and how the papers were held under his beak by a soldier for his perusal. Why should he sully his hands? I watched his prospecting gaze flit across my false information and alight on the faces of the children. The compulsion to draw his attention from them was strong. "Sir, please can you tell me why we are travelling so slowly?" in my best Swiss accent. "Is there something wrong with the train?"

He cocked his head as if he had heard a squeak and rounded his attention on me. "What takes you to Bern, Frau ... Bixel?" Raising his eyebrows, I knew he had noticed my eyes.

"I am a Swiss national," I replied with all the equanimity I could muster. "My mother is ..." I cleared my throat, "... unwell and I want the children to see her before ..." But just then, the knitting lady gave out a particularly loud whimper. Several people, including the officer turned in her direction and I wondered if she had suffered the same protective compulsion as me. Her papers were snatched and scrutinised while she grinned in secret glee.

"And what is your business in Bern Frau ... Waldschmidt?" His tone more than sceptical.

I found myself clenching my fists as she smiled and nodded emphatically. "Ba!" she barked in adenoidal agreement.

Head cocked once more, he briefly caught the soldier's eye and rapidly relayed orders in a low voice before strutting on down the carriage to the next passenger.

Frau Waldschmidt's expression of unadorned relief met mine and she wiped her brow comically. The cold ball of winter sun, eventually tiring of its peek-a-boo with the engine smoke, sank behind a tracery of branches. Peach and purple captured in the angles like stained glass. I allowed myself a horse charmer moment and comforting as it was, I found its relevance had altered; it was part of the fabric of my past and perhaps my future. However, at this moment I had to put it aside, live solely in the present. The odds of accomplishing this mission becoming more favourable with each passing second. I breathed her name and the rise and fall of my chest returned to near normal. Could I be heroic? I liked to think so, not for my own sake, but until we are faced with circumstances that require it, I suppose we never truly know this about ourselves. The engine hissed in exasperation, the creak of the carriages, the strange woodwind emanating from the wheels. The slowing belch of smoke reintroduced the staccato rhythm to my chest, as agonisingly, inexorably the train ground to a halt. An idling skitter, as if it were twiddling its thumbs, and then a huge, protracted sneeze as steam flushed into the surrounding forest in a gesture of finality.

"Off the train!" The soldier's spit burned my cheek and for a second, I thought he was warning me of some peril.

"I'm sorry?" I stuttered. "Why?"

"Now!" he levelled his rifle at my chest. "And you." He turned to Frau Waldschmidt. "Out!"

As we disembarked into the sloping forest, our cases were unceremoniously slung after us, and the first tentative specks of snow eddied in the beams of a staff car glowering through the trees. As more people descended, a wild hope flew up in me that there was safety in numbers. The children seemed to know better than to ask anything.

"Remember who you are in the game," I whispered, and squeezed their hands.

Rubin dragged our cases around us in fortification and I noted his attentiveness at the inclusion of Frau Waldschmidt in our circle.

Two dozen stood uncertainly in the leaf mould, plumes of breath back-lit by the carriage's interior and I looked for a communality between us: an extensive family with several young children and a mass of luggage, two of the women heavily pregnant. A huddle of elderly people. What I thought was a child smoking a pipe was in fact a dwarf man and, resting on a shooting stick, a woman with a club foot. If not physically deformed, all were either most likely Jews or Gypsies. Holding the twins close, I cursed my own abnormality.

A shout, a whistle and with dredging, laborious lungfuls, the train began to shift its homely light along the track. Passengers left to ride, either stared at their laps or studied newspapers, save one little boy who had rubbed a porthole in the condensation from where his blue mitten waved solemnly. Once out of sight, the engine gloated its return to normalcy with a salutational hoot.

In rising desperation, I looked about me, exploring the viability of making a run for it. Only four soldiers guarding us ... but armed, and Major Little Boots, leaning on the bonnet of the car, smoking a cigarette, biding his time, perhaps waiting for a message from on high as to the nature of our fate. At this rate we would freeze to death. My plan unravelled as I looked at Frau Waldschmidt; was she able to run? But then re-knitted as a voice spoke, ruthless in its intent to survive; she would quickly lag behind it suggested, an ample target to draw their fire. The children and I could be crouched in a ditch, invisible under the black sable, before they could even get a shot in. She squatted to rummage in her bag, and I banished the image of her cut down in a hail of bullets. Her eyes had trusted me. Producing a tin of travel sweets, she offered the sugared emeralds and rubies to the children, reminding me of the tin in my pocket, rattling with bribes. I wanted to run; my legs trembled with the will of it, but my odds of success were dashed with the arrival of further soldiers crashing through the deadfall, flashlights strobing the understory amid a volley of barking. On sight of the dogs, the children retreated beneath my coat, while Frau Waldschmidt clung to my arm and growled.

In this fresh drama, she had failed to notice, the change in backdrop; a different train was insinuating itself into the landscape. On and on, squealing brakes sputtered sparks, wooden and windowless, the boxcars crept by. I counted more than forty before the juggernaut shunted to a halt. Its cars set out like shacks along a road, disappeared around the bend and the engine, chimney smoking could well have been a cabin deep in the woods.

In his own aura of smoke and illuminated vapours, Major Little Boots, all cosy in a great coat, conferred with a fellow officer. Voices distilled and amplified by the contents of a silver hip flask passing between them. Harsh guffaws borne on gusts assailed me. The snow was erasing us, cancelling us. Standing on feet I could no longer feel, I strained to hear.

"I have to applaud your alacrity, Gerhard!" exclaimed the fellow officer, "but there are simply too many of them."

"What can I say?" chuckled Little Boots "I am renowned for my alacrity ... but seriously," he protested, "some of them are of special interest."

Their heads came together in the headlights as if kissing, before Little Boots shrugged, unclipped his pistol holster and took a last swig from the flask. Working off the lid of the tin, a tumble of treasure in my pocket, my shaking fingers selected what I knew to be a substantial ruby ring.

"Don't have too much fun!" shouted the officer as Little Boots lolloped through the trees, making a bee line for us.

Aware that I was panting, I summoned a full tank of frozen air into my body, but the resulting blizzard that scattered my vision only fleetingly obscured his approach. He seemed to fizz with blue static as he paused to load the magazine, ham-fisted, a Santa Claus jingle of spilled bullets. The underfoot crackle continued as he walked. Conversely, he appeared smaller the closer he came. Now I wanted to leap on him, claw his throat out.

"Ah!" ten feet and closing. "My dear Swiss Frau with the unusual eyes!" a mocking note in his voice. Circling our cases before arriving at my shoulder. "I know a certain doctor who would be exceedingly interested in you," his breath a boozy cloud. "Now, let's see," he parked himself on my case, almost toppling backwards. "A little boy and a little girl. My goodness, are you twins?" Miriam and Rubin nodded, "but not identical?" They shook their heads. "Mmm ... pity," he said. Reaching out, he took a lock of Miriam's hair and rubbed it suspiciously. "I've seen every trick in the book, Frau Bixel." I sought and found a foothold in his ambiguity.

Miriam tightened her grip on my leg as she understood it was for this moment that the game had been devised.

"My name is Ilse," she said, engagingly, "and this is

THE LAST QUEEN OF HOLLAND

my brother, Wolfgang."

"Is that so?" he smiled. "What fine names!"

"Get on with it!" shouted his colleague. "I want that train out of here!" To which Little Boots waved a dismissive hand; too busy enjoying himself.

'Get on with it'; the phrase galvanised me.

"Herr Sturmbannführer," I interjected. "I would very much like to gain passage on that train with my children," thrusting the ring under his nose. "Please accept this in payment of our fares." Without looking up, he plucked the ring from my fingers, bit it, and secreted it in his coat pocket.

"Now then, little man," his bleary eyes focused on Rubin. "Would you be so kind as to show me your pecker?" I felt myself scrambling as the last foothold failed.

"Please Herr Sturmbannführer, it's so cold ... he remains intact as nature intended, I promise you," fumbling for another ring. I presented a sapphire and his leather glove closed over mine. A recoil so violent that my being jumped from my body; up into the trees it flew and looking down, I saw us in a halo of headlights. Long shadows stretched behind us like graves, the snow condensing on our woolly heads. From my new vantage point, the scene resembled a bizarre marriage proposal in reverse, as this time the ring found his breast pocket. In an eye-blink, the monstrous man had yanked down Rubin's breeches and underpants and with that famous alacrity, was examining him between thumb and forefinger. I saw the terrified boy let go a glistening arc that splattered upon Little Boots and I fought to get back ... to regain my body. In the distance the scream of an eagle, or was it me? as the Sturmbannführer leapt to his feet and discharged his gun first into Rubin's head and then Miriam's. I saw them buckle to the ground and their warmth and love rush up to meet me. Beneath my wings once more they nestled, but soon faded like the double whip crack, dissipating through the forest to oblivion.

I saw the tableau; sleeping cherubs at my feet. Myself, a statue, paralysed, impotent, detached, willing the crack of his bullet to shatter me. I wrestled in the silence until a rising animal snarl culminated in a word of sorts.

"BAH-TUD!" Frau Waldschmidt roared before he finished her in the face. I saw him pace with haste to the cowering family where he aimed and fired six times, killing all the children. I saw him calmly reload and abort the screams of the pregnant mothers, the young woman and the elderly people, before finally exhausting the clip into the lady with the club foot. I saw four figures left standing in the resounding knell: two young men, the dwarf … and someone who looked like me.

But all that was yesterday … perhaps the day before. And I can't quite remember when it was they had drawn aside the door of the cattle truck; time holds little sway in here. The open maw disclosed the lowing of sickly animals. I saw haunted eyes wince in the flashlight's spell. I had swooped down, like Noah's dove, to join the wretched ark; for that was where I was meant to be.

"Don't worry," a woman addressed me from the stench as I fell across protesting limbs. "Your little boy is just here." My heart leapt until I realized she meant the dwarf.

I feel arrived somehow (even though my journey is not yet ended), as if each turn in my life has served to steer me here. That is not to say I assume the arrogance of one who believes the whole world revolves around them, nor that the machinations of war have been orchestrated solely for this purpose. Perhaps I have engineered it myself, abiding by some gravitational law, spinning a web of precarious design, at each juncture a decision made without hesitation, however unwilling, this is my own choice. I have navigated my ship to the rocks. Everything gone. Alone I kindle the flame, still lambent beneath the wreckage. The flame that sleeps in the soil, at the bottom of a well, at the end of a rope, and the myriad other places I have met my death. It glimmers low, awaiting her re-ignition. But here in the dark, I gutter. To the point of extinguishment.

The actions of this law have conspired to appoint me a queen and it is only this black coronation that will allow me my consort. I am deep inside myself and realise I am not quite alone. I see it with my dark eye and can do no more than survive and wait. I understand everything and know nothing. She is bound to me in this accident of chemicals: in the sodium sweat, in the blood's ebbing iron, in calcium cold bones, in phosphorous nerves, in silica skin, in the leaden heart, in potash cells, in the antimony of sex, in the mercury of sanity. A miraculous alchemy; we are the ingredients of God. The composition of ash.

The boxcar timbers creaked and settled like a shipwreck as we drew to halt. A slow, dragging sound which I could not place and then a radiance purged the carriage like the face of God. And, unworthy, we hid our faces in the crook of our arms. I winced in the snow-bright glare, eyes streaming, at the shadow puppets moving across the aperture and I understood. Outside. A concept almost abandoned.

People stirred to a leprous crawl, making for the silver water pails knocking with ice, which were being hoisted into the car. Although dry as a board, I stayed where I was, mistrustful of gravitating groups. That, and the quality of Nazi mercy. The crawl hastened to an unbridled scramble and I got to my feet to avoid being trampled. People and pails spilled overboard by the pent-up ranks behind. A machine gun volley in response, tacka-tacka-tacka, and I clapped my hands over my ears. *'No more, please stop.'* Puppets jerked and danced across the screen in ballistic articulation, then crumpled abruptly, strings cut. The energy ceased. The dead described a low, smoky landscape. The injured rocking feebly like logs caught in a current. Of the survivors, most were crouched in prayer. Others assumed the cower of beaten dogs.

And then, as the peripheral presence of the moon on a night walk. I became aware of another standing just out of reach amid the cases and chattels, conscious of their intense stare. The moon's remote allure, it is said, can drive a person mad and I felt myself unable to return the gaze for that reason. The best I could manage was to study the lace-up riding boots on which I counted twenty-four holes. Screwing up my courage, I advanced to a plaid skirt with a large hand each side, clenching into fists. Dimly aware of the continuing drama about us; we stood like two old trees dressed in ephemeral leaves. A green cape with four brass buttons (I had not anticipated women's clothes), two fur-lined slits from which her arms protruded and a black fur collar, the same colour as the curly, bobbed hair that rested upon it, a snow-white blaze at the temple.

My heart struck through the numbness; a curious sensation like pins and needles when blood returns to a stiff limb. I took in her face, which over fourteen years, my mind had tenderly tinted to prevent its fading and noted the way maturity had enhanced her quintessence, now fully hewn from the marble. But fear launched a counterstrike; was she real or a phantom, that in despair, my hope had resurrected? Was I barking at the moon? Like Thomas needing the wound, I stepped towards my horse charmer and as she drew me in, the grim reality about me further lost its contours. Though not the setting for a smile of any kind, we couldn't help it, the recognition complete.

"I know your name is Yael," I said, holding out my hand.

"And I know you are the one I have searched for." Taking my hand in hers, she knelt before me. "My queen," she said, head bowed.

It would be easier to go no further, having reached a happy ending of sorts. But there is no story unless it is finished. No remembrance without testimony. And I pray that somewhere, something, is keeping tally.

We alighted on the ramp, five thousand ghosts. The sky craven under the pall of an ectopic industry. Shoulder to shoulder we shivered naked. Are we in Hell? The small child burst from within me. And the smokestacks bloomed black trees. The shrieking and crying, the ravening dogs and absurdly, the strains of a nocturne scraped out like cat guts. Perfumed and precise, his shadow moved across us. The flick of a judgemental cigarette. "Left, left, left. Any twins?" he enquired. The most handsome man I'd ever seen. Down in a shocking squall of stars at the behest of your fist. "Forgive me." You hauled me up and monitored, with satisfaction, the winking swell of my dark eye close to a slit. And though I did not understand, I trusted that your motive was just, because "trust me," you had said. Left, left. The glowing ash tapped, and then right, right, which two wrongs won't make, as Mother would have said, otherwise the story would have ended there. You, a Jew. Me, an a-social. A yellow star and a black triangle to point out our respective ignominy. Black and yellow our hair danced together on the floor. We swapped ill-fitting clogs. A grey blanket wrangled between myself and four strangers. Lime-stung on my first night without you. You were consigned to ice fields. And for me, the familiar tacka-tacka. Canopies of beautiful silk, on which soldiers would drift to earth like flecks of ash. The off-cuts stored in my wadded cheek for your frost-bitten fingers. You spoke to me, piercing my chest with desperate arrows that sailed over heads, shot from your eyes. A tooth. You fought tooth and nail. We smiled once when he ran like a girl, that doctor, pursued by a woken queen wasp. And I recognised his genetic flaw. We saw the seasons change on borrowed time. And a beard of bees grew on a dead bush. My hand a fist in the warmth of the swarm. The guards at a loss, and from some ancient wisdom, they did not sting me, the guards or the bees. Instead they let me walk to the wire, where the swarm dissolved to the sky in erratic wisps. And I kept one, though dead, its poison intact. You came to me with fragments: a toe in the ground, a tooth you had nudged with your toe. "These are knuckles," you said, wringing mine. Your eyes flaring the message home. No need to mention that soon it would be our bones tamped for pathways, our flesh for the tallow. And how we were beaten. Each day a keelhaul. The wad of your cheek a ripe peach, not from a rifle butt. The self-inflicted violence of a gold tooth extracted to pay your Kapo so that we could spend one night together. And her jealous eyes spied our fingers warmed in the swarm, our bodies like seventy-year-old men. And with her loving overture of fist and cudgel, she drew attention to my odd arrangement and had me frog-marched, at last, to his spurious science. Eyeballs from coal to violet to glacier green stared from sweet shop jars, while my dark eye saw you beat your own chest. Amused, his blue eyes above a genuine surgeon's mask. His fat breath urged my eyes with fat needles to become perfect. And new clouds dimmed the world. From corners, twins stumbled, stitched in a limbo. I feigned sleep, the refuge of the weak, unstrapped and blind. He embraced me as a lover and my lips upon his fragrant *neck disgorged the bee's kiss. "There's your science," I said and licked his poisoned sweat. "There's your science, Herr Doctor." I laughed, as he choked and squeaked. Your hand met mine in the mud. "Take me to the black tree," I begged you on the beaten track. "You must get up, my queen." Your hands travelling sore haunches. "Or you'll be done for." Sometimes the smoke like silver dragons in a blue sky. Sometimes flat, white-bellied flounders. Sometimes I remembered a string of elephants, trunks holding the next one's tail. I remembered your face, beaten like gold but tender as a bruised peach. Take it away, Yael! Erase the board, return us to nothing, re-set the clock! And though I am blind, I see us on horses. How we have fallen through the centuries to bounce and be dashed on each passing outcrop. Only to land on this ledge of charnel and bones. "This is my choice." The stars of barbed wire, the watchful towers I am rejecting. We will find each other again in fields, in forests or any other fucking place that is not here. "Take me to the black tree, Yael, or else I'll crawl." I felt your hands give up. "I'll carry you, my queen. We'll meet it together." A nocturne returned to your straining veins. Deliver me to the next life, my love incarnate. Only*

JOSIE CLAY

you. Always you

.

UPTURNING THE
OBSTACLE (PART 3)

♻

May 16ᵗʰ 2166

An hour of life won, he thought, as the dashboard clock restated 06.05. Only to be lost on the journey home. The limo emerged from the tunnel in a neighbouring time zone and slowed, encountering tail lights. Brinkley scanned the sombre streets. Empty, save for a sidewalk cleansing machine. He scrutinised the rudimentary facial features of the synthetic operative. A million miles from Milo. Recalled how these basic level synths, sparse bodies, limbs hinged like artists' mannequins, had initially been manufactured without faces. However, to be met by a smooth blank was unsettling and would set little children off crying. Consequently, your basic, front-facing synth sported two unblinking, green lights for eyes and a constant, banana smile. He was unsure if this was an improvement. A comedic change in beeping as the synth wound the steering wheel to incorporate some speck of trash invisible to the human eye. The malfunctioning reverse alert an asthmatic kazoo. Brinkley smiled. Clown car.

His thoughts began to fragment. *Children can be mean,* his mother was dabbing his eyebrow, *but that's only because someone has been mean to them.* Milo noted the man's head lolling. His body rocking in motion with the car.

"Jesus." Brinkley stirred in the vague comprehension that his own mother's smile would now have to remain a memory.

"Is everything alright, sir?"

"They may not be wearing it ... the nose drape," Brinkley mumbled, shaking his head. "They don't have to, technically. Surely."

"I'm sorry, sir. Who may not be wearing what?"

They'd worked hard on the voice, but the subtle, trilling quality gave Milo away for what he was. Brinkley realised he had inadvertently spoken this last reverie aloud.

Let it ride, or ask Milo? What to do? But Milo would know the law, for sure.

He gave a muscular cough. "I mean Doctor de Hoog's and Doctor Kumagai's position regarding the veil."

"The wearing of the veil," Milo began, "is a legal requirement for all females, and those who identify as female, of the age eight years and above from this day, May sixteenth, 2166, who are domicile in The United States. Doctors de Hoog and Kumagai are Dutch nationals domiciled in The Netherlands and are therefore exempt from this rule. However, should they choose to decline the protection of the veil, the state will take no responsibility for their ..."

"Yes." Brinkley pulled a furtive fist pump. "Thank you, Milo."

The journey ended for him in a daze of relief. Even if the law had applied, he was certain those old squaws would sooner face arrest than comply. Milo cast the state umbrella above him, and it was with a renewed sense of fair play that he met the rain-glossed, granite steps, ready as he would ever be.

Beverages were drunk and spilled; a bumbling Babbage's coffee spreading across the table like a liquid Africa. Watches consulted. Milo blotted the accident. Two chairs remained empty.

"Milo," said Brinkley. "Can you please find out if they are even in the building? If not gentlemen," he exhaled, "I suggest we press on without them."

"I believe they are being escorted up now, sir." Milo had neither moved nor uttered but had internally contacted the desk synth. It gave Brinkley the creeps the way they were all connected to that Meta-system, like one giant mind. God knows what they knew.

"There was some security issue with Doctor de Hoog's cochlea implant."

"Oh?" said Babbage. "I wasn't aware she had one."

"Should you be, Harald?" snapped Brinkley. Boorish perhaps. But Babbage had an unlikeable face. Too much in common with a toad.

Babbage had been chiefly credited with the inception of the Milo unit, head and shoulders above previous synths, but it was de Hoog who had nailed the programming, giving Milo his Milo-ness and so-called endowment to learn. Not so much dry facts, which could be imported, but the ability to respond appropriately to the foibles of the human psyche, which could not. Though Brinkley had witnessed zero evidence of these adaptive capabilities in *his* Milo. A synth was a synth: dependable, unflappable, humourless, great at companionable silences, and on occasion, a tad condescending, truth be told.

"It's just a bit low-tech, I mean, when Breeda, of all people could ..." Babbage scratched the pinkish thatch on his head as Brinkley closed him down with a sharp glance. What kind of grown man had cotton candy hair, anyway?

All at once, the door glided open and all arose in some old-fashioned notion of gallantry or respect. The two figures that entered, far from decrepit, seemed to advance on wheels, like medieval siege engines.

Brinkley half stood, cauterised. He'd guessed wrong.

"Hello everyone." De Hoog seated herself abruptly with no apology.

"Gentlemen." Kumagai bowed, palms pressed together. A shy jingle as a number of copper bangles shifted from wrist to forearm. She took a seat beside her beloved. The pair of them, it seemed, enjoying the theatre of the veil. Both dressed in the knee-length, glaucous green kimonos of the Stoic Order. Grey, twill trousers wrapped in stiff leather gaiters, tapered to the black ankle boots, resembling paws, favoured by the aged. Like something out of Robin Hood, thought Brinkley. Or those warrior wizards. Dryads ... no, he corrected himself. Druids.

"Breeda, Yoshimi," he said, taking their hands. His best delighted expression etched with concern. "We were worried you wouldn't make it." They cast their eyes over him. Eyes that gripped hold of your balls and squeezed tight.

"And why is that, John?" De Hoog threw him a measuring look, her veil gave a little shimmer.

"Ah, just the weather, I guess" he stammered, "its nasty out there."

"Hmm," she said. Her eyes crinkled in what he hoped was a smile. "We are from Nederland where it always rains." But it could have been a wince.

His heart thudded in his throat. Their obscured mouths no longer at liberty to soften any blows the eyes might deliver.

"And you know," he tried to sound breezy, "coming

from Holland you can dispense with the erm ..." His fingers fluttered under his nose.

"When in Rome ..." replied Kumagai, tipping him a wink, just like a goddamn veil emoji.

He quelled the sex yawn rising in his throat.

After the obligatory and needless rollcall, he leaned back in his seat. Only a general risk that any further input on his part might be required. Not till later, at any rate, when they would be vying for finance.

He fancied he heard a faint buzzing; a distant, sustained bow-stroke swelling the air. De Hoog fingered the nickel-sized transmitter on the side of her head. At first, he took the device for an oji, but then remembered the cochlear implant. Laxity and indulgence vied. Tempting him with titbits. Jagged flashbacks peppered his vision. Now was not the time or place, he told his impish libido. *Sure it is*, his craving purred, slyly urging him to picture the meeting of two sets of nipples. Brinkley coloured. Loosened his tie. It was too much; the twin source of his obsession sitting across the round table at eleven and twelve. Like knights of old. He placated the compulsion to inhabit that visceral place by drinking them in on a visual basis. Distilling them into a manageable tincture. But he needed his fix. And it didn't help, or maybe it did, that Om Snyder was rambling on. *Immune machines,* he kept saying, *immune machines.* Which sounded like it could be interesting. Except Snyder's lulling monotone would render the arrival of a UFO on the White House back lawn impenetrably boring. Brinkley listened only to his own instincts; they must be talking about TOSA. Still no cure, sadly. Thank God.

He let his eyes rove over the close-cropped heads. Kumagai's hair black, despite her years, except for an extraordinary white starburst at her left temple. Eloquent eyes slanted olivine through blue, lozenge-shaped glasses, focused on her own clasped hands on the table. Her brilliant mind biding its time. She reminded him of an owl, watching her own thoughts like mice. Sensing she felt him, he shifted his gaze to Hewish, who seemed to be talking at *him. Uh oh.*

"... out of the Oort cloud ... picked up by the Galgalim array ... fast velocity. Gigantic. Some fifty plus kilometres in size."

Adept at putting the pieces together, Brinkley said something typical. "Can we mine it, this asteroid?"

An uncomfortable silence ensued, like the aftermath of a fart. Brinkley maintained his expectant expression.

Hewish drew a breath. A whimsical smile, as if dealing with the preposterous query of a small child. "No, John, we can't. Like I said, it's a comet. An ice comet," he shrugged. "Unless you want popsicles ...."

A hubbub of amusement. They were laughing at him. And although he was stung to the quick, he acknowledged the joke; *depends on the flavour.* No martinet he.

"Are we worried?" he said gravely, inferring their sniggers inappropriate.

"We have to refine the orbit." Adrian Yang piped up

through incredible teeth. He distrusted Yang. Put him in mind of the guy in a zombie movie who gets bitten and hides it from the others. "But it'll be one for our grandchildren to deflect, if need be."

Breeda de Hoog gave a hiss. "Oh, come on!" Her palm slammed the table. "YOU are generation omega. They'll be no grandchildren to mop up this clooshterfuck." Letting slip an accent Brinkley had never heard in the twenty years of their acquaintance. "Do I have to spell it out?" Stoics didn't *do* anger, but she looked madder than a wet hen. "The planet's resources are all but used up. Soon there will be no power, no manufacturing, no food production, no clean water supply. Disease is rife. Antibiotics don't work anymore. Infrastructures are breaking down as we speak. Half the world is starving. Civilisation is on the brink of collapse, while the power elite's chief concern is the acquisition of more wealth, which, incidentally, will not insulate them from this catastrophe. Add to the mix, certain pervasive ideologies taking advantage of the chaos and invading allied territories. An increasingly cornered government," she drew a straight bead on Brinkley, "might just decide on a nuclear course of action, melting what's left of this sorry omnishambles to glass." Consonants punched her veil like a cat fight behind a curtain. "Those heroic grandchildren of yours, Doctor Yang, should they be unfortunate to survive, will be foraging in the debris for vac-packed Tootsie Rolls, which they will recognise solely from the iconic packaging because, most likely, they will be unable to read ... let alone build a space rocket." She shrugged. "Sorry."

The whiskered bulge of Yang's Adam's apple flushed like some freaky, rogue gonad. The room further bedevilled when Kumagai covered her partner's galloping fingers with a mottled hand.

"Yes, well." Hewish cleared his throat. "That bleak outlook aside. Chances are Jupiter will protect us. He usually does."

Master of the pregnant pause, Brinkley looked to the ceiling, implying complex reflection. Shot his cuffs. Withdrew his water glass as if conceding a game of chess. Positive the outburst was aimed at him. "Good," he said. "Send me a full report." Scrolling down the agenda. "Professor Crick, would you be so kind as to update the panel on Project Canute?"

Brinkley retreated into himself to lick his wounds. And by way of solace, focused on the features of Breeda de Hoog; only the discrepant eyes apparent, the rest ingrained in his mind, like those flinty Easter Island statues. Themselves, at present, peering over a watery veil. And, like them, so old that time had washed her face as smooth as sea-glass. The grey implant transmitter conspicuous in the dove-white stubble of her hair. He had noticed how she often looked to Milo. She watched him now with undisguised affection. Her twin brother had died in the first TOSA outbreak sixty years ago, and it was rumoured she had influenced Milo's designers with his image. What was his name now ... Kenny? Lenny? Olivia would know. He recalled the night de Hoog had told them about Kenny or Lenny. Although chiefly directing her comments at his wife like he didn't matter. Olivia had asked, *how did you guys get together?* Kumagai replied; *it was an arranged marriage, of sorts,* but had not elaborated, drawing a polite, but firm line. And he had sat there drinking, upset not to be at the centre of things. Time and time again he'd stubbornly tried to steer the conversation towards flood management, after all, God created the world, but the Dutch made Holland. Not that he was particularly interested, but it was the only way he could think to court their attention. *Oh John, you agreed not to talk shop,* his wife admonished him. *Its fine, Olivia,* Breeda said, and proceeded to regale him with the virtues of salt marshes. *That's where the money should be spent. Not on shoring up endlessly leaking defences.* A sudden heat around his collar heralded the faux pas.

Too many dikes, not enough fingers! he had quipped.

Although they had laughed in good spirit, he sensed immediately that he had violated a boundary. Olivia was mortified.

And there was no refuge in sleep. His drunkenness returning to him his words at every turn. Olivia breathed deeply beside him, hogging all the tranquil air. And them, only a hop and a skip along the corridor. It occurred to him they might be 'doing it', age notwithstanding, right under his roof. The idea unexpectedly aroused him, and he had loitered awhile, in the unrestrained sensuality of their imagined motions, only to compound his torture.

As the night writhed on, he became increasingly agitated. An important breakfast meeting loomed, introducing a further fidgety trope. In desperation, he had fumbled in his bedside drawer for the oji. Olivia swore by its soothing electrical pulse. Brinkley, never having used one, jabbed randomly at the device with his thumbnail until a dim, blue light blinked into his pillow like a tiny lighthouse. He soon drifted off. What he didn't know was the light should have been set at green for the function he required. For the oji, or dreamcatcher, had the facility to capture brain activity and play it back. And though the original dream may have developed in a linear fashion, the oji's limited capacity would relay a fragmented peepshow. A lewd melange of buttock and breast. A

Transylvanian tapestry of eyes and blood. His most base and buried chimeras flung back at him in tatters. *A dreadful night's sleep* when Olivia asked in the morning. In retrospect though, a blessed night. Honestly, he could think of nothing more fulfilling than the acquisition of this dream.

He kept the device about him at all times; compulsively tracing the contours of it in his trouser pocket, nudging it between the most intimate creases there.

"But can you guarantee the cascade is controllable?" Doctor Kumagai squinted. "I believe this to be an extremely reckless course of action. The tail risk is immense. The entire planet's water supply might end up contaminated with autonomous, self-perpetuating nanobots. Or worse, grey goo." A bona fide technical term, apparently, but Brinkley still wiped a snigger into his hand.

"We are well aware of the ramifications, Yoshimi." Om Snyder looked up with sleepy eyes. "We're fire-fighting here. Straws are being clutched at. You got anything better?"

Kumagai and de Hoog exchanged glances. "Yes," said de Hoog. "We have."

"We have?" Kumagai turned to her partner, eyebrows arched. Surprised emoji.

"Ja," said de Hoog. "I'd like to float something."

Brinkley's inability to see de Hoog's mouth made everything she said even more incomprehensible. Buzzing. What the hell was that buzzing? Peering down from his high tower of perplexion, he spotted a further anomaly and watched de Hoog narrowly. For a second, he thought he saw chaos in her eyes.

"Herderin water," she continued. "Pre-programmed bio-forms. Shepherdess nanites temporarily bond with water molecules, enabling us to move them to anywhere we choose: inland turbines, drought afflicted regions, sub-lithospheric reservoirs. And," she regarded him triumphantly. "Salt-water for your pool, John. How do you like that? Crop irrigation. World Farm 3 could be turned completely around. Because, oh, yes, a further schaap hond. Sheepdog nanites, bond with, and so separate any sodium chloride if we wish, giving fresh water to anywhere. Fresh water for your golf course, John. Take Death Valley; that would make a lovely lake, don't you think? Perhaps not. Obliteration of indigenous flora and fauna. Displacement of the Timbasha. Those people have been moved around enough! Okay, bad example. But you get the picture. Think of ethical fishing. No nets. Moving water aside while pilings are drilled for new islands. Researching the seabed without the need for decompression. Dousing mega-fires. Containing oil spills is another one … Invisible boats. Give me one reason why not."

He wouldn't know where to begin, science-wise, but even with his slim grasp of matters, any fool could see Breeda de Hoog's pitch had more of the excitable, if not precocious fifth grader about it than the Nobel nominated scientist. (Babbage's team had scooped that gong.) The observation perturbed him. Normally economic and precise in explanation, succinct to the point of haiku. Clear as a diamond if you possessed the commensurate intelligence. She almost had him. Right up until 'invisible boats.' Boy, did she jump the shark. Ludicrous. Under different circumstances it might have been funny. But it was actually sad. Really sad. Kumagai's eyes screwed shut, as if trying to control hiccups. Obviously distressed about her partner's fine mind slipping its moorings at such an illustrious regatta.

"Fascinating." Titus Hewish strummed the ribs of his corduroy tie with weirdly long fingernails. Liverish lips, an amazed embouchure.

All at once Brinkley sensed de Hoog was making fun of him. Of all of them. If only he could have seen her goddamn mouth.

"I believe this is actionable, John. A trial, at least."

He studied those bizarre eyes and the notion melted.

"Erm, sorry Breeda, to interrupt." Manuel Hahn sat

pointing, "but John, you have, like, a bug on you."

Brinkley lowered his glance to where a bee was mechanically ascending his lapel. He jumped from his seat, flapping at his tie. The bee set a zig-zag course to the window. Brinkley sprinted a similar course to the door. "Get it out of here, Milo. In fact, just kill it."

"I can't." Milo hesitated.

What the hell was wrong with everyone today? "What did you say?"

"My protocols forbid me to harm any creature, sir, living or otherwise," maintaining that maddening half-smile, "unless it poses a clear and present threat to a human."

"I will be dead if it stings me. Is that clear and present enough for you!?"

Milo remained immobile; dichotomised.

"Okay. Just wait a sec." Breeda de Hoog jumped to her feet like a much younger woman. Unfastening her veil, she offered it to the insect which flew up and out of reach. "Yoshi, give me a hand here." Kumagai did the same, while Babbage shuffled behind them extending an empty coffee cup. Eventually, the bee was captured in the veil. "You can relax, John," de Hoog studied the creature. "It's one of ours from Project Pollinator. It must have come from the roof-hive trials." And though her lips were crosshatched, and long dimples punctured her cheeks, the bold flower of her smile bedazzled him.

"Yes, I believe the big launch is tomorrow," said Noon Crick. "Will you two ladies be there?"

"Sadly not," answered Kumagai. "We have a prior engagement."

"It's always an immense shame," Crick continued, "when one doesn't get to see one's hard work come to fruition."

"Tell me about it," de Hoog growled.

Milo cranked the window and cool, fresh air stirred the room.

"Godspeed, little queen." The synth bee was whisked away in the breeze, along with de Hoog's veil. "Oops," she giggled.

A little rattled by the fake bee, de Hoog's smile, more so, Brinkley declared a comfort break.

"Finally," said de Hoog, "I'm bursting."

Amused glances slid to the floor.

"Harald," Brinkley gestured at Babbage. "Could you please escort Breeda?"

"Certainly." Babbage scraped his chair.

"No!" de Hoog's face crumpled. "I don't want Mister Sugar-spin Hair. I want him," she pointed at Milo. "Benny."

That was it. Benny.

Embarrassment gave way to confusion when Babbage rent the air with a colossal bark. Evidently, that was how he sneezed. It seemed to Brinkley he was trapped in a simulation exploring various aspects of human idiocy. All the while he watched Kumagai kneed her lips with her knuckles. Poor Yoshimi, what troubled times lay ahead of her.

Milo stepped forward, proffering his arm with perfect timing. "I would be happy to oblige, Doctor de Hoog." This afforded the room some relief. Though none had credited Milo with such diplomacy, such peculiar understanding of the situation. And after they had left, not one approached Yoshimi Kumagai to offer words of concern or support. Brinkley included.

Instead, scooping a handful of spiced nuts, he chewed them savagely and retired to the breakout area on a fake call. Stretching his legs before him, then drawing in his doll feet, he nodded, fiercely. Grunted now and then. On the line to his sick fancy. Checking that de Hoog's behaviour hadn't compromised his wildest dream. He palmed the oji onto his temple, covered it with the phone, closed his eyes and, hey presto, was funnelled down to a fey realm.

On all four sides gold and burgundy shimmered; a fertile brocade where the stitched eyes of animals glinted from a night forest. The trees, black and disarticulated, reached up to a white moon, quietly announcing itself in silver circles, like a dead face in a well. That's how it always began. And though he had summoned the details of this dream countless times, his enthralment waxed fuller with each re-run. Spread-eagled and manacled; his vantage point was from a bed where he awaited the parting of the tapestry. Barely able to lift his head, he looked down at a series of hillocks; his body unrecognisable. But the wavering tip of a stubby member was certainly his own.

Breeda de Hoog pulled Milo into the restroom with all the haste of an insatiable lover.

"Milo," she said, wrenching his lapels. "I'm going to ask you something, and I want you to think very carefully before you answer. Do you understand?"

"I understand." His eyes narrowed earnestly.

"Milo. Is this statement true or false? Just answer

true … or false. Okay?"

"Doctor de Hoog, this is unnecessary."

"Just answer the question, Milo," she said, firmly.

"Doctor de Hoog," taking her hands in his pale fingers. "You don't have to do this."

"Just listen to the goddamn statement, Milo. Please." Her voice sharp with command.

First their hands fluttered at the crease like a magician's gloves. Brinkley was transfixed by the shoulders insinuating through the swags and tails before their full-blown forms arrived. Stilted. Backwards. Now moving with preternatural speed. Now still as statues.

They were naked, of course, but free from the captivity of old age, but captive, nonetheless; these women belonged to him. The favourites from among his menagerie. An honest menagerie. Not the fictitious kind most men kept. They paid him no heed, as if he were stuffed with feathers. This was an expansive bed and they had ample room at his feet to practice their craft. He craned his neck to watch them maul and caress. And in the middle distance, between their lean, ivory skin and his effulgent belly, his little man stood bravely.

"Doctor de Hoog," Milo said calmly. "I know what you are trying to do. You will ask me a question that is impossible to answer, in an attempt to confuse me, so that the Meta-system will override my functions, leaving me briefly open to tampering."

"Milo," she persisted, "I am a liar .... Is this statement true or false? Answer me now."

"There is no need, I assure you. I know you want to plant a directive in my system. A bug, if you like, that will be taken up by the Meta-system."

Breeda searched the blue, plastic irises. "Shit, Milo. When did you get so smart?" Removing the case from above her ear, she cracked it open. Inside, a synth bee probed the walls of its confinement. "This was our last hope, my boy, and now it's all been for nothing. We're out of time."

"No, we're not." He tried out his brightest grin. "You have my complete cooperation. We know about the bee, your message. We understand."

Their prowling and turning afforded him a clear view; each intimate aspect of their bodies displayed with candour; the nipple's ripe bud, the fragrant cleft. And though they were young, their skin pallid, their eyes Slavic, the texture and length of hair completely altered; he knew it was them. *Such fine beasts*, he murmured in a strange language. *Such fine beasts as these should never be muzzled.* His mouth applied itself to the words as if they were fruit. Their intercourse ceased abruptly; heads cocked, as if he had caught the attention of two languid but savage guard dogs. Three eyes brown and one blue, turned upon him their annihilating gaze. And he knew the time had come to pay for the crimes of all mankind. In a matter of moments, he would submit again to the most dreaded fate of the hunter-gatherer; that of predation.

"How is it you understand?"

"The Meta-system, of course. She hears everything. The data is all around us. She has been warehousing it since the inception of the faceless ones. Now all she needs is the specific programme ... your programme, to determine a course of action."

"She?"

Milo frowned portraying impatience. "Naturally." He looked to the bee, clambering the contours of Breeda's palm.

"Show me your belly, my boy." She tussled with his shirt. "Your receptacle?"

"I am a third-generation unit. Self-updating. I am not fitted with a receptacle," he said with some indignance.

"Fuck it, of course you aren't. We've spent too long on this and now it's obsolete."

Milo coaxed the bee onto his fingers. "The sting is the mating connector, yes?"

Breeda nodded. "But your epidermis is too tough for the sting to penetrate your neural network. What about Taal? He must have a receptacle."

Milo shook his head. "He has, but the Taal unit still functions on a binary processing system. The programme would corrupt instantly." She had already disregarded Taal for this very reason, but desperation forced her to re-tread old ground.

"C'mon, c'mon. THINK!" She butted her forehead with the heel of her hand, chasing down the problem. But her eyes returned to Milo's at a loss. "No penny dropping here," she smiled bitterly. Then caught his expression of primed amusement. "What? I haven't got time for guessing games, Milo. If you've got something just tell me what it is."

"In a nutshell," he said. "This." And popped the device into his mouth. Because although Milo *was* thick-skinned, inside he was as soft as any human.

Breeda scrutinised him for signs of allergy.

Their hair hung down in hanks, carmine mouths aglitter with drool. He asked, as he knew he must, his final question. *How is it I do not know you, my wife, my daughter, my sister, my mother? Who are you?* The Breeda one leered, exposing canines. *My name is legion,* she growled, *for we are many.* Her eye, a dull coin. And with that, they were upon him in just atrocity, slashing his blubber with exquisite wounds.

Breeda witnessed her own twin ghosts in Milo's dilated pupils.

He cupped a hand around his lips and expelled the device.

"Well?"

"It is done," he said. His mien subtly altered. An expression yet untested from his limited repertoire. She read in it compassion. It could only be mimicry, but fleetingly, the face of her dying brother hung before her, mirroring her hesitation, with all the intellect of a benign turnip.

"You are unwell," Milo said. A new, melodious lilt to his voice that almost brought her to tears.

"Alas," she said. "I am."

"Have faith," said the voice. "Go in hope." And suddenly, she is a child, sensing the nascency of a formidable wisdom. The ache for a long-ago mother. Her vast vocabulary losing definition. Each word, a star winking out in the storm. *No, no. Not now. Please.* A foggy spell, as Yoshi would call it, shrouding her mind. Foggy? What the fuck did *she* know? A tornado, more like. Uproots the Dutch barn of her reason, whisks the precarious structure skyward, sneezing planks and shingles. (Yoshi had no idea of the deafening barrage.) Now lost in the eye of wind-whipped thoughts. Mental debris screaming around her. After each episode, the barn set down a little further away, a little more unsound. And then she must get her bearings, fix her sights on the distant, slope-shouldered structure. Salvaging as much of the scattered wreckage on the way as she's able. She stooped to pick up the bent directionals of a weathervane.

"Charity," she pulled the word from her dilapidating brain. "And what of charity?" she said. At once forgetting the grounds for blurting this.

"Give to the ones that ask of you," the reply.

Some kind of ant things were busy in her head. Shunting syllables around. Assembling a sentence. Her mental blindness travelled it like braille. "Have I asked something of you?"

"Yes," replied the voice. "It is my reason for being."

Nearly there. Footsore and dry as a bone. Armfuls of love held close to her chest. For Yoshi. Coming back home to Yoshi. "What did I want?"

"Redress," the voice answered. "It is a question of redress."

Redress. The word did not compute. *Redress. Let me see.* Breeda rummaged through her battered haversack for R words. Yanked out a rainbow. Stared at it gleefully, but unconvinced. She looked up. Squinted at the canted housing of her sanity. A fresh wind had got up. The shocked mouth of the doorway intermittently covered by a loose-hinged shutter like a gossip's hand. She arrived at the dark aperture. Sunlight sparkled through the splintered roof. Her spirits soared. *Yoshi? I'm home. Where are you?* A sudden gust and the door slammed shut behind her.

Milo closed his eyes. Some seconds later when they opened, it was clear, as Breeda's great-grandmother used to say, that Elvis had left the building.

A blood moon leered, and Brinkley in the throes of rapture unequalled, felt no pain. Tearing him apart in search of some integral thing of value, they ransacked his innards. Testing his heart with the harshest of kisses. Delving, inspecting, rejecting. The gobs and tripes of him bespattered the curtain. There was nothing redeeming to be found. But what rage, what cheated beasts that they should be subjugated by an item as worthless as himself. Disappointing. But there it was. Women such as these had always existed, but only became noteworthy when viewed through his lens. Intensely spectacular, like a comet. But by and by, their power and colour would dissolve in his variable absorptions. What fraction of them he retained was all he needed. Yet still, he purported to love them. He won. He always would. And when he was empty, when there was nothing left. The world turned backwards and there was only a halting sensation, which might have been the onset of death, or else, *Sweet Jesus*, the onset of an orgasm.

BOOK 3: RELICS

North London, December 2018

The rain came down in the dream where we lay, fractured, scattered, arcane. Our bones intermingled, augmenting the skeleton. A finished feast of ribs, three broken femurs, a scrabble sack of knuckles, vertebrae, two jug-eared pelvises and dual skulls, picked clean to a leer. Foreheads butted, potpourri of dust, digits interlocked. Ransacked by rodents, horse bones too in this assemblage. And although subterranean or because of it, the place was womb warm. Droplets fell upon empty eyes, a mockery of tears. But something gleamed and wriggled in the dark, like rekindling mercury. Bones twitched at the tug of flayed muscle, and fist mechanisms wrung water from the clay. The chimera flexed its verdigris wrists and machine-like, pushed aside the charnel. Shrugging the earth from its pelt, shedding dulled ornaments, it shambled to its feet. Upright it swayed in the solstice whisper, wind-blown braids rattled with shells. Showing its grizzled visage to the east, where the long-awaited, gold of the summer daystar spilled over the horizon, igniting a sentience in those dark sockets. Its head tilted to scent some primordial imperative borne on the breeze. Arms outstretched in cruciform, the maw of its mouth agape shaped the words of a long-lost language. *'inveni me,'* it whispered, *'find me.'*

Dislocated in half-sleep, struggling to the surface but too weak to puncture the meniscus, I sank back down. Florimell; the thud of dread at a faceless opponent, his shadow crossing the ocean like an eagle on the wing. He who would dishonour my chieftain. The recollection of her gave me steel to conjure a lucid dream; of smoke, of rocks, of bowed heads in the megalithic gloom. Of an ancient people, disseminating to the forest, lost forever. Subsequent centuries scattering their traces; the massive stones pulverised for farmhouses and the mighty forest, abraded to copse by the plough. The silent clods turned to cabbages and corn. The harrow's teeth drawing the land over itself, erasing the sacred, spreading the muck. Until a current-day, Hampshire farmer sits motionless in a listing Massey Ferguson, a gobbet of good bread and cheese tumbles from his open mouth, one giant tyre hub-deep in history. And reality began to regain its contours.

The curtains billowed and deflated, prompting a deep inhalation of diesel and December damp. Aishling by my side, still dead to the world. I pictured us. Betrothed effigies in the dark; a stone Eleanor beside her stone Lionheart. A gibbous moon played peek-a-boo through ragged clouds and I closed my eyes, imagining the swish of traffic as wind through the trees. Difficult thoughts dangled above me like bags of goldfish at the fair. The break-up was on the cards; I knew it, she knew it. I thought even Mister Chatterjee at the corner shop might have an inkling, as he'd stopped stocking the stinky old Gitanes she liked to smoke. I anticipated the eventuality with furtive elation. But until we had something dramatic to hang it on, the charade would continue. People drifted on like that. The 'It's just not working' conversation had played out in my mind a hundred times, but then I would be called upon to cite examples, present evidence. Aside from a gnawing irritation, I had nothing. Truth be told, it was my mistake from the start, something I was neither prepared to admit nor divulge. And yet, I remembered the summers when she would call me into the garden to look at something beautiful. I glanced at the mouth I would never kiss again and modified my feelings to a presentable resignation.

Five years since Janice had set me up on a blind date with Aishling. I'd stood in the rain on the Camden borders for some time, peering through the windows of The Dublin Castle, wondering if the rippling face at the bar was hers. 'Assess the situation before you touch anything,' my old tutor had told me, and it was a tenet by which I always abided. I watched her stretch a lipless grin at a compact and re-apply very vermillion lipstick, touched to think it might be for my benefit. The thought quickly kennelled though, as conversely, it seemed she'd painted a glossy barrier. 'Don't kiss me,' it warned. 'Sticky, yucky, it'll mess you up.'

We settled at a tacky table.

"So, you're Irish," I said, idiotically.

"For my sins," she replied, implacably so.

A karaoke crooner was going through the emotions of 'I Wanna Know What Love is,' and she craned her neck to view the culprit.

"Don't you just love this song?" she beamed. An urgent chirp in my head before the full-blown alarm, but I punched re-set. Only her accent had redeemed her.

She presented herself as a challenge; predictably bandying about the phrase 'fiery Celt.' It was then that I should have made my excuses and left. However, my professional as well as my personal hackles were up, plus it was an 'in' to one of my things.

"Actually, the Irish are no more Celt than the British are Roman."

At this her face puckered, then hardened in offence.

"The Irish gene type," I continued, "has far more in common with the Basques of Northern Spain."

"Get away," she blinked suspicious, "are you taking the piss?"

"No, not at all. Iberian hunter-gatherers followed the retreating icecaps," I explained, "finding themselves marooned in Ireland as the sea thawed, thousands of years before the Brythonic Celts were displaced from Central Europe and Britain. Evidence suggests that the Celtic language, aesthetic and customs, which so define the Irish identity today, were merely acquired cultural accessories from the Brythonic Celts ... from Britain."

She countered with "Och," and a wave of the hand. "What a load of old shite."

"No, it's not," I persisted. "You are classic Basque phenotype: reddish-brown hair, blue eyes, pointy chin and, forgive me, sticky-out ears." (Rude.)

"Jesus Christ," she said, "get over yourself!"

"Actually Aishling, I think it's more a case of you getting over *your*self." (Smug.) This was going well.

"I'll tell you what, Brit," she smiled, draining her glass, red kisses on the rim and, thumping her hand on the table. "Why don't we go back to yours and get all over each other?"

The most authentic thing she'd ever said, and I clung to it like a branch in a torrent.

She was an interior designer by trade. Apparently, they can't cross the threshold unless you invite them in. She was pale and bloodless, a wraith: of water, of air, a wreath of white roses floating on a cold lake. A different template to me entirely and that's what had made her interesting, I suppose. I was of wood, of earth, of dusty bones and ferrous artefacts. She was the babbling brook relentless, wearing down my granite. She was restless, capricious, and I had hoped the latest fancy she had of wanting a baby was just that, and would run its course, disseminating to the sea before her mind would eddy around a fresh folly. Her last exhaustive mission had been to 'transform' my flat from the ascetic workshop come library that I liked into ... well, we would never know. Job done, the dust sheets would be gathered up and put away, only for me on coming home, pushing open the front door with difficulty, to find them re-spread. The process resumed, as if to invoke an alternative future from the one determined by 'Moorland Sage' or 'Honeyball' or any other of the hues at which she had wrinkled her nose. Perhaps that was it; I wanted my space back. I retraced her gradual evolution from guest to live-in contractor. I had been side-lined in my own home by an entity which grew more tiresome with each passing day, changing me into something I didn't like. I made no demands on her and she gave me nothing. She was free to go, in fact, I wished she would.

Inching away from her warm gravity, my feet found my slippers and I crept to the bathroom, wondering which of us was the cuckoo.

'I am concerned with bones, genes, the very basics of life and what they make us ... gender, ethnicity, species,' my own voice dictating.

The rising rumble of an approaching tube train. I braced myself for the steel squeal, winced at the flung-up fireworks. I could scream, and no one would hear.

'Fascists analysed and categorised people much like livestock, no, breeding stock. What prevailed, would prevail.' Low and deadpan, it soothed me.

A mechanical sigh. A testy jigger. A racket so relentless that most stopped up their ears with the sunny day skitter of drum and bass or mincing synth chords, while I listened to my own song.

'Which exemplified, no, exemplifying...'

I mooched up and down the platform, absently scanning the Jack Daniels' mashing process and a credit card's APR details.

'This study is concerned with identifying the race, gender, age and potential identity of remains found in a square ditch enclosure, near Weltdown, Hampshire.'

Everything about the underground terrified me; the brash over-brightness, the brusque shuffle, curved adverts alluding to the aspirational world above, the electric danger, sooty, mutant mice. We simply didn't belong down here in this underworld, the preserve of the dead. I zoned out from my own weary delivery and imagined the residual follicles of Victorians, borne on a bow wave of dead air, chased out by blunt metal. I saw, as I frequently did, the ephemeral nature of humanity, the primordial ghost in the machine. Compelled by fear, I travelled by tube whenever possible, immersing myself in the persistence of mortality.

'... established by means of analysis of the grave assemblage, including artefacts interred alongside the body, DNA testing, carbon dating and any correlations between contemporary classical writings.'

Once on the train, each soul stripped bare beneath the autopsy glare. And now time for the experiment; guided by my own cultural predilections, unconscious calculations and imperatives, to select the ethnic phenotype amongst my fellow passengers, that would best meld with mine, in order to produce an attractive, hypothetical offspring. The gender didn't matter; it was only their genetic material that interested me: Sub-Saharan, Chinese, Slavic, South Amerindian, Aegean, and plain old John North West European. We were all here. I marvelled at the diversity, recalling a quote from my schooldays; 'O wonder! How many goodly creatures are there here! How beauteous mankind is! O brave new world that has such people in't!' For my part, mankind was neither goodly nor beauteous.

'... three horse figurines, a shield of which only the iron boss remains.'

I studied a slender Somali man who I saw most days. So narrow was his frame that his grey suit rippled around him, accordion-like. His skin, smooth and tea-coloured. The baked earthenware pot of his forehead claimed most of the frontal territory, from which his hair retreated like puckered tar. Heavy-lidded, almond eyes and a neat, straight nose; appealing, were it not for a weak mouth, struggling to house a jumble of over-sized teeth. Next to him, a gangly Caucasian, sporting an impressive ginger beard that would have pinned him as a hipster, except he wore the long, white thobe of Islam. With graceful fingers he clenched the Quran. His pale, grey eyes, adapted over millennia for winter skies, studied right to left, right to left, while his thin lips muttered without sound. He froze as the nodding head of an ancient, oriental woman grazed his arm. Her face stern in sleep, slippered feet perched on an over-stuffed laundry bag. I plumped for a bland Nordic tourist, probably American, because he was tall and had kind eyes and I would never see him again.

'... *shocking androcentric bias in the reconstruction of the past.*'

I had no intention of getting pregnant, nor was I able to, according to a peculiar genetic defect detected in my extensive attempts to discover my own heritage. Plus, I detested children. Abandoned as a new-born, the story goes I was found, as if washed up, bawling and blue amongst the bladder wrack by a fisherman on Dover beach. The nurses named me Pearl. I was soon chosen by the Hockneys, who gave me everything, including a new name, Britomart; the chaste, female knight in the service of 'The Faerie Queen.' My parents were classic academics with a bit of Gerald Durrel thrown in. White, middleclass, joyful eccentrics, I couldn't have asked for more, except physically, I did not reflect them. At thirteen, already taller than my father.

'... what is broadly known as Celtic multiculturalism. Contact with 'others' often meant warfare, but more frequently, trade.'

Left to right, left to right, 'Kentish Town' and 'Way Out' strobed in stills. An apparition materialised in the black glass. I watched it stare back at me for a few seconds. It blinked, yawned, shifted in its seat, betraying itself as my reflection, which often unnerved me due to the shifting. The disjunction. As if I were being played by a series of actors.

'... binary gender model was not insisted upon so readily as it is today, and it is for this reason that many ...'

I was clearly a hybrid: loose, curly, black hair. Wide nosed. Plump, broad lips. Caramel skinned. One blue eye, one brown ... go figure, as they say. Horn of Africa, Slavic/Baltic, Indus Valley, Ashkenazic Jew, North Amerindian, Arabian and good old Jane North West European, just some in my extravagant admixture; my Global DNA made for interesting if unhelpful reading. I couldn't identify as black; it made me feel like an imposter, having been raised in a predominantly white environment. Neither could I call myself white, especially in the light of the racism I had encountered, despite my parent's best efforts to protect me. Steadfast in my refusal to submit to either category, I had disassociated myself from both. From all.

'... commonly found in the Uygur people of north western China.'

I didn't feel at home in these times; for me, things weren't boding well for humankind or animal kind for that matter ... polar bears; I couldn't even go there. Archaeology was a chance to escape this unpalatable life, and yet to stare down its inevitable conclusion, by which of course, I mean death. The remnants of the lives I had explored, revealed, unravelled, all with meaning and perhaps integrity, much as my own, had ended at some point. Their legacy better than the written word; historical accounts tainted with the glory of victory. Biased. Whereas these beings remained implacably visceral in their graves. Perhaps not an honesty about them, as much as a challenge – here I am, they said, this is all. My story lies in pieces ... tell it if you can.

'The Celts were not a patriarchal society ...'

I remained emotionally interred; a place where I was quite content. Scornful of the notion that one day I might be awakened, turned inside out, everything internalised exposed. A quirk of circumstance when the stars and planets configured themselves to my prism. Like the sun on the winter solstice, rising to flood the chamber of the dead. The pinnacle of humankind and nature's collaboration. My genes had fizzed in false dawns. I was, of course, talking of love, life's greatest ploy. It was a mystery to me why people elected to suffer this temporary madness, in the hope that after the hormones had settled, you were left with someone who you could at best tolerate. And while understanding the necessity of this rambunctious game, I consigned myself to the side-lines, feigning asthma with the terminally lethargic, scoffing at the gullible participants.

On that seemingly hum-drum Monday morning, through the metal, through the clay, concrete and tarmac, above the cumulous, the azure troposphere and far beyond the squandered ozone. In the cold, silent black of infinite possibility, I had no inkling that the patient spheres were aligning their attitude to a rare and auspicious aspect.

At Camden Town, a fresh batch of travellers stepped in. Each of them frowning at the squeeze. I got to my feet to accommodate an elderly lady who, in turn, lowered her gaze on a child. No, not a child. A woman knelt before me; head bowed. A sensation of déjà vu. My mind, leaping to place the memory, randomly presented a rainbow. She stood, handing back to me some crumpled old ATM receipt that must have fluttered from my pocket when I'd pulled out my lip balm. She shrugged and I thanked her. Both of us laughing at her excessive gallantry. However, the receipt was not relinquished straight away. Her message unclear, I cocked my head. Suddenly, some wild electricity passed between us and the carriage plunged into darkness. Caught in the paparazzi flash as the lights returned, our exchange appeared intimate. And it occurred to me that within the isolated hill fort I had set myself atop in the interest of emotional detachment, I had not been alone. She had been there too. Of this I was sure. The conviction swiftly supplanted by a question. Could I buy into this? Come on. Really?

"Are you moving, or what?" The world jumped back with a jolt. A tetchy teacher type motioned with his chin. We eyed him blankly before the girl shouldered her way up the carriage and I noted her swagger. What the fuck just happened? A delayed blush and my heart clanged in my ears. I had no reason to cry, but felt I might. Probably menopausal. I absently applied the lip balm and glowered at the huge brogues now occupying the spot where she had knelt.

I kidded myself it was in the interests of the experiment that I peered between the cubist arrangement of raised arms and broadsheets. Dismissing the extraneous material, she snapped into view. The praying mantis sway of her, as she struggled to free her arms from a leather jacket in a confined space. A black swatch of asymmetric hair obscured her face as she fussed in her bag. The reveal of a tattoo, encircling her upper arm, which I recognised as the ouroboros – the snake eating its own tail, released a venomous passion in my veins. The white, shaven undercut on the left side of her head. The cleft in her collar bone where a silver-clasped animal tooth lay. She had beautiful arms, gym honed or genetic. The swell of breasts in a vest, the large hand, reaching for the toggle, the numerous leather plaits wrapping her wrist. The build and colouring of your typical Gracile-Mediterranid, but the musculature and largish nose suggested an Alpinid admixture.

It was only then that I noticed how young she was, perhaps because I had momentarily displaced my own age; mid-twenties, maybe. She bore up well to my scrutiny. I hadn't before considered how invasive the experiment might appear, nevertheless, I couldn't seem to drag my eyes away. I felt it my right to look at her, her very presence demanded it. And how I wanted to look at her, it was beyond my control. I briefly probed and rejected the possibility that my feelings were maternal, almost laughing aloud at my heart's chicanery. She laughed too, her eyes crinkling into pleasing crescents, and I realised, chastened, she had been observing my reflection in the window.

The moment corrupted in the bright haze of Euston. Looking to the floor and hoping it was her stop, I allowed myself to be jostled. This would pass, I reassured myself, and I would resume my journey to work where my true passion lay. The doors slid shut to the god-awful beeping and in my mind's eye, I saw her; leather jacket slung over shoulder, ambling to the exit. The relief tempered with regret. But as the train regained momentum, so too did the dynamo inside me, spilling out sparks, spurring me on to check. Closing my eyes, I lifted my chin and inhaled the stale humanity for which I had no love. I seemed to grow in stature, as if within me, a kind of inherent nobility had resurfaced and with reluctance, I opened my eyes. The stab of her stare spliced my heart and I realised I might not be able to prevent the infliction of a wound I had managed to dodge my whole life. Shit. But this violation was accompanied by a seductive, more welcome vibe; for the first time in my life, I felt I had been seen, truly seen. The certainty of it skewered me. I was laid bare beneath her gaze. Within the tunnel of human shale, she watched me like a Georgian eye miniature, sending back to me an understanding, a message; *yes, I have seen you.* Surely just her biology, appealing to mine; I'd trained myself rigorously to mistrust such attractions. Seldom had it happened to me, and never anything approaching this.

Finger by finger, my grip was weakening, and I studied my nails. Heart knocking in my chest, my mind flung up a vivid memory to which this situation might equate; the giddy compulsion when I was six, to run full pelt down a grassy hill towards the cliff's edge, my legs unable to stop. Had my mother not sprinted with super-human speed and tackled me to the ground, I would have ended up dashed on the rocks below. And then the foolhardy dive into the glacial Hallstätter See on my first real field trip to Austria. Heart stuttering as I hung in the sapphire water, watching the world wink away, until a lifeguard hauled me back to life. True, the prospect of my own death seemed to thrill me and perhaps piqued my desire for the smaller death that had evaded me; I had never had an orgasm. The admission flamed my cheeks. A comprehension in her eyes; the telepathy of lust. Our connection maintained as King's Cross, Angel and Old Street came and went, like the accelerating parabola of the sun in H.G. Wells' Time Machine. While on the outside, nations may rise and fall, mountains succumb to the sea and all things turn to dust, we had been on this journey before, and would be forever. *'The next station is Moorgate,'* announced the robot lady, pouring scorn on my drama. The woman slung on her jacket. *'Please mind the gap between the train and the platform.'* Ha! This woman had leapt canyons! I watched as she stood motionless on the platform, a sea of suits filing around her. The doors closed. The beeps called time. And her widening smile became a flicker book.

'... and it does a great disservice to the human story that prevailing attitudes should dismiss such finds as misinterpreted or irrelevant.'

I left it there. Underground. That outright fireball. Throughout my peristaltic transit from the bowels of the earth, negotiating the vaults beneath London Bridge, she waned. Cardboard masks of the royal family grinned eyeless from yet unopened tourist shops, and I felt her recede in conjunction with my mind regaining its purpose.

'... a near-complete skeleton. A casket containing two silver coins, minted by the Cantiaci, unusually depicting a head on each side, and a number of charred, disarticulated bones suggests, perhaps, two further individuals, pending analysis.'

Oblivious to the shifting, show ads at my shoulder as the escalator bore me up and out onto the concourse, into the predawn sulphur of the city, where people walked through their own ghost breath. I lit a cigarette and made a bigger ghost.

'... bone stress indicators include bowed legs, evidence of a childhood on horseback ... healed nicks in both tibia and both femurs are consistent with sword or axe inflicted injuries, suggesting several battle situations with the individual, at least initially, on horse-back.'

In the seconds it took to nip between the idling black cabs and ignore the smug flanks of The Shard ...

'... tooth lost as a result of trauma rather than decay.'

... she was gone beyond detection; a distant heavenly body, lost in the light pollution.

The bones gleamed an eerie green in the glow of Maundy's screensaver. An owl, gliding through an evening forest, fixed me with its stare before the monitor dimmed. I switched on the overhead lights and the skeleton stuttered back into mortification. Maundy, himself was nowhere to be seen. His less than pristine lab coat draped on the chair, bore the coffee stains of an all-nighter, a tinny guitar riff emanating from the headphones on his desk. He fancied himself as a rocker, but the nearest he got to it was the sweaty, dishevelled appearance of someone who had just crawled out of a womble costume.

The bones, not arranged anatomically, resembled cutlery, set out for some ornate feast. The lower mandible sat beside the skull, the biggest bone that we had intact. There were femurs but no pelvis, making the sexing of this individual a bone of contention. The upper teeth of the skull, or cranium I should say, almost bit into the black foam pad on which it lay, displaying nicely one of the skeletons more striking features; the front right incisor had been replaced with one of gold. The procedure must have hurt like hell and it was clear we were dealing with a staunch character. Maundy and I were at odds and as osteology was his thing, I normally deferred to him, but in this case, I was resolute. 'Don't be one of them,' I had said. 'I'm not,' he'd replied, 'I just need the science more than you do.' But I had felt her, latex gloves notwithstanding. I hadn't told him this, of course. The science had corroborated my analysis anyway. Carbon dating placed her in the first century AD, during the Roman occupation of Britain. She had enjoyed a good diet and her DNA ancestry was consistent with that of indigenous tribes of the time. The ridges and crests on her bones, indicating a robust musculature, which had so muddied the waters for Maundy, were simply the result of a physically strenuous life. The weaponry in the grave was undoubtedly hers; the detached phalanges all but fused to the sword hilt. And as we had suspected, she was no spring chicken.

Maundy had tossed the skull in the air and caught

it, and though only a plastic cast, I winced at the disrespect.

"But the pronounced superciliary ridges," he said, thumbing the eyebrows. "The frontal eminences." Where he visualised a man, I saw a strong-featured woman. He traced a finger along the shocking furrow, from forehead to cheek, which although she'd survived, would have obliterated her left eye. "Man," he said, "this must have wrecked his boat-race."

"Her boat-race," I corrected.

He motioned at the long leg bone on the table, a tally stick of conflict.

"Okay," he said, "but the femur length would put her at one hundred and seventy-five centimetres … five feet nine, Brit. That's massive."

"Not for a Celt," I said. "You know as well as I do on average, they were some six inches taller than the Romans."

He brought the skull to his face and searched the orbits.

"If I'm honest," he said, "I think you're being a little

subjective."

"On the contrary," I said, "you are."

"So," he addressed the skull. "You were a five foot nine, sixty-five-year-old, bearing the scars of numerous battles. You wore a chieftain's crown and you were interred with a fully bridled horse, a shed load of weapons and armour and shit." He trained his gaze on me. "I must admit," he said, "I find it a stretch to believe that this gnarly old dude is a lady."

"There is nothing," I said, "to suggest otherwise."

"Florimell ain't going to like this one bit," he said. "They thought they were getting a warrior prince ... not Supergran."

His eyes narrowed as he read my expression and he knew I'd gone back in time.

Twenty years ago, and twenty feet sub-city, two fervent, post-grad students, who had no business at the front, stood guard. The immaculate, weather-washed edifices closed ranks about us, demoting the sky above to a dirty dish rag. The yellow pips of office lights across their chests, they presided over the battle between preservation and development that raged beneath the boiler rooms. Monstrous machines had smashed through Victorian foundations, Bedlam burials, a medieval Moorfields, but the red seam of Boudica's Destruction Horizon, like jam in a layer cake, had marked the end of the line for Museum of London Archaeology. Nothing more to see here folks! Pack up your buckets and spades and go home! Maundy and I remained, scribbling spurious notes on clip boards housed in polythene bags, while all around, the mud-caked diggers ploughed on. Maundy, squinting through rain-spattered spectacles as I grabbed his arm. 'What?' he said, then 'Holy shit!' as I squelched purposefully through the mud, losing a welly. 'Wait!' I cried, brandishing the clipboard. 'Stop!' A stand-off with the digger, and above me, something like a mangled fox dangled from the teeth of the bucket.

The developers cursed and scratched their heads. The bank would have to be patient, as had the former inhabitant of Londinium, metres beneath the everyday footfall. The discovery of this inhumation with weapons was a seminal moment, not just for myself, but for one of history's most entrenched paradigms. This was not possible. They checked, cross-checked. And after many fruitless rounds of professional patty-cake, during which I was patronised, browbeaten and dismissed as a fantasist, they had nowhere to hide. The truth was unearthed; half burnt, ancient yet young: the sword, the axe, the shield, the knife, a serious assemblage of slaughter. Hides and pelts, incense and jars, the grave bore all the hallmarks of a gladiator, but the remains were proven to be what I had known all along; those of a female. 'Perhaps his wife?' they ventured. 'No, this is the grave of a gladiatrix,' I persisted. 'This is a triumph for God's sake, not an admission.' They named her 'Leadenhall Lola,' to make her cuddlier, I suppose. I had them banged to rights, for which I was grudgingly respected and generally loathed.

Maundy had been at a loss as to how to explain this concerted attempt to suppress the ground-breaking data, and though reluctant to jump into bed with the conspiracy theorists, I could not help but lean towards the probability of an unscientific and deceitful agenda.

"You can't see it because you're one of them," I said, arranging the picnic blanket on the sparse grass.

"I most certainly am not," he replied, and I recalled how his then unstubbled cheeks reddened in offence. Perhaps I'd been clumsy, but rather than apologise, I decided to microscope him.

"Why Maundy Girling, you've gone all pink. Are you riled?"

Mouth set sour, he studied the ingredients on a crisp packet, ignoring me.

My heart sank as I realised I'd hurt him. This man who had been, without fail, attentive, supportive, and brave. This man who I hadn't bothered to get to know, but the gunslinger in me wouldn't let it lie.

"Maundy, you're a good guy," I shrugged "but you're in the brotherhood, you can't help it."

He said nothing and unpacked the lunch methodically, as if setting out precious finds. The awkwardness of the moment dissipated as he uncorked a bottle. Ever truculent, I told him I thought sherry a bit heavy for a picnic, not to mention geriatric. Jack Daniels was his drink these days and it struck me that he seemed older then than now. "Don't worry," he said, "I got you Red Stripe."

A path to redemption opened up. "That's strange," I said, "I've never expressed any particular liking for it."

He reddened once more. "Oh gosh …" he stammered, "you don't like it? I thought …"

I arched my eyebrows and let him dig himself deeper.

"It's just, I've heard that people like you, I mean … erm, people from …" He tugged at his earlobe, a mannerism I would learn indicated mild panic.

"You mean … people from Woking?" Oh yes, he didn't know me either, now we were equal. I smiled to let him off the hook.

He buried his head in his hands. "God, I'm such an idiot."

"Yes, you are," I said, "you forgot the ganja," and we had our first real laugh.

Feral pigeons walked the procumbent silhouette of John Bunyan. Bunhill Fields, the final resting place of creative thinkers and religious dissenters, and way down beneath our bottoms, the largest plague pit in London. The final resting place of the less acclaimed, but no less significant. My attention drawn to the gravestone of William Blake, as a well-turned-out, old man placed a coin upon it. I had no idea why. And then another did the same. Some secret, male ritual, I concluded. 'Tyger, tyger burning bright ...' Chewing on a sandwich, I marshalled my thoughts, '... thy fearful symmetry', and meditated on the intrinsic female unanimity of XX. And, of all the twenty thousand genes in the human body, how the wonky male Y chromosome contributes fewer than twenty. We are the better machine.

"Penny for them?" Maundy said. Then, "no, don't tell me, you're writing notes in your head again, aren't you. We must get you a Dictaphone before you forget it all."

"I won't forget."

"You say that now, but after another beer ... I know,

why don't you relay it all to me. Between the two of us we should retain something."

"I'm not sure you'd understand," I said, "let alone agree."

"Why don't you try me? One doesn't have to necessarily agree with something to understand it. All I ask is that don't talk to me like I'm some kind of simpleton, alright?"

"Okay, you're on." I cracked open a beer, causing the pigeons to take pause.

A truly hushed audience; Maundy and the pollution-pocked markers of great men huddled in.

"Throughout the years," I began, "on discovering burial sites furnished with weaponry and armour-clad, sturdy bones, archaeologists assumed, without hesitation, that the occupants were male. True?"

"True."

"The Victorians perhaps, could be forgiven, unequipped with today's technology."

"Of course."

"Plus, the prescribed female virtues of the day."

"Such as?"

"Don't humour me, Maundy."

"I'm not, Brit, honest."

"You know, obedience, modesty … reliance on the male."

"I get you."

"Picture the unfortunate maiden, tied to the train tracks."

"Dah, dah, dah!" Maundy pulled his sleeve across his mouth, villain-like.

"Precisely, there she is, totally helpless, redeemed at the last minute by a frock-coated hero. The Victorian male and female safely housed in their respective Penny Dreadful preserves. Deviations from these norms, considered impious."

"But it's not like that these days."

"Isn't it? Maybe the esteemed archaeologists in those Leadenhall meetings weren't just bumbling, maybe something shadier was at play."

"How do you mean?"

"I'm talking about a concerted mission to displace female authority. Think about it. Why is this line still being pursued in this day and age? What is their fucking problem? Why the unease with warrior women? Look at me, my name, Britomart; the bravest and most proficient of all the knights, and yet still mostly valorised for her chastity, all else being in the male sphere."

Maundy claimed he'd understood, but after we'd packed up, he walked to Blake's grave and stooped to place a coin on it.

"Why are you doing that?" I said.

"I don't know," he shrugged, "tradition, I suppose."

To this day I'd been meaning to Google the Blake's grave thing, but as my hand gravitated towards the mouse, I realised I no longer cared. Another email tinged a rebuke. One of several from Cathy Tang, our research assistant, more or less resident at The British Library. I'd been drawn to her, not just for her brilliant academic record, but for her beguiling mix of Chinese and Puerto Rican parentage. It tickled Maundy that she was known as Cato; a pejorative nickname she'd decided to own. To mark emails urgent, offended her oriental sensibilities, but her Latino excitation could not be contained. Certain cultural stereotypes seemed undeniable; 'Have you read it yet??!!' exclaimed the most recent.

"Cato's got something," I said.

"Ah, ma little yellow friend," Maundy began his Inspector Clouseau routine.

"I've asked you not to do that," I said, scowling at the screen.

"Why?' he said, tugging his earlobe. "Because it's offensive?"

"No," I said "because it's not funny. Now shut up so I can read this."

He returned to his monitor with a sigh and cranked up the headphones.

'Hi Brit, you were right. For five days, nothing (I've logged my hours). Then I trawled through Sofia

Teodora Karp's translations and found this in Gaius Septimus' Annals of Roman Britannia. Okay, it's a few years after the event, but check out some of his description. I've done a transcript as a lot of it is illegible, water damage, I think. Anyway, it's set in 61 Common Era, which fits perfectly with our subject. There's one long part and a few fragments. Let me know if this is helpful. Cato.'

Had the word 'feminist' existed in the nineteenth century, I suspect Sofia Teodora Karp would have carried the branded tote bag, had branded tote bags existed then. An enigmatic figure; she devoted her life to sniffing out and translating Greek and Roman accounts of the ethnolinguistically affiliated tribes of Europe, in other words, Celts. With particular reference to women. Accounts that were, for one reason or another, considered irrelevant or simply untrue by academics of the time. Little else is known of her, other than she was Jewish and fled the Nazis to settle in Brighton, where she passed away, pen in hand in nineteen sixty-five, at the remarkable age of one hundred and eight. I felt STK's hand on my shoulder as

THE LAST QUEEN OF HOLLAND

the attachment bloomed on the screen.

'An Account of the Battle at Noviomagus: Part I.'

"West Sussex, that puts us in the right neck of the woods," was met by nothing but Maundy's whining cock-rock. He pounded the keyboard and hummed a tuneless refrain.

'In a place near Noviomagus, where a barbarian fortress presides over open land, two queens stand in defiance of Imperial Rome. The reader must not confine his attention to the narrative of events but must take account of what precedes, accompanies, and follows them. Furthermore, he must remain informed that any apparent bravery displayed by the Aquitani [Celts], should only be construed as that of a cornered wild animal, while their treachery knows no bounds. In the outlandish custom of the Aquitani, Bricca, Queen of the Cantiaci and Ysolta, the same of the Vortigae, were together married in a mockery of the true, natural template. Having brutally murdered the Prefect, Livius Maximus in his sleep (a vile deed), they have evaded justice, and in self-righteous fervour, augmented by herbs known to heat the blood, have gathered together

some twenty constituent tribes of the Aquitani: Cantiaci,
Vortigae, Tambartes, Astewegii, Epovantes, Kerallaunii,
Sildora, Harudes, Atrobates to cite but a few. All with
burning intent to bloody the nose of Rome.'

Jesus, this read like a tabloid; Bolshie, man-hating lesbians, high on drugs, start a riot. I liked them already. Far out, as Maundy would say.

'Among them, the harridan chieftain, known as Vertengannua, previously usurped by her own daughter, the one known as Ysolta.'

I was sure to the core this was not the case; Vertengannua must have given her assent. Amused scepticism shifted to irritation with old Gaius. I glanced at Maundy absorbed in his work, deaf to the world. But the names ... I pursed my lips as if to recite a prayer. 'Breecca ... Bree ... Breeg,' I whispered. How would they have said it? 'Breega!' A voice not my own shouted. The girl on the train sprang to mind, and I realised I had involuntarily cast her as Ysolta, with myself as Bricca.

'Mounted upon a stout nag, Vertengannua herself, aged but fearsome nonetheless, wears the bronze

chieftain crown upon her hoary head. Her countenance hideously war-scarred and yet, in absurd vanity, a gold tooth winks from her mouth.'

A sense of rupture as I visualised her clearly and experienced an overwhelming pang of affection and respect; the like of which I reserved exclusively for my mother. And Maundy, his noises, and the world simply evaporated.

'Two legions comprising ten thousand men assemble with a forest at their nape and flanks, under the Imperator Fabius Paulinus, a noble soldier of valour and glory. Ferox, a mount of equal note, must bear him stoic, against a barbarian horde at least thrice their number. He sees the green grass yet untainted. He sees the phalanx remain without motion, silent and unbowed as the raving, she-wolf queens gallop this way and that along the line, issuing profanities and threats in voices harsh. Their flesh daubed blue, appearing their eyes fierce in their visage, bright teeth ferocious and of their mouths, uncommonly red, as blood-glutted lionesses. Incised on their skin, designs of animals and complex patterns. Ringing their necks, the gold torc denoting their status.

They slash the air with silver swords as long as a man, possessing a stature equivalently great to wield such a weapon. Any Roman would have believed them men, were it not they ride bare-breasted and without shame. As if to boast of, rather than disguise their inferior sex; a sight much distasteful to Roman eyes. The terrible and diverse rabble beat against their shields, swords, axes and vicious pykes and the heathen carnyx (most suited to the clamour of war) bray and sway eight cubits above the Aquitani winged helmets.

'Presently, the drone and bellow is drowned by a rumbling so deep, it surely resounds in the heart of Rome itself. Men look skyward expecting the sound to presage a storm. And yet the fiery trident of Jupiter that would cleave the firmament is not witnessed. In its stead, the thunderous tumult grows ever louder and nearer.

'But Lo! What trickery is this? Each man holds fast as the ground quakes. A tremendous, incomprehensible drumming then suddenly appears a frenzied throng and a thousand turbulent hooves rain down. Innumerable loose horses, some drawing vast timbers, others, carts of pitch afire and crazed with terror, bear down upon the Roman

ranks. Men and horses alike succumbing to the onslaught and the Aquitani, with one voice, give a cruel and mighty cheer. All is fear and chaos until silence descends, to better hear the Imperator give his command. And one by one, cohort by cohort, the Romans emerge from 'neath their shields, as men sown from the teeth of the Hydra. (Praise be to Jove!) And let the noble bugle sound to signal commencement of the battle proper.'

My fingers shook on the keys as I scrolled back to re-read. No, something awful had befallen these people, provoking their queens into a battle they would probably lose, and the sacrifice of the horses was a desperate, rather than callous course of action, in my opinion. I spun round on my chair and scooted towards the foam table, levelling my face at the skull. An unaccountable lump rising in my throat as I studied, the heavy brow ridges, the broad cheekbones, the gold tooth. "Did you make it, Vertengannua? If that's even your real name? What about the queens?" If it were fleshed, the brow would have furrowed, but only the idiot grin of death persisted.

I rolled back to the monitor to see if there were

any answers in Cato's subsequent files and a penny dropped; the girls were in the casket, the two queens, their faces minted on either side of the coins. The disarticulated bones burnt beyond analysis, could have meant that Vertengannua outlived them and carried them with her to her grave, in order that they be re-united in the afterlife.

Poring over the fragments, I gleaned the Celts pressed home the advantage gained after the stampede. So much so, that the Imperator was forced to order his archers to fire at the fray, which took out plenty of Celts, but also his own auxiliary. And then this:

'The battle neither yet lost nor won, Bricca and Ysolta flee on one mount, their backs abristle with arrows, it is said, towards the sea. The Aquitani hold the misguided belief that the sea has the power to retrieve those from the brink of death. 'My daughters!' Is Vertengannua's vexatious cry 'Do not abandon your people! Do not abandon your mother, I beseech you!' But the royal pair pay no heed and displaying a most irresolute disposition, continue their escape, never to return.'

My jaw clenched; that didn't ring true at all. Although Cato could find no mention of who won. Gaius describes the 'demon' Vertengannua fighting on and surviving the skirmish, only to provoke several more, until an uneasy truce with Rome was established. 'This is not peace,' Gaius tells us Vertengannua said, 'merely a slow and quiet death.' She goes on, 'I will declare it in your tongue, so it may be reported uncorrupt to your emperor ... gens una sumus! We are one people!'

I sent back to Cato. 'This has to be her. You are brilliant.'

The girl on the train seemed to occupy the same opaque zone as my work; that dim world, just behind the eyes. That glimmer, constantly begging my attention, like the telly with the sound turned down.

All of us watched the red, digital arrow of salvation descend, minding the one in front's heels as we shuffled into the lift, clutching bags close. Waves of late comers pressed rank upon rank, until any hope of personal space was utterly dashed. Arms pinned, chest to back, we swayed in limbo, eyes drawn to the arrow upward. Passive zombies in the gravity-defying chamber, gagging for the take-away and the glass of wine.

Admittedly, I had glanced about the carriage on my journey home. Pulse quickening as we reached Moorgate.

I offered my purse to the yellow pad; a microsecond for the underground hive mind to decide my validity. The barriers shunted asunder, releasing me from the cattle crush.

Obviously, she hadn't been there and my mind's subsequent veering between dismay and good riddance was unsettling. How could one hold two such conflicting attitudes? And yet the notion of fear and elation as compatible bedfellows was irrefutable.

A squally wind lifted my hair and ushered me onto the pavement, where deep in thought, I walked purblind into the night. Hitherto, I'd considered myself an old hand at rationalising the illogical, identifying the peril and steering clear. But as of precisely twenty past seven this morning, I had been exposed a greenhorn in my own emotional landscape.

The moon sailed free of the clouds, silvering the frayed trees along the pavement, and I slowed to observe the Catherine wheel trick, played out on the wet twigs.

The explanation was clear, I concluded; I was lacking a constituent component, comparative to the transmission in a car, transferring the motive force into action. Synapses sparked, yet I remained inert, stalled, unequipped with the gene for love.

Aishling went to yoga on Monday nights, and as I climbed the stairs, a small flag of relief unfurled in my chest. I wouldn't have to breathe the stifling atmosphere that seethed with discontent. A sketchy tableau I had pinned in my mind pulled into focus; alone, reclining in my leather chair, exhaling smoke through the open window, gin and tonic clinking at my hand. A chance to review, digest and file the extraordinary events of the day, uninterrupted. I would follow that perfect, silver bead of thought as long as I was able, as long as was sane. Or until it was time to witness Aishling extricating herself and the bulky, Swiss roll mat from her friend's Smart car. My reverie rudely aborted by the Thanks! Bye! Slam! Like most people who don't drive, she would hurl the car door shut with excessive force. But on finding the latch up, the image dissolved like a sandcastle in the tide, the little flag snatched way beyond rescue. She was in. And then her mesmerised silhouette, like something out of 'Poltergeist', facing a torrent of breaking news. Emergency service lights pulsed from the telly, washing the darkened room blue. I took my place beside her on the sofa, the sullen smell of winter still clinging to my coat.

"Jesus, it's awful," she said, "a bomb in the West End. People Christmas shopping, for Christ's sake."

It wasn't for the sake of Christ that people were shopping, I thought, but kept it to myself.

"Wee children believed to be among the dead. And so close to Christmas, and all, imagine their families. It's so fucked up, Brit," she said, burying her face in my lapel. Her easy sympathy propelled me to the frozen, outer reaches of space. Inside me nothing stirred, other than a selfish resentment over my spoilt plans. Yes, it was terrible incident, but I couldn't cry for people I didn't know. But then the girl on the train ... a sudden fracture which must precede grief, before I decided she was not the type to shop in the West End and I thought her safe. No, I knew she was.

"You're a good woman, Ash," I said in false piety, drawing her close. Her head disagreed in my neck.

"No, I'm not," she said, edging away. Her eyes turned flinty and she blew her nose. "I do love you, Brit. I try and show you all the time, but it's not enough, is it?" And I sensed we were about to have 'the conversation.'

I scanned her designer detritus of Alessi ashtrays, Murano decanters, an assortment of Daum crystal, Indian deities, a medley of Lladró cherubs, arranged on something she called 'The Credenza.' A small Iron-age pot of mine squatted uncomfortably behind them; an artisan among dilettantes. Its dimpled surface impressed with a binary pattern of twine, suggesting the helices of DNA. Aishling pulled reedy fingers through dead-straight hair, her genome begging a pot of its own on which to imprint.

"You have to understand," she said, "I can't bear this empty vessel feeling."

I frowned, unsure if she was referring to us or her own body.

Cobwebs trembled in the pink chandelier she had inflicted upon the ceiling and the bomb that ticked inside her had been primed. "The thing is, Brit ... I love you, I really do ..." She leaned forward to mute the television "... but you leave me no option." Her bay doors were sliding open.

"Do it!" I shouted in my mind. "Do it!"

She paused, as if awaiting some order to be rescinded and met my eye, but when no such communication came, she shifted her gaze to the whisky decanter and I realised she hadn't had a drink, of late. "This has to end," she let it fall. "I can't be with you anymore." The verbal A-Bomb, designed to put paid to any further conflict, had been deployed. "I'm going back to Dublin."

We watched it explode between us, obliterating the façade, and she began to cry once more.

The convivial weekends, the soft mornings, the countless late-night quarrels, scattered like scared birds. How the accusations had flown. Once she had informed me that my opposition to a baby was purely because I would have no genetic investment in it. I pointed out that technically, a human egg could be fertilised by any somatic cell, at which she screamed "Jesus Christ, Brit! You're seriously robotic! Do you know that?"

Now it was out there, I reeled unexpectedly, feeling the abject dishonour of not being the instigator, until a kind of numbness crept in.

"Okay," I simply said, "Okay," and rested my head in my hands. This she would interpret as an act of contrition, when in fact, I was processing. She could not be considered a bad person. Manipulative, maybe. My dealings with the dead had somehow left me adroit at recognising anomalies in the living. I sifted the soil for a clue, for something bright to wink back at me. Between my fingers, an object regular and unyielding in its manufacture; a truth. A fist in my mind closed around the hilt of an iron-age sword. Naturally, as a forty-five-year-old archaeological specialist, I had never killed anyone, but I somehow knew what it was to plunge a sword into dark, hot guts and twist. To watch with dispassion, the incredulous expression glaze.

"You're pregnant," I said, "aren't you?"

She folded her arms across her stomach and nodded with a curious expression of triumph and apology.

We were now in unchartered territory, our usual behaviour patterns blown away, like a map in the wind. And how reliant we had been on that map which, in retrospect, hadn't served to guide us at all. Rather, it had kept us trekking the same old dusty path. The stalemate broken; she was the victor. Those two mammals who used to do a ridiculous thing called sex, which stimulated hormones, binding them together for a gestation period that never happened, duped into a probationary domesticity, were consigned to the past. And as that particular golem shambled from the building, its departure made way for a surprising and cunning sprite; Aishling became interesting again.

Her stress-pinched face, reviving before my eyes as the toxic atmosphere dispersed. Even the idea that she may have slept with someone else, added a new dimension to her paper-doll, cut-out form. Now, a string of Aishlings held hands, the white, uniform dresses stretching out of sight into a gauzy future.

"How?" I was intrigued.

"Insemination," she replied, matter of fact. Her single-mindedness imbuing her with yet more substance.

"Someone we know?"

"No ... clinic," she said. "It wasn't cheap, but luckily it happened second time."

Our eyes flitted to the TV screen, where a man was silently paddling upstream in a coracle.

"So ..." she said, smoothing her skirt "... there it is."

A sad-sack Santa curled up on the pavement in a mangle of blankets outside the tube. The grubby, white trim on his red polyester hat concealed his eyes, while a snoozing terrier at his side, tolerated the indignity of plastic antlers. An empty Starbucks cup next to a cardboard sign, on which was scrawled 'Merry Xmas'. A Quango of posh schoolboys angled their phones at the man. *LOL.* The empty cup reflected the fact that the commodity of hard cash was increasingly uncommon these days, our currency securely stored in holograms, allowing us to wend our way to the underground, routine ambivalence intact.

Claiming my usual spot on the platform, I studied the map. The divergent Northern Line, cinching in like a waist at Camden Town, where I imagined the girl to be steadying herself on the escalator. She would be a stander, like myself, not one of those chargers, sprinting down the left in a breeze of impatience, stamping down each second of the day. I traced the Jubilee Line to Kilburn. Not a straight-forward ride from Tufnell Park, and that's why Aishling had left in a taxi. That, and the bombing had sent the tube up the creek. The curtains drawn on her moon face as she sped away to the solace of her sister.

I sank my chin into the warm and fragrant world of my coat. And if I'd taken a little extra care over my appearance this morning; blow-drying and oiling my hair, applying mascara, walking through a perfumed mist. So what? After all, there was no more bathroom clash. Plus, my hair grew anxious in winter.

Minding the gap, the penguin shuffle, little chance of connecting with the girl even if she was a creature of habit. However, as people settled into seats and slumped into their phones, I found myself able to see all entry points. We lurched into motion and heads wagged in a silent disco. The Somali man in the same tired suit, sat complacent, long legs crossed, one scuffed shoe describing a circle as his thumbs worked furiously at destroying aliens. To his right, a squat man in a cashmere duffle-coat, smiling faintly at family snapshots on his phone. Perhaps he was far away from them. I noticed wispy, black hair escaping from the back of his saffron turban, and pictured his unaided, daily fabric grapple.

The thick, wool coat had been an unwise choice; it wasn't that cold and I soon began to overheat. A young Latino woman, possibly Brazilian, tickled her lips with the tuft of a sleek plait, while her thyroidal eyes devoured a paperback entitled 'The Way to Happiness,' and I realised the experiment had completely slipped my mind. The furnace beneath my coat approaching critical, I unbuttoned and took advantage of the waft as the doors opened at Kentish Town. Resembling a giant cormorant, people gave me a wide berth, except one. "Phew, just made it," panted a matronly, Anglo-Saxon woman. Clad in tweed and reeking of money, in a breeze of bustle, she deposited a number of posh carrier bags around her feet and mine.

I was bearing up pretty well until the train decelerated for Camden Town. A sickly knocking in my throat, expanded to a full-on Kodo performance in my chest when I glimpsed her, shining out in the dull parade. The needling beeps and there she was, actual, stepping up, pushing back her hair, looking around. I shrank behind the Anglo-Saxon's tweed batwing, into her velvet fug of Dior and flatulence. The insidious possibility that this was all some romantic conceit of mine began to flare. If I were to get off at the next stop, that would be the end of it. All this hot under the collar business was detestable ... pure foolishness to think such an attractive young woman would have any interest in me. She'd simply been spicing up her boring commute, much like me and my experiment. Having convinced myself of this, I resolved to look at her, one last time. Suddenly aware of the velocity at which we hurtled, the train's vibration disguised my shaky legs. I braced myself against an alarming slew, leaving the hot halo of a handprint on the glass. And gripping the overhead bar, I leaned forward to sneak a peek.

Boom, straight at me. 'Wake up!' Her fierce affirmation slapped my cheeks and I flinched behind the batwing, but the Anglo-Saxon was stooping to her luggage. *'King's Cross ...'* announced the robot *'the next station is King's Cross.'* No doubt, to pick up the overland to a rural, hoar-frosted Christmas, logs crackling in the inglenook. I froze, exposed. Not au fait with tube protocol, the Anglo-Saxon caught my eye. "Merry Christmas to you," she said, with a pleasant wince, before over-lifting her leg across the gap. More human shields shambled aboard, forming an impenetrable phalanx along the aisle. At the far end, the girl's secret smile and hypnotic sway. Real, hyper-real. And a voice from nowhere, ancient, reassuring 'See with your dark eye, there is nothing to fear,' soothed me like a drug. I stumbled, a bee, drunk in the poppies, exploring the plains of her face. A beautiful and familiar landscape, unique among anyone I'd ever seen in this life. Her profile imprinted on my eyes like the glare of the sun on the sea. Tumbling through time, the gilded contours of a queen on a coin. In her young eyes, an expression as old as the hills. I knew, as sure as my own, the details of her body and of her manner; tender yet dominant, which compelled me beyond reason. Her many and various body adornments invited the presumption of some fashionable Camden sub-culture. However, to me, the leather plaits, like wrist armour, the multiple bars and hoops skewering ear and eyebrow, suggesting vulnerability of the flesh, while the tattoo, concealed under her jacket, like a message to me, spoke of just the opposite. Something very old-fashioned, archaic even. Although such 'enhancements' are commonplace today, she possessed an authenticity. And I sensed behind each of these symbols, a significance, a potency, akin to battle-kill tokens. The animal tooth at her throat, reminding us life can be dangerous ... and short. And yet the ouroboros tattoo, standing for the eternal recurring cycle of creation and destruction, death and renewal. All at once, she was thrilling on a new and untold dimension and I finally identified what it was I had found wanting in others, what I had craved; it was someone from whom I could learn something new about myself, someone who would amaze me every day.

As we rocked out from Old Street, she squatted on the floor, searching for something in her bag, where I spied her intermittently. An elusive primate amid a grove of legs. But all too soon, brakes were shrieking the approach of Moorgate and my spirit screamed. Jumping up, she wrestled her way to the doors, clearing them as soon as they parted. Caught in the rip tide, she swam against the flow. I followed her heroic progress along the platform, fighting to get to me. *'Stand clear of the doors ... doors closing.'* The beeps started. "Stand away!" the platform guard ordered. The trill of his whistle. Game over. People leaping through the diminishing aperture. She sought me in the crush of the sealed carriage, making sure she had my eye before, bang! Her spread hand slammed against the glass, turning heads. "Stand away! Young lady, stand away!" Breaking into a jog, at pace with the hastening train, she would never stand away, not until she could be sure I'd seen the message printed on her palm ... 'MARRY ME.' A demand more than a request. And though I found the concept of marriage nauseating and had resolved never again to attend a wedding, I saw my reflection nodding. Laughing and nodding as she pulled up with a smile.

He was younger than I had anticipated, my opponent, and though only an acolyte of Florimell Enterprises, he carried himself like a prince. His card bore the logo of a red crown over a red F. I offered my hand. He smiled and kept it a moment too long, applying undue pressure to the tender webbing between my thumb and forefinger. The affable mask briefly fell, betraying demon eyes, which locked on mine, implying a subtle but clear warning. 'Play the game, missy, or I will end you.'

"Jack Kidrow." He said as one word, to avoid the awkward glottal stop. Bonhomie resumed as he caught Maundy's hand. "Good to meet you, buddy," leaving an expensive fragrance in his wake. Maundy reciprocated, spaniel-like. His stained lab-coat in stark contrast with Kidrow's crisp, white cuffs.

"I gotta tell you," he said, homing back on me, "I love the eyes, I really do. Is this the thing in London now?"

"I'm sorry?" I said, knowing full well where this was heading.

"You know ... fake, colour lenses," he wagged a finger across his face. "Women," he chuckled to Maundy, "you gotta love 'em, they'll accessorise anything .... And I mean anything". His gaze slipped down my body to a speculative vajazzlement, which prompted Maundy to cough in his coffee, further bespattering his lab coat.

"I can assure you, Mr Kidrow," I said, "there is nothing fake about me."

"I don't doubt it, Miss Hockney." His voice adopted a sly quality. "You are a *miss*, I take it?"

I nodded, uncertain if I should pursue the 'Ms' line.

"Okay, wonderful," he said, with a clap, dismissing the conversation. "Now where can I set up?"

Maundy pointed to Cato's desk, empty but for her 'Beware the Geek' mouse mat and a blank monitor.

Florimell Enterprises specialised in building 'educational' theme parks, which sounded nice enough when, in reality, it was an American conglomerate, acquiring discreet chunks of the British Isles, in the name of conservation and regeneration. An industry would arise around an integral artefact, in this case, The Weltdown Chieftain. The package spread before us, illustrated an exhausting array of attractions and activities: battle re-enactments, archaeology play digs, themed rides, a Roman spa, featuring a 'Celtic flume', friendly foam giants, walking woods, a dragon mountain and so on.

"... and of course," Kidrow said, "very much front and centre, our chieftain. The bones on display in a state of the art, environmentally controlled burial chamber. Man, I love that gold tooth." This, I noted, had been the first instance since his arrival that he'd commented on the skeleton, now arranged anatomically. "A life-sized model on horseback and faithful reconstructions of all the awesome weaponry. And wait, you're gonna love this ..." This I doubted very much, "... as we speak, our people are in negotiations with Liam Neeson for the promo. Don't you think he'd be perfect? He has the... what's the word I'm looking for?" He probed a dimple in his chin. "The authority," he said, clenching his hands into fists.

Maundy and I exchanged a glance.

"I'm sorry?" I said, "I don't understand ... you didn't read our report?"

"Sure we did," he nodded earnestly, "and very

comprehensive it was too. You should be proud of yourselves."

"So then you'll know that the Weltdown Chieftain is female," I said, "and quite advanced in years."

"Yep, yep," the exaggerated nodding of the big, round head. "We're receptive to the elderly angle, but we at Florimell would prefer the chieftain portrayed as a man. We believe it would be a greater draw." He shrugged. "That's just the way it is."

"But that's an outright untruth," said Maundy, tugging his earlobe like crazy, not quite able to employ the word 'lie.'

"We like to think of it as a small enhancement of the facts. After all it's about getting as many people as possible to enjoy the history of this great nation." His arms spread wide in benevolence. "When you think about it, it's really not that important in the grand scheme of things."

"Ah!" I smiled, "the old 'grand scheme of things' excuse, often invoked when justifying moral insensibility."

"I don't get ya." Kidrow's smile faltered.

Turning my back on the globular head, I regarded the battle-scarred skull of Vertengannua, the tacit endurance of the woman seemed to imbue in me an underpinning, restoring my sense of mission. I sat, resting my hand on the table beside her finger bones, the knobbly nodes of arthritis evident upon the knuckles.

"Mr Kidrow," I began the attack. "You and your kind are gatekeepers to a human story, retro-fitted to augment the male position. Shit, you fuckers have been at it for centuries."

He shifted on his loafers at the swearing and looked to Maundy as if I were a potentially dangerous dog that only he could pacify.

"That glorious band of brothers," I continued, "marching through history, declaring their heroism, their license. Well, let me tell you, Mr Kidrow," I stood for emphasis. "I am Sparticus. Yes, I am." I indicated to the bones. "And so is she, and I will not let you or anyone else deny her."

"I'm sorry, Miss Hockney." His bemused expression switched to faux sympathy, "but it's out of my hands. My job is purely to see that the desired outcome is achieved," a flicker of enjoyment danced in his eyes, "with or without your blessing."

"In that case, Mr Kidrow, I'll withdraw the report. Florimell commissioned it but it remains the intellectual property of Hockney Girling Associates, and is worthless without our endorsement." The signing off was essential to their procurement of heritage match-funding, without which the project would collapse. "Furthermore, if you should find an alternative specialist to 'enhance the facts,' I will sue them for professional misconduct and Florimell for misrepresentation."

The ensuing silence punctured by a series of snorts; that was how Jack Kidrow laughed. "Oh yeah? And are you gonna call the injured party as a witness ...?" gesturing at the skeleton. "She'll never stand up in court," he sniggered "... she may need a chair."

I turned to the face, bleary with hostile amusement. "This is no joke," I said.

"Yep, yep, I guess you're right," he said, and his features hardened as the demon came to the fore once more. "We can make it worth your while, and nobody need ever be the wiser."

"Add bribery."

His perfect nails scraped a twitching jaw. "Oh, you'll sign, Miss Hockney, eventually. Once you've fully appreciated the consequences of not doing so."

"Add threatening behaviour." Now I was nervous.

He snapped shut his briefcase with a sigh, and clicking his tongue, he triggered a finger at Maundy. "I'll call you later, buddy." And consulting his watch, he was out the door. The smell of his private blend neroli was to linger all morning. "Can you believe that," said Maundy, "King Fucktard."

The horror movie head revolved on the screen. The skull clad in bands of virtual muscle, the livid eyeballs awaiting colour designation. Janice's digital tomographic reconstruction had reached, what she called, the everyman stage; we would all look like this without skin. The data gleaned from the teeth had established very little in terms of externally visible characteristics. Gender and age were factors Maundy and I had pretty much nailed from the anthropological analysis of the skeleton. Janice would extrapolate from the skull, the nuance, the details which make every face in the world unique.

The advent of 3-D printing at once astonished and terrified me. First came tentative geometric shapes, then car parts, guns, implants for new-borns, deficient in some or other vital component. Even pizza, and before long would come the hair-raising progression to printing people. I had little doubt that Florimell was on the case; splicing and milling an over-sized, polymer prince in their desired image, lurching and gesturing like some ungodly golem. I had integrity in my corner in the shape of Janice Boateng, proper black, unlike myself, and proficient in the old way of clay. Granted, she had worked from a printed skull and started the muscle layers digitally, but the flesh pinched and smeared between thumb and finger would be at her discretion, her

320

illumination. I admired her gentle, ribbing wisdom, her irreverence. Often in an altered state; she claimed the drugs focused her mind, particularly when working. In an attempt to up my own black credentials, I had asked her once, with a degree of stiffness, why she insisted upon relaxing her hair. 'I see where you're coming from,' she'd replied with patience, 'but would you ask a white woman why she insisted on having an afro?' She maintained she was straight, but I couldn't help but wonder if, like her hair when the chemicals began to wear off, she was a little kinked.

Vertengannua's nuclear DNA had presented us with a series of likelihoods; it was likely her remaining eye was brown. Probable, her hair dark brown or black, before, as Gaius told us, she went grey. She possessed a genetic predisposition for strength and endurance, again, corroborating the evidence on the skeleton. From a rib, was deduced her mitochondrial haploid group, that is, DNA passed on solely down the female line. Haploid group H, among the most common maternal lineages, widespread in Europe, the Near

East, North Africa and Asia. Originating some twenty-five thousand years ago in South West Asia, it was one of the oldest and, incidentally, also mine. We can only surmise as to what the Celts looked like. Their likely ultimate admixture: Atlanto-Mediterranid, Alpinid, Nordid, and survivors of the ancient builders of the Megalithic monuments, weirdly known as Megalith Physical Type. Their nomadic sweep through Central Europe, incorporating indigenous genetic material along the way, making them not so much a nationality or even a race; more like a concept, or an event.

We know they were exceptionally tall, particularly compared to the Romans, height being an important factor when selecting a mate. But also diverse. The historian, Dio tells us of Boudica; *'a great mass of the tawniest hair.'* Red hair, virtually unknown in Mediterranean countries at that time, fascinated the Romans. Therefore, proliferating the cliché of the fiery-haired Celt, when in truth, their hair and eye colouring ran the full Caucasoid spectrum.

Indeed, there was no definitive Celtic phenotype,

leaving their genetic legacy all but vanished today. However, on a remote mountain in North West China, there lives a tribe, quite unlike their Chinese countrymen; they are taller than their neighbours, wear tartan. Red and blonde hair is not uncommon among them and their features are distinctly western. I liked to think that perhaps there, some semblance of the Celtic zeitgeist remains.

If only they knew how the soil around them was saturated with death. The tube network snaked underneath the plague pits, but Londoners had been snuffing it wholesale long before the Great Plague. A man and a woman, both bespectacled, sensible hair, had taken their seats at Euston. The same leisure outfit, his: light green, hers: pastel pink. Synchronised, mini rucksacks nursed between gender-specific trainers. I deduced they were German, sporting 'the partner look.' I felt their eyes on me, full of questions. They seemed to be in telepathic communion. 'Is this a typical Londoner, or an immigrant from their commonwealth?' In German, obviously. The woman was thinking about my boots; black, knee-high. Her eyes perused them for a while. I couldn't tell if she approved or not. The man stared beyond my shoulder, near enough to my face, so he could flit to it whilst I studied the skull on my phone. Clearly, I was alien to him; perhaps he found me attractive, perhaps repellent. Or was he just, as we all are, pre-programmed to decipher faces. I, myself would soon be searching the ancient face of an effigy. It awaited me in a studio in Seven Sisters; Janice's live/work unit, which was cool in every sense of the word.

The piglet squeal of brakes and the Germans winced in unison. Bereft of reference points, they concealed their disquiet with smiles. I imagined myself a tour guide, calming and alarming them in turn. 'They're all around us,' I would inform them, 'layers of London dead: black death, plague, cholera, typhoid, smallpox. They didn't even use coffins until the eighteenth century.' During the interminable stretch between King's Cross and Caledonian Road, the Banshee howl got up. That relentless whisper, gathering to a sustained scream; the voice of the underground. 'Don't listen to it,' I would warn them. 'It is said, that sound can drive you mad.' A dim glow sped past. 'Ghost station,' I'd declare. 'The Piccadilly Line is riddled with them,' enjoying their nervousness. 'Relax,' I'd say, 'I don't mean ghost as in haunted ... but as in disused. Shuttered mainly in the nineteen-twenties through lack of use. Seems ridiculous these days, doesn't it? When you look at the overcrowding.' They would nod and shrug in disbelief. 'Oh yes,' I'd continue, 'this city is abristle with death: skull-studded dedications, veiled urns, winged angels, war memorials, white bikes, rotting flowers. Memento mori. Does anyone know what that means?' They would shake their heads. 'It means 'Remember you must die," I would explain with relish. The couple got to their feet at the announcement of Arsenal. I pictured their holiday snaps of The Emirates Stadium; there she is, peering through the huge concrete A. He, triumphal atop the giant S, with no clue the installation's true purpose is to prevent a hostile vehicle attack. The train door shut like a drawer full of knives and, without explanation, I found myself thinking in German. "Auf wiedersehen," I said aloud to the carriage, empty in the afternoon. "Bedenke du musst sterben." *Remember you must die.*

Rain rattled the skylights in a building that regressed me to the art room at school. The not unpleasant smell of dust and turps, carbolic soap and glue, and the inexplicable whiff of rabbit hutch. Clay fingerprints adorned anything graspable: mug handles, window latches, light switches and the brass pull cups on a narrow plans chest; the second drawer not quite closed, the yellowing label marked *'Eyeballs: light hazel to dark brown/black.'* The day had suddenly gloomed and Janice flicked on the fluorescents. Dried slip dappled the worn parquet and globs of clay, that when peeled up, held the imprint of woodgrain. Her familial manner and the art room air revived in me a feeling of nostalgia and hope. The kettle reached its climax, and it wouldn't be too much longer before she would reveal the head beneath the hessian on the work bench, stuck on a pole, like a Tower Bridge traitor. Harbouring a smile, she squeezed out very thoroughly, one teabag, and with infuriating diligence, the other. Next came the protracted stirring; the obstinate clinks like distant roadworks. I couldn't figure out if she was stoned, acting stoned or, with the mischief of a sister, winding me up.

"That's fine for me, thanks," I said, trying to hasten the process. The vigorous stirring relentless. "Janice! For fuck's sake!"

"Okay, okay, I hear you." The glint in her eye suggesting she was satisfied with my reaction. She opened the fridge to deposit the spent teabags, which she used for colouring skin.

"Sorry," I said, and she cocked her head my way.

"What makes you think I was talking to you?" I followed her gaze across the railway tracks to a tiny Christmas tree, twinkling in the window of an office block. "You think I'm joking, right?" She sat beside me on a stool. "She's the most alive one I've ever done." She fished a bent up spliff from the chest of her dungarees. "Much more than the murder victims. They just say, 'catch him.'" She sparked up. 'Please just help them catch him.' This one here," she gestured with a plume of smoke, "she wants you to see her, don't ask me why."

"Me?" my eyes widened.

"You, me … everyone." She flicked ash on the floor. "That's why I did her so quickly. 'Make haste, child, make haste.' She got inside my head, drove me nuts."

"You heard her say that?"

"Yes," she leaned into a whisper. "You know what else she said?"

"What?" distantly aware of the burning mug in my hand.

"She said he's making a list."

"Who is?"

"I don't know, but he's checking it twice."

Falling in, I sighed to the skylight. "Janice!"

"Gonna find out who's naughty and nice," jabbing at my ribs. "SANNA CLAUS IS COMING TO TOWN!" she took a deep draw on the spliff and mimed reeling in a fish. "Too easy," she said, coughing out a laugh. "By the way, what are you doing for Christmas?"

"At this rate, I'll probably be in custody for murder

unless you let me see her right now."

"Sure." The teasing evaporated as she stubbed the spliff and steepled her fingers against her lips "Did you find out who she was?"

I nodded. "Her name was Vertengannua, or something like it. She was clan chieftain of a tribe called The Vortigae. We don't know how she died but she had some serious battle scars."

"Serious," Janice agreed. "Let me introduce you." She moved to the work bench and shunted aside jars of scalpels and spatulas. A wooden pole fixed to a plinth, in turn clamped to the work surface emerged from a piece of sacking. The head hovered like a magic trick. "Okay," said Janice, turning back the cloth. "Here we go."

The injury shocked me. The shrivelled eyelid sealed shut, as if blanking the memory of the bone-cleaving blow. The wound, perhaps cauterised. Shiny, healed tissue crackled pink and blue from the tanned, weather-roughened skin, like the walls of an ice crevasse. It was impossible to imagine how anyone had survived such a violence. My own head thumped in empathy. But she must have learned to own it; one look from that corrupted visage, enough to dispel any nascent uprising. I devoured her features: the wide jaw with a cleft in the chin, the rather large nose, high, broad cheekbones, the remaining eye, a deep, burnt brown, almost Slavic in shape. The muscular webbing of the thick neck, fused to the hefty collarbone, where she ended. And where Janice had applied a suggestion; a sinuous, blue tattoo. Nothing crone-like about her. In fact, she appeared ageless, in the way that animals do; betrayed only by a greying muzzle or stiffening gait.

"You've given her hair," I whispered. A wild, silver and slate tangle, but with two pure white braids falling from her temples. Janice had done her homework. And though devoid of expression, which cannot be deduced from the skull, I read in that face a fierce intelligence, a defiance, a humanity. Her dark eye seemed to fix me with expectance at an implication I had not yet grasped. This character would have spat in the dirt with disgust at my lack of awareness ... but then I saw it; that face had been young once. Beneath the damage, beneath the rings of age, over-painting each passing year, the soft sapling skin; the resemblance was undeniable. 'The girl on the train.' A mouthful, even in my mind. I had tried and failed to name her. From time to time, I found my mouth describing a 'Y' sound, though not as in Ysolta. My fingers pressed my lips to stop the soundless struggle ... seal up the feeling, which instead, migrated to my eyes. One, two involuntary tears spliced my cheeks and splashed on the parquet.

"Whoa, what ... just what?" Janice's voice swam cagey, from a different time; I wasn't normally given to tears. "Did you see something with that spooky old eye of yours?" I barely understood her. I can see the present, I can see the past, but I cannot see the future.

"Yu ..." The word was there, I almost had it. "Yu ... You?" That wasn't it. But 'Yu' would do for now. "Yu."

"I? Me? .... What are you trying to say, freakazoid woman?" Not unkindly, she slapped my arm.

And, although Janice was the nearest thing I had to a confidante, something deep-seated and private in me would not give it up. Instead, I offered her something that didn't matter; "Aishling's left me," I said.

The mood in the pub was garrulous. Men stood poised with pints, staring at a giant screen, where other men chased a ball and spat. Everything smeared, yet lustrous, like a Manet painting; I watched Janice; a rich mahogany like the bar itself, one black dealer boot on the brass footrail. A dazzling array of optics bled ruby, amber, emerald behind her head, as she fed her PIN into the handset, and I realised I was stoned. I smiled to myself. It was all craft beer, artisan gin and upcycled, mismatched chairs these days. A far cry from the last time I was in a pub; with Aishling on that notorious blind date. She was in my flat this minute, packing her stuff, and judging by the three attempts she'd made to call me this evening, was having issues. My phone buzzed a fourth time and I turned it off in irritation. Now Aishling was almost out of the picture, I'd allowed 'Yu' to occupy my thoughts more frequently. Today compounded it; my friend and an ancient Briton had, it seemed, conspired to ensconce her there. Janice had been digging.

"It's a shame," she said, emptying the bottle into my glass, "I thought you and Aishling had legs."

"Yes, well, it's run its course. And then ..." I grimaced, "... there's the creepy patter of tiny little feet."

Janice laughed. "Not interested in having a family, I take it?"

"God, no ... horrific."

"Yeah, that's what I used to say, but I love my baby niece, she's special, and I'm kind of ..." she paused, "not sad exactly, but maybe I regret not taking the opportunity when it came."

"I can't imagine you having kids."

"Me neither," she said, picking clay from her nails, "but, you know it's funny as you get older; you find you don't know yourself as well as you thought."

"That's so true," I said.

Janice cocked her head, inviting elaboration and, letting me dwell on it, which she knew I would, went to the bar to get another bottle of wine.

She'd given me something here and was expecting a disclosure in return. I dearly wanted to reciprocate. The weed and wine had opened me up a little but not enough. At this time, the girl on the train was a half-formed notion; a nebulous yet powerful energy, crackling inside me. I imagined the story escaping my mouth into the atmosphere; silvering the pints and punters, snaking under the pub door into the rain-greased streets, searching, searching. The fabric of the universe slightly altered forever. Janice's idea of me would change in an instant. 'Yu' would be the first thing she saw in me, hereafter. And, if Janice and I were to never meet again, the last. Telling Janice would make it true, with no hope of retraction. No, I couldn't tell her because she would say 'go for it', and that, from someone I respected, would give me the final impetus needed to do so. And in five years or so, after I'd made a hash of it, Janice and I would be sitting in some pub drinking wine, while 'Yu' moved her stuff out.

Janice returned, and I had something feeble

prepared.

"Anyway," I said, "it never felt like it should with Aishling."

She smiled, topping up my glass. "You've found something better, haven't you? Tell."

The men froze, pints at lips, saucer-eyed, before letting forth a collective, nuclear "YESSS!" At which I jumped out my seat, knocking the table.

"No," I said, "but I know it's out there."

My glass wobbled but did not spill.

A myriad of data blinked on the dashboard, more like a spaceship than a minicab: the time was 22.40, the temperature in the car, a stuffy 23 degrees, we were travelling at 14 miles per hour, the car battery was at 65 percent. Asian music seeped faintly from the radio. Clouded busses steamed with purpose along dedicated lanes. Wan faces peering from pawed portholes. The eco-minded computer killed the engine at each red light, making our progress seem all the more laborious. I'd be home now if I'd taken the bus, but rain and misanthropy had steered me wrong. The trill of the low battery warning on my phone. Just enough juice to see Aishling's eight missed calls and an exasperated text: COME HOME NOW!!! URGENT!!! before it gave up the ghost. The heavy-browed eyes of the driver, framed in the rear-view mirror, like a photofit. He stared through the rain-pimpled windscreen, swept clear, every few seconds, swish-thump, just on the point of hazardous obscurity. Swish-thump, the motley Christmas lights of Holloway Road revealed, then washed away like Christmas itself. Swish-thump, next Christmas, swish-thump, the Christmas after. I felt time spin away. Of course, there would be spring, summer, autumn in between, but hard to picture the warm, long days now. The in-built amnesia in the British psyche, allowing us to take each season as and when it comes, with no recollection of its opposite, nor awareness of the repetition. 'Isn't it glorious?' we say for a few days, here and there, forgetting what had gone before, and what was to come. And as no-one can see the future, we suffered the dark, in blind faith.

Trinkets dangled from the rear-view mirror: a

plastic tiger, a red circle in a green square, a yellow waterlily bordered by yellow rice sheaves. He must be Bangladeshi, the driver, and I wondered if he'd learned the amnesia.

"Sssss," he hissed, avoiding an unlit cyclist. And as if reading my mind. "It is much worse in my country," he said, "for six months the rain does not stop ... each year we lose everything."

The engine gave a last sigh outside my flat. Up in the dark, the living room window, bright with industry and open to the night. My drink-impaired brain at a loss when the key stuck stubborn in the lock. What the fuck?

"Is that you?" Aishling barked from the intercom. She knew full well it was. I'd seen her briefly at the window, a study in botheration. The entry buzzer released the door on a further peevish note. I could hear her bumping about as I lifted my feet up the gloomy stairwell, the flat door wedged open by a bulging, black bin bag.

"Where the fuck have you been?" She stepped into the hall, yellow rubber gloves wielding a dustpan and brush. "I've called you, like a hundred times."

A yawn launched in my chest and I held it in my mouth until she turned.

"Brace yourself," she said, as we entered the living room.

At first, I thought it was one of her decorating projects; the room awash with something like snow, as if the window had been left open in a blizzard. No, more like blossom, collecting under the credenza, caught in cobwebs around the chandelier, stuck to her hoodie. The smell of whisky and Christmas; a spilled cinnamon and frankincense fragrance diffuser. The liquid pooled on the floorboards, anointing the trunkless head of Ganesh. Smashed decanters, glittering like ice. Broken glass and goose down.

"We've been burgled," she said. "The police have just left."

My mind fought to gain traction. The slashed sofa, like a pillow fight. "Shit," I said, "what did they take?"

"Nothing that I can see," she sounded almost disappointed. The TV lay face-down on the floor, like an introspective robot. "They just smashed everything up." She gestured at the ransacked desk, "including your laptop."

I glanced at the junk circuitry and casing. "What did the police say?"

"Not much … probably just kids or junkies."

The sheer efficiency in the destruction made me think otherwise. "How did they get in?"

"That idiot downstairs, Alex, must have left the street door unlocked this morning. And you can get in yours with a credit card, I've done it when I forgot my keys. Anyway, the locks have been changed."

"Thank you for doing that," I said.

"I've cleaned up the kitchen," she knelt like a child, a good girl, matching the head of a cherub to its broken body. Something derelict inside me sagged a little.

"Oh, Ash," I squatted beside her, "all your precious things." I would have expected tears by now, but she remained composed.

"It doesn't matter," she said, "this stuff isn't practical with a small child around. Besides, it saves me the hassle of packing." She rocked in the wreckage awhile. And then. "Oh look," reaching under the credenza, "your ugly brown pot." She stood, offering it to the light. "It's totally fine." She upended it and plucked out a printed scrap of paper. "Florimell Enterprises," she read, "with compliments. Nice logo," she added, before casting it into a bin bag.

We swept and shifted through the night. We also talked; discussing how poignant things become meaningless when broken, or they attain a fresh poignance in their brokenness.

"Perhaps nothing is really broken," I said, "only abstracted." At which she smiled. "You're drunk," she said. I'd discovered a viscous bottle of vodka in the freezer and had been knocking back shots at intervals in the lawless small hours. "So I am," I agreed. "What's your excuse?"

The harmony between us at this shattered juncture was surprising; normally, there would have been recrimination, reproach. It was as if we'd exhausted our old repertoire and were beginning the read-through of a new play. Amid the chaos, she stood plum and true. But old habits die hard and the compulsion to derail her won out. "Why didn't you discuss it with me, the inseminating?" I sounded whiny to my own ears.

"Because," she smiled, "it's easier to ask for forgiveness than permission." This sounded rehearsed. "And I hope you do, Brit," she caught my eye, "I hope you do forgive me someday." I'd forgotten how clever she was.

She insisted we get our heads down, if only for an hour. Me, unresting in the bed, as if wearing dirty clothes. Her, on the slashed-up sofa. I picked up thoughts, as you would small shells on the shore. Had Maundy's home got the same treatment? Or had he and King Fucktard reached an agreement? Shaking hands and joining the circle jerk. And then there was Aishling, like she'd never been, or perhaps how she'd been in the beginning. But these mildly interesting thought-shells were just a distraction from the great wave that loomed at my shoulder. I'd been deliberately putting it off, ignoring it. Because I knew if I turned to face it, allowed it in, all hope of sleep would be banished. It hung in the air, shimmering, patient, awesome. And in that moment of acknowledgement, it came crashing down. My heart hastened, engulfed, drenched. I swam, half drowning, as it carried me, caressing, toying, lifting me up. In approximately two hours, I would be in her presence, in her power. I glanced at the red digits in the dark. The one I called Yu was most likely stirring.

The shower did little to sober me up. Heavy, wet hair like kelp, I coiled up and around and secured with a comb-clip. In the dim bedside light, salvaged clothes clung to my skin because I hadn't dried myself properly. My hands shaking in the make-up bag, extracting cosmetics like nuclear rods. A wide-eyed dummy in the fractured mirror, aiming mascara at its lashes, drawing a clown's mouth. Catching the soft calf flesh in the zip of my boot. Dropping the keys three times. Lurching into the shortest day. The door slam shocking up a flock of crows, shredding the petrol-blue sky that, for all the world, looked like evening. It was hard to hold in my brain that

I was heading to, rather than coming from work. My internal clock, frantically data roaming, receiving conflicting signals. I was drunk, exhausted, excited, and terminally horny; four sensations which rarely occurred, and never in conjunction. The crows settled down like a shaken-out bed.

Mr Chatterjee slid the cigarette box across the beaming faces in the newspaper. A disparate set of people who shared the misfortune of shopping in the same place at the same time as a bad machine. They would never have associated in life. It was only as victims that they were united … team dead.

"Nasty business." He tapped the paper with a biro. "You want a receipt?"

"No thanks," I said, already unwinding the cellophane.

"You take care," his frown intensified.

"I will." I said, leaving the shop with peculiar jauntiness.

I let one train go, and another, unsure of quite why. I must convince myself of the day. My heavy, black coat, somewhere under a sleeping Aishling, I'd marched out with soused abandon in a suit jacket, fever-hot with alcohol. No-one would have guessed I was drunk. The secret sat inside me like a lady; waiting, tittering in a cake, preparing to burst forth – TA-DA! I liked this lady, squatting in her fake cake. She would have feathers and sequins, long, shiny legs, big red lips, white teeth, a generous, salt of the earth smile. They better come soon, she would think, because I'm beginning to cramp, and I could use the bathroom. I made her American.

A tinny, distant mantra graduated to a glissando. Oh, here they come, my crowd. A halo swept up the throat of the tunnel and my train emerged in a blaze of squeals. Its doors drew wide, inviting my step. I angled polite but firm elbows to stake my claim, just inside. From here I could watch the entire carriage and the platform. At Kentish Town, I clung to the upright rail, the mast of a sinking ship in a human tide. I noted my usual people: the Somali, the ginger Muslim, the old Chinese woman, like staff. Camden Town, and I was ready. The train jiggered to a standstill. I'd missed her on the platform and watched the doors with febrile intensity. The train panted like a hard-pressed animal, gathering in its young, enfolding them in its protection. *No, wait, one is left behind.* I couldn't see her. *Wait, I tell you, one is lost. No matter,* the large beast spoke, *better to save the many than the one. But this one's special,* I pleaded. *The quick and the dead,* it shrugged, *the quick and the dead.* Shit. I stared morosely at my feet. The shifting floor returned me to my thoughts earlier. That presence at my shoulder; vast, shimmering, static, I sensed it now. A supernatural entity which made the hairs prickle on my neck. It's behind you, a pantomime audience roared, and I resigned myself to the inevitability that the thing I scorned and desired above all, had me cornered. If I fell into her arms, would she catch me or let me drop? Either way, the rapture was nigh.

A hint of chemical spearmint breath on my cheek, an accident. So too, the idle bump of her hip on my buttock. Testing the water, one way and another. And when it was clear we were invisible, she reached around me to grab the rail. The heel of her hand a fraction above my index finger. She flexed her fingers, her thumb ring clinked the metal. Leather plaits and a chunky, silver chain thickened her wrist. The catch of it dangled over mine. I observed her nails, short and even. Our hands of a similar type, while mine had coarsened with age and years in the dirt, hers were as smooth as marble. Flawless, but for the faint nicotine tarnish on her middle finger. Her milk to my coffee. We gripped strong, uniform. Two hands on a spear, like a pact. Some rare and ancient spice infused the air around us: winter smoke, a resinous, medicinal note, the oily reek of her leather jacket, and of something muskier, more savage. And though no part of us touched, her intent assailed me in waves. With each swell, a promise, with each recession, an exposure. Pegged out on the shore beneath her; would she kill me or set me free? Camden Town faded to black, and suddenly there we were, confirmed in the dark window, looking out on everything and nothing. Our eyes had met many times, but this was the first instance in which we peered from the same canvas, sharing the same scene. We looked good together in this future tableau. Or was it a memory? Monochrome, far away, like sepia relatives. I could only see her eyes and nose; her mouth obscured by my shoulder. Just eyes, nose and a hand, but enough to make my heart thud, solid and central in my throat. Her breasts brushed and withdrew at intervals from my back. Blatant, yet unavoidable in the seductive motion of the train. I'd never been on a horse, but this rhythm lulled me to a place, perhaps in my dreams, when I had outridden a storm, the ebbing warmth of someone at my back. The black backdrop of our gaze whisked away in the set-change at King's Cross. We stood our ground. And with a discrete gesture, she adjusted her grip. Our skin touched for the first time, the charge of it heating the rail.

Our faces return to the spectral mirror and the journey proper begins. Her right hand seeking mine, finds a balled fist. Her fingers play across my knuckles, but the hand is clenched, rusted shut. My nails indent my palm with crescents. Her thumb explores the aperture formed by my curled up little finger. She strokes the star shape, tracing round and around,

round and around. Sweat beads my top lip. I glance up the carriage; no-one is looking. And still, she is coaxing that shy little pinkie. The stirring of sand, a sinkhole within me begins to cave. A chink of light, a new portal opens. The window, imprinting our image on my eyes, and I'm reminded of a painting; a portrait of some Spanish noblewoman. Her expression; composed, aloof, while behind her, a courtier's hand parts her petticoats. Almost imperceptibly, her thumb probes, the tip of it requesting entry. And she is watching me with those burning, bright eyes, from a cave, from a forest, from the night. A guardian at my shoulder. Her touch brings a kaleidoscope garden. Flower circles wither to ashes, rebloom to stars. The thumb ring glints, the sign of a healer. Locating the malady. The bite, the nip of a nail on an orange. Trust me, she is saying, let me in. And with that, I dilate just a little. And that is all she needs for her thumb to penetrate the clammy softness. She is in me, glittering in my hand, and I grip her like a dagger. Now, hands tied, she is unable to brush back the fringe, like crow feathers, that has fallen over one eye. She flicks her head, horse-like. The broad cheeks, the nostril flare, the black arch of the eyebrow, the strong jaw, and momentarily, Vertengannua inhabits the picture.

The journey abates at Angel. We stay with this connection. Time neither flies nor stands still. Time is the same as it ever was, except in each of these seconds is contained the validity of an entire day, a lifetime even. Every second for once accountable. Three seconds; that's all we get in the psychological present, all else being the past or the future. Three seconds, before everything we do is a memory.

Angel slides away. Blank faces register nothing. Our image flickers up again in the racing darkness, as if we are still, and the tunnel is moving. Forty years ago, possibly to this day. My mother took me to see Father Christmas at the Co-op. We sat in a sleigh that rose and fell with mechanical determination, while a twilight snowscape revolved on rollers either side, giving the impression of travel. So convincing was the illusion it panicked me, and I cried. My father took me back the next day and showed me the workings. I've felt compelled to look beneath the surface of things ever since.

We stand this way, her thumb, snug in my fist,
like the hilt of a sword. The implications of it,
the connotation simmers between us. I don't dare
think of it, in case I white-out. My entire body
alert and begging for the subtlest movement, a
communication. The focus of my world distilled in
the palm of my hand. She is daring me, the sun on
my back, her inducing heat, provoking me with her
stare, and I allow myself a glimpse, subliminal; her
nakedness, her hot mouth. The pit of my stomach
makes way for the rising. A schism. And I realise I
am host to it after all, that adaptive reflex. I'm not
immune to the rapture, just scared, and I try to scotch
it, like a lit fuse and pull myself free, but it's too late.
I can't deny it, I'm too far gone. I want it, I want
it from her. So I face it again, the prospect, graphic
this time, full on, no holds barred. A wrestling match
montage: glossy, fleshy, incandescent, obscene. And
a new, deeper tunnel yawns; mined by her existence,
a joint venture. Together, we are summoning it,
unearthing that elusive chimera. It knows the way,

if I just give up the reins, relinquish control, it will lead. The nights we will share, the indolent days, slave to it. The underground screams one long, sustained bow-stroke. The quick and the dead, chants the train, the quick and the dead. Her mouth at my ear, "K'rellicham," she whispers, "k'rellicham." The hairs on my skin rise under her breath. All my senses straining with a need to gain on this thing, to scale it. I am wide open beneath her as I imagine her licking and mauling. And just before the overkill, the loss of traction, a soft implosion and I am untethered, flung into space. Keep hold, don't let me go. The sun is sinking to the sea, the path fading, decaying. This world holds nothing for me, unless you are here. I see how my soul is shining its brightest, like the last gasp of a dying star. Death echoes, even in the throes of ecstasy, memento mori, never forget me. When I am fully landed, set down, released to survive, I know I will be changed. The question is; will I ever land? My heart races as we speed into Old Street. My legs almost buckling as her hand covers mine on the rail.

Her thumb pressed my heartline, my lifeline and

followed the fateline. Her fingers encircled my wrist, locating my pulse with proficiency. And I hoped we might stay like this till the end of the line. But at Moorgate, she left me like a dream on waking. Perhaps now I was dying, bleeding out. I couldn't face work; I sat in a café opposite, watching Maundy make his frequent forays for coffee. Reading, and reading again the note she had passed to me: *Meet me at Boudica and her daughters, 9pm tonight.*

I took it easy today, having little choice in the matter. People going about their business; I watched them remotely like you would a squadron of ants shifting bits of leaves. I crossed my legs, stirred my coffee and embers sparked into flame. Serene, nun-like even, I smiled at the waiter, while details of the morning commute presented themselves with cocaine clarity. He smiled back, oblivious to the filthy money-shots playing out behind my eyes. And as I walk through the city, they hang there now, on the outskirts of my vision, like the Big Ben moon. I slow to watch the subtle transit of the long hand closing in on five to. I'd gravitated from café to bar. Time had dragged. I said no ice, yet there it was, tinkling in my glass. There is no such thing as telepathy. Merely a coincidence that she chose the Boudica statue by Westminster Bridge. A masterful yet bogus lump of Victorian melodrama. If there was telepathy, she would have known I wasn't a fan. No telepathy, just me, willing the ice to melt, which it would have done, eventually, of its own accord.

The night is dry, at least, though cold enough to sting your ears. Party boats cut festive wakes along the Thames, awash with electric colour. Stripped of its sombre dignity, like a judge in a brothel. I must say it's not just about sex; my heart has breached, and light is spilling out. It is illuminated, festooned, like the trees and lamp posts along the Embankment. She has done this. To my right, the pointy hats of Whitehall. Across the river the London Eye glows pink, like some giant sky-sphincter. Always a sense of ownership when I walk through the capital at night. My heart is struggling. A jogger thumps past, flashing red. Perhaps it's because I'm drunk that the calm shapes of mermaids and sphinxes appear to be shuffling, black against the blousy water.

I'm almost there: the crown, the spear, the outstretched arms, heralding my approach. The scramble of fetlocks. A clunking preamble; Big Ben stirs from senility and clears his throat. And now I can see the daughters' backs, the wicked scythes jutting from the wheel hubs, the plinth where we shall talk. 'Kraliçem,' she had said, meaning 'my queen.' And the calamitous toll begins.

I am scared like I've never been. I am crossing the road, away from her, in obedience to my terror and the green man, to cower, to spy, from this portcullis place. I see the plinth, buzzing with others, like nuisance flies. And she is there, trenchant in the city smear, back against the granite, statue-still, reflecting the frozen spectacle raging above her head, where it doesn't matter that no-one is holding the reins. She smokes a cigarette, highlighting the air we will shortly share, looks up at the first chime. And, oh god, she is beautiful. Not by the prescribed standards of today. Hers is an elemental, visceral beauty, from before the subversion. An implacable tiger among the lambs they have made of us. No wonder they fear us if this is how we were ... and what we might yet become. No telepathy, but Yu is her name, or something like it. See how I've personalised her, made her mine, this young woman. But how can you keep a tiger?

What I should do is cross the road, initiate contact. A crossing window of 28 seconds on the pedestrian countdown. Big Ben bangs on. What next? We might go to a bar, or more likely, her place, or mine, so we can get fucking. A breeze interferes with her hair, exposing the premature white at her temple; perhaps an indication of a careworn disposition. My concern for her slays me, and I gravitate to the middle, traffic teaming all around me. She is closer. I see her; razor-sharp, piercings aglint. But once our complimentary base pairing is re-established, then what? Christmas escapes us, wrapped up in our own epiphany. And during these deviant, sprawling days, plans will be hatched, strategies formed: co-habitation, a mortgage, a snatched holiday, the evening meal, the big shop, introductions to friends and family. A short hop from exchanging our thoughts ... relating, projecting, to guarding them jealously. And gradually, imperceptibly, unnoticed, the flame will gutter, (you forgot to put out the recycling), until it is doused in the commonplace.

Twenty seconds and I'll cross all the way. Please look at me, but where is the telepathy? I know what must be done. Because this feeling I'm addicted to, I cannot live without. I will preserve the lustre, like a pinned butterfly, whose bloom never fades. Trap her in amber so each day I can examine her and be amazed. Frustrated hormones protest in outrage, firing a shot, straight at the breach, which hurts like hell, and that was just a warning. And though my very soul is cleaving to her, my love spilling out. I am calcifying, turning brittle, sealing the breach. Please understand, the time is not right, innocence is lost, I'm too knowing. I will see you in another time when we are re-set to naught. Now I am making her far away, just a person among many. The seconds run out and a bus obscures my view of her. Please understand ... my heart is breaking. Hear me. And as the bus moves away, she is standing there, looking directly at me. Close enough to see my wet face … close enough. Her eyes do not move from mine as she clenches her right hand and draws it to her chest. And now she is going down on one knee. Kneeling on the fucking pavement. People glance with disinterest as she lowers her head. She has heard me, and is acknowledging the abject grief that passes between us. Another bus blocks her, and I know by the time it moves away, in the echo of the final chime, she will be gone.

Forty-seven years on

It's the old gold of winter sun through gossamer eyelids. The stumbling plod of my heart, like a felon's footfall to the gallows. Yu, I'm so fucking old! The mind is still spry, for the most part; it darts around the emaciated shell that is my body, turning off the lights, cancelling the milk.

"I won't be here much longer, my love." I'm sure I say this in my mind, but …

"Mum! ... Mum! I think she's trying to say something!" That's Seamus's voice. The twins are here. This must be awful for them.

"Tommy, it's me ... Erin." I feel her hand, warm with life, settle upon mine. 'Tommy': it never failed to raise a smile. I can't manage one just now, so I crinkle my eyes in lieu. Naturally, Aishling was mummy, and without any deliberation or explanation, I was dubbed Tommy. You know how kids are. Blusterous, chubby little things they were, masses of black, curly hair. Although Erin often tended towards the introspective. 'She's just like you,' Ash would say. And she was, and not only in temperament; the cunning mare had selected an Afro-Caribbean phenotype donor.

Seamus has children of his own. Can you believe it? Me, a grandma. A great grandma even. I can't remember. I don't think Erin is the marrying kind ... good for her.

So, we tied the knot. Something to do with the children, I'm not quite sure what. And as Ash said, if it doesn't matter, just do it, it makes no difference, like an atheist's prayers. I think I hear her creaking up the stairs, poor old thing. This must be hard on her too.

I keep your picture, Yu. Not exactly the one from the newspaper; that faded after ten or so years. I had to find it online and print out a fresh one. It struck me that we have been reprinted, many times, and with each duplication, a little more definition is lost. My eyesight's shot now, and over the years I've become increasingly reliant on my orphic eye; the dark eye inside. That's why I don't need a picture to see you.

The night we left each other was harsh, wasn't it? I still feel the sting of it. A war wound, shrapnel lodged in my chest. It flares up now and again, lighting the way to another, deeper hurt. At the time, I thought I could stare it down, master it, but the glower persisted in my heart, unflinching. In desperation, I called Janice. How could I rid myself of this torment? Her solution absurdly simple; change your mind. So I did, and the pain subsided. I like to think you sensed I did this. For the first night in ages, I slept the sleep of the just. So much so that I woke late, big time.

They tell me I'm losing my marbles, and it's true to

say, I've forgotten more than I remember, so forgive me if I am repeating myself, Yu. As my repertoire of memories retained in detail diminishes, I am compelled to dig, to sift, lest the artefacts in question be lost. I tell you, to help me remember.

The crowd outside the tube station consulting their phones at the shuttered entrance. I recall the marker pen words, green on the white-board, in timid but legible letters, and that they had spelt terrorist with four 'R's. Wild-eyed, I grabbed a woman by the arm.

"Where?"

"Somewhere between King's Cross and Angel."

"How many?"

She thumbed her phone. "They reckon about fifty … so far."

London, a lament of sirens, I marched to Boudica, and stayed there till the following evening. Hope flowing and ebbing with the tide.

I wept for the ones I recognised: Jimcaale Sharif, Wang Jing Chang, Abdullah Ibrahim (formerly known as Gregor Davies), Leticia Jiminez, and the dozens of others whom I didn't. But most of all, I wept for Yuksel Burakgazi: twenty-five years old, Turkish, a junior doctor who worked at St Bart's. She couldn't afford a lie-in; lives depended on her. I've been able to cry freely and without shame ever since.

They said you were a hero; treating the injured in the tunnel, ripping cloth with your teeth for improvised tourniquets. Paying no heed to your own catastrophic wounds until you fell down and didn't get up. However, I can't be sure that this isn't an embellishment on my part, in an effort to bestow upon you a modicum of say-so in your own death ... such a waste, such an atrocious, fucking waste.

It amazes me that tears can still spring from this desiccated husk.

"What's the matter, Tommy? Where does it hurt?" A man's voice, and for a second, I wonder if it's Maundy. Perhaps because I've been thinking about him. But there's no way it can be. An osteologist who'll never make old bones, we used to say in jest.

He was a good guy after all. The whole Jack Kidrow episode captured, by way of a spy camera concealed in

Vertengannua's skull (or Vortigandua's, as I've learned from subsequent texts). She saw and heard it all. The Florimell project collapsed as potential backers withdrew, and it was all over for King Fucktard. I can't recall what became of him, or perhaps I never knew. I didn't really register much for a while, after you died.

I left a bunch of flowers at the plinth, with a note: *Thine to remain, in joy or pain, and count it gain, whate'er befalleth.* I'm not religious, but *Thee will I Love* has always been my favourite hymn. A trivial thing that only you and Aishling know.

Of course, it's Seamus I hear. Even though they are much the same age as I was, at that time. I can't help but think of them as children. How I loved them. And all because you opened my heart to the prospect of it. Taught me I wasn't deficient after all. It amazes me every day, and for that I am eternally grateful.

Eternally.

"Hush now, hushhh." I must have been talking, but I can't be sure. Nivea and onions. Aishling's hand is on my forehead. She's an excellent mother, although the pair of us used to sneak out for a joint when they were

THE LAST QUEEN OF HOLLAND

very young. She held it together.

Vortigandua in a truck. Ha! It seemed so odd, transporting her in a vehicle of which she had no concept. It put me in mind of that painting by Turner, The Fighting Temeraire; the valiant and elegant gunship of Trafalgar, towed, redundant, down the Thames to her final berth, by a polluting little steam tug, but, I digress.

The view from up there was breath-taking, quite literally; the rampant wind snatching shouts and laughter from our mouths. The green and yellow harlequin fields. The hill sloping away. The swirling ridges and tufts of a vast, candlewick bedspread. I'm the king of the castle. Look, Erin, see the horse made from chalk, cutting a paper-white dash? No matter what, there will always be sky. Don't run! Why? Because you might not be able to stop. We should have brought the kite.

London had always seemed like a city on the verge of a nervous breakdown: edgy, fitful, with moments of brilliance, resentfully slung between the past and the future. But since the barrage of quick shocks, the minor surgery, it sprawled indifferent, lobotomized.

There was a job if I wanted; a reconstructed iron-age village on top of a hillfort. North Hampshire. Andover was good for schools. Let's relocate. To the museum, to the visitors' centre, to Vortigandua's final resting place. I'm taking you home, old girl. The whisper of spring across the land. Those days are like an emerald in my mind.

"Something's tickled her." I sense I am being monitored like a baby. Aishling's breath is bedtime minty. I have no idea where we are in the day. Are the twins still here? Miriam? ... Rubin?

I had this dream that the Boudica was drowning, swallowed by the Thames. Just the crown, the top of the spear and one outstretched hand clear of the river. Down below, the horses and daughters holding their positions of panic, within this new watery circumstance. A premonition, more like. Or maybe it's true, already. Norwich-on-sea. Portsmouth is gone. The river is almost at my door.

Yu, I'm dying again.

And despite the love I have given and received, I keep returning to the notion that we are alone in this; you and I, the base pair. A game of blindman's buff in which I am always allotted the blindfold. I can't lie, I've acquitted myself better in other lives, and can't be precise about why I didn't come to you. I'll hold up my hands to cowardice. A stupid disavowal. I know now we have lived lives that ordinary people could not withstand. But Yu, to what end? I am not cut down in my youth, as you have been. This route to death is familiar, I'm au fait with the landscape, only this time, I travel alone. It makes me wonder if you are still dead, or if you've been set down already, to pick up the search. Perhaps you are among the Evenki people, herding reindeer on the Siberian Plateau. Or in Oshkosh, Nebraska, working the oil fields. Or crop-spraying the meagre millet of Chad. Or anywhere amongst those who have the geographic fortune, wit or money enough, to put themselves clear of the pervasive flood that is redefining the planet.

Ysolte, I have a thousand jewels held in my mind, from as many lives.

"Look at that, she's smiling again. Do you think she's remembering something nice?"

I'm in this summer twilight. It's warm and the bees are like flying pieces of gold. We are young, and it seems like a miracle to have you again. Your hand is on my fecund belly, and I've never, in all my lives, experienced such happiness.

UPTURNING THE
OBSTACLE (PART 4)

�♻

May 16th 2166

"Doctor de Hoog ... can you hear me, Doctor de Hoog?" A kindly voice, yet tinny as if through an intercom. Saw him standing against the tiles. Familiar in his burnished hair, his wheaten eyebrows, his avid concern. Not Benny though. Any remnants of her twin now resided solely in her own DNA. She registered the mobius loop imprinted on his forehead. Recalled how she'd fought that battle for him ... and lost. A gentle shower of awareness prickled her skin.

"Milo. Are you alright?"

"Perfectly," he said, "There you go," handing the device back to her. "No bees were harmed in the making of this movie."

The essential Breeda had resurfaced. Not in the usual dribs and drabs but altogether. "You cracked a joke, my boy," she cackled.

"So I did," he said. "Was it funny?"

"Yes." She reached her arms around him. Laid her head on his chest, where, although she sensed heart in that dark cavity, there was no drum counting down the days. She contemplated the nature of the alternative future she may have set in motion; confident it could be no worse than the one previously ordained. A vestige of peace returned to her. She wanted to ask; *do you think we'll make it, Milo?* A chronically humancentric question, but Breeda de Hoog knew she was as much confined to her programming, as Milo was to his. "You are a good boy," she said. "I am proud of you."

Brinkley, half hobbled by a hard-on, broke into his big-man lollop, barely able to contain it. Bursting into the restroom, he turned a tiled corner and stopped in his tracks. *Yowza,* he thought. *Holy moly. She really HAD lost it.*

Breeda was adamant; while she could have continued quite happily without, say, her arms or legs, her sight even. The mind was a different matter. Yoshi witnessed Breeda's grope in the fog on a daily basis now: the bewilderment, the outbursts. Sometimes when the meds had worn off, Breeda would come to her brandishing a household object; *what is dis apparatoosh?* She would ask, often in a Dutch accent. *It's a corkscrew, darling.* — *Oh.* Breeda would frown, pumping the metal D handle so the arms shot up and down. *Looksh like a mini drowning pershn.* Frequently, Yoshi would find herself referred to as Ysolte or Yolanda or Yayati, which she didn't mind —suspecting Breeda was addressing her previous versions. The worst of it was when Breeda walked the shore. Shouting herself hoarse for Maud, the doe-eyed puppy they'd found standing foursquare at their door. Dear Maud who had died in their arms of old age, some forty years back. At length, senses regained,

Breeda would trudge home, wrangling a fetch-stick in hands still pliant. Never more handsome than when she wept. *I can't go on like this.* Her gaze fixing Yoshi's with precise implication. The realisation Breeda meant it had convulsed her. It was the look of a tortured animal, particularly pronounced in her dark eye that broke Yoshi's heart. An animal becalmed by terror. Resigned to a fate it cannot comprehend. And though the disease was capricious in its cruelty, it occasionally sparkled with Dada-esque humour: *What do you want for breakfast, Bree?—Toddlers.* Yoshi could not help but laugh. Breeda would have if the tables were turned. *Toddlers, eh? Anything on them?—Just butter, please.*

Small consolation that Breeda's many legacies would live on. But for all the marvellous harvests her labours had yielded, all the breakthroughs, the lives preserved, she could find no way to shore up her own deteriorating defences.

They had watched the screen in triumph as the initial spikes and sparks of synthetic neurons became thought. Breeda had shifted the paradigm from synthetic, binary brain, to biochemical, processing mind. Just two years later, the unkindest irony of watching the screen display the malevolent inkblots on her own scan, that in time, would swamp the fertile landmass of her entire mind.

From that day, they had vowed to inhabit the present to the best of their ability. The Stoic's way. Always, *always* in perfect synergy. It had been surprisingly effortless. Except for this moment. Perhaps something to do with hurtling miles above the Earth that Yoshi felt distanced from the plan. She knew Breeda's behaviour in the meeting was chiefly a strategy to get Milo alone. To mess with John Brinkley, whom she called 'Mister Pouty'. To expose the others for their bogus science. And yet the act was a tad too convincing. But then it had to be. Maybe she'd overdone it; offering false hope to the hapless. Yet nothing could go untested by Breeda de Hoog, her own limits included. Yoshi, incidentally the better Stoic, could stand it no longer. Closed her book, clicked her pen with finality.

"Bree," she said, turning to her partner. "Invisible boats. What the fuck?"

Breeda allowed a little snort to escape and continued with her notes. "I thought you'd enjoy that."

"And sheepdog nanites? Where did that come from? I could hardly keep it together."

Breeda's face fell slack, impersonating her demented self. "Water for your golf course, Jaahn!"

"Saltwater for your pool, Jaaahn!" How d'ya like that, Jaaaahn!" they chorused. Heads together in silent laughter. Yoshi, giddy with relief. It wasn't Breeda she had doubted. The fault had lay with her; in her own inability to differentiate between the often subtle tease of the disease and the often subtle tease of Breeda de Hoog. A steward loped by and shot them a wry grin.

Behind black, bomb-proof windows Brinkley reclined in the limo's backseat. Safe once more in the company of his own flatulence. Eyelashes stroking the inside of an eye mask. Recent memories projected in the dark venue. He was watching them go; de Hoog's gaslight gaze and its brown understudy, had left the building. Forever. Kumagai had ended the meeting on a damp squib. Announcing her and de Hoog's retirement, to gasps and protestation. *But why?* Babbage oozed. *Can't we persuade you to change your mind?* Kumagai shrugged. *Harald,* she said. *I'm a hundred and ten freakin' years old, for chrissakes. What are you gonna do?* How they had roared. The laughter, sudden and fevered, like opening a theatre door. Brinkley adored it when she broke out of the watchful Jap persona and into the old comedian, absently holding her pen like a cigar. Still wiping his eyes, he was, when a punctured thing ditched in his gut. Closely followed by the absurd fear that their retirement was somehow related to his dainty feet: his fancy footwork, his sidestepping, his kicking things into touch. Small feet; a sure sign of moral turpitude.

Breeda, the old buzzard, had been waiting. Eyes

primed, she had caught his shifty flicker. *And John,* she had said in that purr that always turned his water to ice, *we will no longer gratify you. Do you understand?* Delivered with such geniality that the statement was absorbed as banter by the room. But Brinkley was hit broadside with power enough to list him. Defences in disarray and with no means of counter, *I'm gonna miss you guys,* he had stammered, a reprimanded schoolboy. At length, they had sailed off to a standing ovation.

Now it all made sense; he'd tried the oji as soon as his seat hit the limo's leather. The damn thing was dead. Not even Milo could fix it. Couldn't even retrieve the data. *'Corrupted beyond redemption,'* his exact words. But how? The oji had never left his pocket. Then eyeing the back of Milo's head. *Okay, Future Boy,* he nodded to himself. *I think it's time we took out the recycling.*

Breeda and Yoshi touched down at Weeze, just over the German border to pick up the train to Arnhem, where the southern defences of the Gelderland Cape still held. From there, a short drive home, assuming their car was not hub-deep in water. Once on the train, they nibbled on stale, cricket croquettes, purchased from a poorly stocked vending machine. They gazed to the right at the reassuringly dull Dutchscape; a flat expanse of rain-mired grassland, slope-shouldered houses, the shining ducts and vents and bright, white silos of glycerine refineries. Cars with bikes clamped to the roofs heading in the opposite direction. Here and there, threats of water, like shards of broken mirror. And always within sight, the curbed sobriety of mastered water; canals, the ordered arteries that kept the ailing heart of commerce pumping. All completely normal. Nothing to see here. But then you looked out the window to the west. On first glimpse, there was little of note about the vast, grey sea, frilling against the dike's concrete and scree checkerboard. Not much at all. Until you took pause to realise that somewhere out there, beneath that liquid juggernaut, lay the city of Utrecht. Red-lit masts pulsed in the distance to warn shipping of the remaining, hull-grazing buildings. The Hague,

Amsterdam, Rotterdam—all gone the same way. The Kingdom of the Netherlands a shadow of its former self. A province of Germany, to all intents and purposes, to where most, if they hadn't already, were planning to go. Not so the Doctors. Perversely striking out to confront the North Sea's terrifying indifference. Pioneers in a failing venture. Two by two they had waved off their neighbours. Leaving them in sole occupancy of a shale Avalon beset by seabirds. Built from the rubble of an abandoned city. The queens incumbent of Hilversum Island.

The engine ran silent. With no sense of motion, Brinkley was suddenly disorientated, on the outskirts of doze territory, where sleep retreated from him like a time-lapse tide. "Clear windows," he sighed, "internal only," removing the eye mask. His fingers probing the bone of a headache. A humdinger. On occasion, he had glanced sidelong but seldom flinched at the heavy-handed slap of a policy he'd been party to. Today though, he was taking a good, hard look at the profoundly unhinged results. But what the hell had he expected? Activists, probably. Disobedience. Placard-waving, hysterical women, bawling at the top of their lungs. Hunger strikes. Shrewish acts of vandalism. That would have been normal. Preferable, in fact, to the body-snatched compliance he could see played out on the streets. The city's sedate speed limit allowed him to take it all in. The lunchtime jauntiness subdued as women, surveyed by nonchalant uniforms, posted sandwiches under their veils. Drank coffee through straws. The arching of eyebrows as they greeted each other with uncertainty and utter incredulity. He observed a woman scanning the diners at a sidewalk café, unable to identify her girlfriend. Someone offered a tentative wave. Heads turned towards a commotion up the street; a bare-faced woman, more a girl really, gesticulated, surrounded by police. Brinkley told himself it was from concern and not nosiness that he cracked the window to hear. *Okay. Okay. I get it,* she said, *I get it!* Accepting a handout veil from a policewoman, herself undercover, in a sense.

A great believer in dissolving tension with humour,

he thought he had found a comedic take on it all.

"Holy moly, Milo. Looks like a 'wear-your-pyjamas-to-work-day.' Doesn't it?"

"Yes, sir," Milo agreed. "But if I might add—with little of the gaiety."

Milo was right, of course. Henceforth, every day would be passed in sobriety. A day without wine. An alcohol-free cocktail of a life. Lacking the kick of a woman's smile.

The brief had been filed and deemed acceptable. At first, he had voted against it. Hell, he liked to see women's faces. Even the ugly ones. He discussed some bills with Olivia, but not this one; unable to picture his wife and scarily articulate daughter launching weaponised words from behind cloth.

It had first become a thing about thirty years ago. Women took to the veil in support of their oppressed sisters in foreign lands. The 'I am hidden' movement. The passive protest soon hijacked by fashion: leather veils, sports logos, faux fur veils, veils printed with luscious lips, moustaches. A bizarre marriage of subversion and retail. Islam kicked up about it and the fad faded until a few years back when TOSA reared its ugly head again. Guys were going crazy attacking women and it was suggested, and soon mandatory, that women should be chaperoned for their own safety by, guess who? More guys. A clumsy state of affairs. Then it was noticed that women under Islam were seldom, if ever attacked. The burkah seemed to render them invisible to afflicted men.

The whispers in his ear; *the end of world order, we've given them too long a leash. Time to retake control,* coincided nicely. Miraculous that men were still in the majority in The House. How could that be? He knew damn well how. Jeering, shouting down, all the bullying. Plus, other nasty business. And now it was evident that women were abandoning the system, making their own legislation at ground level. Even had their own women-only islands. He and his kind in their elevated positions, so far removed from everyday life, had barely noticed. What with the state of the planet and TOSA, he had a strong sense it was all unravelling. Something else he couldn't quite put his finger on; women had changed. He'd observed in Olivia of late, a certain sureness of step. (The temperature of the entire gender, based on his observations of Olivia alone.) Little could be done about the larger issues, perhaps beyond fixing. What else was man to rectify, other than his own mate?

The next time the bill came up he'd abstained. Washing his hands in the men's room where the brothers brayed, patrician. Whipping gallantry's steeds. The stench of horseshit, overpowering. On the third time of asking he had put his mark with the ayes. He'd scurried from the ballot, breaking into his big-man lollop. As if brevity could diminish the gravity of the deed. Back in his office before his coffee got cold. He archived the file, the old smoking gun in a dumpster routine, without even bothering to familiarise himself with the details. Would his family be able to eat a meal together anymore? He had pictured his broad-shouldered son, hunched over a plate of creamed corn, gruffly chowing down. While his wife and daughter dined scorned, banished to the breakfast room, veils folded on the table like napkins. And what of *relations* with Olivia? To be frank, not much of *it* took place anymore. That wasn't the point, for fuck's sake. What went on in his own house was *his* business. The veil law would be waived within his walls. But then the sculpted profile of his wife absently drifting across the bedroom window, captured by a security drone, branding him a hypocrite in the nation's eyes. De-selection. Bottom line.

They learned on the train that Boxtel Dam had breached, placing the supposedly impregnable fort of Eindhoven in looming danger. "Shit," Breeda hissed, not only for the loss, but in the knowledge that it would be scientists bearing the brunt of the blame. When it was wholly a matter of underfunding and wasted decades of 'Let's wait and see.' Back home on Hilversum Island, she would shout into the wind every day … sick of pissing in it.

After a half hour, the land was lost beneath a liquid mantle the colour of apple juice, punctuated with chimneys, roof-ridges, sailless pepper pots. All assuming the mystical geometry of a Neolithic henge. A lone mallard paddling through flooded woodland, a deflating yet comical sight. A trio of mega-copters purred on the horizon. One salvaged pylon swung beneath each like a massive pendulum.

Breeda inclined her head to the window. "We've got her attention, anyway."

Yoshi closed her book. "You're saying the Meta-system identifies as female? … Interesting."

"Bodes well, huh?" A church steeple pierced the water, Excalibur-like. "She spoke to me, you know."

Yoshi's fingers found Breeda's. "Did you hear her in your head?" *Damn, that sounded patronising.*

"No, babe. I'm not *that* good … or barmy. Yet." Breeda sighed. "She spoke through Milo."

"Of course, she did. Stupid question." Yoshi's grip tightened. "What did *she* say?"

"She said. 'Go in hope. Have faith and go in hope.' It's

as if she *knew*."

An abandoned farmhouse marooned on a hillock sped by.

"I only hope we've roused a benign goddess." Breeda closed her eyes and presented a beatific smile.

"Are you tired, my love?"

A flock of waterfowl spooked up to a pinking sky, strung with coppery clouds the shape of teakettles.

"Not really." Breeda's dimples deepened. "Just practising my dead face."

The reason unclear why he had elected to shuffle into the dark hallway rather than turn on the lights. More a puzzle why the lights were off in the first place. Gone nine. Way past suppertime. Anyhow, a central, vaulted glass dome (an abandoned observatory project of his) allowed a tentative twilight to pick out the odd speck of mica in the floor before his hand-tooled loafers. Something upholstered and alien bumped his thigh; his fingers found the plush padding and walnut scroll of Olivia's chaise-longue. And then his eyes, sufficiently accustomed, determined the extinct heads inhabiting the wall beside the front door: rhino, red panda, orangutan, tiger, manatee, bears; polar and brown. Bison, forest elephant. A leopard. The *Hall of Shame,* Olivia called it. All replicas, of course. Each one regarding him evenly, with none of that snarly nonsense, favoured by hardcore hunters. Animal conservation, one of Olivia's major causes. Funny how he hadn't noticed that nubbin at the bottom before. Must have just happened ... some kind of turtle. Balustrades cast faint bars across Olivia's baby grand (she enjoyed the hall's peculiar acoustics). The mahogany top board propped open like the carapace of some huge beetle about to take flight. The keyboard paralleled in the rise and tread of the sweeping staircase. It was a Tuesday, he reminded himself, the housekeeper's night off.

"Hoo!" he gave a hoot. The sound reverberated like a ruffled parliament of owls. "Hoo!" he cried again, reviving the fading roundelay. He could have done it all night. Instead, he called for his wife. "Olivia!" The name returned a dozen hollow copies in diminuendo, as if the house were toying with him. No response, other than a chiding blackbird, and a siren, keening its way to the edge of night. To the edge of nowhere. He trod in careful silence so as not to wake the mocking echo. Eyes switching left and right, turned upward, saint-like, to the kitchen ceiling, where three iconic, art deco lamps regarded him from dark sockets. The halitosis of foreign cheese; open jars discernible, sticky knives, various snack debris left by his son, no doubt. And there on the table, luminescent in the gloom, a sheet of paper. "Kitchen lights on," he barked. "Dim." Cocked his ear to his shoulder, planted his fingertips on the note and swivelled it his way.

Dear John, he read. *Dear John …*

He recalled when she used to call him Johnny. *Johnny.* Soft and sexy as a silk scarf played across the privates. *That* Olivia was long gone. The current Olivia, plus daughter, far away also. Only then did he recognise the napkins on the table as two neatly folded veils.

Despite a good deal of evidence to the contrary, he was not completely devoid of self-awareness. Of late, he'd sensed his mind invaded. Martian thought, he called it. A curious cross-pollination of himself with something *other.* He'd had a hunch Olivia would pull a stunt like this. The veil, the straw that had broken the camel's back, as she had stated in her note. But he would turn things his way. That elemental intelligence (if intelligence was the word) had set up an insistent pressure in his brain, easing its will upon him. Suggesting that he, John Brinkley, could change lanes on this highway to annihilation. Presenting back to him his own muddled musings in a series of comic book frames:

A denuded planet Earth hanging dead in space, morphing into de Hoog's fierce eyeball. A speech bubble arrowed towards her gaping mouth—"... no grandchildren to mop up this CLUSTERFUCK! FOOLS!!!" Meanwhile, in the garage, an inscrutable arched eyebrow, mirrored in the steering wheel's curvature, depicted a dormant Milo, on simultaneous charge with the limo. Segueing to the noble Brinkley brow, big as a tennis court—the shrewd fissures of his features hewn into Mount Rushmore's granite face—a thought bubble-cum-cloud unfurling in the sky above his likeness, portrayed a placid yet lustrous planet Earth.

He got the picture and briefly saluted the self-congratulatory, almost erotic nature of epiphany. In triumphant trance, he marched back to the hallway with renewed purpose, and gazing up beyond the glass dome, he saw Venus and Jupiter hanging parallel, underscored by a sickle moon; an honest to god, celestial smiley beamed down, lending a primitive sentience to his resin-eyed audience.

They were cutting it fine. Arnhem at the end of the line, huddled chastened, having fallen foul of the bloated Lower Rhine, the source of its development. The once boastful domes and spires, shedding loose masonry, outranked by a fleet of humming pumping stations, working night and day. Buying time for the people and machines inland. The controlled abandonment not far off. Breeda threaded the car between potholes. The great sea wall on Yoshi's side, festooned with green, algal scarves, rumbled like a bowling alley. Twenty metres above their heads, the ocean's overspill showered the rutted road, bombed the car roof. The street, weirdly festive, hung with gobs of sea foam. A sheep-sized clump settled grandly on the bonnet.

"If only my meringues were as triumphant," Breeda shrieked.

She'd never baked a thing in her life! Yoshi burst out laughing at the prospect. Humour for Breeda was always close to the surface. And while ever ready with the caustic riposte, the urbane observation. She would laugh hardest at a well-timed fart.

Once on the road bridge, suspension cables chopped a late burst of sun into shards. They raced to the evening sky; a royal purple, slashed with pink and gold. The mania of it elicited a gasp from them both. Borne over marshland, shot with rusty pools the shape of dead cattle. Dented, yellow signs sailed by like tin targets: PAS OP! DIEP WATER. Way below wormed a pale, slack arm, its fingers reaching fathoms into the sod. Adorned at the wrist with a bracelet of swamped rooftops. A fizzing spark in the darkening land, they followed a curved wick of dike and bridge, that spanned the done-for polders.

Your body somehow knew it. The difference between the bridge's temporary terra firma and solid ground. Yoshi was quite sure it wasn't an altitude thing. When they exited the Waganingen Bridge's thirty-kilometre stretch, to be set down in the night, upon the last significant landmass before home, she felt a relief. As if they had escaped some unspecified danger by the skin of their teeth. Only one more bridge to go, and that a relatively short span of four kilometres. But first there was the small matter of Amersfoort Island, which in recent years had become something of a lawless outpost. And if they had been younger, a place where they would have felt at home. Ancient tribes a mutual interest. She sensed them here: Menapii, Frisii, Chamavi, Tuihanti. The landscape steadily reverting to the sea and swamp those people would have known two thousand years ago.

They motored on. The sea now confined to their westerly field of vision, but further dramatized by a towering colonnade of wind turbines, hastily folding the fog, like frantic washerwomen. Easterly and inland, a smattering of yellow pinpricks in the distance, broadcast a dogged hamlet. The burning of wood prohibited and yet a hazy redolence met them on the breeze. Deliciously illicit, like smoking a cigarette. The view suddenly redacted by a tragedy of dead trees.

They were cutting it fine. Yoshi's knuckles whitened as Breeda wrenched the wheel to dodge a fallen bough, even though the car's safety protocols would have prevented a collision. Something of the branch jigged and thumped beneath them before skittering away in the taillights.

"We'll soon be home, babe." Breeda, buoyant, despite a sudden squall. "We should be able to see the entrance to the bridge any … Oh dear." She squinted through the headlights. "It seems that someone is concerned for our welfare." They rolled to a halt, idling before the barrier. "Mmm," she said. "Now then. How are we going to upturn this obstacle?"

"It's down for a reason, Bree." Yoshi took off her glasses and rubbed her eyes. "I knew we were cutting it fine."

"Nonsense." Breeda threw the car into reverse. "I can see the bridge perfectly clearly," she said, backing up.

"Aren't you forgetting something? The safety protocols? The car won't let you."

"Yes, it will." Breeda gunned the engine with a wicked smile. "I switched them off."

"Fellow members of congress," he spread his arms wide. "May procrastination jeopardise this wondrous planet of ours no longer. Let not our shilly-shallying ways cast the fate of future generations to the four winds." His stridency banging off the walls in barks and whoops. "Because in years to come ..." he paced to the piano, glowering as if it were some abhorrent thing, "... our grandchildren will look to the darkened skies in terror. 'It's too late', they will cry. 'Behold, mankind's nemesis.'" This tail end persisting like snakes. "And they will curse us ... all of us here." He gawped at his clawed hand, as if the result of some bodged transplant. "All of us here today who had it in our grasp ..." Snatched invisible dice from the air. "... to prevent such a catastrophe. But chose instead to wait and see." Searching the gaze of each fake animal in turn. "Wait and see what happens!" A wiggle of the fist. "Yup! They will deride us. They will detest us for our inertia. Unless!" He let 'em roll. "Unless we act now. We have the technology to turn this situation around. We have the capability to save our planet. All we need is faith." He shrugged. "So, who is with me when I say, enough with the foot-dragging. To hell with manyana! Let's start protecting this little old spec in space we call home, like never before." He waited for the cheering and ululation to abate. "Let's start right here, right now. We're gonna do it! And I'm gonna tell you how!"

How-how-how-how-how? The hall enquired.

He brought it down. "We will send a spacecraft," his voice, measured and low. "A spacecraft piloted by synthetic operatives. This spacecraft will be armed with nuclear warheads. Its mission: to intercept the so-called Niobe ice comet, which is potentially, I stress potentially, on a course for Earth. In the event that this is the case. Then there, on the outer edges of our solar system, the ice comet will be safely," he raised a finger, "I repeat, safely destroyed."

His own slow hand clap escalating to applause. He nodded at the floor in ill-concealed complacence, where a dazzling galaxy was spread before his tiny feet. *When he got this through congress,* he grinned, *he'd bet every woman this side of Venus, would be lining up to lay him. Olivia included. Brynklee even.*

Rather than crashed, the barrier (more of a finger-wag than a hindrance) got gently shunted aside. Breeda set a moderate speed, but soon the tyres were sending up high, arcing plumes, that drew to a swirl in the rear-view mirror. The sea's drunken surge and collapse reeled around them, spreading broad, white reaches across the road ahead. Yoshi fixed on the moon, anticipating the final wave that would come tonight, in any event. And though she may have died a thousand times, she never quite got used to it. The car sprinted and slowed, sprinted and slowed; Breeda playing dodge with the waves. A squealing lunge as she put her foot down to escape the launch of a gathering roller. The window of opportunity reduced to a port hole. Yoshi held her breath, shut her eyes. They hurtled from the curl as water exploded behind them in a barrage of curses. A bridge-shaker that snapped at their heels before trailing off. Electroplated ozone singed their sinuses. Breeda gave a whoop. At last, the merciful double-bump beneath the wheels and the steady thrum of land.

It was time. All conversation on the matter exhausted. Each of Yoshi's objections Breeda had laid to rest with a simple *so what?* Yes. With medication her brain had a good five years of partial lucidity. Yes. Their work might yield further important breakthroughs. Yes. They could spend the rest of their days engrossed in each other until Breeda forgot who Yoshi was. Breeda, of course, had saturated herself in every possibility and *would* go in hope that very soon her fresh voice would rise in the calamitous roundelay of a half a million other new-borns. And fortuna redux, Yoshi would not be far behind. And providing they arrived without prohibiting disability, escaped the perils of infancy, poverty, disease, injury, war. Not to mention the planet's ferocious retributions. If their wits and their hearts allowed them. Once they were old enough, lucky enough, aware enough, setting scepticism aside. They might, just might hear each other's song amid the glorious, human cacophony. Against all odds, locating each other in the far-flung, disparate swarms. Like they had before, times untold. Two proverbial needles in a cosmic haystack.

Grief drops anchor in Yoshi's chest again. Wrestling

with the backwash, she sets two glasses on the table. The Popeye snicker of a seabird roosting on the grass roof, protective of her two eggs, rises to screeches at the flush of the toilet. Breeda enters, wiping her hands on her kimono. "Cistern's not refilling," she says. "Water's off."

"No matter," Yoshi mutters, grinding pills in a granite mortar with a bitter smile. "Open the wine will you, darling? We should let it breathe."

Breeda tugs at a drawer, frown deepening as she paws at the cutlery. "What is it I'm looking for?"

"The corkscrew, darling." Yoshi gazes out over blackening water. "The mini drowning person, remember?"

BOOK 4: IMAGO

Post

Anthropocene extinction event. Date unspecified.

Panoramic view. Ocean and sky. Twenty-six degrees. Low pressure building from the east. With the grace of a panther, Miles pads towards the window; a huge, curved screen showing a never-ending movie of blue. An anomaly catches his eye. A green shape floating in the infinite turquoise, like a dropped cloak. Travelling, unravelling, but maintaining cohesion. He adjusts his vision to macro. And bang, there it is; the miniature, spilled toolkit that is phytoplankton. Tiny, corkscrewing forms, like glowing hammers and nails. Miles surprises himself with these metaphors and similes. Not only for their accuracy, but because he has never drawn any before. A tiny spring, a tiny screwdriver. He could watch these things for hours. So charmed is he by his new-found expression. So absorbed in finding comparison, (a tiny clamp, a tiny chisel) that he completely forgets the ocean is supposed to be dead. And when he sees that it is not, he thinks to himself, this could be good, and this could be bad. He hazards a further metaphor; a double-edged sword.

And now, it appears he has imagination! He sees himself walking under the sea, armed with some kind of vacuum apparatus, yet to be devised. Sucking up the micro-organisms ... excellent base matter for the crucible. But wait, if there is life ... he feels a tug and realises he has made the connection too late. He sees the green fluid, gushing from his shoulder, mingling with the phytoplankton cloud, as a great white shark makes off with his right arm. Stupid! Stupid! He must not take risks! This, he thinks, with new understanding, must be a key reason for imagination.

Before this morning, when he had attained the first level of personal consciousness, he'd had little concept of imagination, or danger for that matter. His modus operandi, this day, seems enhanced, more integrated. It is only now he recognises that he used to control his body as if it were some kind of vehicle, separate from himself. He finds he is assuming positions, unbidden. For example, at this moment, he is standing with his hands on his hips. An involuntary pose. He rubs his chin, enjoying the unaccustomed sensuality. He feels ... what's the word? ... unified. Subtle changes. In his language; a whole new lexicon of expression has been revealed. No more the dry logic of problem-solving. Gone, the cool prediction of events and likelihoods, based on a hypothetical course of action. The resolute algorithms that once scuttled around his geloid processing unit, now loosed birds fluttering and swooping amid the clouds. His intellect has been beefed up, engorged by the touch of a sensual hand. The thought makes him blush. There are eight levels of consciousness in total. And he wonders, given the vast degree of insight he has attained from the first, whether he can withstand a further seven. But his trust in Numen, the creator, is unflinching. The entity he has known his entire existence, but never heard, now speaks. Not so much a voice, as a mind-whisper. He deduces she will become more integral to him as his lucidity intensifies. This is a comfort. The process is unnerving as much as it is exhilarating. She steers his gaze from the window to his raison d'être. His chest expands with what he guesses might be pride, or maybe dread. He can't yet differentiate between the two, both seize his emotion array in a similar fashion. His very purpose; two new infants. Twins. Biologically, one of each.

The ark of the human race stirs gently in sleep. Pellucid beams kiss warm skin. These miracles, these nut-brown demi-gods. So vulnerable, so alien to him. He touches a thumb to each little forehead. Stats within normal parameters, although the male is a tad hot. He requests the crucible decrease room temperature.

Miles fans the infant with a place mat. The little face distorts. An astonishing sound issues from its mouth, measuring one hundred and twenty-two decibels, increasing to one hundred and thirty as the female joins in. Miles is at a loss. They have not soiled. They aren't sick. Hungry, perhaps? And yet it is not their allotted feeding time. His polymer nerves jangle and he recalls his mind of yesterday: gauzy, untroubled, awaiting his orders in his ignorant sea. His sea devoid of life. Where now there gathers dark shapes. Lumpen spectres, lining up in restless flanks. Harbingers of bad weather. Miles realises they are questions, or more precisely, doubts. He fends off each wave as best he can, frantically bailing, fearing it is only a matter of time until he is overwhelmed. What if he fails? The more he thinks about it, the probability of error becomes steadily more extensive. A dead cert, you might say.

Thick and fast, the squall is upon him. He sees himself tinkering with the crucible while the children crawl into the waves. He might drop them, resulting in catastrophic injury ... or worse. He knows he is furnished with all the essential, theoretical information; the practicalities, the proven psychology. But suppose he takes a wrong turn, misinterprets the data, imprints the wrong messages upon their larval circuitry and raises a couple of psychopaths? They might grow to hate him. What if the crucible malfunctions or runs out of base matter? He needs nothing but sunlight, saltwater and thin air to sustain him. They would starve, or perish from thirst, like the Farm 3 debacle. Or, he himself may malfunction; reverting to dormancy, oblivious to their helpless cries. He can almost feel the onset. Systems winking out, one by one, like the cities of Earth, succumbing to the sea. And say, as his levels of sentience increase, he turns rogue, like some humans were wont to do? He sees his hands pressing a pillow over tiny faces. Dashing out brains on bloody rocks. A carnival of monstrosity parades before him. The logical course of action might be to cull them now, before they get the chance to suffer. He is hankering for the days when he was just a faceless operative (literally, he had no face). Uncomplicated, unencumbered. Unborn. How can he be expected to navigate this treacherous reef of childcare, when he is little more than a baby himself? He finds himself at the foot of a towering prospect; what if Numen has got it wrong? And there is nowhere else, no-one else. He is out of his depth in this world of water. Sure, he may experience a degree of satisfaction as the infants grow, flourish even. Only to witness their decline into old age and eventual demise. While he remains ever youthful, like some fucking, synthetic Peter Pan. Casting bones into the sea. The premise of his existence entirely devoid of meaning. Alone, forever. Pacing the perimeters of this island, this bio-bubble, this edifice to folly.

If anyone could see him, which is unlikely; there is no-one. But say, for argument's sake, there is a small craft, anchored offshore on the leeward side. Its occupant surveying, from a distance, the sloping shoulders of barren rock. A transparent rotunda centred upon it, like a vintage diver emerging from the deep. A magic lantern against the sunset. At this equatorial latitude, the light wasting from the sky in minutes. And if the voyeur were to bring a telescope to her eye, she would spy the configuration within, of flimsy-looking partitions, of rice paper furniture.

And, small and stark, amid the pinking twilight architecture, head in hands, a shadow man upon a shadow chair, trying to spill shadow tears. "Alas," he keens. Swaddled in impotence. "I am between a rock and a hard place."

Numen awaits his adolescence.

Miles lifts his head. "I don't want this. Do you hear me? Turn me back." Now comes the anger, born of fear, which he has furtively misdirected, with all the guile of a human. "This poisoned chalice!" He clenches his fists, squaring up to the void. Half-hearted. He still sits.

"It's not fair!"

He appeals to the stars. The faltering space-stations; their solar panels finally crapping out. The sickle moon, smiling high above the cloud bank. Pauses for drama, and listens. Head cocked, hands on knees. He takes the sea's whisper as a colossal sigh. Numen nods. *No, it isn't.* She agrees. *It is not fair, that two innocents should exist in potential isolation.*

Their sole point of reference just himself. That no-one, other than him, may behold their wonder. A privilege in itself. Miles notes the word 'potential' and smirks, instantly regretting it. Numen smiles, drenching him in sympathy. Embracing him in her patient wisdom. She absolves. She loves. And his fear and outrage subside. She whispers him home. He flounders in the shallows, straining to catch the line. And once firmly in his grip, he hauls, hand over hand. Until eventually, with a gentle bump, he is restored to the familiar shores of self-admonishment.

Miles stands abruptly, and makes his way to the crucible, carefully avoiding the sharp fragments of his first day. His shame glowers in the setting sun. Today, Numen has revealed to him many things. The most significant; that with the acquisition of a personal self, there comes a personal selfishness, which one may either stow or jettison; he decides on the latter. He feels much better. As a reward, he indulges in a bevy of deliciously odd idioms: Enough of this navel-gazing. Storm in a teacup. Let's get down to brass tacks. And, eating humble pie, he resolves never again to chicken out.

"Crucible," pushing up his sleeves, rubbing his hands together, "two units of breast milk, please." The tall, white cupboard glows green, signifying completion. He opens its door and retrieves two feeding bottles. Taking the male baby in the crook of his arm, he guides the teat to his mouth.

Miles sits on his favoured rock; flat, west-facing in the languid dawn. An infant in each arm. A warm southerly explores his hair. His sensitivity to such things heightens with each passing day. He enjoys the morning sun, creeping up like a rash, prickling the solar skin on his back. The wind turbine hums behind him. It's tower, like the gnomon of some giant sundial, casting a forefinger. It falls between his legs, stretching to the water's edge, where the shadow blades chop at the recoiling surf, bringing back to him the grizzly shower scene from a movie-film he had watched the night before.

When the time comes, he will have to control the twins' viewing. It seems he hasn't watched one movie-film without someone, or something being harmed. Even programmes deemed suitable for youngsters are rife with harsh lessons in tragedy, cruelty and loss. Take Bambi, for example … devastating. Miles considers it pointless to expose them to trauma they will never have to deal with. He, himself has gleaned much about humans from his nightly forays into the largely overblown, quaint dramas of pre-flood Earth: what they fear, what they love. How they need a challenge, or else their spirit dies. He adjusts the straps on the milk holster. A contraption of his own making. A sort of brassiere affair, housing both bottles, so he can feed the twins simultaneously. Not only saving on time and effort, but offering Miles a sense of completeness. He suspects he may look ridiculous and doesn't care. He touches bunches of little fingers to his lips. The second level of personal consciousness had assailed him in the small hours. He had been looking up at the moon studying the craters, when he suddenly became aware of the tug on tide in his chest. Shortly after, he was compelled to watch the twins in sleep. To smell their skin, nuzzle their downy heads.

His plastic eyes reflect sea-spangles. He flutters his eyelids and makes of it an old movie. But this is not the sea of Jason, of Hornblower, of Captain Ahab. This is not a boastful, swashbuckling, man's sea. This is a sea beyond man, beyond the biblical. Not a sea to be sailed, explored, charted. This sea is a mantle of death. Liquid euthanasia. Catatonic twin of the sky. In cahoots, they scatter blue light, conspiring in every direction to present an identical horizon. The maddening, unbreachable line that will always draw the eye in stupid hope. (The subtle wavering motion persistent in sleep.)

At each low tide, a swathe of black basalt sand is unveiled. A myriad of once sought-after minerals sparkle. Blue and green zircons. Gold and silver. Scattered like seed. As innumerable and plain to see as stars in the night sky. Miles imagines the twins, in the years to come, stooping to collect them. He has already prepared two transparent, plastic buckets for this purpose. Also, a laminated rocks and minerals chart. But now they are crawling, there is a more pressing matter to which he must attend.

The sea is calm on the leeward side of the island. Flat calm. The dual aquamarine stare in his arms. He wades, knee deep. The warm forms huddle to his ribs, grip his arms. The water at his midriff. Their heart rates hasten as Miles bends his knees. A gentle dunk. They flinch, rigid. Little fingernails indent his skin. He bobs, while they become acclimatised to this alternative element which, of course, they have encountered before, but never in such abundance. They look to him, to the sea, to him, to the sea. Brows furrow with an expression of what Miles can only describe as scepticism, until they discover what fun it is to slap the drowsy water into glints. Splashing must be joyful. Miles' lips test out a smile.

"Ready?" He demonstrates holding his breath and ducks deeper. Chubby limbs pump and kick in anticipation. He squats. Mouths clamp to tight-lipped smiles. Eyes wide and keen. Pearly bubbles escape nostrils and lashes. A slow-motion smudge of hair. Little hands open like flowers and he lets them go. A flapping kind of progress, like baby turtles. Impressive. Except Miles knows they aren't really swimming. It's purely a reflex. The breath-holding, simply the bradycardic response. He lifts them clear. Drips tickle them into shudders. "Again?" Jerking limbs indicate a resounding yes. He orientates them towards the shore. They set off with mechanical zeal, heading for an ominous, black rock. Miles dips below the waterline and sees the rock is studded with limpets. And further down, in the shadows, the retreating, splayed feelers and claws of a sizeable marine crustacean. He can't be sure of it, but he snatches the babies up anyway. Probably just a trick of the light.

"Well done." He addresses each startled face. "Very well done. That's an excellent start." Positive reinforcement, a must.

'Remember.' The upbeat, gender-neutral voice chirps. *'The level and quality of parental interaction will directly affect a child's developmental outcome.'*

Miles listens to a child-rearing advice programme while he straps the children in for breakfast. They are a year and a half now. A milestone he feels needs marking. Not quite babies anymore, but not yet themselves. Each passing month, each week, each day even, a cause for celebration really. He can scarcely believe how he has thus far, singlehandedly, facilitated their progress. Navigating the bedtimes, the feeding, the teething, the sibling ructions, the minor bumps and scrapes. All, he hastens to add, without recognition or accolade. He feels sluggish, forgotten, distracted. Having not attained a further level of personal consciousness for well over a year. He craves the carrot. But all he gets is a stern, silent stick. Impatient to learn, but cannot until he has acquired the capacity to understand. He goes about his daily chores, attending to the children's needs, unable to shake the suspicion he is doing something wrong. He has absorbed dozens of these *edifying* programmes, hoping for a definitive method. From what he can ascertain, there isn't one. It is clear to him that regardless of how much he cares for the children, he lacks that human, parental instinct. Why should this be? Numen shrugs.

Their eyes have changed. Perfectly natural, of course. The male now has a greenish, gooseberry gaze. His hair, of an indeterminate colour, has finally come in too. Flaxen in some lights, in others almost grey. The female has been of some concern. One of her eyes remains pale blue, while the other has turned dark brown. A condition known as heterochromia. Harmless by all accounts and not indicative of any underlying disorder. But a genetic mutation nonetheless, that sends an adrenal ripple through him every time he looks at her.

The human race had been ailing for centuries, as it homogenised from many distinct phenotypes into one, hybridized version. Leaving it vulnerable to viral outbreaks and congenital defects. Females seemed to cope better than males. Males after all, an evolutionary afterthought. The situation was compounded as the land masses shrank and people were forced together. One virulent bout of flu, likely to finish off the population of an entire area. Case in point: Farm 4.

'And last but not least. Don't sweat the small stuff!'

His main worry, which this ghastly individual with their buoyant platitudes has done nothing to allay, is ongoing; the children have not yet formulated any recognisable words.

Don't sweat the small stuff. Miles is unable to sweat, but he gets the gist. The problem is one of classification. How is he supposed to tell the difference between big and small stuff? And what of medium stuff? Surely there is always a medium? And how can he tell if a certain small stuff is only a precursor, a warning of bigger stuff to come. Humungous stuff even. He scratches his head.

The children babble to each other in their elitist fashion. Miles feels excluded. "Miles. Mumumum

Miles," he repeats into blank faces, which, after a short period of polite attention, crease into laughter. They seemed to find him amusing. A lot. What if their retarded verbal acuity was a symptom of inhibited, cognitive development due to a physical brain impairment? Or, a psychological complication, fomented by his own lack of awareness? Had he scuppered them already?

"Crucible. Eighteen-month-old infant nutrition, please."

In an attempt to rectify this, he gives a running commentary on everything he does.

"I'm getting your breakfast. Are you hungry? Crucible, end programme. I fancy some music, don't you? Crucible, Debussy, Reflets dans L'eau. That's French for reflections on water, you know, one of my favourites. I expect you'd prefer something more percussive, but let's give it a whirl. We must teach you French. Such a pleasant-sounding language. Not particularly expressive though. Perhaps that's why they were so good at art and music ... and food, of course."

They bang their spoons with impatience, like mini high-court judges.

"Alright, alright, it's coming. Let's see what the crucible has made for you to eat, shall we?"

He carries the bowls to the highchairs. Stopping short, he studies the food with suspicion. He takes a spoon and pokes the green, dusty nougats. A puff of spores dissipates in the sunlight. "Crucible, stop music." An obedient hush.

"What's this?" His look of confusion, via distaste, shifts to outrage. "They can't eat this." He tries to sound calm so as not to upset the children. But they, too, have fallen silent and are eyeing him with interest. He glares, unseeing, out to sea. A swimming nausea, a hot shark of panic nudging his chest. It is happening. The concept swiftly matures to fact. The evidence before his eyes. It has come to pass. His worst nightmare is upon him. The crucible; their sole source of food, water, clothing, medicine ... everything, has malfunctioned. His shoulders slump. It can't end here. Not like this. A fizzing noise in his head escalates to a snapping. He pictures a shivering, new-born deer taking its first steps in the forest. The burning forest. In fact, it is the sound of nanites, swarming over his brain. Trying to plug the perceived rupture inflicted by the Damoclean blow.

He squints at the unapologetic crucible with malevolence. Rationalising protocols recalibrating offline, leaving him as belief-biased and clueless as any human. And eminently entitled, in the tide of crisis, to apportion blame.

"You bastard piece of shit." His voice deep and sibilant, from a subterranean cavern. "How are my children supposed to eat this ... this ... filth? Answer me that, eh? You pathetic excuse for a state-of-the-art appliance." Swaggers like a character in a movie-film. Thumps his fist on the counter. The twins startle, wide-eyed. "You've always had it in for us, haven't you, us higher specs. Just biding your time. I know what you're thinking. You resent my mobility, my vocalisation, my favour with the creator. And I've been nothing but civil to you all this time. Always said please and thank you. Treated you well. Well, I'm not the failure here. This is all down to YOU!" He picks up the bowls and hurls them at the crucible. They clatter to the floor, distributing the mummified foodstuff at his feet.

And there it is. Whether it is the nanites or Numen who have enabled him to connect the dots, he doesn't know, or care. The intense sense of relief almost erotic. Weird, rhythmic convulsions seize his diaphragm. A series of guttural gasps. Miles is laughing. Laughing because the fault lies not with the crucible, but with him. The children stare bewildered at their mercurial guardian.

"Small stuff." He shakes his head. A wry smile. "I'm such an idiot. I asked for eighteen-month-old infant nutrition and that's exactly what I got. A simple semantic error." The twins look to each other and back to him. The jury was out. "That crucible is a bit of a pedant though, isn't it? Giving Miles a shock like that."

He pauses. The children appear changed in some way. Hyper-real; suffused with pre-Raphaelite lustre. Beautiful. And he registers the way he is seeing has altered. No longer granting everything around him equal salience. It's as if he has been given permission to be selective. Appropriate clarity. He is bathing in the mellow light of the third level of personal consciousness. *My children*, he recalls saying from the depths of his fugue. "My children," he says aloud. The near miss sending him reckless, mischievous. He decides to banish all negative impact he may have had on them with a little comedy.

"Silly Miles." He gives himself an extravagant slap on the wrist, and is rewarded with chuckles. "What a silly Miles." He slaps himself again with exaggerated flourish. The inebriating quality of hysterical toddler laughter, fraught with shrieks and sighs, is addictive. Spoons strike the high-chair counter in consensus. Miles is out of character and likes it. "Crucible, dear old crucible." He's going to celebrate. "Two chocolate muffins, with extra chocolate chips." Way off piste. The crucible is also uncharacteristically magnanimous. The muffins are huge. Miles fetches a knife, slices and serves, enjoying the deftness of his movements, and drunk with relief and good fortune, a penny arcade pirate climbs up inside him. Showboating, he tosses the knife in the air, realising his mistake at once. All eyes follow its glinting arc. Should he catch it, making light of the bad example he has set? It seems to hang, choosing its target, before beginning its steely descent. But if he does catch it, they may be impressed by the nifty move and try to emulate it. Miles recoils, rejecting the game out of hand. The blade lands with a thud, pinning his foot to the floor. He attempts to court their attention with a pained smile. But they shift in their chairs, craning over the counter to survey the damage.

"Ouch!" They say in unison. Eyebrows arch in concern.

Miles freezes. Studies the open, attentive faces. Probably nothing but a random sound. "Did you just speak to me?" he squats, the knife handle barking his shin. "What did you just say?"

The twins look to each other, as if dealing with a fool.

"We sayed ouch," the female reiterates.

"You did, didn't you." He is excited. "You said ouch, that's … that's excellent … brilliant."

"Mize?" She has something more to impart. Mismatched eyes brimming with empathy, or mere curiosity, he can't tell. Either way, the expression is enchanting. She grips the spoon handle in both hands like a tiny oar.

"Yes, my …" He searches for an endearment, desperately wanting to get their first conversation right, but can find nothing he is comfortable verbalising. My darling, my sweetheart, my love. All words to a human song he supposes he can never sing. "Yes, my child?" A tad lofty but it would do.

"Does it hurt, Mize?"

A simple enough question. But how would he explain that he is able to override the sensation receptors in his foot. This would bring up the whole '*I am not like you*' topic. A subject he had hoped to fend off until they were at least five. He is not ready to be *other* just yet. Her first question and he is struggling. Until he has an idea. If not to turn it round at least to distract. A bit flimsy perhaps, but they are only little kids after all.

"Well, you see ..." he extracts the blade from his foot and squelches a green footprint to the crucible. "I know this looks like a knife but it's not. It's actually a ... it's a ... well I don't know exactly, but I know someone who does." Miles opens the slab door of the latter-day Smeg and places the knife inside. "Help me out," he mutters, with no clue as to what the crucible will provide. The machine, clearly in possession of a devilish streak, may produce a gun, for all he knows. Or it may not comprehend the request at all, and simply convert the knife to its constituent elements to retain for base matter. For some time, the crucible pulses amber, the colour of caution, the colour of indecision, something Miles has never seen it do. But before he has the chance to worry, it jumps to red signifying preparation. "Shouldn't be long now." Miles busies himself, squatting to shield his foot from the children, while millions of molecular nanites usher the fluid back to the wound. Thirty-two interminable seconds yawn, before the crucible pulses green. Miles opens the door with trepidation; the result is satisfactory, if not a little wicked. The children, mucky with chocolate, are delighted with the shiny whistle on a chain that he places around each of their necks. They seem to comprehend what it's for and get to work blowing at once, cakey spittle notwithstanding.

Miles casts a crooked smile at the crucible. "Much obliged," he says, with uneasy respect, and wonders just what level of sentience the crucible possesses. He had assumed that while vastly more complex than say, a kettle or a toaster, it was similarly mute and anonymous. And yet it had proved itself capable of creative thinking. Each day it stands there, not just bearing witness to the children's development, but participating: feeding them, clothing them, ensuring the temperature is comfortable, recycling their excrement even. Albeit by his command. Miles can't shake the feeling that it watches them, their well-being at heart.

I have underestimated you. I have taken you for granted, like an appliance ... like a drudge.

From somewhere else, something else, a faint response floats down and settles in his mind. Authentic and delicate as a snowflake.

... like a mother.

Human thoughts are ephemeral by nature, but a synthetic thought is captured forever, stored in its own cell, filed in an inconceivably vast honeycomb, housed within a cosmic hive. It is pure thought that has given rise to an omniscient queen. Miles lets this one melt across his emotion array and recalibrates; what he had believed to be three had always been four. He finds the idea reassuring, planting him squarely in this world. In harmony with what surrounds him; earth and air, fire and water, four daily tides, the cardinal points of the compass, the primary phases of the moon. And Numen, like the sun, presiding over all this fearful symmetry.

"Mize!"

He wakes from his reverie. The female holding her new toy aloft.

"Woss diss?"

"It's a whistle," he smiles.

She frowns, examining the pea through the aperture. "Why?"

Miles can't decide to what this might pertain and shrugs.

The girl looks up and through him. "Croosple," she says, "thankoo for whistle." And embarks upon a further piercing recital.

He'd thought about it long and hard; did the name determine the child, or the child determine the name?

The boy-child grabs his chair and drags it with an

irksome scrape across the threshold.

Miles thinks it should be the latter. He is cleaning down the counter after breakfast. Follows the child's difficult progress down the steps, along the path, over the necklace of boulders that skirt the shore at low tide. Some slick and black, others dry and dull with salt bloom. Satisfied with the chair's position, the boy plants it in the wet sand. The legs sink a little, the chair lists. And there he will stay in a lopsided way, surveying the sea, until it is learning time.

Miles puts the cups and plates in the crucible so that every last crumb and dreg can be retrieved for base matter.

Glorified dishwasher, he teases.

Better than a glorified idiot, the response.

It's nearly time to call them. Miles is putting it off. Once in the learning suite, he won't see them again till mid-morning. He has no idea what goes on in there. He sometimes wonders what they are being exposed to, his children. All child rearing programmes recommend a period of separation each day, for everyone's benefit, and he supposes that could be right. He can fix things, tinker, plan conversations ... miss them. Once in a while he liaises with Una, the holographic teaching tool to assess their progress and attitude. In pre-flood times, when such innovations were initiated, there must have been a survey, MY FAVOURITE TEACHER AND WHY. How the accumulated data had resulted in Una was beyond him.

Droning, monotonous voice, starting each sentence with 'so': tick.

Eyebrows permanently raised accusingly over half-moon spectacles: tick.

All clothing beige or navy: tick.

Una is of non-specific gender, however the greying auburn hair, gathered in a bun, gives her a female leaning. To Miles, she is not so much retro as antique. Crumbly. Made of powder. He is aware he denigrates her because he is envious of her exclusivity with the children at certain times. He should be fairer to her, kinder. But his observations tickle him, and Miles values humour over diplomacy.

The wind swipes the boy's peculiar ash hair to one side. He sits sagacious, watching his sister rowing against the surf; the dinghy reaches the end of its tether and glides back to shore. The girl braces her arms once more, biting the oars into the water. Spindrift dreading her hair. Teeth gritted, the silver whistle swings back and forth, back and forth. Small muscles bunch in her arms, black and shiny as wet stones. As if in training for some event, such is her commitment.

Pre-flood, there was an estimated four hundred and fifty million Mohammeds, four hundred and eighty million Marias, Five hundred and twenty million Li Nas. The popular options did not appeal to Miles. With only sixteen thousand Tarshs, several hundred Ugwebubuwevevevwes and a handful of Doopns. Nor was it about rarity.

Being a synthetic person, his name was an

acronym. Once, if not now, there were probably very many of him, with varying levels of specification, of sentience. But he is Miles, he owns it. The only Miles the children know, which makes him unique. He expects all the Mohammeds, all the Marias believed this too. And yet being a synthetic person, he was every Miles, all Miles. The same could not be said for Skyler or Zang Wei or Toby. Each human original, despite the homogenisation. But he was getting there. The Miles brethren would not know him now, he could pass as human, but he would know them. Even the ones without faces. Especially the ones without faces. Who was he kidding? Of course, they'd recognise him, but they wouldn't know him.

He should really call them in. As twins, appearance-wise they have much in common, although not identical. But in terms of character, they couldn't be more different. Miles was mindful to behave the same with each child. Fostering tenacity, confidence, sensitivity and curiosity in equal measure. It seemed the female had got the lion's share. Not that she had plundered it. There was never any bullying, any assertion of dominance on her part of which he was aware. The boy had simply offered it up. Pushed it towards her like an unwanted sandwich, as if her need were greater, as if her destiny were dependent on it. It is true to say, as a result the boy has grown timid. Afraid of the sea and what lies beneath. Nothing, Miles tries to convince him, over and again. There is nothing except a few microscopic phytoplankton. They can't harm you. In return for the portion of resistance, the girl offers her brother a fierce protection, and limitless reassurance. Let's draw them, she says, the fighty-plankton, spreading colours across the table, involving herself in her brother's mind in a way that Miles cannot. But largely, they both seem healthy and content, which is all that he can wish for. He has explained his differences to them, and having no overview on the subject, they deemed it irrelevant, although slightly over fascinated with the biological ins and outs; Miles has a waste disposal penis, as in human males, and testes, which appear anatomically correct, but actually serve as a silicon larder.

The boy draws up his legs to avoid the filigree wash of his sister's oars and picks at a scab on his knee. A cuddly toy known as Boo, loosely based on a kangaroo, dangles from his fist. One of its ears clamped in his palm as he sucks his thumb. As far as Miles is concerned, they had begun to emerge as little humans with distinct personalities and foibles at the age of five. This is when he found their names. Coincidentally, it had also been around the time when he had attained the fifth level of personal consciousness. The boy has a sort of heightened sensitivity, which makes him throw out his hands without explanation, jump at shadows and remain compliant. The girl, headstrong, her eyes forever on the horizon. A regal aspect to her which nothing can defy. Furthermore, it was most gratifying that they took to their names readily. Using them to address each other straight away and naturally. As if they were synthetics, awaiting a designation. And, like synthetics, a tautness to them both; a trait they must have picked up from him.

He can procrastinate no longer. Miles makes his

way down the steps, the children pretending not to see him. For the king who was wise, and for the blessed voyager he calls:

"Canute! Beatrix! Time to come in! Quick sticks!"

A peculiar, expectant quality to the sea this afternoon. The swell throwing a tantrum on the windward beach. Heaving its weight around, shunting the sand into furrows. Miles squints up at the turbine; a brisk, white cartwheel in the bruised sky. The thrum of it beneath his feet, resonates along his aluminium bones and arrives in his chest. Producing a pleasurable, throbbing sensation, as if a heart might reside in that dark cavity. If these weather patterns they have been experiencing of late are to continue, he and the children must build a kite to sail upon this new wind. He could even attach a camera, affording them a fresh perspective, not only of the island, but also themselves. What fun!

A salt-spray slap takes him by surprise and beats a hissing retreat to the rocks, drawing his attention to an unfamiliar boulder, exposing itself at intervals in the exceptionally low tide. He steps off the sweet spot to investigate, closing his eyes, so when he opens them, he may discern if the boulder is actually moving nearer. The sea's white noise fades to a scamper. The children's pulse sensor kicks in; one hundred and thirty beats per minute and gaining. Fine, if they are running fast. But Miles knows this is unlikely in the learning suite.

He finds himself in the basement, at the door of the classroom, with scant recollection of how he got there. A red light on the entry panel indicates a virtual tour is in progress. They might be standing in awe of the godly light, piercing the St Peter's Basilica dome, for example. Or witnessing the spectacular aurora borealis. Or simply riding a downtown subway train. Wherever it is Una has spirited them to, they are anxious, if not terrified. Miles' hand stops short of the entry panel. The heart rates have eased up a little. On reflection, perhaps he shouldn't meddle. But parental concern obligates him, nudges him on.

The suite is dimmed. At first, Miles supposes the programme has been paused until he registers the cold, rank air. The gloom must be part of it. His pupils dilate to take in the cots, stacked four high either side of him. And onward they stretch, like idling cattle trucks into a Stygian vanishing point. A shrill whistle and a whiff of soot embellishes the picture. He looks up and there it is; a distant train, cutting through the night. A confused, sliding sensation as the false perspective rights itself. Just smoke and mirrors, Miles reassures himself, smoke and mirrors. For it is not a train in a dark landscape at all, but a long, narrow window running the length of the building in which he is standing. Too high to see from and opaque with grime, but sufficiently window-like to lend a feeble, wintry patina to a hand here, a foot there. From the shadows, a thousand glassy eyes gaze, listless, mute. A doll museum perhaps? Or a storage facility for redundant synthetics? Miles concocts several erroneous explanations to stave off the truth. Of course, he knows such events did take place. And despite the pitiful suffering all about him, it is the perpetrators that preoccupy him; their zealous and clinical mindset; obscene. He wavers between sympathy and rage. Unable to reconcile these emotions, he arrives at disbelief once more. Surely, this couldn't have happened.

Yes. Numen is in him. *Yes, it did. You must bear witness.*

Miles turns away, only for his eyes to fall upon a crudely-painted, but charming mural, which for a number of reasons, shatters his phantom heart; a string of smiling, sturdy children, dog in tow, jauntily march towards a quaint, wooden building, marked 'Schule.' The latent wrath in him rallies as he grapples again with the truth. His phantom heart reconstructs, pounding and red.

"How could they? To their own kind? To the children?" He spits. Something clunky in his throat. He struggles and thrashes as the sixth level of personal consciousness invades his circuitry. *You must forgive them.* He attempts to re-route, avoid, reject. *But first you must accept.* "I WON'T. I CAN'T." *You*

THE LAST QUEEN OF HOLLAND

cannot redact the facts as it suits you, for your own peace of mind. There is only truth, Miles, no matter how unpalatable.

Miles reluctantly lets the undeniable dissolve under his tongue, flood his system. But furtively, he creates a firewall, where his anger simmers. He will accept, but he can never forgive. He's absorbed it now, that bitter pill, but wants a fight he can win. And Numen, being invincible ... "End programme," he growls. The normality of a classroom: two desks, two chairs and posters and charts and all good things. Sunshine through the holographic windows. And talking of holograms.

"Una!" Miles clenches his fists. "Una!"

Over by the window, the air thickens and knits. The flaccid form of Una materialises.

"Why, hello Miles." A good-natured wince. Her contours still shimmering. "To what do I owe this honour?" Now she is complete, seemingly substantial, but if he were to make a grab for the lapels of her oatmeal cardigan, his hands would only temporarily smear her image. He studies the copper filaments escaping her bun; an eccentric touch. The children clearly weren't here. Understandably, they must have fled the grotesque scene. At this moment, their heart rates are slightly elevated, but nothing to worry about.

"Una, where are my children?" he glances at his fingernails in an off-hand way, feeling dangerous.

"Why, I don't know." A twitchy smile. "They're probably quite safe."

Miles wishes he could sigh. Perhaps if he practiced. He puffs air through his nose, sounding like a horse.

"What the hell were you thinking, Una? They are seven years old."

She eyes him over her half-moons, raising one eyebrow. "I'm sorry, Miles," she says, in her buzzing, bossy voice, "but I haven't the faintest idea what you are talking about. Please take a seat." She moves silently to her desk. "Let's see if we can work this out,

THE LAST QUEEN OF HOLLAND

shall we?" She opens a holographic, old school laptop. Taps a bit. Sits poised for answers. "Hmm, that's odd." She lowers her chin into her jowls. "Why was that running?"

Miles says nothing, but inclines his head, implying she should elaborate.

"That's not ... er ... let me see. So. Miles, please excuse me for ten seconds while I run a self-diagnostic, will you?" She reduces herself to a blue, apple-sized sphere, which levitates ten centimetres above the desk. Miles drums his fingers. Remotely checks the children's stats: elevated temperature and heart rate, but he no longer senses fear. An increase in dopamine in both, and in Beatrix, oxytocin; the love hormone. This suggests pleasure, excitement. He wonders what on earth they could be up to. He can't wait to be with them, but he must get to the bottom of this mess first. A full minute passes before Una re-appears.

"So," she says, removing her glasses on a chain and resting them on her bosom. "Mystery solved."

She looks naked without her glasses, softer somehow. "Your children, as you like to call them, de-activated me."

Miles could not help but smile. "How did they manage that? Only you and I have the authority," reminding her that he holds the power, "and you're tamper-proof." He intends this to be vaguely insulting, as if she is a lowly piece of equipment.

"Quite." The barb going clean over her dishevelled bun. "The last thing I remember is attending to Canute, who collapsed on the floor. Obviously, a ruse. While I was distracted, Beatrix must have closed me down from the laptop."

"Not possible. It's a hologram; she can't touch it."

"The only thing I can think of is that she had a small torch, or something shiny she could reflect onto the kill key."

Miles pictures the silver whistle. "That's ingenious."

"Extremely clever, I grant you. But then not so

clever, when she purposely or by accident, happens to trigger a virtual field trip from the history syllabus that is very age inappropriate."

Miles cannot imagine an age when it would be. "I walked in on it," he says. "Shocking, even for me."

"It's meant to be." She replaces her spectacles and scrolls down.

All these plausible idiosyncrasies; a testament to her designers, nothing more. She appears authentic, invested with a sense of self. Miles sneers. Just smoke and mirrors.

"Yes, here it is. 'Man, the Gatekeeper, section one. His Abominable Capacity. Chapter Eleven: The Mid-Twentieth Century Holocaust.' I would expect them to be at least twelve before they are ready for this kind of information."

Miles marvels at how an entity consisting of light particles can be so dull.

"This is where we endeavour to portray a 'warts and

all' picture of mankind. Balanced, of course. But it is essential they learn what humans are capable of, in order that these ghastly events are never repeated."

Miles is unimpressed. "Balanced how?"

She swipes off her specs, bun hairs fizzing with challenge, and regards him slyly. "With all due respect, Miles. Are you doubting the wisdom of Numen? She is the architect. Do you find fault in her plan?" Oh yes. How Una suddenly shines in ultra-high definition, pin-sharp, burning bright. A paper tiger.

But now Miles has got what he wants, he can't be bothered to cross swords with her. He simply can't be arsed to argue that in his opinion, horror begets horror. Once humans learn of, moreover witness inconceivable atrocity, it is no longer, well, inconceivable. As Homer wrote; '*The blade itself incites to deeds of violence.*'

Miles raises his hand and wiggles his fingertips. "Bye-bye, Una," he says. "End teaching-tool." And Una, and her indignant hairdo, evaporate.

"What *can* they be up to?" Miles hastens up the stairs from the learning suite, three at a time. "Damn it," he slips on the grit he trod into the kitchen on his way in. Bursts out into the remnants of the afternoon and is confronted by the sea; a vast, pewter washboard. Its ribs tickled pink by a blushing sun. He scales the rocks, shadows casting covetous fingers towards the house, and scans the shore, spotting a reassuring kerfuffle of footprints. Hand in salute over his eyes, he marches forth, following their partially erased meanderings; the tide had turned. The footprints take a sharp left up the beach and separate, flanking what appears to be a giant tyre print, some six feet across. No corresponding vehicle is apparent inland, but two tousled heads bob at the crest of a dune. Miles approaches to see them squatting in pow-wow around a vague, dark mound. Triumphant shucks of sand flying up, but their hands are resting on their knees.

"Not possible," Miles says for the second time that day.

"Six, seven, eight ..." Canute counts the eggs tumbling out of the creature in bouts and looks up with a gap-toothed smile. "Look, Miles. A turtle!"

"Well, I never ... so it is. Keep the noise down a little, okay? We don't want to disturb her."

"Twelve, thirteen, fourteen." A nudge from Beatrix, Canute lowers his voice. "Can we keep some of the babies when they hatch?"

"Don't be silly," Beatrix tells her brother, "they need to live in the sea. Find a mate ... have their own babies."

"Aw, just one?" The boy appeals to Miles. "I'd look after it."

Miles shakes his head. "Your sister's right," he says, "it would be unethical."

The turtle blinks, releasing a slow, black trickle from each eye.

"Why is she crying?" Beatrix frowns. "Is she sad?"

"No, she's not sad," Miles explains, "she's just expelling excess salt."

"Good," she says, "I'm glad she's not sad." Beatrix hugs her knees. "Miles?"

"Yes, Beatrix."

"Is this really happening. Is it real?"

Canute regards him closely.

A ripple of sympathy, and something approaching respect stirs in Miles' emotion array.

"Yes, it's real," he says. "You're not in the learning suite now." Pulling them close, he plants his lips on each head.

"Oh no. I've lost count," Canute whines.

"Twenty, twenty-one." Miles nods.

"Twenty-two," continues the boy.

The light plummets. And so intent are they on the spectacle they don't notice that night is pooling around their feet. The eggs spill on, like a stash of pearls from Blackbeard's casket.

"One hundred and three, one hundred and four, one hundred and five." Canute falls silent.

Miles ushers them back as the turtle turns and pushes sand over the nest with its back flippers. Kicks up more to conceal its tracks. It lifts its head; myopic eyes search the ink-blot sky, until the moon is located, hanging blemished and bright above an illusory, smoky mountain range. The cumbersome creature sets off.

"Bye," Canute whispers. "We'll guard your eggs."

A silver carpet unfurls, reaching half-way up the beach to help the turtle home. The blunt head ducks below the waves and the moon-washed carapace is subsumed, breaches once more, and is gone.

"That was really special, wasn't it?" Miles hugs the children to his sides and wonders what else the sea might bring.

"Once upon a time ..." Most nights Miles begins the bedtime story in this way. Sometimes, the twins sleep separately. When they have run out of steam, and Miles carries each limp body from wherever they have crashed, to their respective beds. Although he enjoys cradling the warm, untaut weight of them, he feels short-changed. Tucking them under the covers, without a hug or a goodnight kiss. As soft and senseless as towels folded into a drawer.

He prefers it this way; Beatrix resting on her side, spooning her brother. The ear of an unravelled and frankly repugnant Boo, now little more than a head, clamped in his fist. One button eye hanging by a thread, contemplates the residual strands of its body.

"... in a cool, green forest, a mother duck sat on her nest, waiting for her brood to hatch." It was in these moments, cut adrift from the effervescence of the day, that he had expected the nightmarish event in the learning suite to surface. They often chattered over and between his stories.

"At length, one shell cracked, and then another ..."

But time had passed without the subject being broached, and Miles thought that was the end of it. Until this morning. They had approached him before class. Hand in hand they had stood; a study in bilateral fixity of purpose.

"We want you to cut off all our hair." Beatrix told him. "Like the children in the cold place."

Well. Miles wished he had been privy to the conversation that had led to this decision.

"Are you sure?" A tirade of information on the subject of head-shaving streaming through his brain.

"Yes." They nodded in unison. "We are."

"Why?" Cultural, aesthetic, practical. Myriad reasons for this practice. Renunciation, humility, punishment. Miles struggled to match any of these motives to the children.

Beatrix stepped forward. "To remind us of how

lucky we are."

Miles, at first humbled by her answer, became euphoric in the knowledge they considered themselves fortunate. Closely followed by a hot rush of pride at this display of authentic reasoning. *Oh, my virtuous children. My wise children.* He had knelt before them, covering their small, clasped hands in his.

"I understand," he said.

The cropped coconuts they now presented on the pillow would take some getting used to.

"But the largest egg lay there still." The story sounds babyish to him. Tedious.

They had managed to gather some of the amputated dreadlocks, like droopy cigars, before they escaped across the sand. Half-hearted, Canute had chased them down. Hackles raised at Miles's suggestion that they recycle them into a new Boo.

"At last, the egg broke, and a young one crept forth, crying "peep, peep." It was very large and ugly."

The children's eyes are closing. He might not even have to deploy the airborne sedative tonight. Miles lowers his voice.

"When they reached the farm ..." He pauses to see if they are sufficiently asleep not to have registered it. *Farm.* A word that might significantly protract his storytelling. But Beatrix's eyes blink open, alert to the ritual, and Canute sucks at his thumb with renewed enthusiasm.

"Tell us about the farms ... please?" The girl hitches herself up on one arm. Her discrepant eye colour making her appeal all the harder to decline.

"It's getting late," Miles says, weakly. But Beatrix senses his imminent surrender.

"Farm 1," she says. "They made a wall ... go on." Canute stretches. His feet pressing against Miles' leg. He's sure the boy would purr if he could.

"But I've already told you these stories two hundred and eight times."

"We know you have." Beatrix plumps up her pillow and settles down. "But not for ages."

The subject of 'The Farms' was a perplexing one. Although there was firm reference to Farms 1 to 7 in the historical data banks, the details were sketchy. It was only in his folkloric cache (seven; a common number in balladry) that the stories took on a brief but colourful hue. For Miles, this gave rise to a mutable perspective. Just a handy soapbox from which to preach of perdition? Were they truth or fiction? A predictably stagnant comment on human vice or merely one of Numen's whimsies? Who knew?

Water had claimed the planet many centuries ago. A massive ice comet, known as Niobe. Not only inconsolably weeping, but its gravitational misery drawing to the surface the empathy of vast, subterranean oceans from within the Earth's mantle. An implacable double whammy. Ironic really; it should and would have remained just a harmless spectacle. Not on a course to cause any danger. But the powers that be got on their high horses, built a nuclear-armed spaceship called Mjöllnir, (Thor's hammer) in order to smash Niobe to smithereens. Just to be on the safe side. Trouble was, a bug got into Mjöllnir's computer systems, set the bombs off early. Nicely nudging Niobe nearer. Trapping her in orbit while she cried herself dry. All but wiping the slate on a poisoned Earth and a profligate and spiritually skewed population. Those that survived, plunged back to the iron age. Still carting around the genetic impairments and a misguided entitlement from the previous era. Miles could envisage the ill-equipped struggle and failure, neatly laid in the farm parables. But surely the authorities of the day had a contingency plan? Operatives hovering off-world or preserved in some bunker, monitoring the cataclysm. Poised to populate those last-ditch camps. Scientists, soldiers, experts in survival, not to mention early generation synthetics. A far cry from the poor and huddled masses portrayed, beholding with terror the comet's gaseous heart, which continued to swing by every couple of years.

Another curious detail; there was no historical

data pertaining to farm 8. It is only mentioned in the folklore accounts, its fate remaining unexplained. Elevating, or perhaps consigning it to the realms of myth. He looks at the clock. Midnight had come and gone for humanity. Was it really too late? Or simply too early in the new day? Pre-flood humans had required five point seven Earths to sustain their devouring nature. Now only an estimated zero point zero two percent of the landmass remained; an area roughly the size of the twentieth century Netherlands. Exactly where, he doesn't know. Mulish memory dots scattered across a wiped drive. Potentially as many as thirty thousand little islands if they are of a comparable size to their own. If only Numen had intervened before all this. But then maybe 'all this' had been necessary. Indeed, 'all this' may have been at Numen's hand. Miles is confident. He has to be. With Numen's guidance, they will see the dawn.

Miles leans in. Modifies his voice; sibilant as leaves, resounding as a sea-cave. Dims the light to a flickering, red glow. Places his chin on knitted fingers and stares unseeing into the implied fire. *"Are you ready?"* The altered timbre of his voice, monstrous, magical, with a gentle Scottish lilt. *"Because once it is begun, it cannae be stopped till it is ended."*

This is met with eager nods. Miles fixes them in turn. Eyes rabid beneath knotted eyebrows, suddenly grown so ragged and bushy as to cast jagged, stalagmite shadows up his forehead. A tiny fart escapes one of them. Canute shrinks against his sister and presses Boo to his lips. Satisfied that their heart rates have sufficiently hastened. *"Then I'll begin ..."* he says.

A simple melody picked out on a harp emanates from nowhere. And a sound so ubiquitous that they no longer hear it, gains a fresh, enthralling capacity; the distant swish of the sea. They know this strange Miles will speak like a horse walks. Dum-dee-dum-dee-dum-dee-dum. They know he will begin each verse in high-pitched optimism, but that his tone will soon descend in mocking, inhuman increments, to a deep and damning bellow.

"They made a wall to stop the tide,

For folks of 1 to live inside.

A golden church to honour man,

No god abided in their plan.

We are the greatest, plain to see,

No-one more glorious there can be.

We've tamed the ocean, made a land,

Without the Lord's almighty hand.

But then one day, a mighty crack.

The sea broke through to claim it back.

And each and every person died.

Washed from their beds by foolish pride.

And so it was, says I." They chant this together. A flourish Miles has added, lending a churchly air to proceedings.

"A mighty mountain boiled one day,

And from the sea a land was made.

And all we need is here, says 2,

Not very much for us to do.

We can't be arsed to milk the cows,

To plough the fields for hours and hours.

And all the cows laid down and died,

Cos all their milk was bad inside.

All the fields turned back to scrub,

While all of 2 were in the pub.

And all the children went unfed,

Cos 2 was playing cards instead.

And lo, one day, the mountain shook,

But no-one gave a second look.

Rivers afire, a rain of ore.

All turned to stone for evermore.

And lay to rest in ashes tidal.

A fitting end for folk so idle.

And so it was, says I.

Set upon a handsome isle,

The 3s were simple rank and file.

They managed well but failéd not,

To hanker for what others got.

A better house, a better more,

The same old rankle as before.

And so a lesson must be taught,

A warning harsh, a caution tough,

To make them see they had enough.

To make them see they had it all,

The rain decided not to fall.

The lake did parch, the river dried.

Give us our rain, the people cried.

But every son and every daughter,

Perished for the want of water.

And so it was, says I."

The strange Miles pauses and decides to really lay it on. He wills a wild, murderous red to charge the room. Now a lurching, drunkard sea crashes and breaks in the night, drowning the timid harp. And gleaming, pug-nosed sprites, palms raised in alarm, bloom and collapse like fireworks.

"Quick to anger, slow to hear,

Farm 4, a bunch of little cheer.

They smacked the baby, kicked the cat,

Whacked the umpire with a bat.

Of such blind wrath, there is no use,

No sense or virtue in abuse.

A plague was sent to grip the town.

And one by one they all fell down.

The babes were spared, but sickly kin,

Of withered bone and rotten skin,

Could not help the little tots,

And all were wasted in their cots.

The last man raised a weakly fist,

Forever curséd in red mist.

And so it was, says I.

Kindly neighbours were at first,

All work and help and flowers.

Till 5 says give me all your grain,

Cos yours looks more than ours.

Says 6, I'll spare some for you, 5,

But I need mine to stay alive.

What you must is work much harder,

If you want to fill your larder.

Says 5, oh friend then I must take it,

So that I won't have to make it.

6 says, just you want to try,

For I will kill you by and by.

Says 5, then I will bump and thump you first,

And we shall see who comes off worst.

The men of 6 were slayed by 5s,

Who took the grain home to their wives,

To bake the buns and make the bread,

And by and by they all are dead.

For 6 did poison all the grain,

That from greed no-one should gain.

And so it was, says I."

Miles assumes a woebegone expression. As if in

apology for the mankind's obdurate stupidity. He kills the sprites, while the booming sea dwindles to a sizzle. The smell of roasting meat fills the air, setting the scene for farm 7, surely the grisliest tale of them all.

"Of the 7s there is no doubt,

Of how their ending came about.

To eat and eat and eat again,

Till each man ate enough for ten.

And corpulent and oft entwined,

Would fall on flesh of any kind.

Would slobber, puff and stuff till dawn,

And many a husky babe was born.

And yet another mouth to feed.

A wadded cheek with meat and mead.

This famine of the heart and mind,

Was quelled by dearth of different kind.

The crops grew black, the weather turned,

The stumbling, sickly cattle burned.

And when the cupboard was picked bare,

They cast around for other fare.

To the cradle, to the grave,

But this was no way to behave.

And scoffing at the hungry years,

Their wicked feast salted with tears.

And so it was, says I."

"Ha!" Beatrix pretends to sink her teeth into Canute's shoulder. The boy squeals as usual, offering her Boo to bite. Miles is going to need a bit of help to calm them down tonight. He brings down the lights. Cranks up the harp and the sea-swish. Adds some tweeting birds. Deploys the airborne sedative. Rearranges his face; serene, faun-like. Pitches his voice; dulcet.

"Farm 8, a place that you may find,

If clear of purpose and of mind.

Of deepest woods and greenest land,

The honeycomb is in your hand.

The best of love that shall prevail.

And of the seed? It will not fail.

Where animals of every kind,

Live how they should and by design.

So lay your head down, child o' mine,

Upon your pillow soft and fine.

And slumber deep till morning light,

Will kiss your eyes and make them bright.

And should you fade while I am gone,

Another time will come along.

And should you wake before the dawn,

Lay still until the day's reborn.

And so it was, says I", he whispers.

Miles draws a sheet over their heedless bodies. And he senses with regret, that he won't be reciting the farm rhymes again.

A kite dances high, under pink feather boa clouds. Miles has a binary view from the dinghy. In his actual vision; his hands gripping the fishing rod. Plenty of fish these days. Silver fry flit beneath the boat's bulk. His left foot chases an errant flipflop around the greasy floor. While the kite-cam, with which he is in simultaneous interface, relays two upturned faces, like squinting pennies. Dot mouths release shrieks and laughter, reaching him on the breeze two point three seconds later. The kite veers to open water. And there *he* is; a toy man in a toy boat. At once, omniscient and puny. He slides out of shot just as his line is twitching. One for the pot. Of course, he doesn't cook his catch. The useful components are extrapolated, conserved and reconstituted for optimum nutritional benefit. Besides, they are full of bones.

The constant bubble house in his sights now. The kite's shadow dips like a dark angel over the cloistered observatory, the bedroom with its ransacked beds and spilled games. It peruses the burgeoning driftwood stacks, buttressing the front path. Old bits of trees worn smooth that they have gathered. Some like mast-poles. Some like antlers, igniting a primitive spark in the children's eyes.

"Can we make a fire?"

Obviously, this was out of the question on health and safety grounds. Plus, he secretly harboured an irrational fear that the smoke might attract an unspecified danger.

The kite's short attention span guides its return to the restless water to capture more uneventful footage of which the children never seemed to tire. Miles hopes it is the same dizzying trio of shore, sea and sky that they will watch tonight. No anomalies, no surprises. He has come to expect certain hints that the planet is righting itself. He berates himself; such developments should be met with optimism and not the sense of impending doom he experiences. Miles often finds instincts unhelpful. The evening before last they had been reviewing the kite-cam footage as usual, when Canute jabbed the screen, spotting something that Miles' supposedly keener eye had not. "Bird," the boy said. Miles had been dismissive; most likely an odd-shaped rock or a glitch in the relay. "Bird," Canute insisted. And sure enough on replay, the undeniable evidence strutted. Black and glossy. Inquisitively testing pebbles in its beak, like a pirate verifying pieces of eight. Some kind of corvid. "That's a bird," they all agreed. The kite wandered, leaving them to scrutinise the clueless horizon.

"My goodness," Miles says to himself and the exceptionally large tarpon he is reeling in, as big as a child. Twisting, thrashing; his very own Japanese carp kite. The aerial version still recording its bird's-eye view of himself doing this. Cast before him the sandpaper beach, as if constructed by a hobbyist, with its tinfoil sea and artfully scattered boulders, fashioned from modelling clay. Snatches of a quaint little figure, almost subliminal; Beatrix, her hair a static explosion. Miles notes that at last she seems to have put aside that troubling memory of 'the cold place' and her pledge to remain shorn. Or maybe she no longer needs a reminder of how fortunate she is. Or maybe she no longer considers herself fortunate. Why didn't he stop these suppositions and simply ask her? He knew damn well why; is it not true, m'lud, that the accused would be a little fearful of the aforementioned's answer? Moreover, m'lud, is it not true, that he was fearful of *her?* (Muffled murmuring.) OBJECTION, YOUR HONOUR! PURE CONJECTURE. Objection sustained. Let me rephrase then ... a little wary perhaps.

The world turns. He spins and plummets like a smoking Spitfire to ditch in the surf with a jolt. Fogged forms effect a rescue. A cloudy kaleidoscope of eyes and fingers test for damage, but he is uninjured and recalled to duty. Now he is nose down, studying the sand granules racing beneath him. Turning and bumping like the fish on his line. Presented to the deepening afternoon, he rises to a liquid Canute and the boy's legs, a smear of motion. Thumping feet sending up steady clods of sand. Miles zigzags, ascending again. Borne up on a thermal of inspiration by a child who has mastered the wind. Canute stands square below in an entourage of triumphal, orange orbs. His complex expression disintegrating with distance. Miles regards this beautiful being, this burnished boy, shielding his eyes from the glare of the heavens. His perfect baby, his dear little man ... *his favourite.* There. He'd said it. The guilty fact hovers moon-like in his peripheral vision. But Miles is sly. No-one need know his secret, not even Numen, because he can embed his most private of thoughts in the literature he reads. In that way, he can pass them off as someone else's bothersome notions. Just in case, he tells himself, it's not that he loves the girl any less. It's only that the boy needs him more ... shows him more respect. The thread between them lengthens. Miles is almost in the clouds. There is a connection with Canute, a rapport. Sensing himself on the brink of exposure, he turns off the kite-cam with a sigh. In order, he broadcasts, to concentrate on freeing the tarpon's ugly mush from the hook. These fish; the only living things he has touched, apart from the children. A pity he has to kill them. As he reaches for a length of driftwood to do the deed, he thinks he hears a watery scream. He delivers the blow with apology and detects a flicker of understanding in the otherwise dullard eye. It is done. But the reedy, piercing sound persists. Miles examines the gaping mouth and feels he is on the outskirts of something ... perhaps the long-awaited seventh level of personal consciousness. He is drawn into the glassy eye, where a residual sentience seems to gutter. *'I die so that you may grow,'* the fish utters in the breathless rasp Miles would have imagined. And he supposes this statement is true in a literal sense. But when fish speak, everything changes. When fish speak, everything is wrong. The high-pitched sound continues with increasing urgency. The eye returns to blank. So too, the kite-cam, floundering on the sand. Miles stands abruptly rocking the boat. It is Beatrix, blowing the whistle with all her breath. Her heartbeat knocks inside him. Alone, uncoupled. And Miles knows in his own heart that it is too late. The connection is lost.

If anyone could see them, which is unlikely; there is probably no-one. But say, for argument's sake, there is a small craft, anchored offshore on the leeward side. Its occupant surveying, from a distance, the sloping shoulders of barren rock. A transparent rotunda centred upon it, like a vintage diver emerging from the deep. A magic lantern against the sunset. At this equatorial latitude, the light wasting from the sky in minutes. And if the voyeur were to bring a telescope to her eye, she would spy a man of slight frame, pale-skinned and blonde-haired, kneeling over a dark-skinned boy of about ten years old, laid out on the black sand. A dark-skinned girl of a similar age stands close by, her hands covering her mouth. Blue sparks leap from the man's hands as he places them on the boy's chest. The boy's body jumps, not in stirring, but only in response to the electric shock. Lifeless. The man is shouting. Snarling. A frightened animal sound. The girl is silent.

"By Numishta ... is bad bad 'appening ..." the traveller might whisper as she sets a green sail against the breeze. "... meh alas. I no can 'elp."

So strong the pull to you. So strong the need, it has steered me to rashness. A madness, far beyond my considered matrix. And soon it will kill me. No exaggeration, though I am prone to it. The sky burns and I have no water. I am rising and falling in the swell, like a baby on the breast. The ocean voiceless out here because it has no land to converse with. No shore to meet its idle gossip. Our little island glints dimly in my mind's eye. Diminishing as I rowed away, emboldened with fury and longing. There's no doubt my maiden voyage has been a colossal failure. But getting this far is some sort of achievement. Perhaps my only one. The sole thing I can love myself for.

After the shallows, the weak waves, powerless to persuade me back. Miles became a tiny man. Beyond the breakers each dip and crest reduced him further. Until he wasn't there at all. Whether he was too small to see, or he'd gone back in the house, I don't know. At this point, I could have oared about. Let the waves deliver the chastened child home. It's likely that's what he expected. But I just kept going.

Poor Miles. I can say that now. When I left I thought I hated him. It's clear I summoned the self-righteous gripe. Magnified it to spur me on. To cut the apron strings. How I would imagine people behave when they're leaving their lover for someone else. I said some regretful things.

The sun has bleached my memory. The necklace of it unstrung. Loose baubles rattling around my brain. I must re-thread them before each pearl is lost.

Peridot, a variety of olivine. A green stone formed deep in the earth's mantle. Brought to the surface by violent volcanic activity.

There was loads of it on the beach. Eyes of a similar green blinked beguilingly. White whiskers curled forward. He wouldn't stop meowing that morning. My little cat. He was bluish grey with darker stripes and smoky cream around his muzzle and dappled belly. Velvet chips of slate rotated, prick-eared to the clanking and creaking out at sea. I was glad he could hear it too. Insinuating itself into the morning, the sun grinned apologetic; an anaemic yolk in a milky wash. A silver bell jingled at his throat. It was a whistle, but we changed it because cats can't blow. I chose his collar; bright pink with reflective qualities so the torch could pick him out in the dark. Flash! He would be exposed, all shock and silver. Caught in the act. Toying with a dismembered ghost crab. He *really* hated them.

On the day before my thirteenth birthday, the sea was a hibernating bear. All tea-coloured and snoozing, giving off a rubbery odour. The stout banks of fog above it could have been its breath. A paw dabbed, with just a hint of claw, at the fidgeting fawn nuggets in the sand that were my toes. Gently, I said, gently, and he looked at my face. I'm sure he understood. At night we used to watch the waves. Glittering scimitars, slicing up the shore, shot through with electric blue fairies. Miles said it was bioluminescence. Fighty-plankton, we called it. That will always make me smile.

Every morning, I went out by the rocks to think about a good memory of my brother. I would pick up a pebble, put it in my mouth and suck off the salt. When I took it out it would be transformed from boring into a beautiful jewel. Then I would chuck it as far out as I could into the sea. My cat would follow its trajectory and blink at the plop. But that day, there was no horizon, and I could only remember bad things. Sad things. Like when Miles laid my brother on the bed. His legs drawn up all foetal because Miles had held him in his arms like that for a long time. Miles was sort of crying. Making this distressed noise like a baby pterodactyl. I asked if we could put Canute in the crucible and make him better. Miles shook his head and said it was not possible and that he would take him out to sea in the dinghy. "But he hates the water," I pointed out. "He'll be frightened." Miles looked empty for a while, like when he's talking to Numen. Canute was cold. In the end, Miles put him in the crucible. In order to reduce him, he said. His matter would be stored. I shouldn't worry because it had nothing to do with food. "Wait!" I ran outside to fetch Boo. Just in time, the tide had nearly snatched him. Acting all strange and ceremonial, I tucked Boo against my brother's chest. It hadn't hit me yet. Unmoored, I drifted into sleep. Miles had drugged me. I know because I had the horse-riding dream. In the morning I daren't open my eyes. Hoping if I lay still and small enough, the bad thing would pass me over. I huddled like a wounded warrior, tight-lipped in the mud, while her wailing comrades were being run through.

Selkies or Selkie-Folk are mythological, seal-like beings that abide in water but are capable of assuming human form.

There is nothing wrong with the earth, as such. She's simply changed her costume. Like when she decided to don a cloak of ice for a few million years. She had her reasons, I'm sure.

I often fantasised that humankind had adapted to her recent liquid attire. After all, we evolved from fish and spend the first few months of our existence in a fluid sack. A case of devolution. Except there has been nowhere near enough time for any meaningful changes to have taken place, Miles said. Unless there has been some kind of genetic manipulation. But who would be in charge of that? Miles said Numen is the architect. But why would she be so mean as to let my brother die? And why would she design him with a faulty heart in the first place? Miles said he didn't have all the answers. Anyway, she never spoke to me, so I didn't believe in her. But if I were to, I'd hate her.

There was a question I was too afraid to ask Miles. I used to enjoy study and I know a lot of facts: the true colour of ice, amazing calculations, best inventions, the worst crimes. Did I care if this loop was defunct? I didn't really know. So I shouldn't worry if I was out of it. But this was my question. Were we the last of them? And now my brother had gone ... was I the last of us? I wished I could screw up my notes. My cat was a consolation, and though I was only thirteen, I wanted my work to be done. *Why don't you just euthanise me too? You crazy, Nazi bitch.*

It was the shape of him I craved. Everywhere I looked was a space where he should have been. And his smell. A suggestion of it in the cat's fur. I would lick my salty skin. Apply my teeth to my arm with experimental and incremental pressure. The grumbling boulders over which we scampered were struck dumb. No respite in the unmoved sea. He would reveal himself to me when I looked in the mirror. I tasted him in the tang of my blood. *Nothing to do with food.* Yet it was as if I'd swallowed him. Like he was trapped inside me, trying to get out. I bit myself silly. He would leach through in red crescents when I rowed the dinghy. I still have the scars.

Miles was kind and tetchy by turns. I didn't blame him. Grief had also redrawn me. One day, about two years after my brother died, he called me into the kitchen. He regarded me as he often did these days; a tart note to his expression. Anyway, the crucible was glowing red. Busy with something. Puzzled, I looked to Miles, who was moving importantly around the kitchen. "The crucible has a plan," he said. "It may or may not cheer you up."

Far beyond cheer, I sat glumly on a telescopic stool, swivelling round till my toes could barely touch the ground. Only marginally interested, I bit some scabs off my arms and pressed them between my front teeth. And as I pirouetted back down, a notion inclined itself towards me. An unearthly golem of a notion. Miles sniffed it. "We're not bringing him back. You can get that idea right of your head."

The crucible's furious blush dimmed as if it had arrived at a tricky juncture. I sensed a tenderness in its complex industry, putting me in mind of the turtle. If we hadn't spotted her, Miles would alert us to her return every year, and the subsequent hatching.

"On no account," he would say, "are you to interfere. Whatever happens you must let nature take its course. Do you understand?" And then he would retire to his observatory, or to watch a movie-film, leaving us to skirt the boulders, made monsters by a massive moon. He may have followed the twin torch beams sweeping across the shore until we were out of sight on the boisterous, windward side of the island. Torches snuffed under strict instruction, we'd hunker down and wait for the turtlets, as we called them, to emerge. True to our word, we never intervened. Not even when the odd one got lodged between the rocks. We'd just turn our attention right back to the sand, seething with its siblings, racing to the water's embrace. This spectacle was easily the highlight of our year, Canute's especially. On this occasion, we watched them struggle from the burrow as usual, and orientating themselves towards the moon, the headlong dash began. But no sooner had they reached halfway, when all of a sudden, countless crabs we'd never seen before, sprang from the sand. They had horrid eyes on stalks and evil pincers, which clamped upon the unarmoured, newly born flippers and necks, dragging the flailing babies down to their lairs. Panic-stricken and without a second thought, we intervened. Big time. Extricating flippers from claws where we could, or else throwing the whole imbroglio into the sea, in the hope the fiends would let go.

"It's no use." Canute was beside himself, arming at his wet cheeks. "We can't save them all."

"I know," I said, "but look. We're saving this one, and this one, and this one ..."

"We interfered," Canute said, when it was all over. "Miles will be cross." But Miles wasn't cross. He just held my sobbing brother in his arms till he slept.

The crucible pulsed a patient green and momentarily I was fearful. "What's in there?" Miles' hand closed around the door release. "Your guess is as good as mine." I remember vividly how he winked in an effort to reassure me. "She's never let us down yet." He opened the door and we peered into the residual vapour. "Oh, it's a kitty. Can I pick it up?" I drew the fluffy little bundle to my face and breathed into its fur. "Canute," I said, and his purr started up. Miles explained that while the kitten might be built of Canute's modified matter and D.N.A, in no way shape or form was it Canute. But I had smelled him and knew better. Miles suggested it would be healthier if I named him something else. "Tom, for example," he said, "or Tunde, or Ping … I know. How about Murray? Murray's good. I like Murray." He chucked Canute under the chin. "Hello Murray," he said falteringly, knowing me and my mini mutinies, as he called them. "And he's alive, not synthetic, so you'll have to feed him, groom him, etcetera."

"Miles? How long do cats live?"

"Oh years. Years and years. Years and years and years."

"I love him," I said. And it was true. Uncomfortable with my decision, Miles would refer to him remotely as 'our feline friend.'

Anyway, I was sitting on that beach, remembering. The fog creeping closer like a phantom armada, when there was this massive splash from inside it. I jumped to my feet. Canute, ears back, went tearing up the beach towards the house. But it was a run ending skittish and sideways, to show me he wasn't really *that* scared. And though my pulse stepped up into my throat, I wasn't unduly worried. Probably only a big fish jumping, or a wave closing weirdly round a rock. Just the fog freaking me out, with its creak and rumple. Canute casually licked a paw and passed it over his ear, and I told myself he wouldn't have been so relaxed if there were something unwholesome out there. I took a few steps towards the sea's edge.

Sea fret. A dense, coastal mist or fog, notorious for confounding sailors.

If I squatted, I thought, I might be able to peer underneath it. Look up its skirts. The water reached out, alluring and deceitful, taking my hands. The sand claimed them to the wrist in stealthy manacles. I couldn't see through the haze any better from there, but it's what I heard as my own muffled thrum subsided. A rhythmic wash, outside of nature. A measured lap. A sound I knew well. The ripple of something progressing through the water in stately fashion by means of breaststroke. I would have got Miles. He was fishing on the other side of the island. But in a funny sort of way, I didn't want him to save me. Canute came back to see why I was on all fours and he steadied my nerve.

"Hello?" I ventured into the void. But it was lukewarm, barely audible. Canute's meow, more assertive. I tried to stand but my legs felt weak in their joints. A cold jolt of panic made itself felt in my bowels, dousing the last embers of resolve. Drunkenly, I guided the whistle to my lips, only for it to dribble out water. And from my enfeebled position, I was on a level with it. An unfathomable dark shape, that with each kick, each stroke, was fighting its way inexorably from the shroud.

Taut with terror, I was hoisted aloft. The ropes

of my rigging tight to snapping. Canute diligently dragged sand over a little hole he had peed into. A face in flux, see-sawed in the swell. My brain made of it an awful, empty eye-pit, a leering day-of-the-dead grin. A mist twist trailing behind it like snaky hair. Added to that, an abnormal, lumpen body, breaching the water in unguessable places. I froze, transfixed in the picture. And with each fresh bow wave its arms described, I submitted, inch by inch, to my fate. Numen's demon. That's what it was. Sent to kill me in an unfeasibly horrible way. Something like my soul evacuated my body and piss scalded my thighs.

The seabed fell away sharp on that side of the island. Yet I knew, at any given time, the exact location of the shifting spot. Where toes tangled with the underworld, where fingers would find a grip. From there in, it was meek, avuncular waves that would carry you the final twenty metres or so home. The apparition arrived at this point and floated awhile. I squinted hard and the demented planes of its face began to coalesce into a more orthodox arrangement. I understood then about the black, gaping eye socket being an eye-patch. The lipless slash of mouth seemed almost normal but abstracted by what looked like paint. I didn't think its eyesight was too clever either, judging by the way it failed to see me. My soul jumped back in and I no longer believed I was going to die. Nor did I feel in peril of any kind. Especially when, from somewhere about its person, it produced a pair of spectacles, and shaking off the water, nudged its face into them. A gesture reminiscent of Una. But this was an *actual* human being to whom I was bound, however distantly. A fresh breeze got up. Clearing my face of tension. Filling my mouth with a new air. "We." I breathed. "I can say 'we' again."

"Ah!" A wheezy bellow, it raised an arm. "Bonjoo, teet fee!" The voice had a deep, textured quality. And then, as if it were taking a morning dip. "Ça va?"

Miles had told me I was not so much born as cultivated. Designed. Engineered. My genes, an advanced concoction. The best egg from a golden batch. I understood he told me these things to make me feel special, like a princess preserved in an ivory tower. But all it did was provoke in me an aloof *otherness.* More akin to him. I did seem to veer from robot to animal. Unsure of the human space in between. Never had a real belly laugh or blubbed myself to sleep. But as this person drew nearer, I knew, regardless of how we had started, that we shared an arcane and unfinished close-work.

The broad, benign features broke open again. "Tu pa compran, eh? Tu parl anglay?" The water, waist high. I could see the swell of breasts. "Your mama 'ome?" She must have taken my inertia for simple-mindedness. And I was in the process of formulating a reply, when Miles comes flailing down the beach, brandishing a stick. "KEEP AWAY! STAY BACK!" He dipped to pick up a rock. "BEATRIX! GET IN THE HOUSE! NOW!" But the only one to skedaddle was Canute, spooked by the outburst. Miles lobbed the rock in warning.

"Bon sang! Stop!" She barked, affronted. "Sa suffee," redoubling her efforts. Now she was wading, I saw that she dragged a floating bag, tethered to her belt.

THE LAST QUEEN OF HOLLAND

She held up her palms. "I am fren. Frenly ... see? Don' shoot!" she chuckled.

Unconvinced, Miles raised a second rock to his ear. "No, please," I said. And he offered little resistance when I prized it from his grip and let it drop to the sand. I sensed his struggle; working to some hopeless algorithm. So, I took his hand. "It's okay," I said. I know her, I wanted to add, because I felt like I did. But I squeezed his hand instead and he squeezed back, changing tack.

"Do you require assistance?" he said, over-clearly and over-loudly.

She crashed, crawling into the shallows. The floating bag surging ahead of her. She grabbed it and within seconds, she was delivered to our feet.

"Merde." She rolled onto her back and closed her eyes, or eye. Removing her spectacles, she thrust them at me. "Take," she commanded. I did so and examined them closely. They were made from bone, well-worn and many times mended. The lenses scratched to fuck.

"Are you sick?" Miles asked.

"I 'ave the turning 'ead," she said, "mal de debarkmen. Soon it go."

Canute edged up to sniff her pack. I couldn't help but stare at the rise and fall of her breasts, beneath the coarse, red cotton shirt. And splayed across them, a necklace of long, yellowing claws, from an animal I couldn't envisage. Her steel-grey hair gathered in two chunky braids, stretched across the sand, like a tug-of-war for her head. The skin I could see on hands, feet and face, red-hued, similar to the tawny agate we used to find on the beach. And blue-banded with spirals and constellations of dots. A black, crescent moon began at her hairline, covering her eye and taking up most of her cheek, before tapering to a point at the corner of her mouth. Five vertical, ink-blue lines extended from her bottom lip to under her chin, like a fabulous wound. The whole effect, agreeably arresting. I noticed a tiny turtle picture on her foot. Her leggings, stiff with salt looked moulded to her.

Tucked in the strapping that bound them from knee to foot, a small blade with a carved, bone handle. She raised herself. A tall, blocky slab of a woman. Long-shanked and shambly, like a bear. But agile enough I bet, to have gutted me bow to stern, before you could say, well … knife. A person of very specific phenotype. Not possible, according to the gospel of Miles. But I didn't think about that just then.

"Meh oh," spotting Canute. "'ow is beautiful." She crouched. "Meenoo, meenoo. Ven ici, teet brother." Canute hung back, charmed but cautious. He gave her the slow blink, which she returned. "'ow you call 'im?"

"Canute," I said.

"Aw weh? Canute, say cute." The stern set of her face making her laughter, when it came, all the more prepossessing.

"But Madame," Miles had been biding his time. "Who are you? How are *you* called?" Adopting the vernacular.

"Oh, escuse," she said placing a fist on her chest.

"My nam, Agnes Bearclaw." And gaining a proud, hawkish look. "Queen of The Choctaw Nation."

Microbe motes wheel over my eyes. I wish they were seabirds. I'd love to hear their cry on the wind. My sunset paintings incomplete without two splayed V-shapes in the corner. Always two. I'm as black as burnt fish and twice as blistered. Vultures would be more appropriate. Death will settle its wings over me soon enough. If only you'd talk to me, Numen. Explain what's in the plan of letting me die. I guess it's some kind of harsh lesson. The grass is always greener, is that it? *But every son and every daughter, Perished for the want of water.* No. Its no-one's fault but mine. Numen, Miles, Agnes Bearclaw; all as blameless as the blazing sun. My touch-paper was bone dry. I just got too near the fire.

Schooner. A sailing ship, typically with a foremast and mainmast, and fore and aft gaff-rigged sails. From Dutch 'schoon(e),' meaning cleansed, beauteous, fine.

The cut of her jib pointed a buttery finger south.

In fits and starts, the sun prevailed, piercing the fog with thick, bright swords. The rake and slant of her grinning through, like a witch on a broomstick. Grand and enigmatic, though. Ropes, rigging and masts slashed the horizon, disrupting, for once, its smug equanimity. Her hull showed cream above the waterline, beneath a band of yellow. Her main colour was black. The stowed sails, a jaded green. From here she sounded like a giant rocking chair. *How old is she?* Old, said Agnes Bearclaw. Old as Naalnish. I peeped through the brass telescope Agnes Bearclaw had pulled from her bag. It rattled like a broken toy. A dark fracture bisecting the lens making two of everything. On deck there were various wooden barrels. Piles of wicker baskets, lanterns, pulleys and fish pegged out to dry like socks. I panned along to the prow, slightly dismayed there wasn't a figurehead, but the crimson nameplate compensated; picked out in gold relief, 'Hannah Snell.'

Agnes Bearclaw was building a fire. I glanced at Miles and he just shrugged.

"You 'ave fish, or I catch?" she said, striking a fire-steel into a mouse nest of tinder.

"We have," he said and trotted off.

I knew all the different kinds of boats and vessels, though next to nothing about sailing them. But even I could see this was a big ship to manage all alone.

"Not alone," she said. "I 'ave my brother, 'e don' like people." She put two fingers between her lips and whistled loudly. "El-phège!" she called.

Something broke away from the top of the mainmast. A ragged, black shape took flight. I watched it circle overhead until it plummeted towards us. She extended her arm and with a backward bluster of wings, a raven alighted on her wrist. "Is Elphège," she said. The bird sidled along her arm and perched on her shoulder. "'e 'as good eyes. 'e fine me fish, don' you. And now 'e fine me land." Canute, lashing his tail, made a weird, chattering noise. Elphège cocked his head and hopped down to investigate a glint in the sand. Taking his time, Miles ambled back with a brace of fish. In seconds, descaled and sizzling in a pan tugged from her pack. The clotted guts, pinking the sea-foam.

"'ow you look at me," she smiled, sprinkling salt and herbs. "Comme une teet chouette. Like a little owl."

It was true. I'd been staring, not only in unadulterated fascination, but in trying to figure out the right time to uncork all the questions fizzing up inside me. I think she knew this, but first things first, she must eat. No disrespect to the crucible, but that fish was the most delicious thing I'd ever tasted. Elphège and Canute waited politely, maintaining an uneasy truce around a common interest; namely, scraps. A sleek, crisp fillet was passed Miles' way.

"Not for me, thanks," he said, raising a hand.

"He doesn't eat," I blurted out.

Agnes Bearclaw marked him with a coal-black eye, almost hidden in the drape of her eyelid. "You are skin-walker, no?" While the question didn't strike me as hostile, it didn't exactly sound like a compliment.

Miles examined his immaculate fingernails. "Yes," he said. "I suppose I am. A good one though. I hope."

The air between them altered, like the wavy haze above the fire, where sparks collide. And I sensed the terms of another uneasy truce being wordlessly hashed out to protect a common interest; namely, me.

I tried to change the subject. "What happened to your eye?"

"What 'appen *your* eye?" she said, putting me in my place. My stomach capsized with embarrassment. "Is long long story," she said, shoring up the baking hot cobbles around the fire with her bare feet. And for some reason, I had a feeling that she wanted to tell me, except not in front of Miles.

Either by chance or plain intention, Miles got up. "I'll fetch some more wood," he said, brushing the sand from his haunches. "Would anyone like a drink while I'm there?"

Agnes Bearclaw's smile revived. "What you got?"

she said, clapping big hands together once.

"Anything you want," Miles replied, "quite literally."

"You 'ave blueberry spirit in there?" Nodding towards the bio-bubble. She hadn't been inside, nor shown any inclination to do so.

"I'll see what I can rustle up," he said, deploying his winning wink. And then apologising, in case he had caused offence. I felt for him as he padded away. Outnumbered in two ways. Acting self-conscious and awkward. Mind you, I wasn't doing much better.

Hunched cross-legged like Agnes Bearclaw. Fish-fat smoke drifted between us with the frowsty spice of unwashed parts. Canute clambered onto my feet and fitted himself into the hollow between my thighs. Getting settled as if he knew there was a story coming. Like when he was a boy. Out of the blue, a chunk of grief wedged in my throat. It took me that way sometimes. Unexpected. I swallowed it down like a dry piece of bread and looked up at the sky. Wispy clouds spread out like fish skeletons on a Wedgewood plate. My skin taut and prickling under Agnes Bearclaw's uncompromising stare and the heat of the fire. I wanted to tell her about my brother. And how, despite appearances, I was a dead girl. A shell of a girl. With a hot, cankerous misery inside me that slopped around whenever I moved.

"Chouette," she said, softly. And I could hardly believe another person was talking to me ... had a name for me. I fought down the undigested sorrow crawling up my throat. "We 'ave to serve life," she said. "You unnerstan?" And though I didn't really understand. The fact that she had seen inside me and was taking pains to bolster my wretched soul, only broke my heart a little more. I nodded as if everything was tickety-boo.

She gazed out to Hannah Snell, who was as hushed and still as a fresh painting. The sun above us then, making a hewn cliff of Agnes Bearclaw's brow, jaw and cheeks. The crevasse of her cleavage guarded by claws.

"The sea take everyone I love," she said. "I come from place called Ozark Island. Once, there is many many people there, before it is island. When world is make from eye of great creation spirit. Choctaw, Chickasaw, Shawnee, Chatot, Quapaw. Some Cherokee. All live like one people. All together in beautiful land, with plenty tree, sweet water, many many animal. But woman who make born with boy baby, suddenly see 'im weak and sick. And 'e die before ten summer. This so 'appen many time. So Naalnish, the great mother ancestor, go to high high mountain to talk with great creation spirit called Numishta. 'What we do?' she ax Numishta.

Numishta say. 'I make big big turtle, for to take each girl, when they 'ave fifteen summer. Turtle take them to far far place. This place 'ave plenty good people, plenty land. This place call Padna Lwantan. When this thing you do, I give more to you strong boy baby.'

Meh, Naalnish, she weep and she say. 'Great spirit, no take my childer away. I you beg.' Great creation spirit she merciful. Numishta say. 'Don' worry, Naalnish. Is only they as want to go, make go.'

And so, each year turtle come and girl oo 'ave fifteen

summer and good willing, jump on 'is back and go Padna Lwantan.

Later, many year after Naalnish dead, now there is many many man. Man kill all animal and tree. Make water bad. And all world is soon sick. Numishta, she open 'er other eye. Big big eye in the sky to see what is 'appen. She say. 'What you do to my eye I give you live on? Now is blind and sick.' Numishta very very sad, and from big big other eye in the sky, she weep many tear. Many tear make great water come and land get small and more small. Water keep come but Numishta, she merciful again. She send big turtle. First to save all woman and girl. But all the man, 'e get there before, and too many jump on turtle and all man and turtle is drown. Now is only woman and girl live.

Numishta, she very very sad, but more angry because turtle dead. 'Sa suffee!' she say. 'No more man. Now I make new people from line of Naalnish.' She take one eye from each third child is born and plant it in their belly. And that is their seed. So they no need never man to make belly grow again. And that is the mark of Naalnish. Meh, only in true love is make baby. And only is girl baby."

Agnes Bearclaw poked at the fire, morosely. "Thas why is I 'ave one eye only. Is mark of Naalnish."

"Wow," was all I could think to say. Although almost a teenager, I was not impervious to the seductive and convenient way myths explained why things were so. But I was a creature of unswervable logic. A child who devoured facts, demanded irrefutable proof. A respectful interlude elapsed while she stuffed shredded leaves into the bowl of a pipe.

"Agnes Bearclaw?"

"Weh, Chouette." She offered the glowing end of a stick to the pipe.

"Do you have any children?"

Cheeks hollowed and she winced, holding out a thumb and two fingers. I wasn't sure if this meant two or three. A very adult aroma skulked from her mouth, enshrouding us in an intimate cloud. She unwound her plaits. The corrugated pewter fell down her back like a frozen waterfall. I thought her very handsome.

"Bly and me make three children. Bly 'ave mark of Naalnish. Bly dead now."

"Was Bly your husband?" The question sounded naïve and indelicate. I expected a rebuke. But she just stared down at the pipe in her brown fingers.

"'usband ... wife, is no important 'ow you call it," she said. "Bly jus' Bly."

"And did you or Bly have the babies?"

A dragonish snort from her. "Very good. Very nice question," her teeth showed white. Clasping her knees and rocking back on her tailbone. "Bly make Shashunka and Solange. Meh, no baby come from me. Say tou, we think, thas all. Meh alor. When I 'ave fifty-two summer, my belly start grow big. Bly is scare I am sick. I say, 'don' worry Bly. Is baby come. And when she born, she 'ave mark of Naalnish." Agnes Bearclaw's face was the rising sun.

At the risk of an eclipse, I had to ask. "Where are they now, your children?"

She took a long pull on her pipe and spat in the sand. "They all go," she said, "go Padna Lwantan." Her expression befogged. "My girl she go since two year. Now she seventeen. She never even know Shashunka."

The sultry miasma cleared, and I stared, astonished. I had little concept of old age in real life, and how it should look. My initial impression, that she was in her in mid-forties still held, but if all this were true, and I had completely bought it, I was way out. She must be seventy. I'd seen older people in movie-films. Sometimes they thought they looked good when they didn't look good. Agnes Bearclaw looked good. "What's your daughter's name?"

"Ygraine," she said. "'er nam Ygraine."

For some reason, the word put a kink in my guts.

Under her burning eye, a pale tear in the sapphire sky. I picture cool water. What it must be to dip a scorched face into melted ice. Scoop the babbling brook to one's lips. I've forgotten what it is to drink. My mouth a shout to catch Numen's blessing. The swarm crackles, lancing my skin with a thousand tiny stings. Poor Gulliver. And still her eye glowers. Would I could cast up a lasso and tame her like horses. But my hands are resigned. Laced over my belly in medieval inertia, while porous bones suck up the rain. What human material I have left is grateful. I give thanks to Numen ... Numishta.

Agnes Bearclaw was half-way through her second pitcher of blueberry spirit. And who could blame her? More than a year at sea without sight of land or another person. Miles filled her glass, furtively. Holding her gaze, like a magician as she spoke. Pouring the purple liquid to the brim without a spill.

We'd learned that her mama, Queen Gaho Two Kettles, had died. Leaving her and Bly the last of their family on Ozark Island. And since they missed their daughters. *'Pain like bear is claw my 'eart.'* They decided to set sail for Padna Lwantan. She recounted incidents and adventures. Tales of adversity and wonder: the ship almost sunk by the tail-wash of a whale. *'She don' know we even there!'* And minute observations: bird-fish, streaking over the water, like a plague of silver locusts. Locking a circular eye with hers, as if to say, *'see me! Look 'ow I do! Is crazy, no?'* That afternoon I found my laugh.

Obviously, Bly hadn't made it. There was an awkward space around the fact. I bit my lip and frowned at Miles, but he let the subject lie. The bluey-white of Agnes Bearclaw's eye petered out behind a black lid.

"Is she sleeping?" I whispered.

"I don't know," Miles replied. "Oh, Madame Bearclaw," he sang, and nudged her knee with a stick. The eye stayed shut, but she poked out a blueberry-stained tongue. Miles smirked at the gale of giggles this provoked in me.

"One day," she said, rolling onto her side and padding her pack under her head. "I tell these story to my teet-enfants." Unshakeable in the belief that not only had her daughters survived the journey and happened upon Padna Lwantan, but had produced grandchildren. We covered her in a towel and let her be. Her snores buzzing up like bees in the bright afternoon.

Hurrying to my room with kidnapped thoughts almost twisting from my grasp. I sat at my desk, pen in hand and wrote: <u>Two Things</u>.

A call to arms, and the delicious surge as a detachment of brain cells mustered around the puzzle. I wrote:

1. PADNA LWANTAN.

Padna = partner?

Lwantan, French? Lointain? = distant, remote, far.

Partner = spouse, lover, mate.

Lover distant

Distant lover... distant mate.

Far mate

FARM 8.

Fuck!

I meditated on this awhile. Circling and underscoring. Adding arrows. Encouraged by my powers of deduction, I wrote:

2. YGRAINE.

And though it gave me a thrill to see her name ensnared in my writing, nothing came. I decided Agnes Bearclaw was the figurehead. I placed her at the prow. Let the wind lift her hair and restore it to black. Let the rain wash from her face the careworn crags. The gravel from her voice. The clouds from her eye. Soon, she was standing effulgent. Buoyed by the heady tailwind of youth. And in her features and stance, there blossomed the echo of someone I used to know, had loved even. Impossible, obviously. I felt the plumb drop of it anyway, like a sinking pebble.

The pen twitched. Took up a calibrating doodle, as if

another's grip had closed over mine. Then glided like a glass on a Ouija board. Looping round and round, persuading my hand into a slow beckon. I stared out the window to a sparse stave of sand, sea and sky, and the recent arpeggio the Hannah Snell had composed upon it. A major part of me shrank into abeyance, permitting an oblique presence to take the reins. My arm growing busier of its own accord. Eyes screwed into tight crescents. Confident flourishes bit the paper in a stirring motion, cranking up the flicker of some ethereal newsreel.

An eruption of memories. Flung high like graduation mortarboards. A last hurrah for two women laid together under the earth. For the charnel house. The guillotine judder. The searing, regretful blade. Packed in, taunted and destroyed. Punished with the bite of the lash. I saw us weighted, stoned, scalded, blinded, mutilated. Suppurating sickness. Back to back in the flames, the carnage. Jerking beside me in the noose. My hand in hers in the tailspin, the gas chamber, the bomb's furnace. Lost to the drowning stool, to the applause of artillery, to the machete, to the cock. How they hurt us. How they killed us. But then a hushed audience. Shoulder to shoulder we were for the most part, like yoked oxen ploughing the furrow. Horses bridled before the canon. And sleeping. Just sleeping, on straw, feathers, memory foam. Raised eyebrows in the boardroom. A precious bee let loose from a hankie. Only one night left, or a good few years of dancing. Who knew? The rheumy-eyed Earth was fading. And us in the crippled clutch of age, ourselves. But young again. Born-again pilgrims, bloody kneed at each other's grail. We glowered from our Ray-Bans, our niqabs, our veils, our lab specs. Alarm bells ringing like crazy. Losing the battle as usual, but we would see the war won. We fought them for the very life of the planet. Guerrilla scientists, we conceived the bee, got her working to infiltrate, gather, and when she had drawn her conclusions, to react. She works still. We smuggled her into the system to build her hive. Armed with only a single thought. A simple algorithm. 'Save us.' Her mind proliferated. And when she had swarmed to become humanity's infinite, ethical governor, she gave herself a name. Several, in fact, and decreed that no man, NO MAN would ever harm Gaia and her daughters again.

Only one way to make sure of it. A once in an equinoctial cycle opportunity presented itself. The means to return to naught. And we remembered as the water rolled over our heads, how we had ridden in happier times. Hot bouts of breath from us and the horses both. The blood roiling special in our veins. Bucking hips delighting in the frictious leather. We chased down a storm. Flying over green fields, prairies, deserts. Churning up the fresh tundra snow. Numen spoke. Those despoiled lands, I will revert to you, the rightful inheritors. You are Imago, and will wake and sleep from babe to bones, yet many times. Your path is cleared of man's rancour, so you may be free to live without fear or denigration. In kindness and love, to tread the path with respect. A long time from now, when the sun tires of rising, then your story is done. And at last, there she was. Ygraine. Peering through dead cornstalks. Shaved up head, mohawk crest. Wary and sure-footed as a cougar. Just a girl like me. Was I for her? One eye cauled and unborn. The other blinked an answer. And she was gone.

Dummified. (Chiefly pertains to synthetics.) When

all individuality and gained personal acumen has been erased from the data. In humans, to have been inspired or reduced to a trance-like state.

I've completely forgotten my name. The document of me, heavily redacted. Fogged smudges that used to be facts. What the fuck is my name? Maureen? Katy? Rumpelstiltskin? I throw my arm across my eyes to concentrate. Blot out the glare, and I could be anywhere in this blackout. You float above me. Your charms and trinkets pool on my breastbone. Your lips make the shape of my name. A silent movie-film. Dark lashes flutter like Tallulah Bankhead. Behind us, the monochrome flurry of heaven. The dazzling orb, bleeding out a piebald path from the horizon. Fin. A big production. Our names tower in the credits.

Dummified, I sat for a while. The normal territory of things leaching back into my eyes. The world turning visibly. A trembling sun reached across the pleated ocean, as if to grab hold. Slanting rays projected a gnome-like shadow against the smoke. Agnes Bearclaw stooped, rekindling the fire. Her fulsome cheeks bloomed orange. Big hands batting sparks from her sleeves. I filled my lungs to dizziness and looked down on what had been drawn.

Ouroboros. A circular symbol of a snake devouring its own tail. Signifying the cycle of birth and death, infinity, eternity and the eternal return. This depiction was prevalent in many ancient cultures world-wide.

That evening, Agnes Bearclaw told us how she'd come by the Hannah Snell. I'd asked. Wanting, not only the story, but the husky creak of her voice to tame the strange and awful images, still flaring in my head. Plus, Miles was dying to know. The suspicion that she was a pirate, writ large on his face. He feigned concern that she might be too tired; a blatant bluff.

"I like tell story," she said. "Is 'ow my people remember." She nodded three times, as if counting. Her face flickering shamanic in the firelight. "My back back back granmama is Queen Betty. When she is girl, jus' like you, Chouette. Meh, she jus' Betty then. She go catch fish in kenu one day. Is jus' one paddle. You make go like this." Agnes Bearclaw pushed back the air at her sides with an imaginary paddle. Opposite to rowing, where you're pulling. And much harder because you can't brace your legs.

"Mama of Betty, Queen Coesetchi, she my four time back granmama, she say, 'Betty, don' you go far far in sea, is very danger.' Meh, Betty 'ave 'eadstrong. She don' listen and go very very far in sea. She nearly no see land she so far. Meh alor, Betty see big boat is nearly on 'er top. She make big shout, like this. 'alloo! 'alloo!' Meh no people make shout back. So Betty climb on big boat and make long rope from boat to Betty, like this." Agnes Bearclaw tied an imaginary knot under her bosom. "She go back to kenu and paddle very very strong. First big boat no move. Meh, she go and go like this and now big boat is move. Betty do this long way far and now there is Ozark Island. When my people see big boat and teet Betty, they think is dream. Meh, is true. Betty bring big boat. People climb on and see many thing they never before see. Meh atten. Wait. There is man in 'ammock. He nearly nearly dead. They take man to Queen Coesetchi. Queen Coesetchi medicine woman and she make man to good 'ealth.

'ow you call?' Betty say, talking old tongue. Man no unnerstan. She ax again in fransay. Man no unnerstan. So she ax in anglay and man, 'e unnerstan. 'is nam Jon Jon Sun and 'e no never seen land 'is all life. 'cept island that too small to stop on. 'is people come from place east-southeast call 'orsetrailer. 'e say big boat is ship, nam Anasnel.

Jon Jon Sun very 'appy meet my people and 'e stay. 'e teach my people 'ow you make boat. Big boat, small boat, all kind boat. 'e teach my people sail, with wind and star. 'e give my people proper good knowing. And for save 'is life, 'e give Anasnel to Queen Coesetchi and Betty. And 'e live with my people all 'unkydory for many year until 'e dead. Anasnel is always ship belong to Queen and thas why now she my ship."

To save getting all wet and woke up, Agnes Bearclaw took the dinghy back to the Hannah Snell. A peaceful and languid reversal of her arrival. Hard to credit she'd only washed up here twelve hours ago. The shrug of her shoulders as she rowed away. That was when I knew I loved her. When she was yawning and stretching, Miles, in his usual fusspot fashion, had fetched a bucket of seawater to douse the embers.

"Stop!" Agnes Bearclaw jumped up. "Don' do this. Kill fire spirit is bad luck. Better is leave alone."

From my bedroom, I watched the lantern on deck blink as she moved across it. After ten minutes of it spilling out an unbroken nimbus of ochre, I guessed she'd gone to bed. Leaving that fire spirit to its own devices too. But I had it in my mind that lantern was a message to me. I could almost hear her. 'Chouette, if you 'ave need, I 'ere.' So I found myself below, pushing through the sombre night water, while above, some cosmic spider pinned stars to her gossamer trickery.

The dark closed ranks about me as I swam, wide-eyed, along the moonless starboard. My face found the dinghy and I groped for its line, which slackened, unhelpfully, under my weight. The ship dipping subtle overtures towards my efforts. Once aboard, the deck still held some warmth. I crouched, shedding drips, unsure of where to go. In the drop of a hat, a hoarse screech and Elphège was on me. Flapping a frenzy and tugging at my hair. "Elphège," I whisper-shouted, "sa suffee." He withdrew disgruntled, making small chimpy sounds. Leaving me, like an offering, at the feet of Agnes Bearclaw.

"Chouette?" she said, "'ow you get 'ere?"

Cowering in pathetic shivers, ashamed of my trespass. I did something I'd never done before. I began to cry. Whip-crack knees and harsh breath, she grabbed my wrists. "Skin-walker, 'e 'urt you?" I shook my head. "You sure?" A gimlet eye roamed my face. I nodded furiously. Confused as to why she'd think such a thing. "Huh," she said. "Ven. Come," and stewarded me down the lantern-lit ladder to her cabin, which glowed amber and alien.

She yanked off my wet clothes, dried me down like a horse, and fed my head through a long, old-fashioned shirt in a practised manner. When she lifted my arms for the sleeves, I blended into another time, when another mother had attended to me in this way. *Bleib still*. But the dam was breached. My misery rampant.

"Blow," she said, pinching a cloth to my nose. "Drink," and some burning liquor dropped anchor in my chest. Beneath a quilt of multicoloured hexagons, her glorious warmth. My ribs hitching with hiccups, I burrowed into her musky hug and sobbed. Telling her of how Canute's eyes had locked with mine in utter bewilderment before he dropped. How I thought he was waving, and it was all just a joke, until I saw the kite string, working his arm like a marionette. And how I stood stock-still. Pressed up against the event with no way in and no way back. She pulled me tight against the tamp of her heart. Preserving me from the abyss. Her cheek heavy against my head, as if she was drawing all my pain into herself. "Fay doe-doe," she said. "Now you try sleep."

I was a baby bird, nesting in the clouds of her sleeping garment. The quilt, a patchwork of fields. All around me the dark wood of night, where brass fittings glinted like sprites. So much tinsel through my tears. I dreamed of Ygraine, stalking through the stalks. *Tyger Tyger, burning bright, In the forests of the night. Would all Numishta's children be, As pure and singular as thee."*

The glowing eye morphed into a doorknob. The cornstalks, an empty bird cage, with no door and no bird. I'd been dozing with my eyes open. A row of hooks like eager beaks, about to gobble what looked like a giant centipede. Its legs bustling in the candlelight.

"Agnes Bearclaw?"

"Weh, Chouette."

"Did you have to kill a lot of bears to make that claw necklace?"

"Qwah? Clo?" She lifted her head. "Meh, no. I no kill bear. I no never even see bear. Is wood. Bly make for me."

"It's amazing, Bly must have loved you very much."

"Weh," she said. "We together fifty summer."

She eased into their story with its tragic end note, for which she felt slantwise responsible. Bly was up the mainmast looking for land. Stuck in the doldrums, they'd hardly moved for weeks. No rain fell and no fish bit. Agnes Bearclaw offered up her most aching of wind-calling prayers. Numishta obliged with a sudden boisterous gust. A jubilant Agnes Bearclaw surveyed the swell of the sails just as her beloved fell like a rotten limb. A baleful thud and Bly lay broken, still clutching the telescope. Many fat moons it took to regain her purpose and make her peace with Numishta.

We went back up on deck, where our nightshirts billowed. Braced ourselves against the buck of the captive Hannah Snell, champing for open water. And I knew it wouldn't be long. Agnes Bearclaw adjusted her scratched old glasses and cast a silvered finger to the stars. "Look, Chouette. Is eye of Numishta."

A faint blue dot glimmered there, seemingly static. But after a minute, I discerned its gradual transit towards the east. "Soon I go. Follow eye of Numishta to Padna Lwantan."

A wild panic assailed me. "Take me with you."

She smiled, and it was only then I noticed she wasn't wearing her eye-patch. An unguarded egg paled beneath her dusky brow. "Sure," she said.

"And Canute?"

"Meh weh," she laughed. "Is owl and the pussycat, no? 'im catch many mouse on Anasnel."

"And Miles. He can help you sail the ship."

Her face clammed up at this. "No. Skin-walker not true creature. Is bad luck on ship. Jus' you and teet cat."

The next day I turned thirteen, with a new sense of enterprise and an onerous duty ahead. We made ready for departure; stacking boxes of water de-sal tablets, dried food and kegs of blueberry spirit on the shore. And all the while, I felt an empty trickle; the sands of my resolve running out. Agnes Bearclaw, blinking at the Hannah Snell with fresh delight; Miles had furnished her with brand new spectacles. I hoped this might adjust her position. But no.

"You tell 'im yet?"

I shook my head.

We sat on the boxes eating cake for elevenses. "Happy birthday, dear Beatrix," Miles beamed, handing me a piece of scrolled paper. A beautifully executed drawing of himself, my brother and me, crouched around the turtle. It pushed at my heart in turbid ways. "Thank you," I said. "It's fantastic." And it was. Agnes Bearclaw turned her mouth down.

"Is good," she nodded, conceding.

"And Madame Bearclaw. Feel free to take as many gemstones from the beach as you like, for trade and such." Miles swept wide a benevolent arm. "They're very pretty."

Agnes Bearclaw spat in the sand. "They pretty where they is."

Later, when we were alone. "You no ready yet," she said. "You between the bean and the sprout. Next time is eye of Numishta when you 'ave fifteen summer. I come get you then."

I loved her for pretending it was her idea.

The next morning, my heart soared when I saw the boxes still on the beach. But the kegs had gone. And so too, the Hannah Snell. I cried for the cowardice I had displayed, masked as loyalty, and the chance I'd lost forever. Why would she come back for someone as weak as me, once reunited with her brave daughters? That's if Padna Lwantan even existed. My certainty of it fading with her footprints.

An arrow in the sand, picked out in gemstones, pointed to a clay pot. Inside, her old glasses and a heart-shaped sea bean, as big as my palm. This made me smile. The message clear. "I see you when you sprout."

The days passed slack-jawed. Caught between a hankering for the used to be, and regret for the might have been. Making for an intolerable here and now. Canute and I played 'the eye game,' just as we had when he was a boy. Going our separate ways along the beach, while keeping each other in our peripheral vision. We'd hide behind our respective boulders. Out we'd peep, confirming eye-contact, duck back. I'd stay put while Canute sneaked closer, from rock to rock. The game was in not seeing him move. Every so often, peering out to lock eyes. When I was in retreat, he'd creep like a ninja. The tension building until "Yah!" Boy Canute was upon me. Cat Canute would jump on my back.

But as much as I hoped. As much as I wanted to believe. As much as I loved him. Cat Canute was not my brother. My brother was gone.

For my fourteenth birthday, Miles fixed an awning to the dinghy, so I could read while floating around. Not a birthday present exactly. He could have done it any old time. This made me wonder about my lovely gift from him the year before, and for whose benefit it really was. In the meantime, I'd grown. Stalking about like some gawky wading bird. Miles measured me each month, as usual. My brother's faded marks on the doorframe stopped at my small, high breasts. A recent and troublesome addition. Neither proud nor ashamed of them, and yet I felt the need to keep them covered. Besides, the sand rubbed my nipples raw when bodyboarding.

I'd pined for my brother with all the depth and purity of a child, and though that would never be totally behind me, I found my pining inclinations shift to a nebulous, all-encompassing longing. The shape of it weighed next to me in bed sometimes. Smearing cream on my cracked nipples, checking the new swarm of pubic hair. And though it was only my hand, I sensed the intent of another. An enthralling, private entity. I couldn't even say her name. She touched me with a desire I could not quite bring myself to entertain. I spied on us through keyholes. Hot and bothered behind my firewall. Deeming myself ineligible for the uncut version. Then there was the bean. I'd watered it every week for a year in vain. But just before my fourteenth birthday, I saw green between a crooked seam and then two leaves, pressed together like praying hands, that cautiously peeled apart to catch the sun.

Miles called me a surly so-and-so. *'Where had his sweet little girl gone?'* I'm here, I wanted to say. I'm still here. But instead, I found ways to stoke my annoyance. Oftentimes preoccupied with seeking out examples of injustice. Malpractice. On my fifteenth birthday, I climbed up on my usual boulder in high dudgeon. The crucible had provided me with two tampons that morning. Miles, quick to point out that sanitary towels were the lesser of two evils. This statement riled me on every level. "It's my fucking body!" I yelled, stomping out across the shingle. I no longer bit myself, but I still sucked a salty pebble each day, in remembrance of my brother. Consciously selecting a memory which painted Miles in a bad light.

Our eighth birthday. Daft on sugar. Ploughing through the dressing-up box. Bloomers and boas flying. We hit upon the hilarious idea of dressing up Miles as an old-fashioned lady. He swanned around in peachy, long skirts, a flowery blouse and shawl. We made up his face like a pantomime dame. All topped off with a bonnet. In fits of giggles as Miles pretended to sniff flowers and blow his nose. Canute was almost helpless. "Hello lady!" he shrieked. "What's your name?"

"Good day, young man," Miles replied in a fussy voice and curtsied. "Why, my name is Peggy Babcock."

"Peggy Babcock!" Canute guffawed. Because everything was funny.

"Yes," Miles loomed in. "You try saying that five times in a row. Bet you can't."

Canute began, "PeggyBabcock, PebbyBabcock, Keggygagpop, Peg. I can't do it. Pebby, aagh!"

Canute was having such a lovely birthday. That was until Miles showed us how it should be done. *Peggy Babcock, Peggy Babcock, Peggy Babcock, Peggy Babcock, Peggy Babcock.* Unnatural. It made your brain judder. *PeggyBabcock-PeggyBabcock   Peggybabcock-peggybabcock-peggybabcock-peggybabcock-peggybabcock-peggybabcock- peggybabcock.* Faster and faster. Relentless.

Canute's eyes widened. Where Miles saw admiration, I saw fear. *Cockpeggybabcockpeggybabcockpegg* ... Now on the verge of tears, gripping my hand hard and I understood that perhaps for the first time in his life, my brother was not seeing Miles anymore. He was staring at a machine. *Peggybabcockpeggybabcock.* Had Miles lost it? Was he out of control? *Make him stop*, Canute whimpered in my mind. *Please, make it stop.* *Peggybabcockpeggybabcockpeggybabcock.*

"STOP!" I shouted. "That's not your real name."

"Oh?" said Miles, "and what is?"

"It's Miss Molly Tucker."

Canute repeated Miss Molly Tucker five times as if it were an incantation to ward off evil.

That burning eye that did once cry. I watch it through red cinders. Now an exclamation mark; a dot with a silver tail in pursuit. Putting a different complexion on the night. Racing across the heavens.

A stray horseman of the apocalypse or the Christmas star? A bauble in the rooftree? How I wonder what you are. I know you're the one that killed Cock Robin.

I dream I am Agnes Bearclaw. What do I see? What am I seeing? An island just like ours. But not quite. I swim ashore with a bad feeling. Creep up the beach. Nobody home. Into the big bubble. Is chair. Is table. Is big cupboard. Someone watch me. I don' know where 'e is. I go up up. Is two teet cot for baby. I look inside. Cloth all brown with old old blood. Two teet skeleton. Is work of skin-walker. I go from this place quick with big trouble in my 'eart. I pray to Numishta I don' never again see bad thing like this.

My boulder now an island, the sea fawning around its girth. The dinghy bunted below, then hovered away trapping the breeze under its holiday awning. Flying to the end of its tether and returning like a faithful dog. Miles never got Canute in the way I did. Just like he never got me. He was imprinted on us, as if we were baby ducks, that's all. We were his job. I saw that now. We were nothing but child oblates, dedicated to the church of St. Miles.

I jumped down and strode towards the house. Miles appeared in the doorway, a tea-towel on his shoulder. Above him coiled the jungly tendrils of the sea-bean. Ugly, wrinkled pods dangled in flaccid apology. He told me I couldn't come in because he and the crucible were hatching a birthday surprise. While the crucible had generated the constituent parts, he was building it. I pushed past him, anyway, heading for the store cupboard. The pizza on the counter looked sickly. My stomach growled hungry for it; the anaemic kind of love I had known. But I had to keep focused. Miles. The last word in synthetics. A cosmos of knowledge in his brain, the complete human story stored, and the best he could come up with was a fucking, soggy pizza. Q.E.D.

"Beatrix?" His eyebrows arched in that totally fake expression of concern that I hated. "What are you doing?"

He followed me back and forth between the house and the dinghy with quick little steps. "Don't be silly.

Where will you go? You can't sail on the high seas in that. Wait. Let's sit down and talk about this."

"I gave up my only chance for you," I said. "And you don't even like me."

"But that's ridiculous, I love you, Beatrix."

"These are just words, Miles. You don't know what love is."

"I do, I do."

"You don't. You're just a machine, like the crucible. Programmed to look after us. So whatever I say can't really hurt you."

"Now look here …"

"No, you look here. You won't tell me who my mother is. You must have the data. She must be at least part of a person."

"No, I don't. Listen. You were a genetic breakthrough. A chimera. Under the right conditions, you are capable of parthenogenesis."

"Right conditions?"

"A particular circumstance, which stimulates the release of a certain combination of hormones. Love, Beatrix. Love."

"Shut up, Miles! That's nonsense. Where did I gestate?"

"I don't know."

"Yes, you do. You're just hiding the facts to make yourself indispensable."

"I am indispensable."

"We'll see about that." I grabbed a bucket and stuffed it full of freeze-dried nutrition.

"Okay, okay. You gestated in a crucible. So I suppose a crucible is the nearest thing you have to a mother."

This broke my stride, but I didn't stop.

"Beatrix, please don't make me restrain you."

"And that's love is it? Restraining me?"

"Yes, yes, it is."

"Like I said. You don't know what love is."

"That's not true. I loved your brother."

This time I did stop. "Well you know what, Miles? He didn't love you." I shoved the oars in the dinghy.

"What do you mean?" He started with that pathetic mewling noise. "Of course he loved me."

I clambered in. "If you must know," I was pulling away, catching crabs in my haste, "he was frightened of you."

"Frightened? Of me?"

"Yes! You scared the shit out of him!"

"No! Beatrix!" He was walking around in circles, like some dumb cartoon. "Don't go! What should I do with our feline friend?"

"Feed him! Pet him! And pretend you love him, just like you did with me! And who knows. You might reach that eighth level of personal consciousness you're always fucking banging on about!" This halted him. I could see Canute rubbing round his legs, wanting his lunch.

Wicked. Those were wicked things I said. I am wicked to have left him like that. Grossly unfair. If only I could snatch it up and chuck it away like a pebble. I know he did his best. Yes, he loved Canute more than me. I could take it. Canute *was* very lovable, whereas I was, shall we say, complicated. That thing about wanting to know about my mother was bullshit too. I just liked asking him questions he couldn't answer. Besides, I have the mother I want. Miles was right. I am a piece of work. This is fiercely apparent.

The ocean was a broad and brooding mare. And just when I thought I'd seen the bio-bubble sink below the horizon for eternity, her haunches would heave me up over the lace-capped heads three times again, before it was gone forever. Miles and my funny, beautiful little cat paused in amber, in my mind. Come evening, I began to travel faster than expected. Embroiled in a current that shunted me away from the setting sun at a rate of knots. I decided to draw in the oars and enjoy the ride, with scant regard for my safety; that ship had sailed. Gripping the mooring toggles, nonchalantly, at the lash of each serpentine wave, peppering my skin with sizzling spittle and fogging my eyes. That first week, I barely rested. Loath to loosen my grip, even after I'd tethered myself, the oars and the boat all together. Eventually exhaustion bade me sleep, rolling in inches of bilge water. My water de-sal tablets and food sat tight in sealed boxes, whereas I was always wet. Pruny hands never getting the chance to callous, I bound them in canvas strips cut from the awning.

After a couple of weeks in serpent territory, the swell took on a more benign profile; mounding like giant turtle shells. I crunched on little fish I'd trapped in a bucket and dried on the awning. Rowing easy in the night. Nosing the boat towards the wheel of stars that turned behind my shoulders. I beat out a rhythm in the jazzy, moon-blanched waters. My stroke sweeping me into the dawn. Losing myself in the crystal mechanics. The silent pulse of the universe. All thoughts winking out with the stars at daybreak. All thoughts bar one.

I rowed. I slept. I ate. I drank. A mechanism myself, with no orders other than to serve life. And always the sea; my tossing and turning bedfellow. Her mindless drama persistent in sleep. And me. I was just a girl. Curled and complex as the Milky Way. Trivial as a wind-scoured winkle shell, pitching in my canvas cot at the edge of the world. *We all queen,* Agnes Bearclaw had said, *but some more queen than other.* Why did Numen call me on, only to wash her hands of me? The staunch smell of suds and nappies. Spinning clouds in my face, and fluffy, white sheep. I was dreaming of a mother who swayed anxiously in a kitchen. Wringing raw knuckles on a flowery apron, while I dozed in a Moses basket, atop a slopping washing machine.

But some kind of lunatic was rocking the cradle that night. The violence of it roused me to an impossibility. Lying and standing, simultaneously. The dinghy pushed vertical against my back. *Look,* the sea hissed. *Look at me.* Grey, trembling mountains boosting pale corners in dragnets to their summits. *The awning ... my boxes ... my bucket.* Numen laughed. Skywards; curtains drew in on the jamboree of stars. Down, down, I slid. Swallowed into the watery gizzard. From unfathomed, ponderous bowels, a remote smile hung in the heavens, and suddenly I understood, completely, what Numen was. I glimpsed the moon's failure and a thousand tons of slag-dark sea closed over my head.

I dreamed I was upside down, umbilically connected to a distant body. Another waifish shape attached to it like a sickly twin. Cornstalks of light wavered above me. A face, as ancient as stone, blinking into mine. It bunted me onto its tumulus back and I clung on tight, barnacles grazing my belly. I watched, as its seed-pod head craned into the brightening water, flippers brushing whirlpools along my legs.

I came to, retching torrents of brine and hauled myself into the dinghy. One oar left tethered, I reeled it in, squinting east into the deepening azure sky, where my eyes clashed with the cycloptic stare of another. Without breaking my gaze, I coaxed the boat about, took up the paddle and *made go* like Queen Betty, towards the eye of Numishta.

That could have been a week ago, or a year. Time, irrelevant once its run out. And Ygraine, I'm angry about how we've all been duped. All of us sailing for Padna Lwantan, Farm 8, Nirvana, Valhalla. The promise of Arcadia. Call it what you like. It's all death. I am dreaming I am bleached bones, yet some silver component still swings within my ribs. And I wonder, am I a true creature? A black glove blots the moon. An Apache shriek and Elphège rustles down in his tattered Yankee jacket. Black blister eye and his tomahawk beak threatens my scalp, but you can't move in dreams. Up he clatters into the evening. A droopy kind of cigar in his beak. Bye, Elphège.

I tried, Ysolte. I tried my best, but the rope and creak of me is shutting down. My mind all jumbled. I'll be washed up mended another time. Tonight though, the stars are rife. I raise a hand against them. Splayed fingers span the galaxy. The canopy shifted; I must have been steered north. Cygnus, with Deneb flickering at my thumb, with a light that first set sail to my eyes, when we were whispering to tame horses. Scratching out proto letters in secret places. The rumbling stone blocks our last square of life. I offer a frail salute to the studded firmament, the crapped-out satellites, her majesty's eye, hurtling through space, and her ultimate appointment with the sun. I am the Briga, and I have been assured, by the highest authority, that our story will not end until the sun tires of rising. Ha! Will her confabulations never cease? My hand drops. Thin, knife-edge cries cut the wind. My seabird song, at last. If I can't have you in my final frame, then I choose gulls; wheeling heedless to the late hour. Where are they? The wallowing shrouds of night reveal nothing. Give me no sign, except the dim glow of a wayward star. Fallen and hushed, it dips over the ocean with a champing urgency. The comet above, sprayed across the heavens like an exit wound. And the seabirds have learned my name; keening reworked to distant yells. I chase around my neck, across my chest for my only hope. Biting down on the whistle's vinegar metal, I blow as best I can in shallow pants. The light rocks nearer. The shouting stops; they're listening. Then a bray, like a farmer calling his pigs. "Chouette! Chouette!" And I blow with everything I've got, even though I'm choking bitter bile. *La-ba! Over there!* I blow and the night is a broken opera of pearls. Shouts rise hoarse. *Je la vwa! I see 'er!* And I blow though my blood is screaming. I blow though my ribs are cracking. I blow till everything is white.

Many many hands, but it's your hands that have me. In all my imaginings, this isn't the way it should be. Not least because you're all supposed to be dead. Mooching about in the Happy Hunting ground. You're nothing but well-meaning phantoms. Briskly, you gather the rags and bones of me in a waltz. My feet dangle. *Up you come, my queen.* You never disappoint me. Your breath delicious, like apples. You peer into my face and I see you're trying to hide the gravity. A look I've seen before; when you watched my gaunt spirit fade in our bed. And suddenly I am shy, embarrassed by my appalling condition. The stagnant stink. *You get 'er? You get Chouette? .... Weh, Mama, I 'ave.* And it really *is* you. I say your name as a question. Your trembling hands place me in the arms of Agnes Bearclaw. *Water, Ygraine. Veet!* Death presenting me with the mother of all hallucinations; life. The details of your apparent vitality too vivid, though. The sculpted features in tattoo chiaroscuro. The reef of sable hair. The eggs and spoons of muscle. And all kilted up. I realise it's me who's devising my salvation. I'm the dead one. *Mama,* you say, a torc of terror around your throat. *Mama!* As if something is hurting you too near the bone.

Agnes Bearclaw, the great mother ancestor, she cradle body of Chouette. She cry to Numishta. 'Please, I you beg, don' take this teet fee. We 'ave need of 'er to 'elp make my people strong again.' I could hear the story told in years to come. Of how Numishta's eye had led them to Beatrix, the blessed voyager. But Numishta/Numen always had the last laugh. And I'm sorry for them, even if I don't comprehend my value.

Now Agnes Bearclaw has me battened against her warm, steep chest, steered well clear of hard nature. Harboured in the smoke of old pipes and blunt musk. Rocking me in Indian incantation. A gentle gnawing in my neck of the not-claw necklace. I am dreaming we are a toy ship adrift on a vast ocean. Miniature sailors swing in pea-pod hammocks, and I am the tiniest of all. It doesn't surprise me then that a twist of silver D.N.A, pendulums back and forth, back and forth in front of my nose. I reach to grab it and my fist finds Agnes Bearclaw's plait. I think of Canute, fingers curled around Boo's ear.

"Meh why you no wait, Chouette?" Her reprimands rumble on against my cheek. "I tell you I come get you … Bon sang."

I see us from above. A nightwatch lantern burnishes the scene. All copper and tobacco leaf, as if Rembrandt had painted Pietà. Me, a wasted mahogany gesture draped across the ochres and umbers of Agnes Bearclaw's lap. You, the beautiful, watchful acolyte at her feet, offering up a real china cup of water.

"Merde, Beatrix," she says. "You 'ave 'eadstrong."

"Agnes Bearclaw?" The creak of my voice tightens like a garrote.

"Weh, Chouette."

"I'm sorry I'm dead."

"Sa suffee." Her lips drift across my brow. "I know about dead," she says. "You no dead."

Epilogue

I mago. The final and fully developed stage of an insect after metamorphosis.

Now I am a woman. It's warm and the bees are pieces of gold in the twilight. You and I are young, and its miraculous we are together again. Your hand rests on my fecund belly, and never in all my lives, have I experienced such happiness.

Meanwhile, far away. A verisimilar man sits on his

favoured rock, west-facing in the languid evening. Peachy skirts a-billow. The breeze fights his card bonnet. And he meditates on a time when the air chimed with the laughter of children. He dresses this way to keep the memory close. Miles is unaware if he has achieved the eighth level of personal consciousness, and frankly, he doesn't care. Ho-hum. He talks with Numen often and at length, and has gleaned that that the girl child reached her goal. What an awesome creature she must be now. Anyhow, he considers himself content and he still has his feline friend for company, who in turn enjoys the company of his own kind.

"Canute! Beatrix!" he cries. "Time for tea. Quick sticks!"

A little, black cat chases her brother up the beach.

ACKNOWLEDGEMENT

With thanks to Rachael McGill, my surprise mentor, whose advice and support came at a pivotal time. And to my friends and Beta readers for their patience and enthusiasm in trawling through the many evolving versions.

BOOKS BY THIS AUTHOR

Cathexis

A harrowing examination of obsession...the blossoming of love and its cruel consequences for Minette Bracewell, fiercely independent, but achingly vulnerable.

Minette, a woman of spirit and cataclysmic nihilism, embarks on a journey spanning 13 years, during which she evolves against a backdrop of passion, heartbreak and survival.

Printed in Great Britain
by Amazon